# Praise for Robyn Sisman

"A sparky, well-written take on why men and women can never be just good friends." —*Marie Claire* (UK)

"*Just Friends* is just bliss. Witty, warm and wise, it's as good as an old movie for romantics." —*The Times* (London)

"Finely observed characters, vivid set pieces and laugh-aloud wit." —*The Mail on Sunday* (UK)

"With a dash of British humor and an adroit insight into family relationships and what really makes love work, Sisman's lastest offering has what it takes." —*Publishers Weekly*

Robyn Sisman was born in Los Angeles and grew up in various parts of the States and Europe. She is the author of *Special Relationship, Perfect Strangers* and *Just Friends,* all of which were *Sunday Times* bestsellers and have sold worldwide in over twenty languages. She currently lives in England with her husband, the biographer Adam Sisman, and their children.

*By the Same Author*

Special Relationship
Perfect Strangers
Just Friends

# Weekend in Paris

ROBYN SISMAN

A PLUME BOOK

PLUME
Published by the Penguin Group
Penguin Group (USA) Inc., 375 Hudson Street, New York, New York 10014, U.S.A.
Penguin Books Ltd, 80 Strand, London WC2R 0RL, England
Penguin Books Australia Ltd, 250 Camberwell Road, Camberwell, Victoria 3124, Australia
Penguin Books Canada Ltd, 10 Alcorn Avenue, Toronto, Ontario, Canada M4V 3B2
Penguin Books India (P) Ltd, 11 Community Centre, Panchsheel Park, New Delhi – 110 017, India
Penguin Books (N.Z.) Ltd, Cnr Rosedale and Airborne Roads, Albany, Auckland 1310, New Zealand
Penguin Books (South Africa) (Pty) Ltd, 24 Sturdee Avenue, Rosebank, Johannesburg 2196, South Africa

Penguin Books Ltd, Registered Offices: 80 Strand, London WC2R 0RL, England

Published by Plume, a member of Penguin Group (USA) Inc. Previously published in a Michael Joseph edition.

First Plume Printing, March 2004
20 19 18 17 16 15 14 13



LIBRARY OF CONGRESS CATALOGING-IN-PUBLICATION DATA

Sisman, Robyn.
Weekend in Paris / Robyn Sisman.
p. cm.
ISBN 0-452-28490-2
1. British—France—Fiction. 2. Paris (France)—Fiction. 3. Young women—Fiction. I. Title.

PS3569.I75W44 2004
813'.54—dc22 2003053663

Printed in the United States of America
Set in Garamond MT
Designed by Daniel Lagin



PUBLISHER'S NOTE
This is a work of fiction. Names, characters, places, and incidents either are the product of the author's imagination or are used fictitiously, and any resemblance to actual persons, living or dead, business establishments, events, or locales is entirely coincidental.

*For my father*

# 1

Eighty feet below Trafalgar Square the train rattled southward, steepening its angle as it prepared to plunge beneath the Thames. It was Friday rush hour on an unseasonably mild afternoon in early October. The overcrowded carriage simmered with body heat and eau-de-commuter, a musty composite of stale perfume and warm armpit. Wheels screeched. Conversations droned. From all directions came the rhythmic hiss of personal stereos, like a chorus of invisible crickets.

Molly Clearwater stood midway between the doors, wedged between a dandruffy male shoulder and an enormous backpack, with one arm crooked for support around a metal pole. At her feet was a small, worn suitcase. She held a paperback inches from her nose, the pages flat and open. But she wasn't reading.

"A stupid secretary." That's what Malcolm had called her. The tormenting words repeated themselves over and over in her head, and unconsciously she raised her chin, and shook back her tumble of fair hair, like a swimmer coming up for air. She was *not* a "secretary." And how, she would like to know, could you call someone "stupid" who had a first-class degree in English Literature? Plus a distinction for her dissertation ("The Gothic Novel: From Mrs. Radcliffe to Daphne du Maurier"). The image of Malcolm in his exec-on-the-make suit, smirking with the conviction of his own sportswagon-driving, *Men's Health*–reading, investment-checking, cell phone–blathering, hair-gelled *rightness* made her cheeks glow pink. The man couldn't even spell "accommodation."

It was pathetic to remember how excited she'd been, only six months ago, to get this job. No more living at home, being driven barking bananas by her mother. No more slaving for a pittance at Bloom 'n' Veg in Minster Episcopi, sleepiest town in the universe. Destiny called! She and Abigail, her best friend from St. Swithin's comprehensive, had gone out to celebrate at the Horse and Groom in the high street and got so plastered on Bacardi Breezers that Molly could barely ride her bike home. Abigail, who was a beauty therapist now (but a really good one), had conjured up a magical vision of Molly's future—chic clothes and funky haircuts, Notting Hill restaurants and Soho bars, sophisticated men for whom an evening out did not mean a McDonald's and a snog in their van. There would be promotion, her own swanky office, business trips. (Oh, bitter irony.)

The job title was "Marketing Officer," and the advertisement had specified a creative self-starter with degree-level education and superior writing skills—"Right up your *Strasse*," as Malcolm Figg had said himself at the interview. Molly hadn't cared that it was a pharmaceutical company rather than something more glamorous. The point was that she had a job. In London. She was launched on life, big-time.

To begin with, it had seemed a tremendous adventure, joining the commuter rush to work, getting kitted out with free pens and multicolored paperclips, and taking possession of a fat stack of business cards printed with her own name. Determined to make a success of her first proper job, she had obeyed Malcolm's every request, however incomprehensible. She leapt from her desk whenever he yelled, "Hey, you, whatever your name is," ran to the coffee shop for cappuccinos, told callers that Mr. Figg was out when he was in, and in when was he was out, typed pages of handwritten gobbledygook and even—she burned with indignation to think of it now—organized the servicing of his beloved "motor," complete with bull-bars, dangly dice and "Divers Do It Deeper" sticker. She pestered everyone with intelligent questions, and fought to be included in the important-sounding Progress Meetings, held weekly behind closed doors in the boardroom—which, to her dismay, had turned out to be no more than an interminable catalogue of things no one had got round to doing yet.

There had been some wobbly moments, most embarrassingly last Easter when she'd hit the wrong button on her computer and copied in the entire office on an e-greeting from her mother, involving dancing daisies and an animated bunny singing "I just called to say I love you." And possibly she had overdone the literary references in her press release for Trepazamine, though personally she still thought "Do you dare to eat a peach?" a refreshingly original copy line for an indigestion drug.

But the point was that she had worked hard, brought her fine mind to bear on each trivial task, even stayed at her desk throughout the summer while everyone else took time off, returning smug and suntanned with fat packets of holiday snaps. And her reward had come, as she had known it must.

About a month ago Malcolm had called her into his glass box of an office. Swivelling away from his Simpsons screensaver, he looked her over consideringly, gave his breath-freshener gum a few macho chomps, and drawled, "You speak French, don't you?"

Caught on the hop, Molly stared as blankly as if he'd asked her to mend his carburetor.

"Unless you're a lying cow," Malcolm added, tossing her a document that she recognized as her own wildly exaggerated CV.

"Oh, *French*." Molly attempted a confident smile. "*Oui. Bien sûr*."

"Got a presentation coming up in Paris," he told her. "Important medical conference, first weekend in October. I usually take one of the girls with me, to see to all the bits and pieces. No extra pay, of course—it's a perk. You'd have to dress smart, mind, and suck up to those lah-di-dah doctors. This is business, not a frigging holiday. Play your cards right, we could be talking a whole new scenario promotion-wise."

Once she had clarified that he (Malcolm) was seriously intending to take her (Molly) to Paris (France), Molly could have fallen to her knees and kissed his gold signet ring. Her first business trip! All expenses paid. *En-suite* bathroom. Fluffy towels. Mini-bar. Maybe one of those remote-control thingies that enabled you to open and close the curtains while lounging Cleopatra-like in bed. And Paris! She'd never been to Paris—not that she hadn't longed to ever since she'd first read Nancy Mitford when she was about fourteen. But it was a luxury, and so far luxuries hadn't figured in her life.

For as long as she could remember, money—the shortage thereof—had been a problem. Half of her clothes came from Oxfam; her school uniform had always been secondhand. She was the only child to carry her (organic) packed lunch in a wicker basket instead of the regulation plastic box with Disney stickers ("A waste of good money," insisted her mother). "Travel" was by bus or bicycle. "Holidays" meant camping, or borrowed cottages out of season. She was probably the only twenty-one-year-old in Britain who'd never been further abroad than the Isle of Wight; now she was about to visit the most beautiful city in the world. The grandeur of it all made her swell with pride that Malcolm had chosen *her*, and she had worked even harder than before, collating data, sourcing yucky slides of diseased tissue and putting them on disk. She had managed to block out Malcolm's boorish manners, his volleys of contradictory instructions and ridiculous mistakes, by holding Paris in her mind like a beacon of light, growing brighter and more dazzling each day.

"Dunno how you stand that little prick," Fatima in the Art Department commented one day, rolling her eyes. But it was easy. The more Malcolm shouted, the louder she hummed under her breath. *I love Paris in the springtime, I love Paris in the fall* . . . She bought guidebooks, practiced her French, spent money she absolutely did not have on a new "smart" outfit, and polished and pressed everything else into what she hoped would pass for a genuine business person's wardrobe. She applied for a passport and had her photograph retaken eight times in the Boots' booth until she was satisfied that it accurately conveyed her new status.

This morning, the longed-for day had finally dawned. She had arrived at the office showered, nail-varnished, leg-shaved, hair-washed, eyebrow-tweezered and meticulously packed. On her desk was a stack of presentation folders ready to be boxed up, conference agendas, hotel info and the disk containing all the visual aids, neatly labeled, which she placed for maximum safety in her own suitcase, carefully cushioned in the folds of her cut-price pashmina. A car would be coming at five thirty this afternoon to take them to the airport. Tonight—*tonight!*—she would be in Paris . . .

"Mind the gap," intoned a voice from the loudspeakers. Molly felt unknown bodies push past her; then another wave of humanity surged into the carriage. It struck her afresh how Londoners ignored one another, even when pressed flesh to flesh. At home she could hardly step into the lane without someone tooting their horn in greeting or stopping her to describe precisely why their Victoria sponge had won first prize at the flower show, and she had many times longed for blissful anonymity.

But this wilful blindness was shocking. She remembered the first time she'd encountered one of those refugee women in gypsy skirt and shawl, a toddler in one hand and a pathetic note in the other. ("I am from Albania. My husband is killed. My children are hungry. Please help me. Thank you.") Mutely the woman had moved from one unseeing passenger to the next until Molly could bear it no longer and had recklessly emptied her wallet and begged the mother to take her child home at once. The patronizing stares of the other passengers exposed her provincial foolishness. Of course, she was streetwise now. She never gave more than a pound, and then only to women with children, men with nice dogs, and any busker who put an extra spring in her step. But she still found the lack of contact chilling. It was hard to make friends when people wouldn't even meet your eye. Just now she could do with a friendly smile.

It was at lunchtime that things had started to go wrong. Malcolm had gone to the pub with his mate from Finance, leaving Molly with so much work that there hadn't been time even to buy a sandwich. Her only peaceful moment was when she ducked into the ladies' for a moment of quiet contemplation with someone's discarded *Glamour*. She had nearly finished the questionnaire ("Are YOU an 'It' Girl? Ten Ways to Find Out"), and was wondering if she'd lose marks by answering "No" to "Would you sleep with a guy on your first date?" when she experienced that uncomfortable sensation of hearing her name spoken aloud. She recognized the voices of Scylla and Charybdis, the two old gossips on Reception. She thought about calling, "I'm here, actually," or clearing her throat, but instead found herself tucking her legs back out of sight and hardly daring to breathe as she strained to hear what they said over the sound of running taps.

Molly listened, cheeks burning, arms wrapped tightly round

her ribs. She waited until she heard the door swish open and shut again and the nattering voices drift away. Her hand shook a little as she unlocked the cubicle door. Automatically she walked over to the row of basins, put down her magazine and turned on the taps to wash her hands. Then she bent to wash her face, too, slapping the water against her cheeks, eyelids and forehead, as if she could cleanse her mind of what she'd overheard. So Malcolm thought he'd be "in her knickers" before the weekend was out, did he? He'd actually been boasting about it round the office. Apparently he'd succeeded before with other "girls" he took abroad and was confident of scoring again.

Molly screwed up her face and pressed her fingers to her temples. All this time she had worked her heart out, proud of being professional, doing her best to respect Malcolm's position as her boss, preposterous though he was—but to him she was nothing more than a female body to be groped. Molly reached for a paper towel and rubbed it roughly over her face, blurring the makeup she had applied so carefully that morning. Her round pink face with its blue eyes and the swooping eyebrows inherited from God-knows-where looked back at her from the mirror. What had Malcolm seen to make him think she was easy? Unconsciously she put a hand to the open neck of her shirt. She couldn't help having largish breasts. Nobody could accuse her of flaunting them. Still, she decided to do up another button.

But she resented having to do so. Malcolm was a wally. And he was so old—maybe as much as thirty. Anyway, she could never be attracted to a man whose mind she didn't admire. Molly wondered if she could face a long weekend fending him off. Perhaps she should talk to Personnel about sexual harassment? But then she might miss out on Paris.

She squared her shoulders. It was perfectly possible for an intelligent, professional woman to deal with this alone. She was not a prude, after all. A new defiance seeped into her veins as she snatched up her magazine. No, she was not an "It" girl, thanks all the same, and she would not be sleeping with Malcolm on their first date for the simple reason that there wouldn't be one. Malcolm could think what he liked. She, Molly Clearwater, was going to Paris and that was that.

So when Malcolm waved her into his office later that afternoon, expelled a gust of beery breath into the air and announced that he'd got hold of two tickets for the Crazy Horse Saloon tomorrow night, Molly was polite but firm. (She knew from the guidebooks that the Crazy Horse was a Paris nightclub where beautiful girls danced naked—"tastefully," her book said, but Molly suspected there was more to it than just dancing, and any fool could guess where such an entertainment might lead.) "Thank you very much for the offer, Malcolm, but I suspect our notions of cultural attractions are somewhat different."

"Oh, do you?" He glowered at her for a long moment, then swiveled his chair round, picked up something from his desk, and dropped it again with a thump. Molly saw that it was one of the folders she'd prepared for the conference, which he must have taken from her desk. "Sections three and four are the wrong way round," he announced flatly.

"What?" Molly was so horrified by the idea she could have made a mistake that she forgot about everything else. She picked up the folder, leafed through it quickly, and to her relief found everything in order. "Look," she showed him the pages, "it's just the way you wanted it. You gave it a final check yesterday, remember?"

He didn't blink, didn't even glance at the report she was holding out. "Today," he said, drawing out the word in a nasal slur, "I want it the other way round."

"But there isn't time! Everything's been collated and bound.

Besides, it doesn't make sense. Section three has to come first because—"

"Are you questioning my judgement?"

"Well . . ." Molly could feel her temper rising and tried to damp it down. *I love Paris in the springtime* . . . "I mean, surely you can see—"

"What I see is one of my staff disagreeing with me. I don't care for that."

*I love Paris in the fall* . . .

"I don't mean to disagree, I'm just trying to point out—"

"I'm the boss, Molly. What I say goes. Frankly, I haven't got time to sit around arguing with some stupid secretary."

"I'm not stupid!"

*I love Paris in the winter, when it drizzles* . . .

"You're a stupid, inexperienced, uptight little virgin."

"I'm not a virgin!"

*I love Paris in the summer* . . .

"And unless you do what I ask, you're not coming to Paris. Got it?"

. . . *when it sizzles.*

There was a loud *snap!* as the folder slammed shut between Molly's hands. Hardly knowing what she was doing, she marched back to her desk, and flung herself into the chair at her computer. An electric storm flashed and sparked in her head. She could hear the blood pounding in her ears. Was this why she had gone to university—to be patronized by a dur-brain like Malcolm? Was this really her best hope—to be Marketing Officer for some dreary company making money out of other people's suffering? Her chest rose and fell under the buttoned shirt. She grabbed the computer mouse and swept it into position with a trembling hand. Her fingernails skittered across the keyboard. She began to type . . .

"Stand well clear of the doors, please." The pushing and shoving began again as the train stopped at Embankment. Molly realized she had been glaring furiously at the diamond pattern of someone's tie, and felt abashed when she saw the poor man shoot her a nervous look, then check his tie for embarrassing stains.

She'd caught Malcolm's eye one final time, when she'd looked up from her typing and found him staring at her through the glass wall of his office, arms folded, lips set in a tight little grimace of triumph. He thought she was retyping his stupid report. But she wasn't. The words had erupted out of her like red-hot lava. Every phrase, every nuance, every comma was still branded into her brain tissue.

*Dear Mr. Figg,*

*Conscious as I am of the honor of working for Phipps Lauzer Bergman, the time has come for me to move on to a position where my talents will be more fully appreciated and deployed. I accepted this job under the misapprehension that its demands would be concomitant with my educational qualifications. Thank you for opening my eyes. I apologize for wasting your valuable time with my suggestions for improving the efficiency (not to mention the literacy) of the department. For my part, the time has not been entirely unprofitable, as I have been able to gather much useful raw material for my first novel.*

*As of today I am formally resigning as so-called "Marketing Officer" and taking the holiday owed to me in lieu of notice. It will therefore not be possible for me to attend the Paris conference as planned, but no doubt you will manage perfectly well without the help of someone who is just "a stupid secretary."*

*Yours sincerely,*

*Molly Clearwater (BA Hons)*

It was a magnificent letter, if she said so herself. Even Malcolm Figg would feel chastened when he read it. She had been right to stand up for herself. Definitely. To wait until Malcolm was temporarily out of his office, then gather her belongings, press "Send" and sweep out of the office for good was positively heroic. In a film, there would have been "go, girl" music and the whole staff would have stood to cheer her exit.

But this wasn't a film: it was her *life*. Molly felt the first icy trickle of reality. She had no job. Malcolm was unlikely to give her a reference. Without a salary she couldn't afford to stay in London. She was back to square one. It was so unfair! Why should she have to pay the penalty for someone else's character flaws? And she had failed—she who'd got top A levels and everything, and just knew she could be brilliant at something if she could only discover what it was. She gazed down the carriage, scrutinizing the shuttered faces. All these people had jobs; they knew where they were headed; they had friends and boyfriends, wives and lovers; they belonged. She wondered if there was anyone like her in the whole of London, or even in the world. Her glance fell on the advertisements pasted along the sides of the carriage, practically all of them offering late-season holidays in Mallorca, Barcelona, Amsterdam, Venice. There were seductive pictures of beaches, cathedrals, a couple in a gondola leaning close. That's right, she thought, rub it in.

For that was the worst of it: she was not going to Paris. Molly squeezed her eyes shut against piercing disappointment. Everyone else had been to Paris—why not her? She knew just how it would be. The Eiffel Tower, boats on the Seine, old women selling flowers, old men playing accordions on cobbled street corners. Lovers kissing on bridges. Restaurants with art-nouveau mirrors, and waiters in long white aprons. The women were all whippet-thin with names like Chantal and Séverine; they spoke in voices high and delicate as chiming bells and carried small clipped poodles. The men were called Jean-something and pouted soulfully through the smoke of their Gauloises. Everyone smoked and drank and argued and made love with passion and style. They were serious about art and literature. They wanted to live beautiful lives.

*So do I!* thought Molly. She'd been practicing her French for weeks, pursing and stretching her lips to achieve the correct pronunciation. *Arrondissement* (ah-rohn-dees-mahn). Tuileries (twee-lur-ee). Pompidou (pohm-pee-doo). Wasted. All wasted. Molly felt a prickle of tears and swallowed hard. Apart from university she had spent her entire life in a cottage in deepest Yokelshire, just her and her mother, their dog Alleluia, Chanticleer and his hens, and those wretched plants—sheds and polytunnels and windowsills full of them—which dominated their lives from Easter to August bank holiday in return for the most meager of incomes. I have measured out my life with hanging baskets . . .

Of course, she loved them all to bits—but it would have been wonderful, just for once, to escape. She was sick of working hard, behaving nicely, helping her mother, being grateful. She was sick of herself, or the "responsible" person everyone thought she was—as if there was any other way to be when you had to help out at home or go broke, when you had to pass exams however much you wanted to party, when you had a terrifying student loan to repay, when you had no nice daddy to bail you out of trouble—in fact, no daddy at all. What no one understood was that she wasn't like that. Inside, she was a free, adventurous spirit, witty and capricious, passionate and lovable. She burned to do something magnificent.

"Next stop Waterloo," announced a disembodied female voice. How exotic. Molly glanced at her watch: twenty-five to six. She should have been on her way to the airport by now.

Everything was in the bag at her feet: her passport, the new clothes she had bought specially, the guidebooks she knew almost by heart, her plastic envelope of euros.

But, oh, no, instead it was back to Fat Sal and the poky flat they shared in Wandsworth. Molly wished she hadn't made quite such a song and dance about this weekend. Sal was such a party girl that Molly sometimes felt dull by comparison and had perhaps overcompensated. She'd feel a total prat when she walked in at the front door this evening—if, that is, Fat Sal even remembered that Molly wasn't supposed to be there. For Fat Sal, who wasn't really fat, merely opulent of flesh and given to squeezing herself into eye-poppingly small garments, was the vaguest and most easygoing person Molly had ever encountered. She'd found her through a flatshare ad in the *Evening Standard* and liked her on sight, confident that with this large, lazy girl there would be no nonsense about cleaning rotas and dustbin days. Notionally Sal had a job in a public library (hurrah, a literary soul-mate, Molly had thought). Mostly she sprawled on her bed in a litter of glossy magazines, nail-varnish bottles, nibbled chocolates and scraps of garishly colored underwear, planning her social life over the phone, while Molly grazed from her pack of supermarket sushi, watched TV and went to bed with a book. Probably that would be the scenario tonight. Molly's shoulders sagged. No leafy boulevards, no cafés, no Latin Quarter, no "*Bonsoir, Mademoiselle.*" There was no adventure in her life, and there never would be.

The train slowed. Molly folded her book shut, ready to tuck it into the pocket of her suitcase. Its cover caught her eye—a grainy photograph of an unsmiling girl not much younger than herself and the words of the title: *Bonjour Tristesse*. Hello, sadness.

And here was the same old platform, the same old posters,

the same old scrum to get out of the tube and change on to the regional line to—no, not the Champs-Élysées, actually, but Earlsfield. Molly hitched up her shoulder-bag, gripped the handle of her suitcase and trudged toward the exit tunnel. As she approached the ticket barrier, her mobile phone bleeped. Someone must have rung her while she'd been deep underground. She fished for her phone, fiddled with the buttons and listened to the message with an expression veering between affection and exasperation.

"Hello, Mollypops, it's me. I expect you're at the airport now and they've made you switch off your phone. Otherwise the planes crash or something. Anyway. Just to say I love you and have a wonderful time. And don't wander about alone late at night, darling, will you? And do remember to put on a cardigan if it's cold. October can be very deceptive. All right, I'll shut up. Lots of love. Ring and tell me how you're getting on. Alleluia says, 'woof-woof.' 'Bye, darling! . . . Oh. It's Mummy, by the way. 'Bye!"

Molly gave a resigned sigh and deleted the message. She couldn't face ringing her mother just yet: all the questions, righteous indignation, murmurs of pity; the warm reassurance that there would be another time for Paris; the real anxiety that Molly had lost her job. Cotton wool was soft and cozy, but it could suffocate you. She was twenty-one, for God's sake. She *must* be allowed to grow up. By the time they were her age, most of the heroines of literature had lived, loved and even died (and not because of their failure to wear cardigans, either).

She dropped the phone back into her bag, fed her tube ticket into the machine at the barrier, and headed for the escalator. At the top she turned right on autopilot and strode into the mainline station, craning her neck to check the information board for the platform and departure time of the next train for Earlsfield.

She wasn't looking where she was going, and suddenly found she had collided hard with something. Her impressions were fleeting but acute—a clash of suitcases, the sharp tang of cologne, a graceful gesture of apology, a man's voice saying, "*Désolé, Mademoiselle.*"

"No, no. My fault. Sorry."

Molly walked on about ten paces before it hit her. He'd been speaking French. He was carrying a suitcase. That meant he'd just arrived from France. From *Paris.*

She stopped dead, and looked back. Normally when she came into the station she turned right. But to the left there was a sign: a logo of three wavy lines with a bright yellow star, and a single word, "Eurostar." She saw people squeezing into a sleek glass lift that descended into the booking hall—two girls hunched under backpacks, a businessman with his laptop, a middle-aged couple coddling expensive luggage. The lift disappeared slowly from view while Molly stood still in the criss-cross commuter traffic, transfixed by a terrifying and wonderful thought. Her heart began to flutter, to quicken and swell until she could hardly breathe.

She had a passport. She had her euros and a credit card. No one expected her back until Sunday evening.

Freedom. A whole weekend of freedom. If she dared.

But she didn't know anyone. She had nowhere to stay. What if she got lost?

Her spine stiffened. Was she going to lie down under the tractor wheels of fate? Was she always going to do what other people expected, not what she wanted? Did she have a mind of her own, or was she truly just "a stupid secretary"?

*No way!* If she wanted to be a heroine, it was time to start behaving like one.

Her hand tightened around the handle of her suitcase. She walked toward the elevator. Words formed in her head and she repeated them silently, gaining confidence and conviction, so that by the time she reached the ticket booth they tripped off her tongue with absolute assurance.

"Next train to Paris, please."

# 2

It smelled different. That was the first thing Molly noticed when she jumped down onto the platform at the Gare du Nord and lifted out her suitcase: not the cindery fug of London stations but something sharper, more spicy and aromatic, foreign in a way that was both delicious and scary.

The clock on the platform stood at five minutes to eleven. She'd forgotten that France was an hour ahead of England until an official had announced their time of arrival over the loudspeaker system—in English first, then French. At the end he said, "*Merci pour votre fidélité*," which had made Molly break into a smile: much more charming than "Thank you for traveling with Southwest Trains." France was different. Now that she was here, she would be different, too.

She spun right round to look about her, feeling the tug of her suitcase on her arm. Above her head glimmered a high vault of glass and iron, with the night sky beyond. The train she'd arrived on lay sleekly at rest beside a spanking-clean platform, which seemed to curve forever toward a cavernous station that exuded an air of slightly dingy imperial stateliness. Near her a couple of train drivers, jackets unbuttoned, were chatting companionably in French, enjoying a smoke. They looked different, too, dark-haired and dark-eyed, at ease with their bodies. A straggle of passengers was making the long trek to the station, and Molly joined them, anxious not to be left behind.

The transition from England to France had seemed eerily simple. It had been twilight in bosky Kent when the train sank gently into the tunnel; half an hour later, without fanfare, she was in France and night had fallen. Nose pressed against the window, hands cupped against her temples to block out the brightness of the compartment, Molly had just been able to make out a vast, flat landscape of hedgeless fields, across which pylons marched like giant black robots. Occasionally a cluster of lights flashed by, marking distant villages—*French* villages, she reminded herself, with a kick of excitement, full of French people eating things like *ragoût* and horsemeat. (Poor horses!) Once, she caught sight of a spotlit church steeple ringed by bleached trees, and sighed with melancholy, remembering Wilfred Owen's "passing bells" for the First World War soldiers who had "died like cattle" in this part of France. (She'd done the war poets for A level.)

Her biggest worry was finding a room for tonight. She had banked on there being some kind of tourist office where a nice English-speaking person would direct her to somewhere cheap and safe. As soon as she was inside the main building she looked around for signs. Surely there was bound to be such a service in a big international station like this?

There was, but the office had closed two hours ago. Blinds were drawn down behind glass windows. A sign on the door read "*Fermé*." Slowly Molly retraced her steps into the center of the station, put down her case and stood wondering what to do. The other passengers were dispersing with frightening speed. Some had already been greeted by friends or relatives in a babble of French, and hustled away into the night; others were trundling their luggage outside to catch buses and taxis. Everyone else seemed to know where they were going. Suddenly the station seemed very big and gloomy, and Molly felt very small. Soon she'd be left alone with the winos and weirdos lolling against pillars and skulking under arches. She couldn't help thinking of lucky, lucky Linda in *The Pursuit of Love*, who was rescued in this very station, penniless and in tears, by a heavenly French duke. ("I can see you're a woman who needs a lot of concentrating on": she loved that line.) No dukes here, by the look of it—though a dubious trio of bottle-blondes, lightly dressed and heavily made up, was eyeing her with interest. Crikey! Molly picked up her case and gave the jacket of her business suit a prim tug. She'd better get a move on before *she* was mistaken for a prostitute!

She fled outside and, despite her anxiety, experienced a flood of pure joy as the lights of Paris leapt out at her from the darkness. She was standing on the edge of a great sweep of cobblestones that rippled like waves on a lake. Car tires emitted a bass drum-roll as they passed over them—a lovely sound. There were high, ornate lampposts that cast a candlelight glow on to the station façade, a grandiose affair of columns and arches and classical statues in togas, with the word *Nord* embossed in swanky capitals. The air smelled of sweet tobacco and frying potatoes. Along the far side of the forecourt ran a wide boulevard gaudy with signs—*Café*, *Brasserie*, *Tabac*. One or two places were still lit up and their awnings open. Even from this distance Molly could sense the bustle and enjoyment. The blood in her own veins seemed to flow faster, and she was filled with a fierce, almost painful expectancy. It was the oddest sensation, a kind of nostalgia in reverse, as if she was already feeling the emotional reverberations of something that hadn't yet happened. But it was waiting for her here, she just knew it.

"Taxi? Taxi?" Molly whirled round to find a man at her

shoulder, small and Arab-looking. His ingratiating smile exposed a gridlock of yellow teeth. "Taxi?" he repeated, gesturing vaguely into the darkness and stretching a skinny arm towards her suitcase.

"*Non!*" Molly swung it out of his reach and stepped back. "Er, *merci beaucoup*." Chin in the air, she strode back into the station, trying to look like someone who didn't need a taxi, thanks all the same, not because she couldn't afford one but because she had another, much better plan. But what was it?

The station looked even emptier than before. The three blondes had become two. Someone was singing to himself, swooping boozily from note to note. Molly walked briskly, trying not to panic. During the train journey she had pinpointed an area of cheap hotels listed in her guidebook, only a couple of stops away on the underground system, though she'd been nervous of negotiating her way around this alone, especially late at night. And what if all the hotels were full? But now she had no choice. Her eyes skittered from side to side. *Please, God, let there be a Métro station*—and suddenly, miraculously, there it was, a blue-and-white sign hung above steps leading downward. Molly took them at a run, her heels clattering. She would not be mugged. She would not get on the wrong train. She had a brain, hadn't she? Now was the time to use it.

In fact, the Paris system was as logical and straightforward as London's. All you had to do was get yourself on the right line, going in the right direction, feed money into a machine that disgorged a clatter of change and a ticket (a titchy stub of a thing, a quarter the size of a London one), then feed the ticket into another machine that released a turnstile. It was a little nerve-racking walking down the echoing tunnels, but it seemed to Molly that she wasn't nearly so deep underground as she would be in London. True, the first thing she saw on reaching the platform was a man peeing against the wall, but she simply averted her gaze and walked on to sit near some normal-looking people, on a very strange plastic seat embedded in tiles. She studied the posters on the other side of the tracks. It struck her that nearly all of them, whether they were advertising soap powder, hair conditioner or fashion, featured an abundance of female flesh—not, she thought, as a provocative statement but as a matter of course. How very French. Molly felt a thrill of liberation. *Je suis dans Paris . . . en Paris? . . . à Paris?* Whatever.

The train came surprisingly quickly—and quietly, on rubber wheels. It looked clean and unintimidating, two-toned in white and peppermint green. There was a kind of latch affair on the doors, which you had to unhook, but luckily someone opened it for her, and Molly stepped gratefully into the compartment and sat down. She looked around her with interest. Except at the ends of each carriage, all the seats faced forward or backward, not sideways as in most tube trains. This made her feel less conspicuous, and she glanced around at the groups of people, mainly young, apparently friendly, in all shades of white, brown and black, just like London. Reassured, she unfolded her map and started to work out how to get to the street she wanted, once she arrived at her stop.

République turned out to be a vast, forbidding square, harshly lit by traffic lights and speeding headlamps, with a monumental statue at its center and identically wide, straight streets radiating from it in all directions. There weren't many people about, just a few loitering shadows. Molly wondered if she'd made a terrible mistake ("English Girl Found Murdered"), but it was too late now. She started to negotiate her way to the other side of the square, squinting at signs. Ah, yes, rue du Faubourg du Temple. (What exactly was a *faubourg*?) She stepped off the curb onto a pedestrian crossing, then squealed with fright as a horn blared in her ear and a car shot out of nowhere, missing her toes by inches. Another roared close behind. Its passenger goggled at her like a maniac and tapped a forefinger to his temple. Of course. They drove on the right here: she'd been looking the wrong way. She must be more careful. ("Tragic Road Accident—Minster Episcopi Mourns.")

Her case was beginning to feel as if it held the entire *Encyclopedia Britannica*. Every couple of minutes she paused to change hands, fanning her chafed palms. A group of rowdy teenage boys passed her. "*Sprechen sie Deutsch?*" they jeered. "Do you speak Eengleesh?" Molly walked faster. At last she reached a long, drab street lit with a few illuminated hotel signs hanging at wonky angles. "Don't be put off by the crumbling façades," her guidebook had advised and, truthfully, Molly hardly cared now where she ended up so long as she could fling herself onto some bed and stop worrying. The odd whiff of squalor hadn't put off George Orwell, had it?

The first hotel was locked. Ringing the doorbell, Molly finally summoned an old man in slippers, and learnt her first new French word, "*complet*," meaning "full." He was desolated, but wished her a courteous good night before shutting the door firmly in her face. It was the same story at the next two. The fourth was unlocked and Molly's hopes rose, particularly when she saw a large ginger cat sprawled in sleep on the windowsill, its face comically draped by a lace curtain. Anyone who liked animals was bound to be nice. She took a deep breath, stepped into the lobby and walked over to the high reception desk.

A bald man in a cardigan was sitting behind it, watching television. When she repeated her request, he frowned with uncertainty and said he would have to ask his wife. He retreated to a door marked "*Privé*," and in due course reappeared with a woman of about sixty, slap-slapping in sandals, her dumpy figure encased in a flower-print dress whose hem, Molly couldn't help noticing, didn't quite bridge the varicose-veined gap to the top of her pop socks. She and her husband spoke together, so rapidly that Molly couldn't follow. Whatever the man said, his wife contradicted him scornfully, though the scorn seemed habitual rather than malicious—or perhaps the French always sounded like that. Eventually the woman turned to Molly. There was a small room on the top floor. Molly would have to share *la salle de bain* and *les toilettes*. The price was fifty euros per night, payable in advance, not including breakfast. What did she think?

Flooded with relief, Molly smiled her acceptance. No, she didn't need to see the room; she would take it. There then followed a tremendous performance of passport-checking and form-filling, of payment and the issuing of a receipt, of smiling and head-bowing, all executed with such precision and courtesy, and so many *merci, Mademoiselle*s and *je vous en prie*s that Molly felt quite overwhelmed. But at last she was in possession of a key attached to a clinking slab of metal with her room number engraved on it, and juddering slowly upward in the oldest, smallest, most fragile lift she had ever seen.

When she pulled open the concertina grille at the top, she found herself at the end of a musty hall lined with doors. She walked down it, turning her head from side to side, checking the room numbers. Floorboards squeaked and shifted under carpeting thin and brown as cardboard. There were no other sounds. Everyone else must be asleep.

She found her room, unlocked the door and switched on the light. Not too bad. There was a double bed with a shiny floral spread, a wardrobe and shelf made of cheap varnished wood, a bedside table with a yellow plastic ashtray advertising Pernod. Molly dropped her case, walked over to the window and pulled back the curtains, pleased to see that her room overlooked the street and faced a long run of steeply pitched roofs studded with intriguingly shaped dormer windows—arched, pedimented, oval as an egg. She unlocked the catch, pulled the windows open and leaned out. She could hear the thump-thump of distant music, then the wasp-buzz of a motorbike racing down the street. The air was sweet. She could see stars.

Paris was right here, under her nose. She'd done it! All by herself. Molly sighed with satisfaction, then turned away from the window, kicked off her shoes and flung herself onto the bed. She stared up at the ceiling, with its sepia continents of damp. It was good to rest, after all that walking and worrying. Yet at the same time she felt tinglingly alive. If only she was braver, she would go out and do something. But where? And what? And with whom? She pictured herself in one of those mirrored cafés with a cup of coffee before her—no, something more sophisticated like . . . a cocktail, that was it. Maybe a martini—a real one, not out of a bottle. "Very dry," she would say, with cool authority, to the barman, "with an olive." (*Un olive* or *une olive*? Damn. Okay, forget the olive.) She would be reading a book, completely absorbed. (Not a Paris guide, of course: something unquestionably fine, like *War and Peace*.) A shadow would fall across its pages. "Ah, Tolstoy. How *extraordinaire* to find a girl so beautiful and yet so intelligent." And she would look up, startled, into the face of the handsomest Frenchman imaginable. They would talk deep into the night about literature and life, staring into each other's eyes across the table, oblivious to the trivial chatter of the *beau monde* around them, until it was time to get into his open sports car and speed through the boulevards, her hair flying . . .

Molly arched her back and bounced energetically off the bed and onto her feet. What drivel. She fanned her flushed cheeks, extinguishing the fantasy, then heaved her suitcase onto the bed and unzipped it smartly. Just because Paris was supposed to be the most romantic city in the world, you didn't have to be in love to enjoy it: that would be a very narrow definition indeed. There was romance of the mind, for example, inspired by beauty and, er, history. She unearthed her sponge-bag and pyjamas. Tomorrow there would be the Louvre and Notre Dame, the Eiffel Tower and Sacré Coeur. She was *glad* she'd be exploring them alone. Some people weren't interested in culture at all: they only went abroad to wallow in drink and sex. It was much better not to have a companion than one who would distract her.

Anyway, she did have a companion. For after she'd hung as many of her clothes as would fit on the three available hangers, and dumped the rest in piles on the wooden shelf, she had found Bertie squashed into a corner of her case among the shoes. She pulled him out by the tail and smoothed his threadbare badger fur. His glassy eyes winked back at her with their usual cheeky expression. Good old Berts. They'd been together since she was three, when she'd found him peeking out of her Christmas stocking. Here was the bald patch where she'd had an accident with Superglue, and this was the wonky ear chewed by Alleluia when she was a puppy. Molly had cried into Bertie's fur, taught him acrobatics, tested him on his times tables, taken him on holidays and sleepovers and even to college (although she'd sometimes hidden him in a drawer). He was all the brothers and sisters she'd never had. He knew all her secrets. Molly kissed his worn nose and deposited him on the pillow.

Time for bed. Her blue cotton pyjamas lay ready. Somehow they looked terribly English—sensible, schoolgirly, dull. A breath of wind fluttered the net curtains at her open window. She heard an echoing click-clack of heels in the street and a high, flirtatious giggle. "*Mais arrête, toi!*" French women probably wore little silk nonsenses to bed—or nothing at all. Fleetingly, Molly put her hands to her breasts, feeling their fullness, the weight of warm flesh.

*Bang!* Her heart gave a mule-kick of alarm. Someone was knocking at her door.

# 3

Molly stared at the door. Who could it possibly be?

"It's me!" someone shouted in English. The voice was loud, uninhibited and female.

Molly opened the door cautiously. A tall girl in a denim jacket looked back at her in astonishment. "Who are you?" she demanded.

"I'm Molly. Who are *you*?"

"Where's Janine?"

"Who's Janine?"

"Isn't she here?"

"Have you got the wrong room?"

"You mean she moved out?"

"I mean I just moved in."

"But where's she gone? Where's her stuff?"

Even as she spoke the girl was pushing at the door so she could see for herself. Such was her aura of energy and confidence that Molly stepped back and let her, hoping this wasn't some kind of con-trick. She kept one hand on the doorknob, just in case. The girl strode into the middle of the room and plonked her fists on hipbones that were just visible above a pair of perilously low-slung jeans. The silver rings in each ear and her close-cropped hair, so black it must be dyed, gave her a bold, swashbuckling look. Her eyes flitted over Molly's meager possessions, and the weight of her body sagged onto one sturdy leg. "Aw, shit," she said.

"Something the matter?"

"Mind if I take a peek in your cupboard?"

"Er . . ."

But she had already pulled open the doors and was scanning its contents.

Molly scurried after her. "What are you looking for?"

The girl muttered to herself and reached up to rummage behind the spare bedding.

Molly's imagination raced. Was "stuff" a codeword for drugs? What if something illegal had been stashed in her room? She'd be arrested by the police . . . interrogated in French . . . thrown into prison with lesbians and people with funny eyes. No one would know where she was.

"What exactly are you after?" she asked again.

The girl knelt down on the carpet and lowered her head to look under the bed. (Oh, my God, what if Janine was there—*murdered?* Molly pictured herself in the dock facing an implacable French jury. "*Mais je suis innocente!*" She'd never see Alleluia again. Her mother would die of a broken heart.)

After interminable seconds the girl clambered to her feet and dusted off her hands with a clash of bangles. There was a scowl of disgust on her face. "I don't believe this."

"*What?*" By now Molly could practically feel the breeze on her bare neck as she awaited the rasp of the guillotine.

"She's done a runner with my Rollerblades."

"R-Rollerblades?" Molly echoed weakly.

"Except they're not mine. I sort of borrowed them off this

outfit I work for. Now I'll have to pay megabucks for a new pair. And I'm skint as it is."

Was that all? Molly felt quite giddy with relief. Now that reason had returned, it was perfectly apparent that this was no madwoman or con-artist, just an ordinary girl perhaps five or six years older than herself, with an unusually upfront manner and an accent she couldn't place. "I'm really sorry," she said, thinking as much of her own lurid imaginings as the missing Rollerblades.

"Not your fault, sweetie. Only how could Janine do that? We were supposed to go out partying tonight. She's an *Ozzie*, for God's sake. Sydney," she added darkly, as if that explained everything.

"And you're from . . . ?"

"Melbourne, of course."

Molly nodded. Her vague mental map of Australia showed the two cities only about a millimeter apart, but clearly the moral divide was a yawning chasm.

The Australian girl sighed. "I'm too trusting, that's my problem." She rolled her eyes at Molly, twisting her features into a rueful grimace that was somehow comical. "Go on, call me a dickhead."

"Dickhead." Molly grinned.

The girl burst out laughing. "Gee, thanks. I'm Alicia, by the way." *Uh-lee-sha* was how she pronounced it, in an accent as ripe and rich as Camembert running off the plate. "I lived in this place for a couple of weeks when I first got here. Now I'm kipping on someone's boat. Paris is so ace, isn't it?"

"I don't know. I just got off the train from London. I've never been here before."

"You're kidding!"

"Actually, I've never been out of England before."

Alicia goggled and collapsed onto the bed, causing Bertie to somersault off the pillow and roll to a stop in a saggy hollow behind her back. Molly chewed her lip with embarrassment, hoping Alicia wouldn't notice him. She was suddenly conscious of the contrast between this gutsy Australian, who had traveled right round the world and knew how to rollerblade, and herself, in her office-girl clothes with a stuffed toy for company.

"I quit my job today," she told Alicia, with a defiant swagger, "so I thought, what the hell? I'll go to Paris for the weekend."

"Good on you!" Alicia was frankly admiring. "Freedom's my motto. Freedom to go where I like, do what I like, be the person I am."

"Oh, I agree," Molly said fervently. "That's why I'm here. Live a little. Go wild."

"So, what are your plans?"

"Well, I thought I'd start tomorrow at the Louvre—"

There was a scornful snort. "No, I mean now. Tonight."

"Tonight?" Molly faltered. Automatically her eyes swivelled to the pathetic heap of pyjamas and sponge-bag at the end of her bed.

Alicia followed her gaze. "Aw, don't be such a wuss." For a moment she eyed Molly consideringly, as if judging her suitability for some unknown task. Then she slapped her thighs with both palms and stood up. "Come on," she said.

"What do you mean?"

"Since Janine's ratted out on me I'll take you instead."

"Take me where?"

"Get some shoes on."

"But—"

"Grab a jacket."

Molly's ears sang with excitement. Where were they going? What would happen? Who was this girl? But somehow the shoes were already on her feet. A jacket seemed to leap of its own accord from the hanger into her waiting hand. Alicia was at the door flipping the latch impatiently. "Got plenty of money?"

"Yes!" Molly gave a breathless laugh. "But—"

Alicia turned sharply and raised a commanding finger. "No buts." Her eyes locked on Molly's. "This is your first night in Paris—ever. Right?"

"Yes."

"You're only here for the weekend. Right?"

"Yes."

"You want to climb into your PJs and go to bed?"

"No!"

"Okay, then." Alicia grinned. "Let's go play."

* * *

And then they were out in the glittery night, walking between shuttered houses, past humpy cars parked bumper to bumper, under tiers of narrow ironwork balconies. The air was as soft as summer. Molly could smell vanilla-sweet drifts of tobacco smoke, the sour tang of urine, hot fat from a crêperie. There were trees everywhere, the glow and bustle of small cafés sprouting umbrellas, the ripple of French on the breeze.

They were on their way to someone's flat—a French girl called Zabi. Alicia worked part-time in her clothes shop, selling a mixture of retro fashion and Zabi's own designs. This was just one of Alicia's many cash-in-hand jobs, which also included dog-walking, baby-sitting, waitressing and bar work, as well as the Rollerblade tours—anything to keep her in Paris, which Alicia pronounced the coolest city in Europe.

"Have you been to lots of countries, then?" Molly asked enviously.

"Christ, yes. Holland, Belgium, Luxembourg, Germany, all

that Eastern Europe stuff. Italy, the Greek islands, Gallipoli—the whole enchilada."

"Golly." Molly's head spun with all the wonders Alicia must have seen—the Sistine Chapel, the Rijksmuseum, Prague, Venice, the Acropolis. "Er, what happens in Luxembourg?"

"Don't ask me. It was on this stupid bus tour I took when I first came overseas. All I remember is I got bitten by bedbugs in the hostel and spent most of the time itching."

"And Gallipoli? I'm not even sure I know where that is."

"Jeez, Molly, don't you know any history? It's in Turkey. You Brits sent thousands of Ozzie soldiers to their death during the First World War. Mel Gibson, remember?"

"He can't be that old."

"Not fighting, you muppet. In the movie."

"Oh, right." Molly gave her head a little shake. Her brain didn't seem to work properly in France.

But she didn't care. With Alicia at her side the city was no longer intimidating: each unfamiliar sight gave her an electric charge. Her head buzzed: she felt as if she could walk forever. They had turned onto a wide boulevard now, with cars zipping jauntily back and forth. *Beep-beep. Vroom-vroom.* Trees marched down either side of it in synchronized step, each trunk embedded in a wrought-iron circle of fanciful design. Street lamps bobbed among the leaves like high white balloons. Silvery fountains spouted from a small park. There were bright cafés nosing out onto the pavement like jolly glass pleasure boats. Molly spotted one of those kiosks she'd seen in countless photographs: a squat minaret the color of a pine forest at night, decorated with lions' heads and topped by an onion dome. Its sole purpose seemed to be to display advertisements—*Le Figaro*, *Paris-Match*, the Comédie Française. She laughed aloud.

"What?" demanded Alicia.

"It's just so amazing to be here. I feel like Miranda in *The Tempest.*"

"Who?"

"'O brave new world, that has such people in't.'" Molly's voice throbbed with poetry. "That's where Aldous Huxley got the title for his novel, you know—though he used it ironically, of course."

Alicia shot her a suspicious look. "You're not one of those brainboxes, are you?"

"Well . . ." Molly didn't like to boast. "Everyone knows Shakespeare."

"Not in Tullamarine, they don't," said Alicia, and added breezily, "I'm not really into culture and all that shemozzle."

Molly's eyes widened, though she said nothing. Tullamarine: that must be where Alicia had been brought up. It had a romantic, bushwhacking ring to it. Molly pictured a small dusty town with a water tower and a stray yellow dog pasted against a flat blue sky. It probably didn't even have a library! She would get Alicia to tell her all about it. But not now. There was too much to look at.

They left the boulevard and entered a maze of side streets, clearly a hip and happening area, with cool-looking restaurants and noisy bars pumping out Latino music. Who else would be at Zabi's flat? Molly wondered. Would they all be terribly smart and sophisticated? Would her A-level French hold up to a proper conversation? *Bonsoir. Je m'appelle* Molly. *Je suis officier de marketing.* What if they were all snorting cocaine? Or discussing Balzac? Or *both*? She stole a glance at Alicia, shoulders back, head high, striding along like a warrior queen, and tried to copy her careless assurance.

"Mind the dog-poo." Alicia yanked her elbow just in time.

The streets narrowed and darkened; the crowds disappeared.

Molly glimpsed secret stairways and stone archways decorated like molded pastry. Their footsteps echoed between walls shrouded with vines, making Molly think of spies during the French Revolution. If she edited out the occasional parked car or blaze of electric light, she could be gallant Lady Clearwater helping the Scarlet Pimpernel to smuggle aristocrats to England—or perhaps Citoyenne Clearwater, with a tricolor headband and a knife between her teeth, ready to storm the Bastille.

"Here we go." Alicia stopped in the shadow of a deep archway. Beyond it Molly could see a romantically ramshackle courtyard with bicycles parked on the cobbles and a skulking cat. Light from an uncurtained window filtered through the leaves of a much-pollarded tree, under which two African men sat smoking on rickety kitchen chairs.

"We'll have a drink and check out who's here," Alicia told her, "then maybe move on somewhere. You'll love Zabi. She's totally insane."

There was a narrow entrance in one of the vine-covered walls. A dim stairway curved upward. Molly cooled her palm on the iron banister as they climbed, inhaling the smell of damp plaster and a distinct undertone of drains. She could hear party chatter, a screech of laughter, the smoochy beat of jazz. On the top floor they reached a door covered in spray-can graffiti. "Zabi's version of a visitors' book," explained Alicia, banging loudly. "See?" She pointed to one of the lower panels where her own name appeared in a lime-green flourish, with orange stars instead of dots over the *i*s. "She says it's an interactive artwork that will sell one day for millions."

Molly was wondering just how insane the insane Zabi might be when the door was flung open by an extremely pretty girl wearing a lacy white ra-ra skirt and black fishnets. Barely five feet tall, with burnished hair sheared into a bad-boy crop and a tiny jewel sparkling in the curve of one nostril, she looked like a naughty fairy.

"Alicia! *Salut!*" She threw her hands into the air, then pulled Alicia close and kissed her enthusiastically on each cheek. "And who is this?" She turned to Molly. Her bright stare was not unfriendly; nevertheless, Molly felt that, in one laser glance, every millimeter of her body shape and clothing had been expertly assessed. The next moment, before she could even try out a tentative "*Bonsoir*," her hand had been grasped and firmly shaken.

Alicia explained Molly's presence as they stepped inside. Her French yowled and twanged with distinctly un-Gallic vowels, but it was impressively fluent. With suitable hand gestures she outlined the disappearance of her Rollerblades along with the *méchante* Janine, while Zabi gasped at the *horreur* of it all. Molly stood between them in a daze. The small square room seemed full of people, all smoking, all talking at top speed in a language that seemed to bear no relation to the one she had studied at school. There was a stuffed owl in the fireplace and a wirework scorpion hanging from the ceiling. One wall was adorned with an enormous poster for a Johnny Hallyday concert dated 2000—hadn't he *died* in about 1963?

In a voice at least an octave higher than Molly's, Zabi called to someone to bring some drinks. Meanwhile, a group had drifted over to listen to the Rollerblade drama. More people shook Molly's hand—a pair of prancing French girls with fluting voices, a black man so elegant and sinuous that Molly could hardly stop staring at his beauty, a Spanish girl called Kiki who designed shoes to die for, an older man, whom Zabi introduced as her guru, dressed from head to toe in white and glowing as if from an all-over spiritual suntan. "I adore blondes," he confided to Molly, caressing her hair.

"Beer or wine?" asked a voice.

Molly accepted a glass of red wine from a Frenchman with a ponytail who informed her that his name was Didier and that he was a merchant of biological vegetables. "How very interesting," she replied.

So: she was from England? Didier could tell by her accent. He hoped her poor country was at last recovering from its terrible crisis. Or did it still suffer?

"Not *too* much," Molly answered cagily, having no idea what he was talking about. She took another slug of wine.

For his part, he could not imagine the horror of living in a country full of stupid cows.

"Really?" Molly bristled.

Luckily France had taken special measures to keep each and every stupid English cow out of France.

"Well, *I'm* here," Molly told him defiantly. "And I'm not stupid."

"Give the guy a break," Alicia's voice rumbled in her ear. "He's talking about mad-cow disease—*vache folle.* He runs an organic veg stall."

Molly clapped a hand to her mouth to stifle a giggle. Fortunately, Didier seemed to have decided that this was an example of the famous English sense of humor, and started laughing too. Molly felt a surge of adrenaline. She was witty—in French! She grinned at Didier (crazy name—crazy guy!) and raised her glass to her lips again. Oh. It was empty.

Alicia steered her toward a table covered with bottles. "Come and meet Gilbert. He's lost his job, too—one of those dot-coms. The French piled onto the techno-wagon a little late and just fell off with a wallop."

They passed the guru trying out his technique on one of the prancing girls, who had stopped prancing and was lying on a sofa among rumpled *faux* furs. His clasped hands pressed on her stomach. "Breathe, breathe," he intoned, while she squealed and squirmed.

Gilbert *(jeel-bear)* was a broodingly handsome guy in designer black jeans, smoking furiously. "I am a martyr of the new economy," he told Molly, with tragic eyes. "For two years I sat clicking like a moron. I worked ninety hours a week. Lunch was a *baguette* at my desk—can you imagine? And now—*pouf!*" He tapped his ash. "The best I can hope for, it's a job in one of the ministries with the gray-hairs. I'm going to have to buy a suit."

"That's very sad," Molly agreed, admiring his cheekbones. "Here, have some more wine."

"You know, you're a very sympathetic girl."

Was it the booze or could she hear an electronic tune playing? Molly thought she recognized the "Marseillaise." Gilbert slid a mobile phone from his shirt pocket and pressed it to his ear. "*Chérie*," he pouted, "where are you?"

Oh, well. Molly turned away and surveyed the smoke-hazed room. It was all very different from Minster Episcopi, or even Earlsfield. Travel did broaden the mind.

Zabi got her to sign the front door in purple and silver. A man in glasses, confusing her with Alicia, gave her a brief lecture on the physiology of the kangaroo. French people spoke French to her, and she answered them back. Absolutely no one wanted to know that she was an *officier de marketing.* There was no quiz on Balzac, though she did find herself drawn into an impassioned argument between one of the prancing girls and the organically minded Didier. *Non!* insisted the girl. It was only humans who were entitled to possess a donkey. *Mais écoute*, Sylvie, had not the good Lord created all life? Why shouldn't an insect—or even a tomato—have its own donkey? What did Molly think? Eventually, Molly clicked that they were not talking about donkeys (*ânes*) but souls (*âmes*). Her own soul was stirred by the loftiness of this discussion. It was true what they said about the French being intellectuals. She rather thought that France might turn out to be her spiritual home.

Now Alicia had caught her eye and was waving her over. Zabi was with her, and as Molly made her way across the room she felt, once again, the scrutiny of those black eyes. "Zabi's talking about going to a club," Alicia told her. "There's this new DJ who's really hot."

"Great!" Molly's eyes sparkled.

"Only there might be a problem."

The problem, Molly discovered, was herself—or, rather, her clothes. This particular club was infamous for its bouncers—*les physios*—who took a sadistic pleasure in excluding anyone failing to meet their capricious criteria of cool. ("*Salauds!*" Zabi tossed her head in disgust.) Molly looked very *nice*, Alicia went on, in fact, pretty enough to look good in almost anything, but . . .

Molly glanced down at her polyester-mix work suit and the smile faded from her face. She could almost hear the elation hiss out of her, as if from a punctured tire. It was always the same. It was always other people who wore great clothes, had fantastic jobs, went to cool clubs. Not Molly Clearwater, oh no. Once again she felt as though a magnificent play were being enacted on stage—lights, color, drama—while she waited, waited, waited in the darkness of the wings for a cue that never came.

". . . but Zabi can fix you up, no worries," Alicia was saying.

Molly turned in confusion to Zabi, who was fluffing out her skirt, looking excited. Fix her up how? Fix her up where? And why? But already she could feel a hand in the small of her back, propelling her across the room. "You won't believe Zabi's bedroom," said Alicia's voice.

A door was opened, a light switched on. Molly gasped. There

was a bed as big as a galleon, a crumbling gilt mirror propped against one wall, a tailor's dummy half dressed in a zany patchwork coat, and rack after rack of clothes: black leather, white silk, damson velvet, vintage lace and aged denim, boots with buckles, belts with studs, sequins, fur, hats. They couldn't all be Zabi's. This was obviously an overspill from her shop.

"*Alors*," Zabi steered Molly to the mirror and planted her in front of it. "What do we think?"

Molly thought several things at once—that they couldn't, surely, mean to lend her special clothes just to go to a club; that she would rather die than undress in front of the terrifyingly chic Zabi; that however hard they tried she was going to wind up looking silly. She had the vertiginous sense of teetering on a precipice, wondering if she dared jump off.

"I totally love this dress." Alicia, who had been rummaging in the racks, brought over some slippery red thing.

"Tsk, tsk." Zabi waved it away. Her face was a sharp little triangle of concentration. She slid off Molly's jacket, and swept the hair back off her shoulders.

"Or this?" Alicia thrust a hanger under Molly's chin.

Molly stared aghast at a zebra-print dress about two feet long, with a hole where the front should be. "I can't wear that!"

But even as she spoke she could feel Zabi's deft fingers at her zipper. The next second her skirt lay in a pool at her ankles. Helplessly Molly stepped out of it. Zabi, with a searing glance at the label, folded it expertly and placed it on the bed. "And the shirt," she commanded.

Once again, Molly found herself obeying. A familiar figure in chainstore bra and tummy-toner tights stared back at her from the mirror. There was dead silence.

"Look, Alicia," Zabi said finally, in the tone of a scientist pointing out an interesting phenomenon under the microscope. "The breasts, they are very pretty, *non*? And the legs?" She fluttered a tiny hand. "One could perhaps do something."

The two of them walked around her, as if examining a piece of livestock. Molly found the experience unnerving yet strangely thrilling. The nearest she had ever come to being "dressed" was when a languid shop assistant had drawled, "Oh, that *really* suits you." (Often this turned out to be demonstrably untrue.) But here she sensed she was in the presence of professionals. Morever, everything was happening to her in a foreign language. There was a soothing impersonality about French—*the* breasts, *the* legs, *the* bottom (which, alas, was multiple in French—*les fesses*)—as if none of these body parts had anything to do with her. French also had a cunning trick of making everything impersonal—*il faut . . . on doit*—so that it was not Molly who was trying on clothes, but the clothes that must be tried on.

Actually, the zebra dress didn't look at all bad. Molly felt cheered until Zabi rejected it with one withering glance. Next she tried a slinky black number ("*Not* black," Zabi ruled), then pinstripe flares with a creamy chiffon blouse ("*une catastrophe*"). Garment by garment, Molly felt herself yielding to the seductive narcissism of the moment.

Suddenly, Zabi smacked her hands together. "Gold!" she declared. "With the hair, the skin—you understand? Quick, Alicia, the little skirt. And the crocodile sandals. Ah, I can see it all. I am a genius! *Vite, vite!*"

In a moment Molly was stepping into high heels with thin straps that crossed at the ankle. Next, she slid a miniskirt of soft, shimmering gold leather over her hips and drew the zipper closed. It fit perfectly.

"Oops, VPL alert," said Alicia, pointing to the visible groove in Molly's hips made by her knicker elastic. "You'll have to just wear your tights."

"*What?*"

"Hurry up or we'll miss the DJ."

Molly started to make the necessary tortuous adjustment. Meanwhile, Zabi had skipped over to the racks and was yanking back the hangers, muttering to herself. She returned with a bustier made of shot silk that gleamed bronze and gold where it caught the light. She held it against Molly and sighed. "I am inspired! Of course, the bra must not be worn."

No underwear at all! She couldn't go out in public like this. Well, maybe she could. The bustier felt cool and slithery against her bare skin. It hooked up the front, moulding her figure into a miraculous shape.

"You see?" said Zabi. Her eyes snapped with pleasure.

But before Molly could see properly, Zabi pulled her over to a plain wooden chair and tilted a lamp beam on to her face. "A little more drama with the eyes," she murmured, applying a stub of pencil. "And something at the neck." She rummaged in a drawer and pulled out a thin velvet ribbon which she fastened under Molly's hair. "Now, shut your eyes." There was a hiss, a smell like hairspray, the tickle of tiny droplets on Molly's bare skin. Finally she handed Molly a jacket of worn velvet the exact colour of coffee beans. "There," she said, relaxing at last into a satisfied smile, "you are perfect."

Molly stood up slowly, balancing on the unfamiliar heels.

"Uh-oh, boys, hold on to your lunchboxes." Alicia popped out from behind the racks where she'd been rummaging for accessories. She'd given her hair a purple streak and found a wide, ferociously studded belt to sling round her hips. "Molly, you look sensational."

"Do I?" Molly slid her arms down the silky lining of her jacket and teetered toward the mirror.

Zabi was readying herself now, filming her lips with dark crimson, puffing a cloud of perfume into the air and letting it rain down on her upturned face and arms, finally wriggling into a tight uniform-style jacket with brass buttons.

The girl in the mirror stared at Molly with smoky eyes. Her legs were long and slender, her breasts like two creamy pillows. Her hair and skin sparkled with gold dust. Molly leaned close. Who was this sultry siren, this golden goddess, this confident, curvy, glamorous, glittery stranger?

The answer bubbled up from a secret place deep inside her. *Me!*

# 4

It was too far to walk to the club, Zabi decreed, especially in their perilous heels, and the Métro had stopped long ago. In the end Didier gave them a lift in his rattletrap veg van, with Molly and Zabi squashed into the front seat and Alicia nobly volunteering to perch in the back on a case of organic mushrooms. Didier boasted that he had twelve different varieties to sell. (*Twelve!* Molly couldn't have named more than five.) Their musky smell made her head spin. So did the wine she had drunk, the blur of lights and buildings, columns and statues, fountains and trees, and the lurching excitement of speeding through a foreign city in the middle of the night, to an unknown destination, with people she hardly knew, wearing someone else's clothes. And no knickers! What could she be thinking of?

But there was no time to think. A light turned green. After a nanosecond Didier jabbed the car horn, and suddenly they were on a bridge, crossing an inky blackness that flickered with tiny sparks of reflected light.

"It's the Seine!" Molly squeaked.

"*Ouais,*" Didier agreed carelessly.

Molly gazed through the grimy window as Paris spread itself out around her like a magic carpet. She could see another bridge farther along, its graceful curve decorated with twin rows of lampposts like candles on a very grand birthday cake. If this was the Seine, in a few moments she would actually be on the Left Bank. Her heart swelled. That was where Hemingway had written in cafés because he was too poor to heat his lodgings, where *Ulysses* was first daringly published, where Gertrude Stein had lived and Oscar Wilde died. Its picturesque streets teemed with student cafés, romantic attics and underground jazz clubs—or so she had always imagined. Truthfully, as they reached the far side of the river and turned onto a busy highway, all she could see was the hulk of a railway station and an eruption of tower blocks.

What was happening now? The van veered off the highway and plunged down a dark sliproad, heading straight for the river. Molly clutched her seat as they rumbled and bounced over cobbles. There was nothing down here but boats and groups of shadowy figures hanging around in what struck Molly as a sinister manner. A chilling thought occurred to her. What if there was no club? What if Zabi and Alicia were members of an international vice ring, and everything that had happened tonight was an elaborate ploy to kidnap her, sail her down the Seine to—well, wherever the Seine came out, and sell her body to some oily sheikh of unspeakable depravity? She'd read a book like that once. She sneaked a look at Zabi, who was humming to herself as she polished her nails on the sleeve of her jacket. That could be a bluff.

The van wheezed to a halt and the engine died. Molly could hear a thumping noise. Was that her heart? "Always tell someone where you've gone, and make sure you've got your bus fare home." Her mother's familiar words tolled ominously in her head. Stealthily she felt for the door handle and began to ease her feet out of her shoes, prepared to run for her life.

A metallic rasp made her jump. Didier had put on the handbrake. He turned to her, his face in shadow. Zabi looked up from her polishing and leaned toward him as if she was about to whisper an instruction.

Molly shrank away from them, the van door flew open under her weight, and she toppled out sideways. Zabi screamed. By a miracle of balance and a rather unattractive ape-like stagger Molly avoided crashing to her knees. Meanwhile she could hear Zabi and Didier demanding anxiously what had happened. Was she hurt? That imbecile car! It belonged in a cemetery. Molly straightened slowly. Fresh air gusted into her lungs—and into her brain.

Of course no one wanted to kidnap her. Didier didn't even get out of his van; he'd be setting up his stall in a few hours' time, he said, and had decided to get some sleep. Zabi had whispered nothing more sinister than "*Merci*" as she kissed him good night. The shadowy figures were clubbers, checking their finances or stopping for a snog. The thumping Molly had heard was not her heart but Alicia demanding release from her fungal fug. And this was no seedy dockside, but a wide and beautiful esplanade dotted with trees that followed the graceful sweep of the Seine. On one side a high wall protected its serenity from the rushing highway; on the other, boats strung with fairy-lights rocked gently on waves of black glass.

The club was on a boat—one of many that had been turned into restaurants and clubs now, each with its own character. Tottering past on treacherous heels, arm in arm with Zabi and Alicia, Molly heard jazz drifting into disco, rock overlaid with rap, until they reached an old lighthouse boat painted sizzling red, with a squat glazed tower flashing like a beacon.

Unquestionably this was the coolest club of all. At the gangplank a small but fervent crowd jostled for entry, waving bank-notes at the *physios*—whose name, Molly discovered, had nothing to do with their build or the physical harm they could inflict but was short for *physionomistes*; in other words, they were experts at reading character in the face. What would they see in hers? she wondered. Suddenly she wanted passionately to get into this place, where music pounded and colored lights streaked across the portholes. She wanted to be part of this excitement, to drown in it, to let go of everything that made her feel small and cramped and disregarded.

Zabi smuggled her way to the front of the line and tilted her chin at the bouncer, a surly Goliath straining at his black suit. Her stance was at once coquettish and imperious as she addressed him in rapid, bantering French. She gestured to her companions, summoning them forward to display themselves. Molly, forgetting she was supposed to be cool, beamed her sunniest smile. "*Je suis australienne,*" Alicia announced, as if that would clinch it.

And perhaps it did. For after long seconds of jowly scrutiny the bouncer stepped aside and jerked his head. They were in. Molly set one fragile heel on the gangplank, feeling the music judder through the boards. A cool updraft from the river tickled her thighs, unfamiliarly exposed, and she tugged at her skirt to hold it decently in place. Then she was on the boat, conscious of its subtle sway as she followed Zabi and Alicia through a hatch to the top of a narrow companionway. A sea of sound roared up to meet them, crashing in Molly's ears like surf. The air was steamy, infused with alcohol, perfume and sweat.

They stopped to wait for a couple coming up the narrow stairway, a dark young man holding the hand of a fragile girl in black, drawing her up behind him like Orpheus leading Eurydice out of Hades. At the top of the steps, quite unselfconsciously, he turned and pulled his partner into a passionate embrace. Inches from Molly's eyes their lips met and melted together. There was no giggling, no pawing, no slobbering—just a kiss so intense that the soles of Molly's feet tingled. Zabi, she saw, was watching respectfully, without impatience, even though they blocked the way. Was love, then, so important?

The couple drew apart. Unhurried and rapt, they brushed past Molly and moved toward the open air, hip to sinuous hip. She couldn't help turning her head to watch them go.

"C'mon, let's groove!" Alicia's heels clanged on the metal steps as she called over her shoulder. Zabi had already disappeared into the teeming pit below. Jerked back to reality, Molly gripped the handrail and plunged after them.

Her first impression was that there was no room to move, not one inch. Bodies pressed close in the half-darkness. A synthesized beat slammed into her chest. The floor bounced under the weight of dancing feet. A man thrust his grinning face close to hers and shouted something she couldn't understand. Molly smiled vaguely and pressed on, holding her bag protectively close to her stomach. There had been a warning in her guidebook about pickpockets.

For a panicky moment she thought she had lost her friends. How would she ever get back to her hotel? Could she even remember its name? Then a hand grabbed her arm and drew her out of the crowd to the edge of a gleaming bar.

"We must order a bottle," Zabi shouted in her ear. "If they think we have money to spend they'll find us a table."

"I'll pay," Molly offered recklessly, rummaging for her credit card.

In a miraculously short time the three were seated at a tiny round table wedged among others between the bar and the dance floor. A waiter in jeans and black T-shirt brought over a tray bearing three glasses and—*eek!*—a bottle of champagne, whose label he deferentially displayed to Molly. She nodded numbly, trying to erase the mental picture of her bank balance whirling into reverse, while the waiter unwrapped the cork, eased it from the bottle with a polite *pop* and poured her the tiniest drink she had ever seen. She looked up at him in puzzlement. How come he was just standing there holding on to the bottle when poor old Zabi and Alicia hadn't even a drop? Were the French mad?

An infinitesimal movement of the waiter's eyebrow redirected her gaze to her glass and, with a thrill of embarrassment that raised hot prickles all over her skin, Molly realized she was supposed to taste the stuff and pronounce judgement. Hastily she grabbed her glass, took a gulp of bubbles, and just managed a jerky nod before erupting into a choking fit. Alicia thumped her on the back.

"I'm fine," Molly croaked, wiping her eyes and pretending to be absorbed in the dancers.

She could see the top half of the DJ now, spinning his decks, presumably on some kind of stage at the far end of the boat. He was wearing a floral shirt and headphones, head jerking forward and back like an idiot pheasant on the run. But the music was great, and the crowd was cool. No one had their T-shirt off or was vomiting on the floor. The women were racehorse thin, groomed to perfection, wearing minimalist black dresses and a don't-mess-with-me expression. The men were dark and streamlined with soulful eyes, mobile eyebrows and imperious noses. It struck Molly that the French really were a different race, not just another nationality. By comparison the English were pale, mousy and . . . porridgy somehow. Nor did Englishmen have that air of refined carelessness Molly found rather attractive. Insouciance, that was it. (From the French *souci*, meaning care, Molly explained to herself. There you go, the English didn't even have a word for it.) Whoops! A man had caught her looking at him. He scanned her from top to toe with a sweep of dark lashes, then granted her a swift, smouldering smile. Bloody hell.

Molly turned back to the table and cooled her blushes with some more champagne. Perhaps he thought she looked tarty. She began to have second thoughts about her borrowed outfit. Even though it was stifling in here she didn't dare take off her jacket. What if someone noticed what she was wearing? (Or not wearing.)

"Okay, girls." Alicia leant close, eyes alight. "Targets for tonight: who do we want to drag home and eat for breakfast?"

"I haven't really come for that," said Molly, crossing her legs.

"You big kidder. Come on, let's show them what we've got."

"Yes, let's dance," agreed Zabi.

Within moments Molly was stripped of her jacket and pulled onto the dance floor. Suddenly she was in a swirl of black dresses and white shirts, flailing arms and floating hair, half blinded by lights that scythed across glistening flesh and bounced off teeth bared in ecstatic surrender.

"Bring it on!" yelled Alicia, pumping her fists in the air.

Molly wished Alicia wasn't quite so . . . well, *Australian.* She wished Zabi wouldn't keep twirling her skirt like that. She wished she herself wasn't so tall, so blonde, so . . . fleshy. Viewed from above her cleavage looked wantonly exposed. And her skirt barely covered the tops of her legs. Basically, she was wearing a lampshade.

Who did these French blokes think they were, staring like that? She'd soon fix them. But her famous withering-scorn glare didn't seem to work here. Instead of jerking their heads away, like English boys, they just went on staring—not exactly rudely or lecherously but with a frank, almost professional appraisal that was new to Molly. Take the good-looking one over there, for example, dancing with his girlfriend. Every time Molly looked at him, and she couldn't have done so more than five or six times—well, *glanced*, really—he flickered his eyebrows appreciatively, as if giving her marks out of ten. The nerve of it! He wasn't *that* good looking. Molly tossed her hair, turned her back on him, and put an extra wiggle into her dancing just to show she didn't require the approval of any man.

Nevertheless a glow of confidence spread through her. The fabulous creature she had seen in Zabi's bedroom mirror—that was *her*. Molly had often observed how easily men could be bamboozled into finding a girl attractive simply because she wore revealing clothing, and strongly disapproved of this cheap trick. *But it worked!* And it was liberating to wear so few clothes, to feel her body writhe in their slithery embrace as she abandoned herself to the music. Everything was pulsing to the same rampaging drum-and-bass rhythm—the bottles on the bar, Alicia's earrings, the hem of Molly's Cinderella skirt flashing gold against her thighs. This was how life should be: color, music, energy, sensation, freedom.

*Wham!* Molly nearly overbalanced as Alicia did a bum-clash with her. Alicia had worked herself into superkinetic overdrive now, whipping her hips, stamping her heels. Molly could almost believe that Alicia's arrival in Europe owed nothing to conventional air travel but to sheer seismic force of character, propelling her straight through the earth's burning core to erupt in Paris. Her face shone with perspiration and unaffected enjoyment. With a rush of affection Molly grinned back. Oh, help, another bum-clash coming.

Zabi was right about the DJ: he was brilliant. Every time Molly thought she would have to sit down or die, he ratcheted up the music another notch until the whole place was at fever-pitch. At some point a vision in white appeared: Zabi's guru jiggled sweatily beside them for a few minutes before leading Zabi off to another table. (He was probably too old to dance, poor thing.) A couple of laddish types, who had been clowning their way around the dance floor, now made a move on Molly and Alicia. One wore a cowboy hat, the other a daft shirt with flashing lights. "We are crazy boys," they shouted, leaping up and down. "I lurve *yooo*." Molly giggled so much she had to bop back to the table to refresh herself with another slug of champagne; when she returned they had gone.

She danced on with Alicia, maybe for ten minutes, maybe for forty. Her head was a bubble of sensation. She felt sinuous and all-powerful, a golden tube of liquid energy. When the music finally eased into a more relaxed tempo and everyone had cheered the DJ, she floated back to her chair on a cloud of euphoria.

She'd hardly sat down when a folded piece of paper landed on the table in front of her nose. She opened it and read in French, "You are a beautiful woman. Telephone me. Claude," followed by a string of numbers. She swiveled round and caught the eye of the man who'd tried to flirt with her on the dancefloor, now on his way out of the club *with his arm around his girlfriend!* The sneaky devil. Wordlessly Molly passed the note to Alicia.

"Gee, Molly, this kind of thing never happens to me." But there wasn't a hint of jealousy in her voice. Instead she stood up and said, "Mind if I go after that guy in the cowboy hat? He looked a bit of a spunk to me."

"Fine, fine." Molly waved her away. "I'm too hot to move anyway." And thirsty, too—if there was anything left. Reaching for the champagne bucket she discovered that the bottle was practically full again. How odd. But how lovely. *I get no kick from champagne*, she hummed happily, refilling her glass to the brim, then congratulating herself on knocking back the lot without mishap. What a marvelous and desirable being she was. She screwed up the note and tossed it heedlessly over her shoulder. No two-timers for her, thanks.

The truth was, she was feeling rather dizzy. She decided to go up on deck and cool off. On the way two men asked her to dance. "*Non, merci!*" How easy it was to be flighty in French. She swayed up the companionway singing, "I feel pretty, tra-la-la, oh so pretty . . ."

The fresh air acted like a calming hand laid across her forehead. It took a few swaying moments to adjust to the change in environment. Then she wandered to the offshore side of the boat and leaned on the rail, looking out across the water to the lights of the Right Bank. Paris! How delicious it was to stand here in the middle of this mysterious, magical city with stars glowing out of a vast dusky sky and the air on her skin, warm as an August night in London.

The sour green tang of the river conjured up a sudden memory: her tenth birthday party, delayed for some reason until the summer holidays, held at a favorite place on her local river. There was a rope that hung from a fat, tilting willow. You could launch yourself from the muddy bank and swing out over the brown water, as far and high as you dared. Molly could remember the swoop in her stomach and the exquisite terror of letting go and dropping down, down, into the cold depths, with the ooze of mud between her toes. Other children had swimming and trampolining parties at the leisure center, followed by plastic pizza and Coke, or a disco in the village hall where you learnt the moves for "YMCA" and "The Barbie Song." Molly had not been at all sure that a dirty old river, games on the bank, veggie burgers and marshmallows cooked by her mom over a campfire would be cool enough for her schoolfriends. Yet the party had been a wild success. It was the last time she could remember feeling such pure, uncomplicated happiness.

She sidled down the broad deck, trailing her hand along the rail. The frustrating thing about arriving here at night was that she couldn't see anything properly. Where, for example, was the Eiffel Tower, whose ubiquity in photographs suggested it was visible from every square inch of Paris? She followed the deck as it curved round to the front of the boat, stopping every few paces to crane her neck left and right, not even knowing where to look.

A faint movement in the semi-darkness made her stiffen. She registered a fruity tobacco smell. Then a voice said, "*Vous cherchez quelque-chose?*" You are searching for something?

She knew he was smiling even before she looked round, just as a prickle of goosebumps between her shoulder blades told her that something extraordinary was about to happen. He was leaning back against the rail a few feet away from her, smoking: thin, twentysomething, heart-stoppingly handsome, with dark hair carelessly swept back and hot, pinched eyes that rested on hers as he waited for an answer to his question.

"No. Well, yes," she replied, so flustered that she momentarily forgot how to speak French. "I was looking for the Eiffel Tower."

"*Mais alors*, one can't see it from here." His voice was wonderfully scornful. "It's over there, behind the mountain of Sainte Geneviève." As he indicated the correct direction, Molly saw his profile briefly illuminated by the lighthouse turret: sloping forehead, straight nose, yesterday's stubble shadowing the angled plane that ran from ear to chin, a boyish smudge of eyelashes.

"I didn't know," she said, stepping closer. "I only arrived in Paris this evening."

He picked a piece of tobacco off his tongue. "Tourist?"

Molly's chin rose in protest against this label. "I am here," she said in careful French, "to—to regard the beautiful things of history and of culture."

"*Ah, oui?*" He took a drag of his cigarette and narrowed his eyes against the trickling smoke. "And the beautiful men?" he inquired.

Her skin tingled. This man had insouciance in spades.

"Perhaps. If I find any." Molly thrilled to her own audacity. But she was a beautiful woman: she'd had it in writing.

He cocked an eyebrow. "You are English?"

"No, I am from Turkey."

For a moment he seemed to half believe her. Then he caught the mischief in her face and they both burst out laughing. He had white, even teeth. When he smiled his eyelids stretched into sensuous upward curves.

"The Turkish girls, *quand même*, don't have the beautiful blonde hairs like you." He examined her in silence for a moment, then took his cigarette out of his mouth, held it between thumb and index finger, and flicked it into the river. Uncrossing his legs, he eased himself off the rail. "*On danse?*"

There it was again, that insidious impersonal pronoun. He didn't exactly ask her to dance; she didn't exactly agree. It was simply going to happen.

Instead of leading her back down into the hold, he grasped her hands and started to dance with her right here on the deck. Out in the open air the music was muted, and so was his dancing, a kind of slow jive she'd seen other people do but had never dared attempt.

"I don't know how to do this," she apologized.

"It's easy." He drew her forward, pushed her away, turned her round, dropped her hands, reached for them again. It was like playing a game—a slow, silent, sexy game. Molly watched the way his body moved under his jeans and shirt, and felt she was being hypnotized. Her body began to respond to the rhythm. Soon she was snaking past him, sliding back to back, twirling in and out of his lazy embrace.

While they danced, they talked. So: she had come to Paris for the weekend. Alone? Yes—though, of course, she had friends here. She worked in London. Her job was very interesting. Quite a lot of responsibility and international travel and—and so forth. What about him?

He was born in Paris and had lived here all his life, though naturally his family had a country place too—nothing special, just a *gentilhommière* in the Loire. Until last summer he'd been studying art at the university, but he'd had to drop out. Money problems.

"*Quel dommage*," Molly murmured, and remembered to slip in the fact that she, too, had been to university. She didn't want him to think she was a birdbrain who just went clubbing. All the time, as his eyes glanced down into hers and she watched the mobility of his mouth and dark eyebrows, she felt the pressure of excitement building in her chest, in her throat.

At the end of the song they stopped and faced each other.

"I am called Fabrice," he said.

"And I'm Molly."

"*Bonsoir*, Molly." He reached out and shook her hand with a teasing formality that made her smile.

But he didn't mean good-bye, did he? Not now. Not yet.

"Tell me about Paris," she said quickly. "Where should I go? What should I see?"

"You mean 'the beautiful things of history and of culture'?"

"Yes! Don't laugh at me. I can go to a club and still be an intelligent person, you know." Unconsciously she placed one hand flat across her chest, hiding her cleavage. "I've never been here before. I want—I want—" She stopped, unable to articulate even to herself the magnitude and urgency of what she wanted.

"Never?" Fabrice looked amazed. "Is that true?"

Molly nodded.

"*Alors, viens.*" He grabbed her free hand, suddenly full of energy, and started tugging her toward the gangplank.

"What are you doing?"

"We are leaving." He turned, eyes teasing, and bopped backward down the deck, pulling her with him.

"Wait!" laughed Molly, though a wild exhilaration swept through her. "Where are we going?"

"To see Paris!"

"*Now?*"

"Why not?"

"But it's dark. Everything will be shut."

Fabrice stopped. "*Enfin*, Molly, one cannot shut a city. It lives, it breathes, like you and me." His own breath was warm on her cheek. "It's at night that Paris reveals her secrets. Just like a woman."

Molly's head spun.

He was jingling some keys. He must have a car. It would be utterly crazy to go off in a car with a strange man in a strange city.

His eyes were like melted chocolate. His fingers against her palm delivered shocks of pleasure to hidden places.

And he *was* an art student.

"I'll grab my jacket," she said.

# 5

Wind rushed in her ears and swept up her skirt. There was hair in her mouth, folds of leather jacket clutched in her hands, a fairground flutter in the pit of her stomach.

It wasn't a car, it was a motorbike—one of those scooter things with wide running-boards curving up to the handlebars and a coffer under the seat from which Fabrice had extracted a spare helmet. His own helmet, Molly thought, made him look as heroic as a gladiator.

"Hold tight!" he called over his shoulder, as he accelerated up the esplanade.

Tentatively Molly moved her hands to fit more firmly on his waist. It felt very intimate sitting so close, with her skirt rucked up and her knees nudging his thighs. Fabrice reached round and drew her hands closer still, until they met under his rib cage and her breasts pressed against his back. He opened the throttle wide.

Instead of taking the sliproad down which she'd come, he headed toward the river. They sped along the edge of the stone bank, perilously close to the dark gleam of water. Powerful currents rippled its surface, like muscles under skin. The danger was intoxicating.

There was a bridge ahead—and beneath it a tunnel. Fabrice

beeped his horn as they raced into it. The engine was suddenly as loud as thunder. A yellow beam from the scooter's headlamp flashed across massive stone supports banded with a green tide-line. "*Eeeeeh!*" Molly shrieked, and heard her voice echo around the mossy vault.

A few meters out of the tunnel Fabrice stopped showily, with a squeal of rubber. "You are frightened?"

"No," she gasped. "I love it."

"*Gentille petite Anglaise*," he murmured, and slid one warm palm up and down the outside of her thigh, as if soothing a horse.

He revved the bike to a roar and took off along a path that meandered up and down between mown grass. Jagged metallic sculptures, looking as if they had been ripped from sheet metal by a giant's hand, lined the way. Was this a park? An outdoor museum? There was no time to decide before Fabrice turned the bike onto the grass, bounced hair-raisingly downhill toward the river and careered into another tunnel. On the far side he slowed the engine to a sputter and stopped, keeping the bike balanced with his feet. He pointed forward. "*Et violà, . . . Mademoiselle la Touriste.*"

Molly brushed the wind-tears out of her eyes and leant past his shoulder. "Oh . . ." she breathed.

Straight ahead, rising out of the river in a golden haze of spotlights, was the cathedral of Notre Dame; she recognized it at once, though she'd had no idea it was on an island. Despite its stupendous size it had an airy fragility, almost as if it floated on the water. With tapered buttresses like billowing sails and a mastlike spire soaring into the sky, it might have been a dream ship conjured by Coleridge in an opium trance.

"Not bad, *hein?*" Fabrice grinned. Suddenly he looked much younger than the mysterious stranger on the boat.

He's actually *nice*, Molly told herself, as well as gorgeous. "It's fabulous," she told him.

He gunned the engine and they were off again, up a juddering ramp, then back into the glitter and swish of late-night traffic on the riverside highway. Where now? Molly wondered. Somewhere a clock was chiming: half past something. Half past Friday? Half past Paris? Half past her life? Could this really be the same night she had arrived at the Gare du Nord?

And was this really her, an unemployed office-worker who'd never even been abroad before, zooming through Paris with her cheek laid against the warm back of a tantalizing Frenchman? Yes! She was not a nobody from the provinces. She was not a stupid secretary. She was a wild woman loose in Paris. *Une femme sauvage. Grrrrrr.*

They had left the highway now and were climbing steeply, away from the river, past shuttered shops, tall houses slumbering shoulder to shoulder, the dark bulk of a church, a mysterious high wall that made Molly think of the secret garden where Cosette and Marius had pledged their love in *Les Misérables*. (She'd spent one interminably rainy holiday sobbing over that book.) The narrow streets wound upward, dark and deserted. Molly would not have been surprised to see the furtive shadow of a monk whisking down an alleyway.

Instead they were suddenly bathed in an unearthly light as if an alien spaceship had landed, though it wasn't a spaceship but a great golden building, domed like St. Paul's, standing spotlit at the center of a vast square. A palisade of black railings emphasized its austere magnificence. There was no sound except the putter of Fabrice's engine as they circled it and came to a stop at the entrance. Molly craned her neck to look at the columned façade. There was some writing high above the entrance; it seemed to be a kind of monument to the "*grands hommes*" of France. She frowned. "What about the great women?"

"Are there any?" he teased.

"Of course," she said, racking her brains. "Simone de Beauvoir . . . Marie Curie, er . . ."

"In any case, that's not why I brought you here. Look the other way."

Molly turned her head. From here a road sloped downward, wide and straight as a die, to some distant gates. Sticking up above the horizon, as familiar and heart-lifting as a friend, was a soaring shape outlined in a filigree of tiny golden lights. "It's the Eiffel Tower!" she cried. "Isn't it beautiful? Oh, thank you, Fabrice." Impulsively she tightened her arms around his waist to hug him clumsily from behind.

He swiveled round and gave her a slanting smile that practically made her fall off the bike. Their faces were very close. For an electric moment she thought he was going to kiss her. "Are you tired?" he asked.

"No!"

"Okay. Let's go."

* * *

He sailed the bike gently down the hill. Molly watched the Eiffel Tower shrink smaller and smaller, then slip beneath the horizon. He probably wanted to take her to some special place. Well, that was fine. She was beginning to understand Frenchmen. They might do that looking thing, but that didn't mean they had to grab. Being French, they recognized that there was a pace to love, a concept she was sophisticated enough to appreciate. They would kiss when the time was right.

Anyway, their helmets might have clashed.

Wherever they were going, it was a long way. They returned

to the river by a different route, crossed over to the Right Bank on a bridge she didn't recognize and entered an area of triumphalist avenues and one *place* after another as grand as Trafalgar Square. The buildings here were puffed up with self-importance to monumental size, splendiferous with pediments and flags. They reminded Molly of Victorian grandees in top hats and tailcoats eyeing each other superciliously through *pince-nez*. Yet there was an exuberance about the gilded domes and scrolled pillars, the frivolity of metalwork and profligacy of trees, even the outsize statues of noble men (and their noble horses) that filled her with delight. *Liberté, égalité, fraternité!* (Especially *fraternité.*) Street by beautiful street Paris was opening its heart to her. Molly could do no less than fling her own wide.

Métro stations flashed past, with their pretty arched entrances and exotic names. There were intriguing shopping arcades, bandbox-neat theatres with posters outside, half-lit antiques emporia displaying opulent gilt chairs and lifesize statues of Nubian slaves. Gradually the smartness deteriorated into a zigzag of nondescript streets. Once they crossed a petrol-fumed avenue, still awake in a razzle-dazzle of neon, before entering a maze of ever-narrowing streets. All the time they were steadily climbing.

Finally the scooter stopped. Fabrice turned off the engine and removed the key. The silence was absolute. They were in a small, lopsided square of pretty houses painted white, with a tree in the middle. A scattering of leaves glinted yellow under an old-fashioned lamppost straight out of Narnia, and there was something about the stillness and small-scale charm of the place that gave Molly the same sense of entering a magical world.

"Where are we?" she asked, climbing stickily off the bike. She took off her helmet and shook her hair free.

"Montmartre."

Fabrice stowed both their helmets and tethered his bike with a thick chain. He was even handsomer than she remembered. Just watching the deft movements of his hands—the play of knuckles and wristbones, those delicate, supple fingers—made her sigh. "But isn't Montmartre very touristy?" she said quickly, to cover up.

"That's why we come at night. Anyway, the tourists only want to see the Sacré Coeur." He waved to somewhere in the distance. "This is the real Montmartre, where people live and work and have children and drink a *coupe rouge* with their friends. It's like a village. Come. I'll show you."

He guided her toward a flight of steps while fishing in his jacket for a cigarette. Molly watched him wedge it loosely between parted lips, then angle his head to light it with a click of his lighter. The small flame glowed on his cheekbones and lowered lashes. He pouted slightly as he released a twist of sweet smoke. Molly dimly remembered that she disapproved of smoking, but for the moment couldn't remember why.

They strolled slowly up twisting lanes, down precipitous stairways, from pools of light to the deep shade of trees, past ivied villas, terraced gardens and even a tiny vineyard, which Fabrice said produced wine like piss. A freshness in the air told her they were high above the city fumes. Sometimes she heard the gush of water from a small fountain or hidden rivulet. Otherwise, it was so quiet that they might have been the only two people in the world.

Fabrice told her why Montmartre was called the hill of the martyrs, and something about Napoleon, and showed her the house of a French film star she hadn't heard of. He was very intelligent. Molly scoured her brain for something impressive to say in response. All she really wanted to look at was him. All she wanted to know was whether he liked her.

"And, of course, this is where all the painters lived," she managed at last, "like Picasso and—and all the, er . . ." Oh, God, was it Cubists? Or Surrealists? It would be terrible to make a mistake.

Fabrice rolled his eyes and gave a groan of laughter. "Molly, you and your culture. You are adorable."

"Am I?" She smiled back tremulously, longing for it to be true.

He seized her by the shoulders, swung her round to face a row of cottagy houses and jabbed his cigarette toward one at random. His breath tickled her ear as he lowered his voice portentously. "It was in this very house that *stupidisme* was founded by Cliché and Maladroit. Note the intricately carved *hors d'oeuvre* above the door."

"Stop it." Molly giggled.

He swung her round to face the other way. "And here we find the studio of Champignon. He later combined with Huîtres in the shocking Flageolet Exhibition of 1925."

Dizzy with laughter and his intoxicating touch, Molly leant into the warm circle of his arm as he strutted clownishly down the street. He stopped in front of a squat pink house with shuttered windows. "*Et voilà!*" he announced, with a dramatic flourish. "The famous bar where the experimental poet Croque Monsieur used to come with his mistress, the *chanteuse* Muscadet, until she left him for Roquefort. All dead now—*hélas!*—and buried in the Cemetery of Bouillabaisse."

"Don't!" Molly shrieked, fighting for breath. Even Fabrice was chortling and snorting at his own jokes.

There was the screech of an opening window, and a torrent of furious French poured into the street. A woman in a nightie was leaning out from an upper story, screaming at them like a demented witch. Molly didn't understand all the words but she got the gist. Couldn't a decent woman be allowed to rest quietly in her own bed at night? What was wrong with young people these days?

Fabrice replied in a sulky mumble. They were only taking a little promenade; it was not a crime, after all. Crazy lovers! the woman yelled back. They ought to be ashamed of themselves. Unless they went away at once she would call the police. The window banged shut.

Molly and Fabrice looked at each other and exchanged guilty giggles. He took her hand and led her back up the street in an exaggerated stealthy tiptoe, finger to his lips, relaxing into normality as soon as they were out of sight. At the top there was a tiny raised square, wedged into the angle of two streets. Though hardly bigger than an average living room it contained a precise and perfect arrangement of three trees, one ironwork bench and a statue of a couple embracing.

"Could we sit down a minute?" said Molly. "My shoes hurt."

"Of course." He shepherded her up the stone steps and sat her down on the bench. As soon as she had eased her feet out of the (too small) sandals he gestured impatiently. "Poor feet. Here. Give them to me." He pulled them on to his lap and began to massage them gently.

At first Molly was rather embarrassed. She hoped there wasn't too much of an *odeur*. But then the most delicious lassitude oozed through her body. No one had ever stroked her feet like this before. She hadn't known they were an erogenous zone. Or was she kinky? Leather skirt . . . no underwear . . . French foot massages: was there a rogue gene she didn't know about? She lay back against the bench in a sensuous stupor, watching Fabrice's beautiful hands squeeze and press her flesh. If she wasn't careful, at any minute she was going to sob aloud with pleasure.

"Who are they?" she asked, pointing at the statue.

Fabrice shrugged. "I don't know." He looked up and gave her a sly smile. "Crazy lovers, maybe?"

Molly's eyes flickered to his and away. But as soon as his attention returned to her feet, she looked back again. She couldn't help it. She was mesmerized by the little kink at the corner of his mouth and the way his hair slithered down across his forehead.

"Is that better?" he asked.

"What? Oh, yes. Thank you." Molly put her feet back onto the ground in a daze and fumbled with the straps of her sandals.

"Good. I have one more thing to show you."

The streets wound upward. There were more shops here, shut, of course, but full of trinkets and the usual tourist junk. How very superior it was not to be a tourist but to have her very own Frenchman—Parisian—to show her the city. Not that Fabrice was exactly hers. But he did like her, didn't he? She remembered the look he'd given her when he had said "crazy lovers" and felt a quiver of anticipation. Already she was imagining what would happen tomorrow, and the day after—and weekends to come—and even wondering what Fabrice would make of Fat Sal when he came to London.

She was so busy with her thoughts that she didn't take any notice of where she was going until he stopped and pointed his chin at the view ahead. "You see?" he said.

They were standing at the edge of a high stone platform from which the ground plunged steeply. Below them and all around for miles and miles, as far as the eye could see, stretched the lights of Paris, with the river looping through them like a fat black snake. There were domes and steeples, turrets and belfries, apartment blocks and skyscrapers—and the Eiffel Tower! It was fantastic.

"But don't look behind you," Fabrice warned.

Of course Molly turned round at once. A couple of hundred yards away, Sacré Coeur glistened brilliant white like a gigantic wedding cake.

"It's an excrescence," said Fabrice, pushing out his lower lip. "A bastard of architecture. Any fool can see that."

Molly nodded solemnly. She thought it was lovely, rather like the Taj Mahal.

They turned back to look at the view. Far to the left there was a smoky red glow on the horizon—a factory, perhaps, or something burning. "What's that over there?" she asked, pointing. "It's not a fire, is it?"

"That's the sun, you silly baby."

"What?"

Her gaze swept across the Paris sky, east to west, from pinky gray to starry black and back again. He was right. It was tomorrow.

"It's going to be another beautiful day," he told her. "You are lucky."

Molly gave a secret smile. Of course she was lucky. Of course the weather would be perfect. Hadn't she met Fabrice? "My first real day in Paris," she murmured dreamily. "What shall we do?"

He looked at her blankly.

"I mean, if you want to. If you're not busy."

He looked down into her face in that careless, casual, moody-broody way he had.

"We can do anything you like," she told him. "Anything," she blushed.

"Molly." He sighed. She loved the way he said her name—*Mer-lee*. "Okay. I have an idea. Here, I'll write it for you." He had a pen but no paper, so he tore a strip off his blue-and-white cigarette packet, wrote something on the blank side and tucked it into her jacket pocket. "And now," he said, "I will take you home. You are staying at a hotel? A hostel?"

After her earlier scare, when she thought she'd lost Zabi and Alicia in the club, Molly had memorized both the name and the address. He said it was on his way. Soon they were back to where he had parked the scooter. Molly climbed onto it and smiled to herself as Fabrice revved the engine importantly.

"You want to go back fast or slow?" he shouted.

"Fast!" She knew it was the only answer.

They jolted down the cobbles, gathering speed, heading back toward Sacré Coeur. The scooter's headlamp glowed feebly; the sky was already lightening to gray. He swerved and steadied the bike. Molly saw it was pointing straight down toward a succession of steep stone stairways.

"No!" she shrieked.

"Yes!"

The bike tilted sickeningly to a forty-five-degree angle, then they were bumping down the steps at terrifying speed. Molly squeezed her eyes shut and held tight. The bike straightened out, then swooped again—and again. She heard someone call out, and looked up in time to catch a snapshot impression of a man holding a basket of oysters as they shot past. His astonished expression made her laugh. She thought of Didier setting out mushrooms on his stall.

Finally they reached a broad, straight boulevard and joined a trickle of early-morning traffic. The sky was no brighter than pearly gray but it was definitely morning. The day was beginning to hum. Molly laid her cheek against Fabrice's back and closed her eyes. Her world shrank to the warmth of his body circled in her arms, the feel of his ribs under her fingers, the thrum of the engine, the muted honk and hubbub of cars.

When she next looked up, color was seeping into the scene

around her, and they were stopped at a traffic light in the place de la République, where she'd emerged from the Métro probably no more than eight hours ago. It no longer seemed big and gaunt and frightening. There was a small carousel—how had she missed that? A waiter in a white apron and black waistcoat was setting out wicker chairs in front of a café, dusting them down with a flick of his cloth, meticulously adjusting their position. As Molly watched, he caught sight of an acquaintance. "*Salut*, Bernard!" he called.

"Eh, Martin, *salut!*" The two men shook hands.

The bike moved into quieter streets. The news kiosks were opening. She saw an old man in slippers buying his paper. Small gray vans were parked along the pavement, bottoms tilted into the air, doors open at the back to display crates of grapes, curly lettuce and ribbed tomatoes, galvanized tubs of lilies and carnations, boxes of black lobsters slithering in slow motion across crushed ice. Another kind of van, green and much bigger, lumbered down the street scouring the gutters and spraying the pavements clean. A cartoonish picture on its side-panel showed a human figure triumphantly holding up a small bag. The slogan underneath read: "I love my neighborhood. I pick up my dog's turds!"

Molly recognized her own street, narrow and quiet. The cat was sitting on the doorstep of her hotel, washing itself in the pale dawn. "It's here," she said, close to Fabrice's ear. But when he stopped outside she couldn't bring herself to get off. She wanted to stay like this for ever. "I'm too tired," she moaned, clasping her fingers tighter and snuggling her face into his jacket.

"*Arrête, toi*," he said, with a little laugh she could feel under her hands. He smiled at her over his shoulder, then reached round to grasp one elbow and help her off the bike. She stood beside him, swaying gently. "Poor Molly," he said.

He propped the bike steady and climbed off himself. Molly felt his fingers flutter against her cheek as he undid her helmet and removed it. He smoothed back her hair carefully, a palm on either side of her head. "You know, Molly, you are very beautiful."

"No, I'm not," she whispered.

"I like your hair. And your little English nose." He ran a finger down it.

"That tickles."

"And your smile." A knuckle brushed her mouth.

Her eyelids drooped. She was melting, turning to butter. Then his lips were on hers, warm and searching. He pulled her tight and pressed harder, sliding his tongue into her mouth, tugging and twining until her head sank back in surrender and her body arched into his. She felt his thighs hard against hers, his chest beneath the thin shirt pressing against her breasts. She could smell his skin and feel its masculine rasp against her own. They were breathing each other's breath, tasting each other's taste, matching each other's heartbeat.

Finally he set her upright. "Until tomorrow," he said.

She nodded dopily. "Today," she reminded him.

"Go on," he smiled, "go to sleep. *Au dodo*."

Molly stood on the edge of the pavement, watching him loop the scooter back the way they had come. His jacket billowed out behind him. She loved the angles of his knees and elbows, the serious way he held the handlebars. Just as he reached the corner, the first beam of sunlight glanced across the freshly hosed street, turning drops of water to diamonds. High in a tree a bird was singing its heart out. From somewhere came the sweet smell of freshly baked bread. It was like the beginning of the world.

# 6

Malcolm Figg sat at the poncy gilt table that served as a desk in his hotel room, and tapped his pencil impatiently on its glossy surface, waiting for his call to be answered. Although there was a perfectly good phone in the room, he was using his mobile: quick, cheap, no mucking about with foreign instructions and, above all, confidential. There were no flies on Malcolm Figg.

Which reminded him. After that time he'd given an entire presentation with the tag of his Spurs boxer shorts caught in his trouser zipper, it was always best to check. No, everything in order and under wraps. Practice makes perfect. Detail, you see. That's how he'd got to where he was today. He didn't intend to let some snotty graduate with a diploma up her arse throw him off course.

Was she ever going to answer the phone?

It wasn't until late last night, while sorting through the conference material Molly had prepared before staging her ridiculous walk out, that he'd discovered the graphics disk was missing. Malcolm had lain awake in a sweat of panic. On Sunday at noon he was due to stand up in front of four hundred assorted medics to kick off the presentation of Phipps Lauzer Bergman's new wonder drug for ulcers, then introduce a panel of distinguished scientific experts. It was the first time he'd been chosen for such a key role, which hinted at a definite leg up career-wise. Following a "Tips for Success" article in *Men's Health*, he'd bought a new suit specially, had his hair styled and his hands manicured. He'd rehearsed every audio-visual cue, from the fanfare accompanying the PLB logo to the lab shots, and coordinated with the white-coats to ensure that their spiel would be accompanied by the correct images of viruses, tissue sections, organ scans and whatnot. It would be the slickest presentation anyone had ever been privileged to witness—with the disk. Without it, he might as well resign now before he was fired.

The bloody cow! He'd tried her mobile dozens of times, but she'd either turned it off or switched it to voicemail. He'd already left three messages. Had she gone out, or was she still in bed at nearly midday? Okay, ten thirty, English time. In the early hours of this morning, tossing and turning, he'd had a brainwave. As early as he dared, he'd rung up a junior colleague in London and virtually twisted his balls off to go into the office and find her home number, stuffed somewhere with her job application into one of Malcolm's filing cabinets. What with London being an hour behind Paris, the process took forever. It was already eleven before Malcolm got the number. Each passing minute tied another knot in his gut.

At last! He heard the scrabble of a receiver being wrestled from its cradle and a sleepy groan. He'd woken her up. Good.

"Yeah?" croaked a voice.

"Molly, you bitch! Is that you?"

"Sal here. I'm asleep. 'Byee."

The line went dead. Bloody hell! He punched the call button again. If the only way to get hold of Molly was to wake up the flatmate, or whatever she called herself, so be it. Perhaps Molly was a lesbian. That would explain a lot.

"Yeah?"

"Can I speak to Molly? It's urgent."

"Not here. Sorry. 'Byee."

Unbelievable! She'd hung up again. Malcolm banged his phone on the table—not too hard. He didn't want to damage the new fascia he'd bought by mail order. (The "executive" model, burred walnut effect, pricy but worth it. Respect yourself and others will follow.) He jabbed the green icon again, reconsidering his strategy. There was a mirror above the table. He smoothed his tie, limbered up his facial muscles as recommended in the "Customer Relations: Advanced Techniques" course he'd recently attended (Smiles Mean Sales), and prepared to ooze charm.

"Yeah?"

"Sa-a-al. Malcolm here. Good to talk to you again."

"Look, who is this? You're not one of those perverts, are you?"

"Ha ha ha. This is Molly's boss speaking. Malcolm Figg. Two *g*s. I trust I'm not inconveniencing you, but I need to contact Molly as a matter of urgency."

"I told you, she's not here." There was the squeak of bedsprings and a heavy sigh. "You've woken me up now."

"I do apologize. Might I inquire when you expect her to return?"

"Dunno, really. Er, what day is it today?"

Malcolm placed a hand over his eyes. "Saturday."

"But Molly doesn't work Saturdays, does she?"

"No. Well, yes. I mean, she would if—" Malcolm clamped his jaw tight. Girls always did this to him. Brains like spaghetti wriggling in all directions, tripping him up, tying him in knots. He tried the deep-breathing exercise (Calm Means Confidence).

"Hey," she said, suddenly perky, "you're not the Malcolm I met in Scheherazade a couple of months ago?"

"No."

"Or it might have been Viva Tango."

"No!"

"Only you sound just like him."

"Well, I'm not."

"Thing is, he went off to get me another Vodka Red Ball and I lost him. I quite fancied him, actually. Bit of a brute, gorgeous brown—"

"Look, I'm going to give you a number." (Seize the Initiative.) "It's very important that Molly rings me ASAP."

"Wait! I've just remembered. She's gone to Paris for the weekend."

"No, she effing well hasn't!"

"Oi, mind my hangover."

"That's the whole point. I'm in Paris and she isn't, and I need something she's got. What's more, if I don't get it back by the end of today, I'll be pressing charges for misappropriation of company property."

"Come again?"

"To say nothing of dishonoring her contractual obligations."

"D'you know, darling, I haven't the faintest clue what you're on about."

Malcolm ground his teeth. Unfortunately he'd skipped the anger-management session in favor of crazy golf. "Let's just say it could be a police matter."

"*Police?*" For one glorious moment he had her full attention. Then she spoiled it by adding, "Come off it. Not Molly."

"I said 'could.' You get her to contact me, and we'll see."

"Oh, all right. What's your name again?"

"Malcolm Figg. Two *g*s. PLB Pharmaceuticals."

"Farming what?"

"Jesus! Look, forget the company. Just say Malcolm. She'll

know who it is. She's to ring me on this number. Have you got a pen?"

"I'm in bed, darling. If you say it nice and slowly I'm sure I'll remember it."

Malcolm did his Hannibal Lecter face in the mirror.

"Ooh, look, here's a lipstick. Orange Carnival. I'll write it on my *Vogue*."

By the time he cut the call Malcolm's hair stood up in spikes and sweat prickled his back. He tried to calm himself by playing Snake on his phone, but his nerves were so shot he couldn't even get to three hundred. He scrolled down the menu to check his top score. Six hundred and fifty-seven, wasn't it? It was. Bloody good.

He was a smart boy, no question. One day his potential would be recognized. One day he'd have his own parking space and a sleek car to put in it, with leather seats and that Japanese stereo system he'd seen featured in *FHM*. He'd own a loft overlooking the river, with one of those showers that sprayed water at you from all directions, and an enormous bed, where he'd watch twenty-four-hour sports on his home-cinema system. Or, even better, a house in the sun with its own pool, somewhere relaxed where he could go drinking with his mates, drive around in a convertible (or an off-roader? Tricky one) and pick up a willing, suntanned blonde whenever he chose. He'd run his own business and call the shots. Never again would he kow-tow to corporate fat cats, or be patronized by posh idiots with a lot of letters after their names, or let some butter-wouldn't-melt secretary whip the carpet from under his feet.

Molly Clearwater had been a mistake. She'd looked bright enough on paper, in fact wildly overqualified, and she'd put in the hours, he'd give her that. But she had no office savvy. For example, she'd take messages for him, nicely presented with the time and phone number and all that crap, but never seemed to get the point of them and initiate the necessary action. Half the time she acted like a startled deer; then she'd go all exasperated on him, as if she could run everything much better, given the chance. Her niggling corrections drove him mad. Who cared if "phenomena" was singular or plural? Work was about having a bit of a laugh, doing a job adequately and moving up the status ladder.

He'd only chosen her because of her looks. No point hiring a dog, was there? A man needed attractive women around him. He owed it to himself. Normally he wouldn't go for that wide-eyed English-rose type, but there was a ripeness to Molly that had excited him. Banked fires, he'd thought, under that virginal exterior. He'd like to see her begging for it. Alone with him in Paris, what with his experience and a few drinks, she wouldn't have stood a chance. Not a chance, Malcolm repeated to himself, blotting out the memory of the way she had sometimes looked at him, as if he was a cross between an escaped lunatic and Attila the Hun.

Christ! Look at his hair. He couldn't go back to the conference like that. Malcolm grabbed his gel, slicked it over his scalp, then combed his hair smooth apart from an erect cowlick at the front. Sex-ee.

Molly had fancied him, all right. Why else would she have done those extra jobs for him, rushed out to buy his favorite coffee whenever he asked, stayed late most days? She couldn't have missed the signals he'd sent her—complimenting her on her clothes (especially those shirts with the straining buttons), letting her drive his motor to the garage (bet she was dead impressed by the turbo charge), then this Paris trip, with the prospect of the best night of her life at the Crazy Horse Saloon, and himself for afters.

What was it with women? You did one tiny thing wrong—so tiny you couldn't even guess what it was—and they were off. Molly Clearwater had dropped him right in it. Time of the month, probably. By rights all this stuff littering his floor should be in her room, with her to sort it out. Malcolm glowered at the brochures, reports and folders emblazoned with the words "XIIIth International Meeting of Gastroenterologists," at the boxes of blank name tags, customized pens and freebie umbrellas with the PLB logo. What a circus it all was.

This hotel was stuffed with doctors from across the world—mainly consultants and "opinion formers," with a sprinkling of young turks—plus big-wigs from Phipps Lauzer Bergman and the other drug companies who were sponsoring this conference. The doctors all pretended they were coming to discuss new research and read each other mind-bogglingly boring papers about the small intestine (between six-course meals and lavish entertainments). The drug companies, who paid for the damned thing, knew better: this was their chance to "persuade" doctors to prescribe their drugs, offer funding for research programs and cozy up to the boffins in charge of clinical trials—all of which might result in millions of pounds of profit. The golden rule for drug companies was to present themselves in the most flattering light possible. Without that disk Malcolm was going to look a complete prat—and his company likewise. His bosses would not be pleased.

He'd kill Molly if he ever saw her again. At the very least, he'd make sure she never got another job in this industry. As for a reference, he could hardly wait to write it.

Meanwhile, what was he going to do for female company? There hadn't been time to organize another girl from the office. Two very expensive tickets were awaiting him at the Crazy Horse saloon, which meant that this was some bird's lucky night. The only problem was finding her. He'd have a discreet word with that *concierge* bloke downstairs—slip him a banknote, ask about *les girls*, wink wink. These things could be done. All it took was a little *sav-wah fare*, as the French said.

Malcolm checked his watch. Time to go. He switched his phone to "vibrate" and slid it into the inside breast pocket of his jacket. Pausing before the mirror, he adjusted the position of his Mensa badge and gave himself a last squirt of Tiger. Looking good, Malc, he told himself, and hurried to join the conference.

# 7

Oh, no . . . please. She didn't want to wake up. What brute had switched on the light? Molly turned over with a groan and nuzzled her pillow. It felt unfamiliar, unyielding, as if it was packed with sand. There was something odd about her bed, too, made with sheets and a tickly blanket instead of a duvet.

She opened her eyes a crack, wincing at the light. But it wasn't a light, it was the sun, forcing its way through the thin curtains and invading her room in a yellow blaze. Not *her* room . . . a different room . . . a hotel room. Molly's eyelids flew wide and her heart gave a leap.

Paris!

*Fabrice!*

She jumped out of bed, ran naked to the half-open window and pulled it wide, draping herself with the curtains. The morning was already well advanced. Warm air flowed across her skin. The sky was happy-go-lucky blue daubed with innocent white cloud. Sunshine danced along the pale walls and peeling shutters of the houses opposite, turning window-panes to crystal and imparting a magic to each tiny domestic drama being enacted on the small balconies: a woman beating dust from a carpet she'd draped over the iron balustrade, an old man tenderly picking over his scarlet cascade of geraniums, a white terrier running back and forth, barking at something in the street.

Leaning out, Molly peered down at the shiny roofs of parked cars: one provided a sun bed for a paunchy cat. Outside the *brasserie* opposite, a trio of girls with sunglasses perched on their heads sat gossiping at a metal table; she could hear the swoop and twitter of their voices. An old woman in black, grey hair coiled at her neck, walked with slow dignity down a narrow strip of shade, hauling shopping bags sprouting with greenery. Molly could smell hot pavement, fresh coffee, a gingery tang from the takeaway place next door (*spécialités chinoises—thaïlandaises*). Inhaling deeply, she tilted her face to the sky. Somewhere out there, across the rooftops, over the chimneys, was Fabrice. She felt so happy she could explode.

She was in love! Madly, passionately, helplessly. Had there ever been anyone so handsome, so romantic, so intelligent—so *French?*

And Fabrice: was it the same for him? Might he, too, at this very moment, be leaning out of some high attic window festooned with vines, dreaming of her? Molly turned from the window, blinking away sunspots. They said men were different. How was one supposed to know? What would it be like to be loved, really loved, by a man?

He'd said she was beautiful. Molly padded across to the mirrored doors of the wardrobe, and stared at her milky reflection smudged with pink, at her tangle of tawny hair and the darker scribble between her thighs. She slid her palms slowly down the curves of her hips, back up beneath her rib cage, over the silky undersides of her breasts and across the already hardening nipples. A hidden fuse sparked as she remembered the smell of his skin, the dark languor of his eyes, the lick of his tongue against hers.

What was she doing? What was she thinking? Molly snatched her hands away, yanked on her dressing gown, and decided to take a quenching shower. Of course she wasn't in love—not after one night, not with someone she could barely talk to. It was ridiculous. Key clutched in one hand, sponge bag and towel under her arm, she stalked down the corridor toward the bathroom.

But look at Romeo and Juliet. They'd fallen in love at first sight.

And killed themselves shortly afterward.

Well, anyway. All she knew was that she'd never felt like this before, certainly not with Gavin "I am a genius" Thorpe, who'd managed to monopolize half her time at college and blighted the rest. Molly locked the bathroom door behind her. Who was to judge what love was, or how swiftly it could ignite? As Shakespeare had so rightly said, "Tell me where is fancy bred? Or in the heart or in the head? Tum-te-tum . . . et cetera." She might not have known Fabrice for more than a few hours, but so what? She'd been able to talk to Gavin all right, and certainly vice versa—but that had turned out not to be love. Not at all. Cautiously Molly turned on the tap marked "C," cleverly remembering that in French this did not stand for "cold." After a few painful experiments she was standing in the yellow-stained bathtub holding a shower-head above her scalp. As the water alternately drizzled and spurted, her thoughts trickled back to the big, windy campus on the hill, the seminar rooms with their polecat fug, herself eager, intense and slightly plump in her new Gap jeans with daisies embroidered on the hems. Ah, how naïve she had been in those days.

Though she could no longer remember exactly how or why, from about the age of eleven Molly had formed the determination to get to university—a proper one, not some fancily rechristened institution that handed out degrees in Food Technology and Tourism Studies. She'd dreamed of a different world, a world bigger than local gossip and what had been on TV last night, where you could discuss books and ideas and not worry about wearing the right brand of trainers. It had taken a great deal of effort to achieve the necessary exam results, and almost as much again to sort her way through all the different courses and application forms. Her teachers, though vaguely encouraging, provided no real guidance; neither did her mother, an art-school drop-out who always claimed to have been "useless" at school. Money was another hurdle, though by taking out a student loan, and working weekends and in the holidays, she had scraped together enough to see her through the first year on the tightest of budgets. She hadn't possessed the temerity even to think about Oxbridge; the offer of three places elsewhere, including one at a northern university famed for its English department, was like being showered with gold. Her expectations had been accordingly sky-high.

She had wanted to *learn*—to engage with other minds, to feel intellectual sparks fly. It had been a shock to discover that most other students just wanted to drink and muck about. In a big city far from home, awed by the size of the campus and terrified of failing, Molly had initially kept her head down and worked. Beyond a small circle of friends, mainly girls, in whose company she was relaxed enough to be herself, it felt safer not to be noticed. And she wasn't, until she met Gavin.

It was a perfect spring day at the beginning of her second year. She'd been sitting on the library steps, half luxuriating in the sun, half reading *1984* for her Literature and Politics module, when a voice behind her said, "Brilliant book, isn't it? An absolutely excoriating denunciation of Stalinism." Molly jerked herself upright and turned to see an eager-looking man in glasses crouched a couple of steps above her beside a battered, bulging briefcase: a tutor, she assumed. He was too old to be a student.

"Actually, it rather reminds me of the Blair government," she'd replied, showing off. "All those slogans and news management and saying the opposite of what you mean. Winston Smith's a kind of spin doctor who sees the light."

"My God, you're right!" He ran his hand excitedly through sandy curls, revealing a forehead of noble proportions. "What a brilliant insight. Though, of course, historical contextuality has its own critical validity."

"Absolutely." Molly hadn't a clue what he meant, but she was so flattered to have been called "brilliant" that she was hardly going to ask.

For the next forty minutes they talked about Orwell and dictatorship, death camps and the power of television. It was the best conversation she'd had yet. He didn't look at her breasts once. Moreover, it turned out that he was a Cambridge graduate writing a doctoral thesis on D. H. Lawrence. When he asked if Molly would accompany him to the opening night of a new play that weekend—he'd be fascinated to hear her opinion—she accepted without hesitation.

The theater date was followed by an art exhibition, then a concert of Baroque music ("certain stylistic tendencies in 17th–18th cent. arts," according to Molly's dictionary), then dinner at his flat where, with some ceremony, he served her *daube provençale* (stew, basically). Gavin wasn't handsome in the conventional sense (or, some might have said, the unconventional). What Molly found overwhelmingly seductive was being taken seriously by an older man. Gavin talked to her of critical theory, Thatcherism, the situation in the Middle East. He played her German opera and avant-garde jazz, often with a finger raised to alert her to a particularly fine phrase. He told her about his journeys to New Mexico and southern Europe "along the Lawrentian trail," as he put it. Wherever he traveled he carried a Krugerrand sewn into the lining of his safari jacket in case the local economy should unexpectedly collapse. Molly was dazzled.

His thesis was provisionally entitled "The Plume and the Serpent: Themes of Androgyny in the Works of D. H. Lawrence." Although it was not yet finished—still, in fact, at the complex and unendingly fascinating research stage—Molly soon shared Gavin's conviction that it needed only the transposition of ideas into words to land like a bombshell on the international academic scene. She had been thrilled to find herself by no means too inferior to carry out the more pedestrian aspects of his work, to spend long hours discussing the different psychosexual makeup of men and women and, in due course, actively to research these between the burgundy sheets of his double futon.

By her second year she had more or less moved in with him. (The fiction of a flat shared with other girls was preserved to stop her mother flapping.) It felt wonderfully grown-up to talk together in the evenings over a meal she had bought and, increasingly often, cooked, then retire to their separate desks to work. Sometimes, when he wasn't too busy, Gavin offered to read her essays, which he did with fastidious concentration and a poised pencil while she nibbled her nails. Of course they went to parties, too, but their relationship did not depend on such fripperies. This was a meeting of minds.

Molly squeezed a blob of shampoo onto her hair and vigorously massaged her scalp, trying to obliterate the picture of herself striding across the campus like Joan of Arc among the unbelievers, averting her gaze from the posters advertising discos and Beer Nites. She had been so convinced she had chosen the Higher Path that it hadn't occurred to her the lower path might be more fun.

It had taken a weekend visit from her schoolfriend Abi and a disastrous meal *à trois* to cause the first tremor of doubt. "He's a saddo." (Abi had never been a great mincer of words.) "Boring and old and selfish. You're a billion times cleverer. Honestly, Moll, he's turning you into a middle-aged housewife. And D. H. Lawrence! How uncool is that?"

Abi had returned home early after a major bust-up between the two friends, leaving Molly shocked, hurt and defiantly enraged, not least by an unwelcome piece of self-knowledge that told her she had half invited Abi (then studying Beauty Therapy at the local college back home) to impress her with sophisticated university life.

But the spell was broken. Almost as soon as the words "boring" and "Gavin" had been used in the same sentence, Molly realized just how bored and boring she had become herself. She *hated* German opera. Who cared if the name Gavin was morphologically connected to Gawain of green-knight fame? How could it take anyone so long to not-actually-write a thesis? Where was the romance in doing a man's academic research, not to mention his laundry? Within a week she had ended the affair. Shortly afterward, she was rewarded by seeing him with a pretty first-year—shy, smiling, flattered—and recognizing herself with bruising clarity. Belatedly she woke up, moved into a mixed household of students her own age and tried to grab herself some fun. But by that time she was in her final year, with exams pressing. Determined to salvage something from the wreckage of her illusions, Molly had thrown her energies into her work and, by sheer willpower, managed to scrape a first.

But she hadn't got a first in men. More like an F: F for failure, F for fool. Molly turned off the tap, squeezed the water from her hair and stepped onto the pink shagpile bathmat. How could she have made such a colossal, humiliating, wasteful mistake? No doubt a psychoanalyst would come up with some guff about a father substitute (although, to be fair, Gavin had been only nine years older than her), which just showed what crackpots these shrinks were, as she'd been perfectly happy being brought up by her mother.

Anyway, that was the old Molly, English Molly. She twisted a towel round her hair, swept it on top of her head turban-style and tucked in the ends. This was new, French Molly. Coquettish Molly. She wriggled into her dressing-gown. Desirable Molly. For a moment she allowed one shoulder to remain bare, and imagined Fabrice nibbling his way up her neck. Then she frowned severely, gathered her belongings and unlocked the door. Clutching the dressing-gown spinsterishly tight under her chin, she checked the corridor for perverts and peeping Toms and scampered barefoot back to her room.

She had just stretched out on the bed to massage cream into her freshly razored legs when her glance fell on something she half recognized: a stiff circle of gold leather, concertinaed on the floor. Next to it a spiky-heeled sandal lay on its side.

Molly sat bolt upright as a chunk of memory rushed to the surface of her mind, bobbing wildly. Zabi's party . . . borrowing the clothes . . . the club. Last night, when she'd retrieved her jacket before zooming off with Fabrice, she'd had just enough sense to tell someone what she was doing. She remembered finding Alicia on the dance floor (in the cowboy hat!), swearing to return Zabi's stuff the next morning and—oh, help!—agreeing to meet Alicia at some café at noon. She bet it was nearly that now.

Hastily smearing the remains of the cream across her stomach, Molly leaped to her feet, yanked off her dressing gown and zigzagged back and forth across the room, simultaneously trying to comb her hair, drag on some clothes and find her watch.

She had one leg in her knickers when she spied it in the Pernod ashtray. Hopping across the carpet with the comb in her teeth and hair spattering her bare back, she grabbed the watch, turned it the right way up, and let out a wail of panic. She was already five minutes overdue.

# 8

Twenty minutes later, hair still damp, cheeks pink from running, hugging a bag of Zabi's clothes under one arm while wrestling with a street map that refused to refold, Molly pushed open a heavy swing-door and was instantly engulfed in the beguiling smells and roaring chatter of a café at full weekend throttle. Glasses slammed on zinc. Trays clanged. There was the sizzle of cooking, the clink of spoons stirring sugar lumps into coffee, above all a fervor of conversation conducted with such decisive gestures, so many cigarettes swooping and soaring in passionate emphasis, by such a well-dressed, multiracial, cool-looking crowd—and all in French, too—that Molly was momentarily daunted. She paused by the bar to survey the high-ceilinged room, thronged with tables and brown leather booths. Its crude wooden panelling, pewter chandeliers and mottled mirrors suggested that it must once have been a working-man's haunt, though the stylish clientele and waitresses in jeans swaying sexily past blackboards offering cocktails and "Le Brunch" screamed boho chic.

"*Excusez-moi, Mademoiselle.*" A barman, nimble as a dancer, snaked round her, hoisting a tray of bottles and glasses, miraculously balanced. Molly scuttled out of his way, and scanned the tables once again, hoping that Alicia hadn't got fed up with waiting and left. This place looked fun. Besides, the sight of plates whisking past, piled with *frites*, parsley-flecked mussels, and hamburgers oozing pink juice reminded her that she was starving.

"Oy, Molly! Over here."

From a seat near the window a figure was sweeping both arms through the air in huge arcs, as if guiding in an aircraft to land. Molly recognized Alicia, reincarnated this morning as a slightly more butch Audrey Hepburn, complete with black polo-neck and flicked-up eyeliner. There was a momentary blip in the decibel level as heads swivelled first to Alicia, then to Molly, who sketched a wave, ducked her head self-consciously and hurried over.

"Sorry, sorry, sorry," she panted, sliding at last into the chair opposite Alicia and cramming her bag under the table.

"Yay, you made it!" Alicia beamed her searchlight grin. "Thought you might still be, you know, in bed." Her eyebrows flickered suggestively.

"No, of course not," Molly said, a little stiffly. "I overslept, that's all."

"Oh, yeah?" Alicia's throaty giggle implied that sleeping was the last thing she'd imagined Molly doing.

Molly sucked in her nostrils. Honestly! Just because one accepted an invitation to see Paris by night, it didn't mean one was the sort of girl to, well, not on the very first date . . . although the idea was not wholly—not that she'd even thought about it. (Hardly.) So there.

"You have chosen?" A willowy brunette had wafted to Molly's side, order pad poised.

Flustered, Molly picked up the menu that lay on the table in front of her and gazed at a blur of foreign words and euro symbols. "Er, *je ne—je n'ai pas—*"

"If you're hungry, go for the brunch," Alicia interrupted. "It's totally yummy." She guided Molly through the various choices—coffee, tea or champagne; bagel, salad or eggs Benedict; fruit juices in mouthwatering flavors—and ordered for them both, concluding with a breezy "*mur-see*."

As soon as the waitress had gathered up the menus and left, Alicia leaned forward, elbows on the table, round blue eyes alight with curiosity. "So?" she prompted.

"So what?" Molly stalled.

"So how did it go? Last night, remember? We took you to a club and you buggered off with some gorgeous hunk."

Molly frowned at this crude description. Had Heathcliff "buggered off" with Cathy across the moors? Was Mr. Darcy a "hunk"? Australians obviously had no concept of romance.

"At least, I assume he was gorgeous," Alicia persisted.

Molly picked at her red-and-white-checked table-mat, trying to quell the treacherous smile that tugged at the corner of her mouth. "He was—very nice. Very intelligent. An art student. We went round Paris on his scooter. It was extremely . . ." she fumbled for the right word ". . . interesting," she concluded lamely.

"I bet it was!" Alicia gave a loud, dirty laugh. "All that throbbing under your bum. Whooh! Enough to make anyone wet their panties. Not that you were wearing any."

"Shush!" Molly flushed and furtively checked the adjacent tables, hoping no one understood English.

"Well, you weren't. You can't pretend to me. I've got them right here, in this bag. Want me to get them out and show everyone?"

"*Alicia!*" Molly whispered, in agonized protest.

"Then get off your high horse and tell me what happened last night. Come on, girl, give. It must have been special. Or do you always dump your friends and disappear with strange men?"

"No! And there's nothing 'strange' about Fabrice."

"Ooh, *Fabrice*."

"*Et voilà*." To Molly's relief, the waitress was back, bringing coffee and hot milk in silvery jugs, a plate of miniature muffins, and two tall glasses of fresh, frothy juice. Molly had chosen raspberry. She took a deep, cooling gulp.

"So, did you shag him?"

Molly spluttered, choked as her juice went down the wrong way, gasped for breath, then coughed half the juice back into her napkin. She could feel her face turn to boiled beetroot. Tears squeezed from her eyes. Everyone was looking.

Alicia had come round the table to pat her on the back, and hand her a glass of water.

"I hate you, Alicia," Molly croaked, between sips.

Alicia merely returned to her seat with a smug smile. "No, you don't. You want to tell me all about him."

She was right. Molly allowed the wild happiness she had felt all morning to burst her defenses and flood into her face. "Oh, Alicia," she sighed, "it was the best night of my whole life. We watched the dawn come up over Sacré Coeur. He showed me the Eiffel Tower. He even massaged my feet."

"So you *did* sh—?"

"No, I didn't!" Molly slapped the table furiously. "Not yet."

Hearing what she'd just said, she clapped a hand to her mouth and stared at Alicia, appalled.

Alicia snorted, then giggled, then burst into loud gleeful guffaws, pointing her finger wordlessly at Molly until she, too, was overtaken by hysterical giggles and the pair of them were practically bent double, clasping their stomachs, rocking helplessly on their chairs, pounding their feet on the floor. Molly had almost regained control when Alicia pointed her finger again and cooed, "Fabree-eece." Once again they were off. "*Mais quand même!*" someone muttered in haughty disgust from a neighboring table.

Finally the girls wiped their eyes and looked at each other in perfect friendship.

"Right, then," said Alicia. "Do we gather you at least got a snog?"

Molly nodded, and allowed herself to let loose another long, dreamy sigh.

"Tongues?"

"For God's sake!"

"And you're seeing him again?"

"This afternoon. Half past three." Molly felt a twinge of doubt. That was the time they'd agreed, wasn't it?

"Ooh, this is so exciting! I knew something was up when I saw you come in looking all dewy."

*This afternoon.* The breath caught in her chest. What if Fabrice hadn't liked her after all? What if she couldn't think of anything to say? What if he didn't turn up? Molly watched the waitress's hand remove the muffins and set down a plate bearing an artful arrangement of eggs Benedict flanked by *saucisses* and frills of crisp bacon. What if he just grabbed her, tore off all her clothes and—

"Guess you're going to miss out on the old Louvre, then."

"Hmm?" Molly bit absently into a sausage.

"You know, the place where the paintings are?" Alicia pinched her features into a hoity-toity expression. "'First thing tomorrow I'm jolly well off to the Louvre for some culture.'"

"Oh, shut up." Molly giggled. "Actually, I think I'm meeting him, er, Fabrice—" she blushed to say his name aloud "—at some kind of museum." She fished in her handbag for the precious strip of cigarette packet he had given her last night and handed it across. "Maybe you can tell me where that is."

"Bloody hell!" In an instant Alicia's face had changed to fury. She jumped to her feet, sending the table rocking and cutlery slithering to the floor. Ignoring Molly completely, she charged through the café and out of the door.

# 9

Molly stared after Alicia, aghast. What had she done? What had she said? Was Alicia ill? She half rose from her chair, wondering whether to go after her. But they hadn't paid the bill. The waitress would think— She sat down again. Not knowing what else to do, she picked up the fallen cutlery and arranged it neatly on the table, pondering Alicia's extraordinary behavior, feeling anxious and unhappy.

A terrible realization made her go cold. Alicia still had the bit of cigarette packet. Molly couldn't remember what was written on it. If Alicia didn't come back, she wouldn't know where to go. She pictured Fabrice waiting for her, checking his watch as hope and happiness drained from his face. He'd think she wasn't coming, that she didn't care. There was no way to contact him. This was unbearable! And she'd never, ever see him again. Molly almost sobbed aloud at the thought, and hid her agitation by taking a large swig of coffee.

Then a much grimmer possibility made her drop the cup back into its saucer with a rattle. Alicia had rushed off at exactly the moment Molly had handed her that address: why? *Because she had recognized Fabrice's writing!* In a blinding flash Molly could see it all. Alicia and Fabrice had been lovers—no, *were* lovers—no, no, Fabrice would never be so perfidious as to pick up another girl, namely herself, if he was already involved. So. They'd been lovers. (Perfectly possible: they both lived in Paris, both liked going to clubs. Alicia was perhaps a little on the old side, but hey.) Anyway, it was all over for him, but Alicia still cared. She hadn't realized that Molly's Fabrice was *her* Fabrice, too, until she'd seen the telltale writing and felt her whole world crumble. Poor Alicia! Molly sank back in her chair, winded by the tragic irony of this scenario. How often momentous events turned on a single tiny detail. It was just like that brilliant bit in *The Golden Bowl* where the wife realizes that her husband and best friend have been—

"Sorry about that," chirped a familiar voice, at her shoulder. "Bloody Janine. The nerve of it! Sailing right past the window on *my* Rollerblades. She was too fast for me this time, but I'll get her in the end." Alicia seated herself calmly, looking slightly puffed but otherwise normal. "Now, where were we? Oh, yeah, that address." She pulled the scrap of cardboard from her trouser pocket and scanned it casually. "Funny writing these French have. All loops and whirly bits." She handed it back with a reassuring smile. "You'll be right. I can tell you how to get there."

Molly gazed back at Alicia's strong, friendly face, her bright, guileless eyes, her kooky voodoo earrings, and felt a wave of remorse and embarrassment wash over her. How foolish she was! How stupid and selfish and ungrateful! "I've been thinking," she began hesitantly, "you know, about last night."

"Again? By the way, the French for condom is *préservatif*."

"No, seriously. I had the most fantastic time, not just Fabrice but everything else—Zabi's flat, the clothes, the club. It was all wonderful. And none of it would have happened if you hadn't been nice enough to take me with you."

Alicia pulled a silly face.

"So I just wondered if I could, er, make a contribution to a new pair of Rollerblades so that you won't have to—I mean, if money's a problem—well, basically so you won't keep abandoning me in restaurants."

Alicia reached out and squeezed her arm. "You're a doll. But I couldn't take money off you. Tell you what, you can book in for my Sunday morning roller tour. *Balade*, they call it here."

"But I don't know how." Molly pictured herself waving her legs like a flipped beetle on some posh Parisian *trottoir.* And she might be busy with Fabrice (in a not dissimilar position). How testing life was.

"Beginners welcome. Plus I get a percentage of every customer I introduce." Alicia grinned at her hopefully.

For a moment Molly teetered on the knife-edge between what she wanted to do—hoard every minute for Fabrice—and what loyalty and friendship told her she must do. Her conscience spoke loud and clear. "That's it, then," she said lightly, feeling a painful inner wrench. "I'll be there."

"Yay! You can bring me up to speed on the great hunkerama—" Alicia broke off suddenly and cocked her head. "What's that noise? Is it your mobile?"

"Can't be. I put my calls on 'divert,' so I wouldn't have to pay to receive them." But instinctively Molly was reaching for her bag. "Oh, look, can I give you Zabi's things? And give me my stuff, before you go around showing my knickers to everyone." They swapped plastic bags, then Molly scrabbled around for her phone. She could have sworn she'd turned it off on the train, but now she, too, could hear its insect bleeps. "Got it!" she cried triumphantly. "Oh, it's stopped. But I've got a text message. How weird."

"No, it's not. They don't get diverted because they cost the same to send anywhere in the world. I'm always texting my mates in Australia." She leaned across nosily. "So, who's it from?"

"It seems to be from Sal, my flatmate." Molly was hunched over the phone, staring dopily at the letters jostling on its tiny screen. Whatever Alicia said, it felt weird to be sitting here in a café in Paris, with the sunshine outside and Fabrice filling her thoughts, then suddenly be jolted back to her old London life. "Something about the police!" she exclaimed. "And all these Roman numerals."

"Here, show me." Alicia grabbed Molly's wrist to pull the phone into view.

Together they scrolled through the message, which read: "MLCLM [angry face symbol] SEZ GIT ASAP OR POLICE! ROUK? *werubin*? XOX SAL." After the words came a long string of digits.

"Let's see . . ." Molly frowned. "M is a thousand, and L is fifty, I think—"

"They're not Roman numbers, you drongo. Look, do you know anyone called Malcolm?"

Molly made a face. "Only my old boss." Then she jerked upright as her brain finally crunched into gear. "Christ! Malcolm!" She read the message a third time. According to Sal, Malcolm was very angry and wanted her to get in touch as soon as possible—or he was calling the police! Why?

"So, Moll, what did you do?" demanded Alicia. "Run off with the petty cash?"

"No! All I did was resign." Molly pictured her drab, sunless workstation, all those piles of dreary reports and press releases, Malcolm's cocky little walk. Suddenly it seemed incredible that she could ever have taken that job in the first place, or lasted as long as she had.

"Not your problem then, is it?" Alicia said breezily. "Oh, beauty, here come the waffles."

They had finally reached the last course of their magnificent brunch: two crisp waffles overlapped in a pleasing geometric pattern, with a strawberry placed at the exact center on a blob of whipped cream.

Automatically Molly picked up a fork, then stared blankly at her plate, unsettled by Sal's message. Surely it wasn't a crime to resign. Should she have informed Human Resources first? Perhaps Malcolm was upset by her letter. It wasn't libelous—was it?—to tell someone they couldn't spell. "I don't get it," she said, stabbing the strawberry. "Why the police?"

"I dunno." Alicia poured lavishly from a small jug of maple syrup. "Call him up and find out."

"I couldn't!"

"Why not?"

"He's so horrible. You have no idea, Alicia. He shouts."

"All men shout. I've got five brothers and I know. Just shout back."

Molly shook her head vehemently. The very thought of speaking to Malcolm made her stomach churn with fear. She remembered uncomfortably that there were at least two pens in her possession bearing the company logo, and possibly an eraser. She pictured herself getting off the train at Waterloo tomorrow night . . . a posse of uniformed officers tramping toward her . . . a beefy hand laid on her shoulder. "Excuse me, Miss, may we take a look in your bag?"

"What could I have done wrong?" she burst out.

Alicia looked at her, laid down her fork with a clatter and gave a resigned sigh. "Want me to call him for you?"

Molly gaped at this dazzlingly bold suggestion.

"Come on, hand over the phone. I'll pretend to be your secretary or something."

"But I haven't got a secretary!"

"Your lawyer, then—PR person. Does it matter?"

Molly laid a hand reverently on her heart. "God, Alicia, you are so-o-o brave. But not on my phone," she added quickly. "He's got this number. If my name flashes up on his screen he'll know it's really me."

"A pay phone, then. They've got one here, I think, out the back. Eat up your waffles and fill me in on this Malcolm dude. Then we'll go and phone. You can listen in."

Five minutes later, heartbeat quickening in anticipation, Molly followed Alicia as she sauntered down the aisle between the tables. The wafty waitress, suddenly about as wafty as steel, stepped into their path and raised a suspicious eyebrow.

Alicia gave her a cheery wave. "*Nous retournez dans un minute. Téléphone.*"

"*Ah, bon.*" The eyebrow returned to normal.

The pay phone turned out to be one of those cool super-designed things, all brushed steel and digital screen, with a see-through acoustic hood. The two girls squeezed underneath it together. Alicia produced a telephone card and slid it into the slot. "*Patientez SVP,*" flashed the screen. Molly chewed her thumbnail. What if Malcolm was so beastly that Alicia broke down and told him where Molly was? He might come after her. She might miss her meeting with Fabrice!

"Wakey, wakey," Alicia gave her a nudge. The screen had changed to "*Numérotez.*"

Molly read the number off her mobile and Alicia punched the buttons, then held the receiver so that they could both listen. They waited. Molly wished she'd gone to the loo first. Oh, God, she could hear it ringing.

"Yep, Figg speaking."

It was him! His voice was low and crisply businesslike against a background roar of voices. He must be in the actual conference.

Alicia pulled the receiver close so she could speak into the mouthpiece. "Hi, Mr. Figg, how are you doing? This is Ms. O'Connell, phoning on behalf of Ms. Clearwater." She gave Molly an enormous wink, and angled the receiver back again.

"*Molly Clearwater?*" He uttered the name with such fury that Molly flinched. "Where the fuck is she?"

"Now, Mr. Figg, we're not going to get very far with that sort of language, are we?"

"And who the fuck are you?"

Alicia raised an eyebrow. "If it comes to that, who the fuck are *you* to be threatening Ms. Clearwater with the police?"

Molly marvelled at her steely calm. Even Malcolm seemed impressed. After a small pause his voice came back on the line tinged with a new respect: "Her boss, that's who."

"Ex-boss, according to my information," said Alicia, unperturbed. "She's considering bringing a suit for sexual harassment and constructive dismissal."

Molly's jaw dropped.

"Bollocks!" Malcolm snapped. "I'm the one who's going to be suing—for bloody stealing."

"Oh, yeah? And what's she supposed to have bloody stolen?"

"She knows. Did it deliberately, the cow."

Alicia turned inquiringly to Molly, who spread her hands and hoisted her shoulders in a desperate mime.

"Could you be a little more specific, Mr. Figg?"

There was a pause. Then his voice came through slightly muffled, as though he'd turned his head away, oozing smarmy matiness. "No. No problem, Jerry. Hot to trot. Catch you later." They heard him blow out his breath. Then he said in a tight, furtive voice, "I'm going to have to take this call in—in another room."

The babble of voices receded. There was the squeak of a swing door, the click of shoes on tiles. Malcolm's voice came back on the line, aggressive but strangely echoey: "Now, listen to me. I don't think you realize who you're dealing with here. I represent one of the UK's leading pharmaceutical companies—"

"What, you personally?" Alicia cooed. "You must be very important."

"Yes, well, I do have considerable responsibility for strategic thinking, market-wise, within the global economy, plus an extremely large—"

He broke off and they heard an unmistakable whooshing noise. Molly caught Alicia's eye and exchanged a look of wide-eyed glee.

"An extremely large . . . ?" Alicia paused delicately.

"Budget. Which is why," he hurried on, "I need those graphics. I've got the cream of international medicine here, the boss breathing down my neck, and no disk!"

At the last word Molly let out a little squeak. Too late, Alicia jammed her palm over the mouthpiece.

"Who's that?" Malcolm pounced. "Molly's *there*, isn't she? Molly, get on the line this instant or I'll—"

Alicia lowered the receiver, cutting Malcolm off in mid-rant. "Do you know what he's talking about?" she whispered.

Molly nodded. She remembered now. She'd wrapped the disk in her clothes, packed it in her case. "In the hotel," she whispered back. "I forgot."

Alicia rolled her eyes and lifted the receiver again.

"—never work in the industry again!" Malcolm was shouting.

"Just shut up a minute and listen," Alicia interrupted. "I may be able to locate that disk for you."

"Ha!" Malcolm said triumphantly. "Now we're getting somewhere. Right, then. I want it couriered over to me in Paris, top priority, and don't whine to me about the expense."

"As it happens, Mr. Figg, the disk is already in Paris."

"You're kidding me." It seemed that for once his brain was working, for almost immediately he added, "Do you mean to say Molly's *here?*"

Molly made frantic signs of denial.

"I'm afraid I am not at liberty to divulge her whereabouts. But talk to me nicely and I could have that disk at your hotel within the hour."

Utter silence. Then a dazed voice said, "Fuck me."

"Is that what you call talking 'nicely,' Mr. Figg?" Alicia's voice was like honey.

"How do you want me to talk, then, Miss Bossyboots? Er, I assume it is 'Miss'?"

"You could always try calling me Alicia . . . Malcolm." Alicia shot Molly a look of wild mischief. Molly gaped back, horrified.

"Oh, ho. Alicia, is it? Well . . . Alicia . . . I can tell that you're a very formidable lady."

Molly clutched her throat and stuck out her tongue. She could hardly wait to hear Alicia's put-down.

"Am I?" Alicia said silkily. Molly couldn't believe it. Alicia was actually *enjoying* this.

"Oh, yes." There was Malcolm's smug chuckle. "I can hear it in your voice. As it happens, I'm quite an experienced judge of women."

"What a coincidence. I'm quite an experienced judge of men. . . . And both of us in Paris, too."

"*Ooh, là là!*" Malcolm said friskily.

This was disgusting! Molly made a grab for the phone. Alicia snatched it back and jabbed her, really quite sharply, in the ribs, then pressed the receiver so tightly to her own ear that Malcolm's side of the conversation faded to an unintelligible drone. Molly tugged at the phone cord. Alicia held it firm.

"Tonight?" she was saying, passing a languid hand over her hair. "No plans in particular. What did you have in mind?"

Worse and worse! Molly put out her finger to cut off the call, and was shocked when Alicia slapped her hand and made a shooing motion. Reluctantly she ducked out from under the hood. But she could still hear Alicia.

"And where exactly is your hotel, Malcolm?"

Molly cleared her throat ostentatiously.

". . . No, no, a show sounds great."

Molly plucked desperately at the hem of Alicia's sweater.

"I might be blonde and I might not. You'll have to wait and see."

Now Molly was jumping up and down, signaling wildly. She slashed a finger across her neck, stuck a finger down her throat, scratched her armpits like an ape, smooched her lips to the Perspex hood and crossed her eyes. Alicia simply turned her back and went on talking.

Finally she put down the phone, retrieved her card and turned. Molly blocked her path. "Alicia, you can't! He's a creep. He's got tufty hair and a signet ring."

Alicia grinned. "He sounds quite a laugh. Anyway, my dad wears a signet ring."

"You know where he wants to take you, don't you? That ticket was supposed to be for me. It's . . ." She lowered her voice and looked around carefully. "It's the Crazy Horse Saloon."

"So?"

"You don't understand. There are *naked women* dancing around with—with feathers and snakes and stuff. It's a *sex show.*"

"Really? Might give it a go, then."

"Not with Malcolm. He'll leer, and make smutty remarks."

"I can handle sexist men, Molly. Remember, I'm Australian."

Molly stared at her, thwarted. "Well, at least take your mobile, so we can contact each other. Let me know if things get out of hand."

"That's so sweet." Alicia patted her head. "Come on, let's nip in here." She waved to a door marked "*Dames*." "I'm busting for a whiz."

Molly gave up, and slowly followed Alicia inside. This morning she'd wondered if she'd ever understand men; now it turned out she didn't understand women either. Great.

Still, there were more important things to think about. As soon as she emerged from the cubicle, Molly made a bee-line for the mirror and peeled off her cardigan to reveal a skimpy red dress. She'd bought it months ago, egged on by Abi who'd insisted that this particular holly-berry red was absolutely "her" color—but Molly had never yet had the nerve to wear it. The neck was deeply scooped (too low?), the skirt short (too short?) and flared, the fabric stretchy and figure-hugging (did she look fat? Those waffles!). What would Fabrice think?

There was the rasp of a bolt. Alicia strolled out, heading for the basins, then did a double-take. "Whoa, knockout dress."

"You really think so?" Molly was sucking in her stomach so hard that her voice came out hoarse as a crow's.

"Not so sure about the shoes, though." Alicia turned on a tap. "And that cardy should be burned. Haven't you got a groovy jacket?"

Molly was itemizing her limited choices when Alicia checked her watch and interrupted: "Malcolm's hotel is on the other side of the river, you know. If you're going to take that disk back and still make your rendezvous with Fabrice you'd better get a move on."

"*Me?*" Molly was astounded. "I'm not taking the disk."

"Yes, you are. I promised Malcolm he'd get it within the hour—you heard me—and I'm a girl who likes to keep my promises. Have a heart, Molly. The poor guy's frantic."

"But I thought *you*—"

"No way. I've got to get back to Zabi and the shop. Some of us have to work, you know."

"But, Alicia, I *can't.* The place will be crawling with my old colleagues. It's too embarrassing. What if I run into Malcolm?"

"What if you do? He's just a bloke. Like Fabrice is just a bloke."

Molly blanched at this heresy.

"Anyway, all you have to do is hand the thing in at the desk and rush out again."

"I can't," Molly said stubbornly. "I won't. Someone will recognize me."

Alicia went on washing her hands. Molly watched her clean her nails, one by one, then smooth the thin arcs of her eyebrows with a damp finger, and wished she'd say something. Instead, Alicia moved over to the drying machine, leaving Molly staring at her own unattractively sullen reflection. She ran hot water into the basin, trying to drown the sulky echo of her voice, knowing she was being childish. But the idea of entering some posh hotel foyer and facing all those people terrified her. Alicia didn't understand. She was older and braver and—and Australian. She had five brothers who shouted. Why couldn't *she* do it?

Then Molly felt ashamed. Alicia had been generous to her beyond all expectation. She was warm and funny and terrific company. It was because of her that Molly had met Fabrice. Now Alicia wanted to meet Malcolm (God knows why). It was pretty obvious that their date would go a lot better if he wasn't still waiting for his stupid disk.

Molly joined Alicia and thrust her hands into warm air. For a moment their fingers touched, and Molly looked up and smiled. "You're right," she said. "It's no problem. Of course I'll go."

"Good on you." Alicia gave her a quick hug. "And stop worrying about it. I've just had a brainwave."

# 10

The windows were full of wonders. In one, rivulets of diamonds and avalanches of pearls poured onto dark velvet. In another, female torsos paraded in filmy lingerie of every sorbet shade from lime to raspberry. Molly passed whole shops devoted to truffles, or caviar, or mosaics of baby vegetables embalmed in gelatin; to rosebuds and bronze-leafed dahlias still glistening with garden dew; to carved plinths of chocolate supporting miniature sculptures of lemon peel and crystalized violets. She saw floor-length cashmere coats and leather bags supple as babies' skin, displayed against limestone-and-glass interiors where exquisite assistants palely loitered. Emblazoned on flags, or coyly framed by clipped box trees, were designer names she'd only read about in back issues of *Vogue* while waiting for a trim and blow-dry at Snipz, Minster Episcopi's trendiest hairdresser. This was the natural territory of American and Japanese tourists, confidently eyeing the credit-card signs, though they were easily outclassed by the Parisian women, coiffed and creamed, toned and taloned, carrying themselves like duchesses.

*Lèche-vitrine*, they called it in France: not window-shopping but window-licking. But for Molly the most mesmerizing sight—and the main reason she stopped so often to gaze in appalled fascination—was her own reflection. The Cleopatra wig was Alicia's idea, filched from Zabi's shop. The sunglasses they had bought together, not far from the café, from an Arab street-trader peddling designer rip-offs; almost as large as the mask of Zorro, they had starlet-black lenses and fake tortoiseshell rims. Alicia had also insisted on lending Molly black mid-calf boots with criss-cross laces, and one of those super-cool denim jackets that looked as if it had been immersed in seawater, pegged out to dry in the Sahara, then lightly singed. Along with the red dress, it was a striking ensemble.

She heard what she thought was a derisive snigger, and turned sharply. But it was only a tiny beribboned dog, whose yapping head protruded from an elderly woman's handbag. "*Mais qu'est-ce que tu as, mon petit bijou?*" clucked the woman, and tapped her little jewel's nose with a crimson-tipped forefinger. Molly moved on, avoiding eye contact. Despite the disguise, she felt as conspicuous as if she were naked. The wig itched. She longed for this whole ordeal to be over.

The ritzy shops were now giving way to less intimidating department stores and kitchenware outlets, with "*Prix choc!*" signs pasted to the windows. At the entrance to one of these, Molly stopped and pushed up her sunglasses to consult her map. One more block north, turn right, and she should be there.

The hotel was unmissable, one of those turn-of-the-century monstrosities built for wealthy travelers arriving at the nearby railway station, now downgraded to accommodate the *hoi polloi* of conferences and tour groups, and vulgarized with a Marie-Antoinette Bar and concession gift shops. Nonetheless, a veneer of grandeur remained in the ornate portico, red-carpeted steps and uniformed flunkeys summoning taxis. Molly's throat tightened. For the umpteenth time she checked that the disk was in her bag, now sealed in an envelope marked "For the attention of

Mr. M. Figg (Phipps Lauzer Bergman)." All she had to do was hand it to the receptionist and walk out again. With a final uneasy glance at the peculiar person keeping pace with her in the hotel's street-level windows, Molly raised her chin, put an extra swagger into her step and, looking to neither right nor left, swept up the carpet and inside.

Crikey! The lobby was enormous, as big as a ballroom and at least three stories high, with an abundance of marble, gilt, and crystal chandeliers, and a broad staircase twisting up to galleried landings. Scores of people milled about by the desks variously labeled "Information," "Exchange," "Concierge." Lifts pinged. Porters wheeled trolleys of luggage. Women in sensible shoes and draped silk scarves chatted among potted palms. A huge banner welcomed the *Congrès International de Gastro-entérologie.*

But where was the reception desk? Molly walked forward a few paces, lost her nerve and veered purposefully left. By a glass display case she mimed an artistic double-take, then pretended to admire a selection of Hermès scarves while scouting out the territory. There was no one she recognized. Phew! Eventually she spotted a long curve of mahogany set with bulbous glass lamps, with a bank of pigeonholes behind, and men in black suits attending to a stream of queries and requests. She sidled up to the extreme end of the desk and lurked behind a vase of lilies until it was her turn.

"*Oui?*" A sallow-skinned man with slicked hair cocked his head with professional politeness.

Molly leaned forward and explained her mission in a low voice. She spoke in French, but her accent couldn't fool an old hand: "Certainly, Mademoiselle," he replied in English. "I will see that 'e receives it."

With a rush of relief Molly reached into her bag and took out the envelope. She was just stretching out her arm to hand it over when the man's gaze slid over her shoulder and he gave a cry of joyous surprise. "Ah! But 'ere is Monsieur Feeg now!"

In a frenzied panic Molly ducked behind the flowers and shot in the opposite direction at a low, crouching run, the envelope still in her hand. Her head swung left and right, as she searched for escape. Where should she hide? What should she do? Into her field of vision came the back view of a man—tallish, grey jacket, heading for a doorway. She rushed up behind him and slid her arm into his. "*Au clair de la lune, mon ami Pierrot!*" she gabbled breathlessly, as if greeting a long-lost friend.

The man halted in astonishment. He was middle-aged, ordinary: sweater and casual shirt under the jacket, a badge ineptly pinned. Molly felt his arm pull away, and locked her elbow in a vice-like grip, propelling him forward. "*Ma chandelle est morte. Je n'ai plus de feu!*" She gave a vivacious laugh.

Her bonkers behavior had been enough to get them through the doorway and out of the lobby. A long, carpeted corridor stretched ahead: if Malcolm followed, she might still be trapped. Molly could feel her companion's surprise turning to annoyance: any second now she would be denounced. There was an opening on her left: low tables, dim lights, red plush. "*Le bar!*" Molly cried ecstatically, and frogmarched the stranger inside.

Here he wrenched his arm free, swiftly frisked the breast-pocket area of his jacket, and confronted Molly with mingled puzzlement and suspicion. The barman looked up from his glass-polishing, sensing a drama. Molly shifted from foot to foot in an agony of indecision—longing to hide, wanting to explain, infuriated to be mistaken for a pickpocket, terrified that she was about to be publicly accused.

She lowered her voice to a heartfelt whisper. "*S'il vous plaît, Monsieur, excusez-moi. Je regrette*, er, *beaucoup* . . ."

The barman had slithered, eel-like, to their side. Did Monsieur have a problem? His damp eyes lingered on Molly's bare legs and fetishist boots. She was horribly reminded of that scene in *Pretty Woman* where Julia Roberts got fingered as a prostitute by a hotel manager.

After a long look at Molly, the stranger shrugged as if to say everything was fine, and gestured to her to take a seat. There was a hint of irony in his extreme courtesy, which she found disconcerting. Feeling rather as if she was being escorted to the headmaster's study, she led the way to the farthest, darkest corner and slid into a banquette. The man sat down opposite her and folded his arms.

"So what on earth was all that about?" he asked calmly.

Molly jerked her head in surprise. He was English! For the first time she looked at him properly. Blue eyes, a bit saggy but quite intelligent-looking; mid-brown hair showing the first flecks of grey; indoor skin; a mouth that suggested he smiled more often than not; sophisticated in a way she couldn't quite define, though not a vain man, to judge by his clothes. Her eyes fell on his badge. She couldn't read it through her super-dark sunglasses and, anyway, it appeared to be upside-down. But he must be with the conference—perhaps even an employee of PLB. She'd better be careful.

"You *are* English, aren't you?" he insisted. "Despite the rather inspired use of French nursery songs."

"No. Not at all. I'm . . . Australian." Molly injected her vowels with a nasal twang.

"Really? Your French seems remarkably good. I thought Australians learned Japanese these days."

"My family's originally from Frahnce, I mean Frans," Molly improvised.

"Ah. No doubt that explains your splendid dark hair."

Baffled, Molly raised a hand automatically to her head and

encountered something that felt like the coat of an Afghan hound. Of course: the wig. She smoothed it casually, then wished she hadn't as she felt something dislodge.

"And what do you think of Paris?" he asked.

"Oh, it's—it's fair dinkum."

His eyebrows rose slightly, but all he said was, "My own view exactly."

There was a silence. Molly plunged in: "Look, I'm terribly sorry to have grabbed you like that. You must have thought I was mad—I mean, crazy as a bandicoot." She tried to imitate Alicia's rollicking laugh. "The thing is, there's someone here I don't want to see. But I did. So I had to get out of there fast, without being spotted. I know it was incredibly rude and stupid but . . ."

His eyes rested on her, not exactly disbelieving but wary. "And who was it you didn't want to see?"

"A man."

"Boyfriend?"

"Certainly not."

"Someone more . . . official, perhaps?"

"No!" What was he implying? "Just a man."

"Hmm." His tone was skeptical.

"I know what you're thinking," she said hotly. "That I'm some kind of hustler who sneaks into hotels and—"

"Would you like a drink?" he interrupted.

Molly saw that the barman had reappeared with his pad. "No, thank you." Her tone was frosty.

"But I insist. You're the one who dragged me in here, after all."

"Oh, all right. Do you have Appletize?" she asked the barman.

His nostrils flared at this barbarity.

"Orange juice, then."

As soon as he was out of earshot, she leaned across the table and continued, in an indignant hiss, "I promise you, I am not after your wallet, or a free drink or—or anything else. You obviously think I'm some dangerous criminal on the run, but I can assure you I was simply trying to deliver a package."

"A package?"

"Yes! The package I need to give to this man."

"The man you don't want to see?"

"Yes! No." Molly sighed at this nit-picking. "I want him to get the package, I just don't want to give it to him personally. Look, it's here, if you don't believe me." She pulled out the envelope and slapped it theatrically on the table. A second later she flipped it the other way up to hide Malcolm's name.

"You're some kind of courier, then?"

"Well . . ."

"You're not a spy, are you?"

Molly had a feeling he was laughing at her. She turned her head and gazed haughtily into the distance, not deigning to reply. Then her face brightened. "Cool! Look at that." Her orange juice was arriving, complete with a wedge of fresh orange, a maraschino cherry, one of those straws you could bend in every direction, and a cocktail umbrella. She was shocked to see that her companion had ordered Scotch, though it was barely afternoon. Perhaps he had an alcohol problem.

They sipped their drinks in silence. Molly's was delicious, though every time she bent her head to the straw her sunglasses slipped annoyingly down her nose, and she had to wedge them in place with a forefinger.

"I hope you don't mind me asking," he said, "but is there a problem with your eyes?"

"No. Why?"

"I thought you might like to take off those glasses. It really isn't too dangerously dazzling in here."

After a moment's consideration Molly did as he suggested. Instantly, her face felt cooler, more normal. The room sprang to life, right down to the fleur-de-lis carpeting and gilt mirrors beset with cherubs. She looked carefully round the scattering of tables and peeped over the back of her banquette to check the entrance.

"If the man you don't want to see comes in," he said, "scratch your left ear and I'll create a diversion."

His expression was deadpan, but she caught the glint of humor in his eye and couldn't help responding with a small smile. He wasn't so bad, now she could see him properly. His pale coloring and rumpled appearance were reassuringly familiar among all these dark, natty foreigners. It was comforting to hear an English voice; his was educated but not lah-di-dah. She might have chosen someone much nastier.

Suddenly she remembered the time and jerked back the cuff of her jacket to check her watch. Forty minutes until she was seeing Fabrice, she calculated: better get going soon. But what about that damned disk? Alicia had promised it to Malcolm "within the hour"; the deadline had passed fifteen minutes ago. That's probably why he'd come into the lobby. If he was really desperate, he might still be waiting, ready to pounce. Molly gnawed at a nail, then realized she was being observed.

"Sorry. It's just that I'm meeting . . . someone. I mustn't be late." But instead of making a move to go, she put out a hand and fingered Malcolm's envelope. She must do something *soon.* But what?

He watched her over his Scotch. For some reason she noticed his hands—broad and capable-looking, with clean, rounded nails. No signet rings. "You're not in any trouble, are you?" he asked.

"No, no. Well, apart from delivering this package." She poked it with a fingernail, then nudged it infinitesimally in his direction. "I suppose . . . I suppose *you* wouldn't hand it in for me?"

He thought about this. "What's inside?"

"It's not drugs, or a homemade bomb or anything, honestly, just some boring PR stuff for a pharmaceutical company." She turned the envelope over and pointed to Malcolm's name. "Look. He's in their marketing department. You can check if you like. He, er, forgot this stuff and I promised to bring it."

Molly could tell he knew he wasn't getting the whole story. She was beginning to be sick of all her lies.

He hefted the package, put it to his ear and gave it a rattle. She looked up hopefully.

"Okay," he said. "I'll deliver it. In person, if you like. I'd quite like to meet this Mr. Figg."

"Oh, thank you, thank you, thank you!" Molly pressed her palms together as if all her prayers had been answered by God Himself.

"So long as you swear it doesn't contain the secret locations of Australia's nuclear arsenal."

After a moment's confusion, Molly remembered she was supposed to be Australian. She blushed a bit, and they both laughed. He was quite funny, really, for an old guy.

"And would you mind terribly not saying it came from me?" she asked.

"That's easy enough. I don't know who you are, do I?"

"No." Molly twisted her hands in her lap. It felt rude not to give her name, but Malcolm mustn't know she was in Paris. Imagine him muscling in on some romantic moment with Fabrice and bullying her back to the conference to take a memo or set up a stand. "You needn't even say a girl gave it to you," she suggested diffidently.

"I won't. Not even under torture."

Molly smiled. She wondered what he was doing here. He didn't seem like any of the Phipps Lauzer Bergman brigade, with their flashy self-importance. "Are you with a drug company, too?" she asked.

"God, no. I'm a doctor, lowest of the low."

Molly raised her eyebrows at this. At work everyone had always spoken of doctors as if they were capricious gods, to be cajoled and appeased. "Then shouldn't you be, you know, conferencing?" Molly nodded at his badge.

"Probably. The truth is, I don't usually come to this kind of conference and I'm rather bored."

Despite her horrid experiences at Phipps Lauzer Bergman, Molly felt a perverse prickle of annoyance. To think of the hectic preparations for this conference, all those pages of typing, her mega-drama with disks, and he was "rather bored." "What's wrong with it?" she demanded.

"Too much marketing, not enough science."

Molly frowned severely. "I'd have thought you'd be grateful to learn about all the useful drugs they're producing."

He burst into laughter, as if she'd said something naïve. "Actually, it's the other way round. People like me develop the drugs they make a fortune out of. If I'd only had the wit to buy shares in the companies selling the drugs, I'd be a millionaire by now."

This sounded convincing, if rather arrogant, but his hilarity at her remark still stung. Molly bent her head to her straw and sucked up the last drops of her juice, producing a satisfying gurgling noise from among the melting ice cubes. Then she looked up challengingly. "I know why you came here," she announced. "You wanted a freebie in Paris."

She was deliberately cheeky, expecting a smile. Instead, he sighed. "I expect you're right," he answered dully.

Perhaps he was tired. The newspapers were full of articles about doctors' long hours. He did have quite a lot of wrinkles.

"What's it like being a doctor?" she wondered aloud.

"Frustrating. Exhausting. Sometimes interesting. Very occasionally thrilling. I've never known anything else." He tossed back the last of his whisky. "Listen, shouldn't you be going?"

"Golly, you're right." Molly grabbed her bag.

"I'll come out to the corridor with you." He picked up Malcolm's envelope and stood up. "There's a side entrance that brings you out right by the Métro, if that's useful."

"Yes, please. I've only got half an hour to get there." Molly was already on her feet, jiggling with impatience. She couldn't believe she'd been sitting talking to some old doctor about a stupid conference when Fabrice was waiting. Still, she must be polite. She followed the doctor to the bar and watched him pay the bill while listening to his instructions about how to get out of the hotel and which Métro line to take. "It's only a few stops," he told her. "You'll be fine."

They walked together out of the bar and halted. "That way." He pointed down the long corridor. "Right, left, and you're there. I'm going back through the lobby."

Molly nodded, bouncing on the balls of her feet. "Thank you so much for agreeing to deliver the package," she said, "and for the drink, of course."

"A pleasure. I've enjoyed meeting you." He put out his hand for her to shake. "Have a good time, wherever you're going."

"I will." Her nerves were already tingling.

Something must have shown in her face, for as he let go of her hand he added abruptly, "I hope he's nice to you."

Molly had to bite her lips to stop herself smiling too ridiculously. Turning away, she flipped a small wave. "'Bye."

Round the first corner she broke into a run. No one was

about, so she tore off the wig, stuffed it into her bag and let her hair stream free. Joy swelled in her chest. *Fabrice!* There were large medallions woven into the carpeting at regular intervals, depicting the face of some Louis or other in a clasp of laurel leaves. With exuberant leaps she cleared them easily, one by one.

Another turn. Here at last was the exit, a revolving door gleaming with polished brass. Not a flunkey to be seen. Heartbeat thudding in her ears, Molly pushed at the heavy mahogany and spun herself out into the sunshine.

# 11

"I am desolated, Monsieur Feeg." The reception bloke spread his hands and gave another of his irritating Froggy shrugs.

Malcolm twisted his signet ring in frustration. This was the third time in the last ten minutes he'd escaped from his duties in the exhibition hall to check whether the girl, whoever she was, had reappeared. His boss Jerry was beginning to notice: "Got the runs, mate? Too many *es-car-goes?*"

Ha bloody ha. Malcolm leaned aggressively across the desk. "Sure you haven't missed her? She must have come back by now. What could she be doing? Where did she go?"

"I told you, she disappear. *Comme ça. Pouf!*"

Poof was right, thought Malcolm, eyeing the Frenchman's pouty lips and flapping wrists. Bloody ballet dancers, the lot of them. Even if the girl did come back, he'd probably be too busy pirouetting about the place to notice.

Malcolm fixed the receptionist with a steely Clint Eastwood stare. "Tell you what I'm going to do. I'm going to wait over there for five more minutes." He jerked a thumb at the group of low sofas and coffee-tables behind him. "My eyes will be on you, mate. As soon as you see this girl, you tip me the wink.

Keep her talking, right? And this time make sure you grab that envelope. *Comprendo?*"

"*Oui*, Monsieur Feeg."

With the macho deliberation of a cowboy unholstering twin pistols, Malcolm jerked his shirt cuffs free of his jacket—first left, then right—holding the Frenchman's gaze to be sure he got the message. You didn't mess with a guy who wore twenty-four-carat Gucci cufflinks. Monogrammed. Then he swiveled abruptly, walked stiff-legged to a beige leather sofa and sat down, remembering first to unbutton his jacket to avoid unsightly creasing.

Where was she? More to the point, where was his disk? Crunch time was rushing toward him. Jerry would be at tomorrow's presentation, along with Jerry's boss and Jerry's boss's boss. If he screwed up, it would be *steak au Figg* for lunch.

Malcolm's left foot jiggled violently, then the right. He stared at the ceiling, checked on the receptionist, frisked his ears for excess wax and furtively flicked the findings onto the carpet. He examined his watch, whose multiple dials included a solar compass, an underwater depth gauge, a digital calendar and the current times in Tokyo and New York. None of these gave him comfort. The second hand swept implacably round and round. No one approached the reception desk.

The girl had sounded so convincing on the phone. She, or at least some "foreign" female, had actually come to the hotel with a package to deliver. She had asked for Mr. Figg by name. The receptionist had seen the envelope himself—bigger than a letter but not too bulky, just right for a disk. He'd almost had it in his grasp. Then the girl had vanished. Why? Where? Malcolm's eyes bulged, his ears buzzed with the maddening mystery of it.

He jumped to his feet, automatically rebuttoning his jacket and smoothing it over his stomach. He paced to the furthest potted plant and gazed at it intently. I am a leaf, he told himself, practicing one of his stress-management techniques. A nice, big, shiny leaf, calmly hanging in the air. He unclenched his fists. A Figg leaf. No, it was impossible. He gave one of the leaves a vicious flick with his fingernail, retraced his steps and sat down again. He unbuttoned his jacket.

Black hair, the receptionist had said. Red dress and boots. Young. Very pretty. It couldn't be Molly, despite his suspicion that she was somewhere in Paris. But what about the other one, Alicia? "I might be blonde and I might not." Cheeky bitch. Was she having him on, or might she be up for it tonight? He liked the sound of those boots. Bet she knew a trick or three. He had no problem with that. Bedroom-wise he was in peak condition, especially since taking those capsules advertised in the back of a men's magazine. He'd even entered the competition. Photographing himself for the "Before" and "After" snaps had been tricky, but worth it for the chance of winning a red Lamborghini Diablo ("0 to 60 in 3.8 seconds"!). Malcolm pictured himself squealing to a stop outside the office, the awed faces of his colleagues pressed to the windows, girls begging to—

"Excuse me, are you Malcolm Figg?"

A tall geezer was looking down at him, giving him the once-over: posh voice, superior manner, a linen suit that looked as if it had never seen the inside of a trouser press.

"Who wants to know?" Malcolm snapped back. The man was blocking his line of sight to the reception desk. The girl might turn up at any minute.

"My name's Griffin, Dr. Jonathan Griffin. But that's not important. All I—"

A doctor! Belatedly Malcolm noticed the badge. He rose swiftly and smeared a smile across his face. "My privilege, Dr. Griffin." Deftly he slithered his jacket buttons into place while wiping any traces of sweat from his palm, then held out his hand. "Malcolm Figg, marketing executive, Phipps Lauzer Bergman. How may I help you?"

"It's more the other way round, I think," the doctor said coolly. "Shall we sit down a moment?" He gestured to the sofa.

"Of course. Be my guest." Malcolm waited for the doctor to sit, then pinched up his trousers and perched on the adjacent cushion. "I must warn you, however, that I may be called away at any moment. I'm expecting an important delivery."

"Not . . . this, by any chance?" The doctor produced an envelope, seemingly from nowhere, and held it up tantalizingly.

Malcolm's mouth went dry as bark. He could read his own name hand-printed on the outside. "Where did you get that?" He itched to grab it.

The doctor gave an infuriating smile. "I'm afraid I'm only the messenger."

"A girl gave it to you, didn't she? Black hair, red dress."

For answer, the doctor tipped the envelope within Malcolm's reach. "Perhaps you'd like to check the contents?"

Of course he bloody would, seeing as how it was his property, addressed to him. Malcolm mustered a graceless "Thanks," snatched the envelope and picked roughly at the glued flap, careless of his manicure. Finally he managed to insert a finger and rip open one end. A sharp shake, and the disk slid into his palm, smooth and precious as a wafer of gold. *Yes!* Malcolm turned it over to check the label, but relief was already flooding through him, pumping him full of confidence. Figg was unstoppable. Figg was a winner!

The doctor was watching him. "Everything all right?" he asked.

What was his game, Malcolm wondered. Why wouldn't he say who the girl was? Did he know anything, or was he just a "messenger," as he'd claimed? Doctor or no, Malcolm could willingly have throttled the truth out of him. But he was too canny for that. Oh, yes. However much stress he had suffered from all the palaver with Molly and the disk, he didn't want any funny rumors going round the conference, any hint that Figg had lost control. Best to play it cool.

He flapped the envelope carelessly against one palm. "Secretaries, eh?" He gave a dismissive snort. "Drive you nuts. Heads like sieves, gabble-gabble-gabble in the ladies' toilets, whining for promotion after two minutes. Then, just when they might be of use, they bail out and leave you up shit creek without the proverbial."

"I take it that's the missing paddle." The doctor nodded at the envelope.

"What? Oh, yeah, got you. Stupid girl forgot it, didn't she? Didn't even have the guts to give it to me herself. Too frightened."

"I wonder why."

Malcolm looked up sharply, but he saw nothing in the doctor's expression except curiosity. Malcolm eased himself back against the cushions. "It's a tough old game, marketing," he confided. "My bosses are tough bastards. I'm a tough bastard. I have to be." He narrowed his eyes and nodded confidentially.

"See, a creative unit is like a pride of lions," he elaborated, half remembering a pep-talk given by some weirdo Yank in a baseball cap on one of his training courses. "The top lions are top because they fought their way up. They're strong, they're hungry. Sometimes they may look as if they're lying around half asleep, but they're thinking, right? They need the other lions, er, lionesses to go out hunting for them, to provide *without question* what they need to keep the pride ahead of its rivals. That's the deal. You don't get a lioness moaning, 'Do I really have to kill two gazelles today? Wouldn't a zebra do instead, or a—a—?'"

Malcolm's store of knowledge about the wildlife of the savannahs suddenly failed him.

"Warthog?"

"Jackpot! You're quick. That's why you're a top lion." Malcolm gave an approving nod. No harm in buttering up the old quack.

"But your secretary?"

"That's it, isn't it? Couldn't get into the pride ethic. Didn't like it when the top lion snarled at her." He sighed. "Molly just didn't have the killer instinct."

"Molly? Is that her name?" The doctor leant forward. "Molly what?"

Before Malcolm could answer, they were interrupted by a tinny rendition of the *Indiana Jones* theme tune.

"My phone." With a possessive smirk Malcolm reached into his breast pocket. "Could be important. Be with you in a tick." He stood up, punched a button and put the mobile to his ear. "Yep, Figg speaking."

"Oh, Mr. Figg, thank goodness I've reached you!" A female voice wittered down the line. "It's Fran Clearwater here. I'm terribly worried about my daughter Molly. She didn't ring me when she got to Paris, as she'd promised, and when I contacted the hotel this morning they told me she'd never checked in! She's not been home either. Her flatmate gave me some garbled story about . . ."

Unbelievable. Malcolm muffled the squawking with his hand and rolled his eyes at the doctor. "I've got the bloody mother now. I ask you!"

Rocking on his toes and casting exasperated glances about the lobby, Malcolm waited until the woman finally ground to a halt. "All I can tell you," he said crisply, "is that I last saw Molly yesterday afternoon. She did not, in the event, accompany me to Paris, and she is no longer in my employ."

"Why not? What happened? Did you upset her in any way?"

"Did *I*—" Malcolm choked at this upside-down version of events. He clasped his forehead with all the histrionics of a footballer shamming injury from a non-existent tackle. A sneaked glance between his fingers confirmed that the doctor was watching. "Suffice it to say," Malcolm enunciated, "that her work did not reach the high standard expected by Phipps Lauzer Bergman, professionalism-wise."

"What nonsense!" The mother practically burst his eardrum. "Bloom 'n' Veg thought the world of her. No one had a better eye for a ripe melon. I don't think you're being straight with me, young man."

Malcolm gaped at this outrage. "Completely mental," he whispered to the doctor, jabbing a finger at his phone. Secretly he was relishing this little drama, with his captive audience of one. He strutted back and forth on his miniature stage of carpeting, raising his eyebrows, flexing his shoulders, tapping his foot.

"The fact is, Mr. Figg, no one has seen Molly since she set off for work at *your* office."

"May I ask exactly what you are inferring?"

"I'm asking for your help! Molly was working for you. She was going to Paris with you. Suddenly she's disappeared. Have you no sense of responsibility?"

"I'm her employer, not her father," Malcolm shot back. "Ex-employer, at that."

That silenced her. Malcolm looked triumphantly at the doctor, inviting his approval, and was unnerved to find the blue eyes watching him stonily. The yattering started up again in his ear.

". . . must be very wrong. I know my daughter. She would never go off like this without telling me. Never!"

Typical mother. No idea what their kids were up to. If Molly wasn't in Paris, how come he'd got that disk so quickly? Malcolm couldn't resist giving a knowing chuckle.

"What does that mean?" the mother pounced. "You know something, don't you?"

"All I know is that your daughter is over twenty-one, and if she wishes to divulge her whereabouts to you, she will no doubt do so."

"Are you telling me she's in Paris after all?"

"I don't say she is and I don't say she isn't."

"For heaven's sake, Mr. Figg, please help me! I'm going crazy here."

"Unfortunately that is not my concern. Now, since I have nothing more to add and my time is at a premium—"

"You've got her there somewhere, haven't you? Oh, my poor baby!"

"I am not prepared to bandy words with you any further, Mrs. Clearwater. Good-bye!"

With a flick of his thumb Malcolm cut her off. He swung round to gauge how his performance had been received and was gratified to see that he had the doctor's full attention. The man was half out of his seat, mouth open, eyes wide with what could only be admiration. Malcolm could barely refrain from taking a bow. His mother always said he'd made a lovely Toad at Wanstead Primary, and could have hit the big-time in Hollywood if Marketing Studies had not claimed him first. He contented himself with a modest smile of acknowledgement and the merest flourish of his "walnut" phone before dropping it back into his pocket. His inner lion roared. Figg had triumphed again.

# 12

Act normal, Molly told herself. Stop smiling that idiotic smile. But it was impossible. She heard his name in the whisper of wheels and sigh of brakes as the Métro train swept her through dark tunnels. She saw his face in the fathomless black of the windows, and felt his fingertips on her neck with every draft of opening doors. Now, as she emerged from the station and climbed into daylight, the shadows of maple leaves on the pavement seemed to welcome her like waving hands. Sunshine poured its warmth onto her hair. The air was heavy with the narcotic sweetness of afternoon. Each breath was like a swoon.

*Concentrate*. There was a billboard-style local map bolted to the railings outside the station. Molly took the precious fragment of cigarette packet out of her bag, and double checked the address Fabrice had scribbled last night: Musée Rodin, rue de Varenne, 7e. She carried it over to the map and with her forefinger traced a route from the "*Vous êtes ici*" arrow. It gave her a jolt to see how close she was, and instinctively she turned her head as if expecting to find him already at her shoulder. But the pavement was empty, apart from a foraging pigeon. A glance at her watch showed that she still had five minutes in hand. She set off southward under a rustling canopy of trees, matching her pace to an inner beat of happy anticipation. How romantic it was to be meeting at a museum. It showed that Fabrice respected her as a woman of intelligence, not just a pick-up in a club.

Who exactly was Rodin? Molly scoured her brain for facts. She was fairly sure he was a sculptor, maybe a painter too. French, obviously. Nineteenth-century, probably. Dead, anyway. *The Thinker*: that was Rodin, wasn't it? And the little ballet dancer with her nose in the air—or was that Degas? Why, oh, why hadn't she consulted her guidebook? Fabrice would think her ignorant and trivial. And she wasn't!

Should she take off her jacket or leave it on? The Métro ride had made her a little sticky, but she still wasn't quite comfortable in the red dress. Might it seem too blatant to turn up with half of her body on show? ("Are you *kidding?*" she could practically hear Alicia bellow in her ear.) Molly compromised by keeping the jacket on but sliding it back to semi-expose her shoulders, in a manner that might look casually sexy while secretly cooling her armpits. She prayed that, after the magic of last night, her appearance in daylight would not disappoint him too much.

Here was the rue de Varenne already. The sight of the navy enamel street sign, with its bold white letters, squeezed her ribs tight. As she turned left she could see railings, the entrance to a large house obscured by topiary, a huddle of middle-aged tourists at a ticket booth. That must be it. There was no sign of Fabrice.

Nevertheless, expectation caught in her throat and fine-tuned each nerve ending. She was acutely aware of a slight give in the hot tarmac under the soles of her boots; of a policeman standing in silhouette under a distant archway, wearing a cap shaped exactly like an upside-down saucepan; of the spicy-sweet scent of roses drifting from an unseen garden. Her knuckles hurt. Molly discovered that she had crossed the fingers on both hands so fiercely that when she shook them loose, bloodless patches still showed white on the skin.

She was here. Where was Fabrice? She dithered by the ticket booth, scanning the shifting groups that thronged the entrance, unsure whether to buy a ticket—or two—or simply wait. It was exactly half past three. You couldn't say he was late. Not yet.

* * *

And then she saw him, sauntering toward her from a stone bench where he had been waiting for her in the sun. A current of pleasure rippled out from the pit of her stomach and up her back. He was wearing sunglasses, a long-sleeved T-shirt that drifted loose at his waist, his leather jacket slung over one shoulder. The sunglasses made him look wonderfully dangerous, but she couldn't read his expression. Would he still like her? Did she look okay?

"*Salut*, Molly." She wasn't sure if she had moved forward, or if he had come to her, but suddenly he was standing in front of her, the cleft of his chin and the long curve of his lower lip level with her eyes. He put his hands lightly on her shoulders and kissed her on both cheeks, French-style. He smelled faintly, deliciously, of sweat.

"*Salut*." Molly darted a smile, and tugged self-consciously at her skirt.

They stood awkwardly in silence. Last night's familiarity had receded. He looked different—taller, his face broader through the cheekbones and narrower at the jaw than she remembered, his hair longer. She wished she could see his eyes.

"Shall we go in?"

As Fabrice gestured toward the open gates, Molly saw that there were two tickets in his hand. She wanted to thank him, or offer to pay. She wished she could think of some easy, witty remark to make him smile, and recapture the intimacy of last night. But for the moment any fluency in French had deserted her. Tongue-tied, she paced beside him along the gravel, and for the first time took note of the scene around her.

Ahead lay a two-story mansion, serenely proportioned with tall windows, a central pediment and matching turrets, built of a mellow stone on which slanting sunshine bestowed the fuzzy bloom of ripe apricots. It was very beautiful. Molly could see through the open doorway, right across an airy hall and out to a seductive-looking garden at the back. Here at the front was a lawn, too, its immaculate condition preserved by a sign that warned, "*Pelouse interdite.*" It was flanked by severely clipped hedges, and flowerbeds running in dead-straight parallel lines. Those must be the roses she had smelt. (Hybrid teas: how her mother would scoff!)

Fabrice had stopped. "I adore this place," he announced, with a fierceness that evoked an answering leap inside Molly. Imagine if Fabrice were a great artist—imagine living with him in such a house, possessing all this beauty and spaciousness in the heart of Paris. She pictured him toiling in his studio while she wrote great novels upstairs, the two of them strolling together through the garden in the evening light, discussing their work, perhaps picnicking under an ancient tree (she would be an effortless cook), before mounting the steps to a breezy bedroom where—

"Rodin is a passionately interesting artist," Fabrice continued, turning away from the main path to lead her toward a group of clipped yews where a few tourists loitered. "At every visit one sees something new, even in the most familiar works."

Molly followed meekly. It was silly to expect him to pay attention to her. People went to museums to look at the exhibits, not to talk and hold hands. Besides, she had nothing interesting to say.

One of the tourists had stepped back to raise a camera to his eye. Molly realized that she was staring straight at an enormous bronze sculpture set high on a plinth. "*The Thinker!*" she exclaimed, without thinking. "*Le Penseur*," she said—was that the correct French? Belatedly she saw the words carved on the plinth in letters large enough for a four-year-old to decipher.

Fabrice did not bother to acknowledge her statement of the obvious. He was prowling around the statue, examining it intently. He even took off his sunglasses. Feeling faintly snubbed that he had not done the same for her, Molly prowled after him at a respectful distance. The figure sat, massive and brooding, at least half again as large as life, gaze abstracted. He was unashamedly naked. Molly noted the muscles of his angled back, the spread of his toes, the jut of flesh between his legs, the lifelike manner in which the knuckles squished his lips as he supported his head on one hand.

"I wonder what he's thinking," she heard herself say—a daft, trivial, girly question she would have snatched back if she could.

But Fabrice answered at once: "The sculpture represents Dante, thinking about his poems. You know Dante?"

"Of course." *The Inferno*, Beatrice, et cetera.

"But it's symbolic, you understand. It could be any man—any woman," he added courteously, though without conviction, "engaged in the creative effort."

Molly nodded, and looked again. There was an arresting tension between the inwardness of the pose and the physical potency of the figure. She felt a stirring of interest, outweighed by the consciousness of her vast ignorance. She turned to Fabrice and asked humbly, "Tell me about Rodin. Show me what you see."

He made a puffing noise, as if so much explanation was beyond him—or, worse, beyond *her*. Molly might have felt crushed if at that moment she had not caught sight of something marvellous over his shoulder. "Look!" She pointed.

The sun had projected a shadow of *The Thinker* onto one of the cones of clipped yew, perfectly framed within the tawny green. The sculpture's shape was intriguingly distorted, but so sharply outlined that one could distinguish the separate fingers of the figure's resting hand. At first Fabrice didn't understand what she was showing him. Then his face lit up. *Ah, oui!* It was fantastic. He'd never seen that before. How fascinating, how instructive to observe a three-dimensional shape reduced to two. "You see," he told her, with a teasing smile, "you have a good eye."

"No." But Molly felt herself revive under the warmth of his smile, like a statue come to life. For the first time today she felt a connecting thread spin out between them, and hold.

As they strolled toward the house, Fabrice told her about Rodin: how he had failed to get into art school and was forced to work as a decorative plasterer and ornamental stonemason for the buildings of Paris; how his sculptures were repeatedly rejected for being ugly, pornographic, even too realistic for, *bien sûr*, Rodin had also taken anatomy classes to understand the configuration of the human body (the accusation that he had cast one of his figures from life had been *un grand scandale*); how, even when he was famous enough to be offered commissions, the work he produced was nearly always judged unsuitable or remained unfinished. It was only toward the end of his life that he became internationally famous, and not until after his death that one recognized he was, in fact, a genius. But that, said Fabrice, with a magnificent shrug, was always the fate of the artist.

His French came at Molly in a rushing tide of rising and falling sound, full of precise consonants, liquid vowels and purring gutturals, too fast for her to understand everything. But she understood his enthusiasm. She understood the fire in his eyes as he spoke of his hero. She loved the expressiveness of his hands and the sensual thrust of his lower lip when he groped for the next thought with a "*Mais, euh . . .*"

Despite her intention as a conscientious tourist to check out the Louvre, museums were not usually Molly's favorite haunt. She felt she was not a visual person, and that her ignorance rendered her views pointlessly subjective. Windowless galleries leading one into another made her claustrophobic. But she was prepared to love this museum because Fabrice did, and as soon as she entered the house she found it was easy. The airy proportions of the rooms were in themselves a delight. Windows were flung open to birdsong and greenery on every side. There were burnished parquet floors, fireplaces and cornices of restrained, pleasing design. The sculptures were arranged so that one could walk right round them and peer close. Though one could not touch them, their tactile quality was immediate and intimate. It took a while for her to realize that this was because of the work itself. Nudes predominated: a naked male torso in mid-stride, a marble woman curled in sleep; flying figures, beseeching figures; bodies lustfully entwined or unbearably strained in struggle. The nakedness in itself was powerful. But more than that, passion rose off the sculptures like steam. These were not just bodies: they were human beings caught in the extremities of emotion.

To begin with, she felt faintly embarrassed to stand beside Fabrice as they gazed at the more explicitly erotic pieces. It was impossible to look at so many bodies in wanton display and not be aroused. Fabrice's presence gave everything an extra charge. When he told her that, even for his clothed figures, Rodin had often made a nude study first, so that he could be sure how the clothes would hang, she could not help looking at Fabrice himself in a new way, observing the twin curves of his shoulder blades under his T-shirt, the taut stretch of jeans between his hipbones and down his thighs.

Fabrice led her from room to room, full of talk and expansive gestures. In this group of apparently different men, he showed her, the figures were in fact identical; they had merely been positioned at different angles. Wasn't it remarkable how a change in physical perspective elicited such different emotions? And this pair of hands, upright and almost clasped, the fingers not quite touching: had she noticed that they were not, in fact, a pair, but two right hands? *Comme ça?* He seized her right wrist and raised it diagonally to his own in demonstration. "Rodin thought it was more graceful not to have the same fingers opposing each other," he explained seriously. Then his expression softened. "But look at your little tiny hands." He pressed his palm flat against hers; the tip of his middle finger projected a good inch beyond hers. He smiled and Molly reeled, as if she'd been plugged into the mains.

From time to time he drifted away to examine something more closely, but Molly no longer felt neglected. The work exerted its own emotional forcefield; Fabrice colored her responses to everything she saw. In one of the downstairs rooms she came across *The Kiss*, the sculpture of a naked, embracing couple she'd seen in countless photographs but never in its full-size, three-dimensional reality. Now she noticed the way the woman's foot pressed on top of the man's as he pulled her close, a detail of such tenderness and sensuality that she felt her own body stir.

There was one piece she kept returning to, a woman folded facedown on the ground, her spine gently curved, long hair flowing forward from the nape of her bowed neck to reveal one exquisitely delicate ear. A printed caption explained that this represented a mythical story about a young woman in hell, condemned to pour water forever into a bottomless vase. Molly leaned her cheek against her fingers, her imagination caught, her sympathy engaged. The marble was lustrously smooth and polished, showing every swell and ripple of the beautiful young body stretched in despair. When Fabrice returned to her side, she found she had tears in her eyes.

He looked into her face. "Are you crying?"

"No." Molly turned her head away. "A little. It's just so beautiful, and so sad."

"Ah, Molly." He brushed a finger under each eye, and took her hand. "Come. We'll go into the garden."

They stepped out into the warm sun and wandered down a pathway overhung with lime trees. Two little girls with impossibly shiny blonde hair skipped ahead of them. In the distance Molly could see a small café arranged outside, in dappled shade; from the girls' happy shrieks she gathered that ice cream had been promised. With her new eyes, she noticed the sheen of their smooth calves and the fragile structure of their ankles. She was intensely aware of Fabrice's hand in hers, and tried to imagine how Rodin might render its contours of flesh and ingenuities of bone to capture everything she felt about him.

"What about *your* art, Fabrice?" she asked him. "Do you want to be a sculptor, too?"

He shook his head. "I don't have the talent. Drawing and painting are what I like best, especially the human body. But that's unfashionable. My friends think I'm crazy. They tell me I have no originality."

Molly's eyes kindled with outrage. She was quite sure that Fabrice was brilliantly talented. She remembered him telling her that he'd dropped out of art school. "That's not why you've given up, is it?"

"No." His face darkened. "It is my father. He refuses to pay the fees."

"But why?"

Fabrice shrugged. "I failed some exams."

"But that's so unfair! Rodin failed his exams, too, you told me, and look what a genius he turned out to be."

"That's true. But it's no good arguing with my father. He's a very rigid man. I can't talk to him. He won't even help pay for a studio. I have to share a room with some other guys. Unheated. Filthy."

Molly sighed with sympathy. But it was hard to be too depressed. They had reached the end of the lime avenue, and now turned to follow the curve of a large pond, with one of Rodin's most tortured sculptures at its center, and two more positioned on either side. There were wooden benches here, at the end of the garden, facing back toward the house. In harmony of mind and body, Molly and Fabrice sat down on one, and stared in silence at the view. The house, pleasingly symmetrical, glowed back at them across a long strip of smooth, untenanted lawn ("*Pelouse interdite*"), its topmost pediment reflected in the still water of the pond. Sunshine slanted from the west, still meltingly warm. Unselfconsciously, Molly took off her jacket and relaxed against the bench. Through half-closed eyes she watched tourists, encumbered with cameras and plugged into audio tours, crunch up and down the gravel paths, moving from statue to statue with the dazed, meandering gait of giant herbivores on the brink of extinction.

"I like your dress," said Fabrice. "That color is fabulous for you."

Molly smiled lazily. After a moment, he shifted closer and slid an arm around her. His fingers fluttered against the skin of her shoulder.

"*Alors*, you think I'm a genius." He said it as if it were a joke.

"You never know until you try. Maybe your father simply can't afford the fees."

She felt Fabrice's chest heave as he gave a derisive grunt. "He's loaded with dosh." (*Bourr, de fric*: the phrase was unfamiliar, but its meaning was easy to decipher from the way he shook out his fingers from the wrist, and blew a whistling breath through pursed lips.) "He's just stingy. He thinks only of himself. I bet your father's not like that."

Molly didn't answer.

"Well, is he?"

"My father's dead." As always, when she said these words, a fist seemed to tighten around her heart. She stared at the gravel.

"*C'est vrai?*" Fabrice jerked forward to peer into her face. He seemed profoundly agitated. "Poor Molly." He put his other arm around her and hugged her close. She could feel his lips against her hair. "My mother, too, she is dead. She died when I was fourteen years old."

"Oh, Fabrice, I'm sorry." Molly curved a hand up to his forearm and rubbed it gently, feeling the tension in his muscles.

"I detest funerals, don't you?" he burst out. "Everyone in black. Those hypocritical priests. The smell of incense. I don't like to go inside churches now, even to look at paintings."

Molly felt unbearably sorry for him—and guilty, too, unworthy of his pity. "It's different for me. I—I never knew my father."

"He died when you were a baby?"

Molly made a small movement of her head. She didn't deny it.

"That's tragic."

With a bitter exclamation he turned to stare at the calm house floating above its sea of green. In profile he looked broodingly intent, and so handsome that Molly imagined herself grabbing his face and wildly pressing her lips to that hollow under his cheekbone. She dug her fingernails into her palms. What was happening to her? She should be ashamed of such thoughts at a moment like this. His mother was *dead.*

"Do you miss her very much?" she asked.

"Every day I suffer."

Molly was moved by his simple statement. *Je souffre.* French was so direct and unembarrassed.

"And you suffer also." Fabrice captured her hand and held it tightly. His marvellous, melancholy eyes gazed into hers. "You and I," he told her solemnly, "we are twins of sorrow."

*Jumeaux de la tristesse.* How poetic it sounded. How persuasive was the image it conjured up of herself and Fabrice, bound together by the shared experience of a dead parent. But it wasn't true. She had lied to him. She always lied.

Her eyes slid away, as she struggled against a painful confusion of feelings. She hated her deceit, when Fabrice was so open. She felt inflamed by his hot hands pressing on her flesh, and chilled by the old, cold secret she carried alone. Her mind teemed with Rodin's images of bodies caught in the throes of ecstasy or agony—breasts offered for caress, mouths wrenched with pain; muscled legs, rounded thighs, hands fisted in despair. Everything seemed so much more emotional in French.

"Don't move!" Fabrice commanded.

But the urgency in his voice made Molly turn to him at once.

"You moved." His thick eyebrows were drawn accusingly. There was a new intensity about him that made her a little frightened.

"What's the matter?" she asked.

"Your face just then . . . the light . . ." He zigzagged his hand through the air, scooping invisible shapes. "It was extraordinary. For a moment, it was as if I could see into your soul."

Her soul! (*Âme*, not *âne*.) Molly's eyes widened.

"Come." He jumped up, and pulled her to her feet. "I want to paint you. Now."

Molly tottered on her boots. He wanted to paint her! But she had no bone structure. Would she have to take off her clothes? "But how?" she asked. "Where?"

"We can go to the studio. It's not far." He yanked impatiently at her hand. Molly resisted, tugging him to a standstill while she tried to think.

Fabrice stepped close, pressed his body hard against hers and kissed her roughly on the lips. She could feel his teeth. His fingers dug into her spine. When she opened her eyes again, the light dazzled. A green horizon tilted, and steadied. Fabrice rested his forehead against hers. She felt their eyelashes brush. "You permit me?" he asked.

Molly didn't say anything because she had no breath to do so. She wiped a trembling finger across her bruised bottom lip, and nodded.

# 13

There was a butcher's shop at street-level, displaying flayed rabbits, ducks in full feather hanging by their iridescent necks, and black sausages wound in snaky coils. Their gamy smell pursued her as Molly climbed upward after Fabrice, past silent apartments whose half-glazed doors, shrouded with lace, allowed a grayish glow to seep onto the landings. Wooden steps sagged rottenly under their tread. At the top, Molly waited in the gloom while Fabrice, still in a fever of artistic impatience, tussled with a padlock. Finally, it yielded. Fabrice pushed the door wide, and Molly followed him into a long, narrow attic.

The floorboards were bare and dusty, splodged with paint. There were no windows, only squares of wire-meshed glass let into the roof, on which pigeons' feet scrabbled. Canvases lay in disarray against the sloping walls; an overflowing waste-bin squatted in one corner, surrounded by empty beer bottles. The furniture consisted of four easels, two wooden chairs, an ironwork daybed with a mattress and tattered bolsters, and a large metal table piled with artists' clutter: rolls of paper, stacks of board, old tins jammed with paintbrushes, spray cans, sticks of charcoal, crumpled rags, misshapen tubes oozing pigment, and a blackening banana that Molly felt sure must once have formed part of a still life. It could not have been more romantic.

"Over here, where the light is good." Fabrice was energetically dragging the daybed under one of the skylights. Molly hurried to help. She saw that he had already taken off his jacket and hooked it on a nail by the door. Other garments hung beside it—paint-smeared overalls, someone's raincoat, exotic folds of peacock-blue silk that looked like a woman's kimono. Of course Fabrice must use models: that was only to be expected.

Molly felt a flutter of nervousness. On the way here, swaying on the back of his scooter, she had decided that she would be prepared—if necessary—to pose naked. It would take courage, but sometimes personal scruples had to be sacrificed for a greater good. Rodin's example was hot in her memory. The voluptuous poses that had caused outrage a hundred years ago were now universally admired. Fabrice, too, would have his own creative vision, which ordinary people like herself could not grasp. Even thinking about the wanton positions Fabrice might force her to adopt had made Molly give a little gasp (fortunately drowned by the timely toot of a car horn). But she must not be prudish, especially in France. If Fabrice turned out to be a genius—well, he *might* (the thought had made her squeeze her eyes tight and hug him with excitement)—she would be immortalized. It was a great responsibility. Thank goodness she had shaved her legs this morning.

"Take off your jacket," said Fabrice.

Here goes, Molly thought.

But all he did was carry it off to a spare nail, then stride over to the big table and start rummaging for materials. He seemed brusque and absorbed.

Feeling superfluous, Molly wandered round the room. At the far end there was a narrow door, set into a flimsy partition wall.

She opened it and peeked inside, only to withdraw her head quickly from the sight of a murky lavatory and a wash-basin evidently used for cleaning brushes. She continued her prowl past the canvases, peering with silent respect, wondering which were Fabrice's. One painting was still propped against an easel. It looked like a very complicated paint-by-numbers kit, with the contours of a giant female face crudely outlined in black, and strange mathematical calculations scrawled in each white space.

"Those are the chemical formulae for each of the pigments," Fabrice explained, noting her interest. "My mate François believes that art must at all costs avoid the obvious. But, then, he has a spider on the ceiling."

Molly glanced up anxiously, then remembered that this was an idiom, like "bats in the belfry." She was relieved that the picture was not Fabrice's work. She had a vision of herself drawn like one of those posters of a pig's carcass at the butcher's, with dotted lines dividing "Chop" from "Loin."

"Come on. Quickly." Fabrice had his easel in place now, a fistful of brushes in one hand. His sleeves were pushed up to the elbow, his hair raked back.

Molly swallowed, and walked awkwardly toward the daybed, agog at what he might now ask her to do. "Like this?" she asked, gesturing vaguely at her dress. "Or do you want me to, you know, change?"

"What?" Fabrice glanced up impatiently. "No, no. The red is good for painting. Sit down."

Molly perched on the edge of the mattress, knees together, hands in her lap, and watched him squeeze different colors onto a bit of board. Purple! What on earth was he going to do with that?

Fabrice raised his eyes and fixed them on her with such intensity that Molly couldn't help smiling back. He was so lovely to look at, with the light from above making his face a wonder of sharp lines and angled planes. She should be painting him—except that she didn't have the talent.

Fabrice gave an exasperated sigh. "Not like that. I'm not taking your photograph, you know."

"Sorry." She crossed her legs and leant back a little. "Is this better?"

She could tell from his expression that it wasn't. Oh dear. She was already a failure: not beautiful enough to paint naked, or indeed at all. "I'm sorry," she repeated helplessly. "I don't know what you want."

Fabrice waved a hand. "Don't look at me. Concentrate on something else. Take off your boots. Relax. Dream. What were you thinking about in the garden? You had such a beautiful expression, *très mélancolique.*"

Molly bent obediently to unlace her boots, and cast her mind back to the sunny bench. What had she been thinking about? Fabrice, of course. Fabrice's mother, who had died. His ogre of a father. *Her* father . . . She eased her feet free, swung her bare legs onto the mattress and stretched out on her side, settling her elbow as comfortably as she could on one of the bolsters. She wondered what would have happened if she'd been brave enough to tell Fabrice the truth about her father.

"Eyes higher," he commanded. "Look at the wall . . . Relax your other hand . . . That's it."

He sounded remote, withdrawn. She wasn't even allowed to look at him. It was too late for talking. Deep down, she was relieved. To share her secret would be to lose its addictive mystery. It gave her a strange shiver of pleasure to know that, however good an artist Fabrice might be, he could never paint what was inside her head. Dream, he had said. Molly leaned her cheek on her hand, thinking about the lie she had told him, and the truth as it should have been. She let her eyes drift out of focus until the patch of grimy wall evaporated to a smoky nothing, and waited for the pictures to come.

She was standing on stage in a large auditorium, accepting an award. Applause thundered in her ears. Spotlights danced in her eyes. It was a very glamorous ceremony, but she felt calm and in control because she, too, was glamorous. With all the hard work that had gone into winning this award, her body had miraculously toned itself and the weight had simply melted away. Her dress was perfect.

Walking triumphantly offstage, she was immediately engulfed in a babble of congratulations from her many friends and colleagues. Someone handed her a glass of champagne. As she raised it to her lips, she couldn't help noticing a man standing on the fringes of the group, staring at her with admiration and intense curiosity. He was around fifty, tall and handsome, with distinguished graying hair, and an air of cultured elegance that hinted at sophisticated European origins. Though Molly was sure she had never seen him before, she felt an inexplicable tug of familiarity. While she chatted gaily she was aware of him watching her, but he bided his time until the crush had subsided and he was able to find his way to her side. He had an intelligent face, and kind eyes in which Molly thought she could detect a hint of sadness. As they talked, she felt once again a strange prickle of recognition. He told her his name: Jackson Carruthers. It meant nothing to her, of course, but when he asked if he might take her round the corner for dinner, she cast all her other invitations to the wind, and accepted.

Now they were in a restaurant, small and intimate, with exquisite food. It was extraordinary how well they got on. He was intelligent and charming; she had never been so witty, so sparkling, so articulate. It turned out that he was in the same business as herself, though he had been based in Italy for many years, and only rarely returned to England. Molly asked him about Italy—naturally, she had traveled extensively abroad—but began to notice that the conversation kept coming back to herself.

He wanted to know everything about her—school, jobs, childhood. What was odd was that the more she told him, the more agitated he became. Eventually he interrupted her in mid-sentence. Exactly how old was she, if she didn't mind him asking? Twenty-one? He thought so. And was her mother's name Frances? Astounded, Molly could only nod dumbly.

And then he put his hand on hers, and told her he was her father. He had been searching for her all his life, but had never been able to discover where she lived. It was a miracle that, by sheer accident, he had found her tonight. He had never dreamed she would be so talented and beautiful. He begged her to come back to Italy with him, just for a few months. Of course, he understood that her work was important, but they had so much time to make up, and Tuscany was so beautiful at this time of year.

"That's good," Fabrice murmured, in an abstracted voice. "Stay like that."

Molly blinked. The studio snapped back into focus. She felt the lumpy mattress under her hip-bone, an ache in her flexed wrist, and gave a tiny, inward sigh.

It was all nonsense. She would never be thin, and never win an award. Her father did not think she was worth finding, or he would have done so long ago. Probably he wasn't even aware that she existed. He might be dead. She didn't know. That was what gnawed away at her: *she didn't know.*

She could hear Fabrice's brush dabbling stickily in paint, rustling across canvas. The linseed smell tickled her nostrils.

In her first year at school, the teacher had told the class that they were all going to make a Father's Day card. Molly was just learning to read and write. She'd found it exciting to copy the chalked hieroglyphics from the blackboard onto her sheet of bright paper, on which she'd painted a huge head with a smile like a U-bend and legs looping straight down from the chin. "How lovely!" her mother said, when Molly proudly brought the card home, and pinned it without further comment to the corkboard in the kitchen. But there was something tense and over-bright in her manner that had made this moment stick in Molly's memory—the moment when it had first occurred to her to ask, "Where's *my* daddy?"

"Oh, he lives a long way away, darling."

"Why?"

"I expect he likes it."

For the time being this satisfied her. Gradually she came to understand that many of the parents of her schoolfriends had split up or divorced or remarried. It wasn't uncommon for "Daddy" to be replaced by a series of boyfriends. But the other children knew who their daddy was. Even if they didn't see him, they had a vague idea of his job and where he lived. They knew his *name*. But Molly always got the same smiling evasion, so breezy as to make her feel foolish even to have asked. "Oh, sweetheart, what does the name matter? He's never going to be a part of our lives. We don't *need* anyone else. Aren't we happy just as we are?"

Yes, they were happy. They told each other so, often. Mummy and Molly. M and M. They had their special games, their silly jokes, their domestic rituals and favorite foods. Within the cozy confines of the cottage, it never seemed important that Molly couldn't produce a competitor for the Fathers' Race, or a name to fill the blank in My Family Tree.

But the outside world was tougher. Already, Molly was aware of being different. Her mother spoke "posh," listened to Radio 4 instead of watching television, disapproved of supermarket food and package holidays in Tenerife, and drove a diesel van full of plant-trays and spilt earth with a "Save the Barn Owl" sticker on the rear window. And, of course, she was beautiful, in a gypsyish, outdoorsy, barefoot way, which other mothers weren't. It was impossible for Molly to admit publicly that she didn't know who her father was. That's when she began to make things up.

Early on, she'd been caught out in stupid, embarrassing lies: the new bicycle her father was sending for her birthday, which never arrived; her trip with him to Disney World one summer holiday, when it was obvious to everyone that she'd never traveled further than Minster Episcopi. Quickly, she learned that it was easier, in fact almost glamorous in a spooky way, to tell people that he was dead. Molly didn't believe this for a moment. She talked to her father secretly, at night. She met him in dreams, though afterward she could never remember his face. She imagined how they would meet, and made up names.

Jackson Carruthers: a ridiculous name, though Molly was still fond of it. At various times there'd also been the Count of Montepulciano, a cross between Max de Winter and d'Artagnan, whose exotic name she'd read on a wine label (alas, he was already married and could not endanger the succession to the Montepulciano estates by acknowledging his bastard daughter); Doug Michaels, a Wall Street zillionaire with an uncanny resemblance to Michael Douglas (too busy for babies, although there would turn out to be a very surprising clause in his will); Ricky Radical, a seventies rock guitarist of stupendous talent and charm (tragically OD'd at the Glastonbury Festival). For many years her favorite had been Tex, who bred Appaloosas on a ranch in America, where she galloped across the plains on a stallion no one else could tame, and watched as much television as she liked. (Her mother had refused to move to a place with no Radio 4 reception.) In the election fever of 1997 she had even briefly toyed with the notion of Tony Blair as her father, on the flimsy basis that he was the right sort of age, had a connection with Edinburgh (where Molly's mother had spent some time as a student) and would be understandably reluctant to admit to an illegitimate daughter.

At one level she recognized that these were fantasies; at another she believed in them passionately. (The scene in which she was smuggled into Downing Street, nobly forgave Blair for choosing politics over paternity, and swore to carry their secret to her grave, had once moved her to tears.) Each new book she read, each film and newspaper story fueled her imagination. Was her father in prison, like Roberta's daddy in *The Railway Children?* Was he living in America with her long-lost identical twin, as in *The Parent Trap?* Would a mysterious seafaring man turn up in the village pub one day, inquiring about Miss Molly Clearwater? *Great Expectations* became a favorite book, read and reread. A great sigh would escape her at the end of the scene in which Pip tells the dying Magwitch that Magwitch's lost daughter lives, that she is a fine lady, rich and beautiful, and that Pip loves her.

But Molly did not want to wait for a death-bed revelation. Nor did she want a convict for a father, though the older she got, the more fearful her speculations became, erupting in violent dreams of masked men leaping from the shadows. "Why won't you tell me?" she raged, in her early teenage years. "I need to know." But by some sleight-of-hand her mother made it seem quite normal to keep this knowledge to herself, and insensitive of Molly to ask. Wasn't she loved? Didn't she already possess the really important things in life? Molly saw how hard her mother worked, how heroically she held together their fragile existence, how proud she was of their female independence. It seemed disloyal, ungrateful, to ask for more. Imperceptibly she, too, was drawn into the conspiracy of silence. When, at fifteen, she sent off for her birth certificate, she did so in secret. "Father: unknown," read the vital line.

Molly was sure her grandmother—her mother's mother—had known something. Once or twice, when they had been alone together, there had been the tiniest hints, no more than the intensity of an expression or an extra vibration in the air, that had made Molly hold her breath. But six years ago Granny got cancer and died. Even so, Molly had half expected the arrival of a letter—perhaps even a lawyer, like Mr. Jaggers—to unravel the mystery. But her eighteenth birthday, then her twenty-first, had passed without revelation. There was no Grandpa to ask: he'd run off to London with another woman when Molly's mother was ten, causing such unhappiness and financial ruin that his name was mentioned rarely, and always with scorn. Thanks to him, the beloved family house had been sold, her mother expelled from its paradise of green meadows and sun-gilded, tick-tocking rooms, and her gentle grandmother forced to find a job while her grandfather played hide-and-seek with his creditors, and partied away the family money. *That* was how fathers behaved. Perhaps it was how all men behaved. Molly didn't know. *She didn't know* . . .

"*Voilà*. It is finished."

A floorboard creaked. Molly turned her head. Fabrice was standing back from his easel, frowning appraisingly at his work. With his hair in disarray and paint-smeared hands, he looked very romantic and stern.

"Can I see?" Molly sat up, rubbing the stiffness in her neck.

"No. Now I want to do some drawings. Take off your clothes."

"What?" Molly stared in shock.

"Your clothes. Take them off." There was an edge of irritation to his voice. He barely glanced at her.

Molly stood up slowly, arms hanging at her side. Her bare toes clenched the dusty roughness of the floor. She couldn't undress here, just like that, with him watching.

Fabrice was gathering up his brushes. He carried them over to the table, poured some liquid into a tin can, dunked a brush. He gave her a sideways look under his lashes, dark and intense. "This is art, Molly."

"Of course." Her head bobbed up and down like a nodding dog's.

"The human body is beautiful. One must not be ashamed."

"No." But would one be allowed to keep one's underpants on?

"You can go in there, if you want." He indicated the squalid lavatory-cum-basin room.

"Okay."

She gave a bright, social-worker smile, padded over to the door, opened it and shut it behind her. Once inside, she stood still and stretched her eyes wide at the tiled wall. What was she doing? *I'm in Paris, in a horrible loo, taking my clothes off.* Right. She drew a deep breath, crossed her arms, grabbed her dress at the hem and peeled it off over her head. There was a hook on the back of the door. She turned the dress the right way out and hung it up. Next she unhooked her bra and slung it over the dress. She looked down. There they were, Gloria and Esmeralda. (Did other girls name their breasts?) Gloria was the sexy one, Esmeralda more reserved. If she kept her shoulders back, maybe they wouldn't loll too much. Next, her knickers, a white lacy pair not yet sabotaged by the washing-machine, designed to be admired. But how often did one see a life drawing that featured pants? Molly slid them down her thighs, then did a little wriggle until they dropped to the floor. Stepping out of one leghole and leaving the other hooked round her ankle, she flicked her foot and caught them neatly in mid-air. They joined the dress and bra.

And there she was. Naked. With Fabrice waiting. Molly wished there was a mirror. She gave her hips and bottom a quick massage to erase any lingering trace of elastic, smoothed down her pubic hair and twirled the ends into a corkscrew curl. She felt exposed, super-sensitive to the caress of air on her skin. But this was art. *L'art*, she mouthed to herself. *Lahrrrrr*. She tipped back her head, fluffed out her hair, and before she could think any further about what she was doing, opened the door and stepped out defiantly.

Fabrice had his back to her. He was still by the table, dangling a pad of thick, outsize paper from one hand and choosing charcoal sticks from a tin with the other.

Molly cleared her throat. "I'm ready," she announced.

"Good, good. I'll be with you in an instant. Go and sit down."

Back to the daybed. Fearful of wobbling too much, Molly sneaked past him with a shuffling, pigeon-toed gait, as if her legs were glued together from knee to thigh. She kept one arm crooked across her breasts, the other hand splayed protectively over her crotch. Quickly, she lay down on her front, propped on her elbows. After a moment, she bent one leg and pointed her foot in the air, then the other, then twiddled them about. Fabrice hadn't even looked at her! Thank goodness. She peered over her shoulder to check that her bottom didn't loom too enormously.

Oops, he was coming! Molly sank flat on to the bed, crossed her palms and laid her cheek on them. She peeked at him through her hair. He stopped about six feet away, stared at her in silence, then lowered his eyes and spent a lot of time fussily balancing the pad at the correct angle against his hip.

"Okay," he said. "We can start like that. But I must say to you this one thing. You must rejoice in your body. I want you to move around, do as you feel. This is not a formal pose. I want to make lots of sketches, improve my technique."

Lots! Move about? *Rejoice?* "Mmm," Molly murmured doubtfully.

"Don't think of me as a man. I'm not looking at you like a man—not the way a man looks at a woman. I am looking at you like an artist. The artist must always be invisible and impersonal, like—like God."

"Hello, God." She waggled a foot.

"Legs down," he ordered. "Cross your ankles. Pretend you are sleeping."

Molly did as he asked. How peculiar this was, to be lying naked in a French attic with her eyes closed, being stared at by a man she hardly knew, listening to the soft sweep of charcoal across paper. Peculiar, but not so bad . . . After what seemed like a minute, but was probably five, she heard a tearing sound as he stripped the paper from the pad and wafted it on to the floor.

"And now?" he said.

Golly, another position. After a moment's thought, Molly rolled onto her side—with her back to Fabrice—supporting her neck with one hand and discreetly draping the other over the hollow at the top of her thighs. Again, there was silence. Then came the same faint stroking noise, sometimes soft as a cat's paw, sometimes sharp and scratchy as a claw. Molly had the odd sensation that she could feel the tip of Fabrice's charcoal on her skin, smoothing its way over the curve of her hip, rippling down her vertebrae one by one. Out of the corner of her eye she could see her breasts, spilling from her rib cage like mounds of whipped cream with strawberries stuck on top. What would she do when the time came to turn round? They weren't easy things to hide. But Gavin had never paid much attention to them. Perhaps Fabrice wouldn't notice.

There went the paper again, gummily unpeeling. This time Molly sat up, still with her back to Fabrice, supporting herself with one palm pressed flat and clasping her ankles with the fingers of her other hand. Back straight. No lolling, girls. She hardly dared breathe.

Scritch-scratch. Scribble, scribble. There was the faint squeak of trainers on wood. Then, so unexpected that she jumped, she felt his hand touch her leg, adjusting its position. In a second he was gone again. There was a smudge of blue paint on her calf. She wondered if he had peeked at her front. Damn. She'd forgotten to suck in her stomach.

She was running out of ideas for keeping her back to Fabrice. Any minute, as soon as this sketch was finished, it would be time to turn round. The strange thing was that she was almost getting used to being naked. There was a freedom to it that made her want to stretch like a cat and let the air play on the parts usually hidden by clothes. She told herself that it was no good being coy at this stage, and resolved to come out with all her guns blazing.

There it was, the crackle and rip of paper. A pause. Molly rolled smoothly from one haunch to the other, swung her knees over and rearranged her hands, adopting the mirror-image of her previous pose. But how different it felt! She could *see* Fabrice, sinuous and dark and beautiful. She could see him looking at her. When their eyes met, it was as though she was sitting in a shower of sparks. They danced and sizzled on her skin, licked into flame, fanned into a forest fire.

Fabrice bent his head to the paper. His movements were bold and sure—a flowing line here, a squiggle of shading there, a semi-circular sweep (could that be Gloria?). He glanced up, then quickly down again, avoiding her gaze. His lips were pressed firm, his eyebrows drawn down in an expression of deep concentration: improving his technique, no doubt.

Molly was finding it hard to sit still. Her flesh tingled, her breath came louder in her ears. How could Fabrice act as if she was no more than an intriguing arrangement of iron girders? Didn't he want to come closer, to touch? Without waiting for her cue, she moved both hands behind her and leant back. Her head tipped back, her breasts thrust forward.

He glanced up, hesitated, then tore off the previous drawing and stood frowning at her from his little island of wood, across white waves of curling paper. She saw his eyes drop to her breasts and linger. So he *had* noticed.

He started to draw again. "*Enfin*, Molly, you can't keep moving around like that."

"Why not?" She observed that he was holding the pad lower than before, shielding the zip of his jeans.

"The concentration, you understand . . . For a man it is difficult." The movements of his hand across the paper were becoming jerky. "When one sees a sensational body . . . *euh* . . . the thighs, the hair, the breasts . . ."

*A sensational body!* His words coursed down the center of her like warm syrup, spreading outward, spilling over. She stretched her arms languorously, clasped her hands behind her neck, arched her back and smiled at him.

His charcoal snapped.

Molly laughed, heady with her own power. "Don't think of me as a woman," she taunted.

"Molly . . ." Her name was wrenched out of him. He lowered his pad and took a step toward her. Molly strained forward. Then he stopped, his attention arrested. "Stay like that—just a moment." He raised the pad again, grabbed another stick of charcoal.

"Fabrice . . ." she pleaded.

"Wait!"

"I can't."

"Neither can I. But we must. This will be good—the best. I can feel it."

With a sigh, Molly held the pose. It was unbearably exciting. Now he was really *looking*. He drew as if in a fever, slashing across the paper. Tendons stood out on his wrist, muscles pulsed in his forearms. His eyes on her flesh felt as if he was stroking her all over with a feather.

Ri-i-ip. Thump! He finished the drawing, threw down the pad, and in two urgent steps was at her side. Molly leaned toward him, straining for his touch. He ran his thumb down her cheek, then reached out and drew a finger lightly under the nipple of each breast. Molly swayed dizzily. She put out a hand to steady herself, grasping at the waist of his jeans. Her knuckles grazed his flesh. She stretched her fingers down against the smooth, tight skin. Fabrice groaned.

"Put your clothes on," he said.

"What?" Molly's head jerked up. How dare he suggest such a thing?

"We will make love," he told her, gently drawing her hand out of his jeans and pressing it to his lips. "But not here. You get dressed. I'll pick up the drawings." His eyes burned into hers. "Hurry."

# 14

The room was dark, except for slats of sunlight that glowed on the carpet like rows of gold bars. It smelled of beeswax and woodsmoke. Molly tightened her grip on Fabrice's fingers, laced with hers, as he guided her round lumpy shapes of furniture.

"Where are we?" she asked, in a half whisper. "Is this your flat?"

"Wait. You'll see." He disengaged his hand. She heard him fiddling with catches.

Bereft of his touch, Molly longed to snuggle herself against his back, nibble his shoulder, breathe in his smell, but Fabrice had gone silent and mysterious again, and she didn't quite dare. She had no idea where they were. Their brief scooter ride had passed in a blur of Saturday traffic and crowds, from which she'd retained only random details: spurting fountains, curvaceous balconies, obelisks and spires rearing into the sky, bridges splayed above dark hollows and gushing water. Fabrice's hips rocking under her hands as they took corners. His thighs jammed against hers. The taste of his hair in her mouth.

She was vaguely aware that they had crossed the river onto an island, before stopping beside an arched stone entranceway, massive enough to admit a coach-and-four. There were huge wooden gates painted dark green, into which a smaller door had been cut. Fabrice had tapped a code into a discreet entry-box, pushed open the door, humped his bike over the threshold and propped it in a cobbled courtyard. Molly followed in a daze. She seemed to have lost the ability to think, or the will to move. Fabrice had to unbuckle her helmet for her while she stood limply, then lead her by the hand into a cool corridor. He tapped more buttons, opened a door. The next moment, they were rising silently in a lift of black glass and brushed steel, while Molly's stomach turned back-flips. At the top Fabrice produced a key and slotted it into the lock of a panelled door. Inside, it was so shrouded and still that Molly felt like a trespasser.

"What is this place?" she asked again, giving the back of his T-shirt a stealthy tug.

But at that moment, with a rattle and clank, Fabrice pushed open door-length shutters and stood aside to let Molly step onto a narrow balcony.

"Oh, wow," she breathed. There was the Seine—right below her!—sparkling past like a torrent of diamonds. Through a filter of greeny-gold leaves she could see people sunbathing and fishing on the quays. To her right, almost close enough to touch, stood Notre Dame. On the far bank a line of old houses rose gracefully, balcony by balcony, to steep gray roofs inset with circular windows that seemed to mimic Molly's round-eyed astonishment.

She felt Fabrice clasp her waist from behind and put his mouth to her ear. "It pleases you?"

"It's fantastic!" She leaned her head back into his shoulder, wrapping her arms around his. "But who lives here?"

"It's my father's apartment. But he's not at home," he added quickly, feeling her start of alarm. "He's gone to the country for the weekend."

Molly turned in the circle of his arms to face him. "But I thought you didn't get on with your father. Doesn't he mind you bringing, er, friends here?"

Fabrice shrugged. "I am his son, after all." He let go of her and stepped back into the room. "All these things, I grew up with them." He swept his hand in a wide arc, inviting her to look. "They are mine as much as his."

Molly followed him inside. The unknown territory she had crossed in the darkness turned out to be an elegant living room, poised just above treetop height. Watery sunlight, reflected from the river, washed over ancient beams and decorative plasterwork, gleamed richly on antique tables, shimmered across finely wrought silver and glazed china, turned Persian carpets to jewels. There was a grand fireplace of marble, embossed with fauns' heads, a carved bookcase packed with glossy hardbacks and odd-looking paperbacks with stitched spines. At any other time she would have been curious to look more closely, but now her mind welled with questions. What were they doing here? Why hadn't they gone to Fabrice's own place, wherever it was? Was he ever going to kiss her?

Fabrice seemed jumpy. He picked up objects and set them down in different positions, flopped for a moment on a plump cushion, then stood up again, leaving it dented. One moment he flashed her a smile; the next, he stood hunched at the window, staring out, his hands shoved into the back pockets of his jeans. Molly decided that he was giving her time to absorb the messages of this stylish, civilized apartment. He wanted to reassure her that he wasn't just anyone, but from a "good" family—as if she cared! But the French were like that, as she knew from Proust. She wondered what Fabrice would make of her mother's cottage, with muddy trainers drying on the back of the Rayburn and Alleluia's hairs shed all over the foam-rubber sofa.

"It's lovely," she told him. "Your father must be successful, even if he's so horrid to you. What does he do?"

"He's an architect. Fairly well known, I suppose." Fabrice made a disparaging face. "But one could not live in such a place on the income of an architect. The Île St-Louis, you know, nowadays it is only for rock stars and rich Arabs. My father cultivates the air of an intellectual, but he likes the good things of life. A *gauche caviar*, you understand?"

Molly took a moment to decode the phrase, then nodded. "Champagne socialist. We have them in England, too." Though not, as far as she knew, in Minster Episcopi.

"The money comes from my mother. Her family is very wealthy. My father sold our childhood home a couple of years ago, and I moved out to start at the university. Some things he brought here, some he sold." Fabrice frowned.

*Our* childhood home, he had said. "So do you have brothers and sisters?"

"Two sisters. But they are much older. The nearest to me in age is thirty already, married, with little children. They occupy themselves with their houses and husbands, and lead *la vie bourgeoise*." He jerked a shoulder dismissively, and toyed with an object lying on a sideboard: a small silver candle-snuffer. "This, for example, belonged to my mother. Eighteenth-century. It must be worth a thousand euros. My father never even uses it."

"Never mind," Molly said softly, wanting to smooth away the hurt on his face.

Fabrice looked up and gave her a sudden, melting smile. "Shall we drink something?"

"If you like."

He started to leave the room, then abruptly circled back to her, cupped her jaw in his lean fingers, and gave her an urgent kiss on the lips. The next second he had disappeared, leaving her reeling. What was he up to? She didn't want anything to drink, she wanted *him*. Was that very wicked? Henry James had been quite right about Paris: it turned one's ideas of sin upside-down. Look at what's-his-name in *The Ambassadors*, who was sent out to Paris from some God-fearing, narrow-minded part of America to rescue a young man from the clutches of a foreign temptress, but ended up convinced that the "loose" woman, and the society in which she moved, were far more civilized and life-enhancing than the arid existence that awaited the young man back home. "Live all you can," was the message of the book. "It's a mistake not to."

Molly nodded to herself, reassured by this precedent. She used to believe that, no matter what other girls did, *she* would never go to bed with a man she'd known less than twenty-four hours. And now she couldn't wait! Molly was ashamed of her impatience. How crude she must be, how unsubtle, how *English*. The French, of course, were experts at *l'amour*. She must follow Fabrice's example, and prolong the moment of delicious expectation.

It was impossible to keep still. She roamed the room, noticing the unfamiliar details of a real French house: its tall, narrow doors with pull-down handles, the walls covered with fabric instead of wallpaper, windows that opened inward and shutters that opened outward, the exact opposite of the cottage at home. She examined paintings, peered sideways at the spines of books, touched a display of stunning blue hydrangeas, massed in a vase, to see if they were real. (They were. A petal fell off. She hid it under a magazine.) She caught sight of herself in a gilt-framed mirror, looking flushed and tousled as if in the grip of some tropical fever, though quite pretty, she thought. But she was still wearing her jacket. No wonder Fabrice wasn't concentrating on her. She took it off and tugged down the neck of her dress as low as she dared, in case he needed reminding. No, no, how could she stoop to such vulgar tricks? She jerked it up again.

On a small, inlaid table she found the photograph of a woman, very slim and chic, with dark hair drawn back. Molly picked up the silver frame and studied the face. The woman was beautiful, with molded cheekbones and dark eyes like Fabrice's: his mother, Molly was sure, though she would not be so insensitive as to ask. She sighed with pity. It was all so clear: the beloved mother, dead; the older sisters, too busy to bother with their brother; the cruel, spendthrift father, ignoring his son, throwing him out of the house. Poor Fabrice. She would make him forget, if only he'd let her.

There was the sound of quick footsteps, a musical clinking. Quickly she replaced the photograph in its exact position, and whisked herself to the other side of the room.

"Champagne!" Fabrice announced, entering with two gold-rimmed goblets wedged between his knuckles, and a bottle swinging from his hand. His physical presence, eyes alight, moodiness gone, drove all other thoughts from her head.

He set down the glasses. Molly stood by him and watched his long fingers peel gold foil from the mouth, untwist the wires that secured the cork and slip off the little cage. Holding the bottle cocked at a forty-five-degree angle, Fabrice revolved it gently while holding the cork tight, until the two parted with a soft *pop!* and a ghostly mist of spume. He poured the champagne. Bubbles foamed to the top, then subsided to liquid topaz in a shower of fine spray.

He handed her a glass. "Nineteen ninety-six," he announced importantly.

He looked so ridiculously serious, so absurdly handsome, that Molly nearly burst with love. "A very good year," she replied, mimicking his tone.

He took a drink, eyeing her suspiciously. "Bad girl. Are you teasing me?"

"Of course not." Molly batted her lashes innocently and gave him a naughty smile over the top of her glass as she drank. She saw his eyelids lengthen into a slow, smoldering smile. The corner of his mouth curled. They were flirting! Molly felt lightheaded with delicious danger, like someone standing on a high cliff, momentarily tempted to jump for the sheer exhilaration of falling through the bright, blue air.

"You think I'm funny, *hein*?"

"*Mais non*." Molly tried to pout, but her lips wouldn't stay in position. He stepped close, pretending to look menacing. His eyes danced under dark lashes. The blood began to hum in her ears.

He put down his glass and grabbed her playfully by the arms. "What do you know about champagne, you little English girl?"

"Nothing!" she squealed. "Mind my champagne." It slopped out of her glass and trickled down her front. "Careful, Fabrice. My dress . . ."

"What dress?" asked Fabrice.

She felt the glass pulled out of her hands, and heard it chime against some hard surface. Then his arms were around her, jerking her hips to his so tightly that she swayed off-balance and her head sank back. His breath was hot on her face. His lips grazed her mouth as he repeated, "What dress?" His hands curved over her bottom and yanked up her skirt. She felt them slip inside and slide up her flesh, peeling the dress from her skin. Molly's arms drifted up helplessly as he pulled it over her head. Somehow her bra came off too.

Fabrice tossed them both aside and looked her over with scorching eyes. "I like you like that," he said. "Just the boots and *la petite culotte*. Oh, look, there's champagne on your breasts. I will lick it off."

Goodness, what was happening? He lowered his head with a growl. Molly twined her fingers in his hair as she felt him licking, nibbling, kissing. She grabbed at the back of his T-shirt and at last got her hands on that peekaboo strip of flesh that had been distracting her all afternoon. His back felt like warm suede. She pulled the T-shirt higher and higher, running her hands over the silky temptations of his ribs, his shoulders, his muscled neck, until Fabrice ducked his head out of the collar, and the shirt came off in her hands. She flung it away. They stood back from each other, panting.

Then Fabrice took her shoulders and spun her round to face the mirror. "Look how beautiful we are," he murmured, nuzzling the curve of her neck.

Molly saw his golden arms wrapped around her marbled skin, his dark hair entwined with hers. "I thought you didn't like me earlier," she said, to his reflection.

"I like these," he said, sliding his hands up and doing a bit of juggling.

"Stop it!" Molly giggled.

"All right. I'll be very gentle. Hello, my little kittens. How's that?"

Molly sagged against him, staring at the mirror through half-closed eyes as she followed the mazy, drifting, tantalizing tracks of his fingers back and forth, under and over, round and round. A rosy flush swept across her skin. She was hardly breathing. One of his hands sneaked over her rib cage, down her stomach toward the strip of white lace, dipped beneath it for an electrifying moment. "Time for the bedroom," he declared.

With his arm around her shoulders, she stumbled blindly across the room, staggered as he stopped and bent down for something. "We'll take the champagne," he said. "It tastes even better on your skin."

There was a corridor, a door, a small room with a vast bed. Fabrice banged the bottle down on a table, tore off the bed cover and flung himself onto the bed, pulling her down on top of him. She felt the rasp of his jeans against her bare legs. He swept the hair back from her face and kissed her cheeks, her eyes, her nose, her mouth. Molly kissed him back with all her heart, wanting him to love her, to fill every crevice of her body and mind until there was no room for anything else. He was so beautiful! She snuffled the silky hair of his armpits and kissed her way down his golden chest, worshipping each curving rib, the taut concavity of his stomach. When she reached his navel she raised herself up until she was sitting astride him. The heels of her boots dug into her bottom: too late to take them off now. She shook back her hair to look at him. His face was intent, his eyes dark and mysterious as moorland pools. Holding her gaze, he reached for one of her hands and placed it on the rivet of his jeans.

Molly flipped the straining button out of its hole. Her thumb and finger squeezed the tongue of his zipper, ready to tug. She paused. Oh, no. She'd forgotten the French for condom.

# 15

Préservatifs: that's what the garlic-guzzlers called them. But where were they? This place was supposed to be a chemist's (*Pharmacie* in Frog-speak), although it looked more like a cross between a beauty salon and a giant medicine cabinet, with a refined, reverential atmosphere that made him feel he should be tiptoeing. The staff was all female, intimidatingly young and well groomed in white lab coats, very different from the hatchet-faced harpies and gormless school-leavers at his local Boots. They reminded him of those masseuses in old James Bond films, who turned out to be wearing no more than a suspender belt and a suntan under their uniforms. Strict but sexy: just what he liked. But he couldn't ask them for condoms, could he?

Avoiding their inquiring gaze, Malcolm skulked up and down the aisles, scrutinizing the unfamiliar products. One thing was for sure: the French were a bunch of raving hypochondriacs. You didn't need to be a linguist to understand the words *tonique*, *vitamine*, *hygiénique*, *dynamisme*, that shouted to him from the shelves. He'd never seen so many different types of bandage, and freaky surgical aids involving rubber tubes and suction bulbs. The graphic packaging of bottles, capsules and powders betrayed a nation paranoid about ricked backs, dodgy kidneys, dicky digestive systems and something mysteriously called *la grippe*. What was more, he got the nasty feeling that some of the remedies were not to be swallowed but shoved up your you-know-where. Barbarians. How lucky he was to be English.

Things improved in the female section, thanks to the posters of naked girls languishing in bubble bath, or rubbing their perfect thighs with something that looked like a giant Brillopad. There was a lot of kinky stuff about *régimes* and *le corps gymnastique*. One cheeky brunette wore nothing but a tape-measure strategically twined round her body: "*85, 60, 89!*" boasted the caption. Blimey, she was a big girl—or was that centimeters?

Ah, this was more like it. Malcolm examined a display of small Cellophane-wrapped packets, disappointed to see that they weren't all that different from what you'd find in England. He even saw one advertising itself as "*sensible*"; there couldn't be many takers for that. Alicia would expect something very *un*sensible, judging by the sound of her. Would unusual colors impress her? Or flavors? Or the ones with "extra features" sometimes advertised in the back of his men's magazines?

He was just reaching for something called *superglissage* when he became aware of the tippety-tap of approaching heels. Quickly he snatched away his hand, scuttled back down the aisle and tried to hide behind the cardboard cut-out of a svelte blonde placing electrodes on her pertly presented bottom. But it was too late. There was the soft rustle of stockings, and a frighteningly attractive woman of about thirty bore down on him with a pink, glossy smile. Her skin was dewy with perfectly applied makeup, her dark hair swept up into some complex bun affair. A spotless white coat skimmed her figure from cleavage to knees. She stopped a few inches away from him, eyes shining with professional fervor and good health. Malcolm stared back glassily. ("Turn over now, Commander Bond.") Her lips parted.

She leaned toward him, exuding enough perfume to make his head spin, and in a soft, siren's voice asked if there was anything Monsieur desired. Smiling weakly, Malcolm mimed the action of brushing his teeth.

Half an hour later, sweating with nerves and exertion, he was back in his hotel room with five toothbrushes and a packet of something called Everest, bearing a misleading picture of a mountain peak with a flag on top, which turned out to be mints. Fortunately, the sixth *pharmacie* he visited had been staffed by a man, so he was also in possession of a variety-pack of condoms (*Sélection Exotique*).

But it was already nearly six o'clock. In half an hour he would have to be back on duty downstairs, for drinks and a stint of brown-nosing with the PLB-sponsored doctors and their spouses. ("Excellent work on the spleen! I gather congratulations are in order" . . . "May I top you up, Madam?") That would take him until eight, when Alicia was due. There was barely time to smarten himself up for his hot date. Meanwhile, his room looked more like a secretary's office than a seducer's den, and he still hadn't rehearsed his speech for tomorrow. Trying to suppress rising panic, Malcolm undressed quickly, hung up his suit, grabbed his sea-moss exfoliator and headed for the *en-suite* shower.

The gushing water cleared his head. *Confidence, Malc, confidence.* After all the work he'd put into it, his presentation was going to go down a storm. First off, he'd decided to do something different from the usual bland introduction ("delighted to welcome" . . . "another excellent year for PLB" . . . "go forward in partnership with the medical community," yakkety-yak). With all the big bosses there, he'd be mental to miss the opportunity to make his mark, to show he could think outside the box. So he was going to put on a real show, no messing, following the tips he had picked up from speech-writing manuals. Even little things helped, like making sure you looked good ("Always check yourself in a *full-length* mirror"), and standing up straight. ("A mere five minutes a week with a large book on your head will develop a posture that gives you instant presence." He'd been practicing with the new Terry Pratchett.) There were some brilliant pointers on how to pep up your talk: "Draw in Your Audience with a Relevant Personal Anecdote," for example. That had been dead easy. Gastroenterologists dealt with stomach and bowel disorders, right? What could be better than the hilarious story, well honed now after many riotous retellings in the pub, of his holiday in Turkey last year, when he'd had a runny tummy on the twelve-hour coach ride from Istanbul to the coast? Malcolm soaped his chest hair complacently.

"Set Your Audience At Ease with a Joke" had proved more tricky. This was an international conference, with doctors from all over the world, so it had to be a joke they could all relate to. Luckily, he'd remembered the one about the Frenchman, the German and the Irishman who go into a pub and find a goat behind the bar. Using his Visualization Technique, Malcolm could see himself standing triumphant at the podium, the roar of a standing ovation in his ears, before he stepped down modestly and handed over to the boffins with their scientific guff. There was a smile on his face as he reached for his Follicle-thickening Finish Rinse (as used by the cast of *The X-Files*, so he'd read: not cheap at thirty-seven quid a bottle, but what was good enough for Scully and Mulder was good enough for Figg).

The only thing still worrying him, as he toweled himself dry and leaned a hand against the bathroom mirror to trim his armpit hair (a grooming tip that reduced body odor by half!), was that he hadn't yet checked the graphics disk. Not that he didn't trust that Dr. Griffin, though it was weird the way he'd asked so many questions about Molly—but who was to say the stupid girl hadn't muddled it up with one of her own CDs, and he'd wind up blasting the conference with the *Bridget Jones* soundtrack. Now that *would* be embarrassing. He decided to nip into the exhibition hall as soon as he was dressed, and test it on one of the computers before he presented himself for drinks.

And—Christ! He'd better ring his mum. She liked to know he was safe when he was abroad, and it would be a right cock-up if she rang him later, when he was . . . busy, though he had her pretty well trained now. Still, he wanted to remind her to have his Paul Smith shirt ironed for Monday morning. She was a bit slack sometimes, even though she had nothing to do all day. Some of his mates teased him for living at home, but it made sense, didn't it? Domestics taken care of, no mortgage to eat into his disposable income, proper food like toad-in-the-hole and treacle pudding, and the prospect of a nice little property when his mum popped off. He bunged her the odd wodge of notes from time to time, but he needed most of what he earned to maintain his lifestyle: clothes, car, holidays, pension—and girls, of course, who banged on about equality and "paying their way" but always ended up costing him. He was going to think very carefully before selecting the future Mrs. Figg. Malcolm pulled up his trousers over his lucky jockey shorts, white with a huge red St. George's cross front and back, and tucked in his shirt. Only his shoes to go, and he'd be ready. He checked his watch. Yeah, he reckoned he could spare his mum a minute, especially if he styled his hair and slapped on his aftershave at the same time.

But all thoughts of his mother were driven from his head by a horrific discovery. His bottle of Tiger was empty! He couldn't face another *pharmacie*; besides, there was no time. Then he had a brainwave. Quickly he grabbed his briefcase, rummaged through it until he found the magazine he'd bought at the airport and thumbed through the pages. Jackpot! There was one of those ads where you peeled off a tab to get a whiff of some new product. Malcolm ripped it free and pressed the impregnated page to the skin behind his ears, then undid his second and third shirt buttons and smeared it across his chest. He looked at the crumpled page. Calvin Klein, the latest fragrance, very expensive. Alicia would be dead impressed.

Unless she didn't turn up. Malcolm rebuttoned his shirt thoughtfully. And what if she was a dog? The guy on the reception desk had called her "pretty," but he was French, one of the same beret brigade whose high spot music-wise was "La Mer," and who thought a horse was something you ate. Malcolm didn't want to get stuck with a fatty in glasses, as had once happened to him on a blind date. He could still remember the agony of sitting opposite her in a bar and watching her chins wobble. In the end, he'd had to fake an "emergency" call on his mobile, and she'd burst into tears and sobbed about her thyroid. He shuddered. The best plan would be to tip the *concierge* the wink, and hang about in the lobby to check her out. If he didn't like the look of her, he'd scarper. The way he was looking tonight, he ought to be able to pull another bird, easy. There were even one or two query shaggables among the doctors' wives.

But Alicia would be a goer: he could feel it in his bones. Picking up the disk, Malcolm gave himself a last admiring glower in the mirror. He patted his pockets to run a final check: breath fresheners, emergency comb, wallet ostentatiously fat with credit cards. Truth to tell, he cheated a bit by bulking it up with his AA card, Blockbuster Video membership, Sainsbury's loyalty card and his rail pass, but many was the time he'd seen a girl stare open-mouthed as he flipped through the multiple plastic folders. An Australian wouldn't recognize the cards anyway. Malcolm felt a ripple of excitement: he'd never had an Australian before. Maybe she had yet to discover the privilege of going to bed with an Englishman. They were strangers in a strange city: who knew what would happen? But it was a fair bet that the Crazy Horse Saloon would give them both some pretty wild ideas for games they could play with his didgeridoo.

# 16

She was floating on a cloud, unimaginably high in a sky of hazy gold. Her arms were outstretched, her legs sprawled in delicious lassitude. Somewhere out of sight she could hear birds calling. How odd that they could fly this high. If she raised herself to peer over the edge of her cloud, she might be able to see what kind they were. But she was too contented to move. And she was naked. Why was that? she wondered. It didn't matter. Nothing mattered, except—except something was missing. She chased a sweet, elusive memory. What was it? She mustn't let it slip away.

Molly's eyelids fluttered open. There were spots of tawny light on the ceiling. She watched them glimmer: pale, then bright, then pale again, lacing themselves into fantastic patterns. Idly, her gaze slipped down to walls covered with fabric, traversed the panels of a narrow door, focused on the outline of a bottle; there was something familiar about its shape. Then a seagull shrieked, raucously close, and consciousness returned in a rush. She turned her head on the pillow, already smiling at what she would see. But Fabrice had gone!

Molly sat up in bed and looked wildly round the room. She felt desolate. She peered over the edge of the bed: his jeans and shoes were missing, too. But what was that, half tucked under the empty bottle? Reaching over, she drew out a piece of paper, obviously torn from a pad and faintly criss-crossed with lines, like graph paper, with words and drawings sketched across it. As she turned it the right way up and started to read, a smile spread across her face. He'd drawn her a strip cartoon! The first box showed his head on the pillow, yawning as he woke up. Next, the focus widened to show him full-length on the bed, with Molly beside him looking like a mermaid, with cascading hair and an undulating body (her breasts weren't *that* big!), her legs draped by a sheet. A bubble emerged from Fabrice's head, filled with hearts and exclamation marks. How lovely . . . Now a close-up of Fabrice's face, smiling wistfully as he thought about smoking a cigarette; then another, more anxious face, and another bubble in which a giant box labeled "Cigarettes" radiated lines of urgency. There now followed a flurry of drawings depicting his search for his cigarettes—checking the pockets of his jeans, then his jacket, finding the packet (oh, joy!), discovering that it was empty (*hélas*), tearing his hair. Eventually, he appeared fully dressed, tiptoeing out of the apartment. The final box showed him back in bed with Molly, contentedly smoking. A scrawled arrow pointed to his watch, with the hands set at six twenty.

Molly reread the cartoon with smiles and croons of delight. She kissed the paper. How marvelous he was! She found her watch curled on the bedside table, and saw that it was already twelve minutes past six: not too long to wait. Probably his shutting of the door had woken her up. She gathered the pillows together and flopped back in an orgy of down. Above her loomed an elaborately carved headboard with gilded rosettes; she felt like a queen lounging on her throne. *Arise, Sir Fabrice.* Molly giggled at her joke and stretched luxuriously, relishing each small ache, each tender spot, as if they were battle scars from a magnificent victory. A faint breeze drifted across her skin through the open window. The light slanting through the shutters was dusky orange. She lay cocooned in happiness, listening to muted footfalls in the street, birds returning to their trees, the pleasurable sounds of a city catching its breath before the excitements of night.

But now something much louder began to obtrude. A thrumming noise, as from a giant refrigerator, grew to a growl, a roar. Molly jumped out of bed, padded across polished boards, and pushed open the shutters just in time to see a tourist boat—a *bateau-mouche*—approaching down the river, fat and wide as a gigantic water-beetle, with a glass carapace sheltering throngs of sightseers. As it trundled level, a disembodied monotone floated to her across the water from multiple loudspeakers. ". . . And on our right we can see the Île St-Louis, known as the Island of Cows until the seventeenth century, when Louis XIII allowed it to be developed for housing. It was here that the famous composer Chopin . . ." Molly leaned out of the window and waved vigorously, thoughtless of her nakedness. A surprising number of people waved back. How friendly of them! "Hello!" she wanted to shout. "I'm Molly Clearwater. Isn't Paris wonderful?" She watched the boat pass, its twin wakes turning fiery as they caught the evening sun, and followed a line of ripples to the far bank, where they set barges rocking. One day she would like to live on such a barge, with geraniums on top and a cozy stove inside, and sit on deck on evenings like this, under a turquoise sky shredded with pinky-gray cloud.

Leaving the shutters open, she returned to the bed and lay back with her hands clasped behind her neck, gazing complacently along the length of her body. This afternoon she had done several things she had never done before, and some she'd done but had never seen the point of. Now she knew what love was like: irresistible, overwhelming, frantic, uninhibited. Molly hovered for a moment over the word "love." Then she remembered the urgent tussle of limbs, his shadowed face above hers, the sound of their voices rising and falling together, and gave a secret smile. Never again would she be ashamed of her body. She would rejoice in something that could receive and give such intensities of pleasure. When Fabrice returned, she would not hide herself with a sheet. In fact, she was going to lie right here, in the most provocative position she could think of, to give him a surprise.

She heard a small sound. Was that him already? How quick he'd been! She pictured him running back through the streets with his precious cigarettes, bursting out of the lift in his impatience to return to her. Yes, that was the heavy front door slamming shut. With a look of mischief on her face, Molly grabbed the champagne bottle and placed it upright between the tops of her thighs and her *foufoune* (another new word to add to her vocabulary). Quickly she flung herself back onto the pillows in a position of abandonment. "Yoo-hoo," she cooed. "*Je suis ici-ee. Dans le lit-ee.*"

She heard footsteps. The door handle angled downward. The door opened, and a man she had never seen before stepped into the room.

With a screech of fright, Molly scrambled to the headboard in a tangle of limbs and hair, and crouched defensively, clasping a pillow to her breasts. In her rush she must have kicked the champagne bottle. It fell off the bed with a clunk, rolled thunderously across the floor, and rocked to a halt by the man's immaculate shoes. "Who are you?" she demanded, in a high voice, clawing desperately for the sheet. "What are you doing here?"

He looked at her with a resigned expression, his hand still poised on the door-handle. He was quite old, well into his fifties, but very good-looking, with haughty features and silvery wings to his sleek black hair. "I suppose my worthless son has been here again." He sighed.

"What do you mean?" Molly reared up so aggressively that one of her breasts popped over the top of the pillow. She recaptured it quickly, and yanked at the sheet until at last she had enough material to tuck under her armpits.

Cold eyes flickered over her. "I am Armand Lebrun, Fabrice's father. This is my home. I would like you to leave, please." He turned to go.

"One moment!" Molly staggered to her feet on the wobbly mattress, and kicked a tangle of bedding free of her ankle. So this was the monster who was ruining Fabrice's life! This was the man he couldn't talk to, the only parent Fabrice had, who refused to educate his son while he himself lived in wild extravagance. How dare he call Fabrice worthless? "How dare you call Fabrice worthless!" Molly shouted defiantly, tugging at the sheet as she tried to drape it round her bottom. "He's *not* worthless. He's marvellous! He has shown me beautiful things. He has talked to me about art. He's intelligent and kind and—and *I like him!*"

The man was looking at her with mild interest. "Ah. An English girl."

Molly tossed her head at this irrelevance. No doubt he found her accent amusing. "Fabrice thought you were in the country," she told him. "It was a mistake. Anyway, why shouldn't a son be allowed to visit his own father's apartment?"

"I decided to come back early. Tell me, how long has Fabrice been here? Should I count the spoons, I wonder?"

Molly gasped. Her eyes blazed. "Are you suggesting that Fabrice would *steal?* From his own father?"

He shrugged off her outrage. "At all events, he does not appear to be very attentive. Where is Fabrice, by the way?"

"On the contrary, Fabrice has been extremely attentive, thank you. He went to buy some cigarettes, that's all."

Fabrice's father rolled his eyes.

"You see?" Molly said accusingly. "Even his smoking makes you cross. No wonder Fabrice can't talk to you. No wonder he calls you '*rigide*.'"

"Does he?" He frowned. "Is that what he says?"

Molly caught a note of uncertainty in his voice and decided to press home her advantage. Perhaps she could effect a reconciliation. At the very least she could try to explain Fabrice to this coldhearted man who was obviously more concerned with his personal grooming than with his son. Who but a pampered peacock would wear cream slip-ons and knife-creased trousers to the country? His attempt at a tweed jacket was ridiculous. She could smell his cologne from here. Back home, he wouldn't even make it to the bar of the village pub.

But he was Fabrice's father. It was her duty to make him understand the pain he was causing. Molly hitched up her sheet and addressed him earnestly. "Monsieur Lebrun, you're a cultured man. I've seen the books on your shelves. Balzac and Proust, John Updike, Julian Barnes. How can you, a man who loves literature, treat your son so cruelly?"

His eyebrows rose in astonishment. Probably he wasn't used to hearing the truth. No doubt other people kow-towed to him as he sat around eating caviar with his so-called lefty friends, spending his dead wife's money. But not her. She was not ashamed to speak out for what was right. "Fabrice is so talented. And all you do is make it impossible for him to show his brilliance. He doesn't even have a proper studio. You've stopped him taking classes."

The eyebrows rose higher. "Is that—"

"Remember Rodin!" Molly wagged her finger at him.

"Who?"

"Rodin. The famous sculptor. He didn't have any money either, and was forced to take menial jobs. He was *dead* before his genius was recognized. Is that what you want for Fabrice?"

"You are suggesting that my son is a genius?"

His supercilious smile enraged her. "How can you laugh? It's not funny. Fathers are supposed to love their children, not make jokes about them. Imagine how it feels to have a father who doesn't care about you, who abandons you with no money while he goes off and enjoys himself with—with rock stars and so forth."

*"Rock stars?"*

"Fabrice has already lost his mother. He *needs* a father, a real father who will encourage him and appreciate him, not call him worthless. Nobody is worthless." Tears of passion stung her eyes. "Nobody," she repeated.

There was a silence. Molly wrapped the sheet more tightly around herself, folded her arms and gave a defiant sniff.

"May one inquire your name?" Fabrice's father asked at length.

"Molly," she told him. "Molly Clearwater."

"It must be said, Mademoiselle Clearwater, you are not quite what I expected when I saw you lying there with the champagne bottle." He bent to pick it up from the floor, and glanced at the label. "One of mine, I see."

"Yes. Well." Molly blushed. "I'm sorry about the champagne. I agree, we shouldn't have drunk it. In fact, I would like to pay you back for it."

"No, no. Please." He looked pained.

"I insist. One would not, after all, wish to be accused of stealing!" Head high, Molly trampled across the bed in search of her bag, stepped on the end of her sheet and would have toppled over if she had not grabbed the headboard in the nick of time. It creaked ominously under her weight: another priceless heirloom, no doubt. Her bag, she now realized, was still in the other room. "I'll find the money in a minute," she said, with dignity.

"Don't be absurd. Allow me to offer it to you as a gift, from an old Frenchman to a charming young English girl."

Now he had the audacity to smile at her. Molly raised her chin. She was much too clever to be beguiled by such obvious French flummery. But when he smiled, he reminded her of Fabrice. And it had just occurred to her that she had very little cash left, and that champagne was expensive, especially the sort that this man would drink. "Well, all right. Thank you." She gave a queenly nod. "Now, if you will allow me to dress . . ."

"Of course." He returned her nod, and withdrew.

Half a minute later, as Molly was on her knees searching under the bed for her knickers, having discarded the sheet, there was a knock on the door. "Mademoiselle?"

"What?" she demanded, flustered.

"Since you are getting dressed, I thought you might want these." The door opened a few inches, and a hand appeared clutching her jacket, dress and bra, with her bag dangling from his wrist.

Molly crept around the edge of the room as if avoiding sniper fire. From behind the door she reached a hand round to take her clothes. "*Merci.*"

"*De rien.*" The door closed again.

While Molly was dressing, she heard Fabrice return and waited anxiously for him to come to her. Now that she'd had time to reflect, it occurred to her that there was a certain element of embarrassment in being found in someone else's flat, naked and uninvited. Imagine if it was the other way round, and her mother had returned unexpectedly to the cottage and found clothes strewn all over the sitting room, and a strange Frenchman lying naked in her spare bedroom. Of course, that didn't excuse the father's arrogant, unfeeling behavior; nevertheless, Molly felt a twinge of conscience about her intrusion, and could not altogether rid herself of the sordid impression made by the tangle of sheets on the bed, and the coverlet of antique lace carelessly crumpled on the floor. She needed Fabrice to put his arms around her and tell her everything was all right. She needed him to confirm the magic of their afternoon together.

But he didn't come. She heard a rumble of voices from the other room: the pompous, hectoring tones of his father, a defensive outburst from Fabrice, then both together, rising to an angry pitch. Poor Fabrice. He was being told off. She must go and help him. First, as quickly as she could, she made an attempt to put the room in order by roughly folding the sheets into a pile and smoothing the coverlet over the mattress. Then she unearthed her hairbrush from beneath the Cleopatra wig in her bag (she hoped his father hadn't seen that!), and brushed ruthlessly through the knots, her face growing stern as she listened to the mounting quarrel next door. Fabrice was being bullied: she couldn't bear it. She *wouldn't* bear it. Slinging her bag over her shoulder, she hurried down the corridor and into the living room.

Instantly, they fell silent, but their body language was expressive enough. Fabrice's father sat in a throne-like armchair, his face thunderous, while Fabrice stood by the window, shoulders hunched, jerkily smoking a cigarette. His features were pinched and mutinous.

"Ah, Mademoiselle." Fabrice's father made a show of courtesy by rising to his feet.

Molly marched straight past him and up to Fabrice, took his

face in her hands and kissed him boldly on the lips, determined to show that she cared about him, even if his father didn't. She stroked his cheek and smiled into his eyes. "Don't worry," she told him.

Then she turned to face the father. "I suppose you want to speak to your *son* now." She gave the word a bitter emphasis, reminding him of the fatherly duties he had so selfishly neglected.

"*Euh*, Molly—" began Fabrice.

"No, Fabrice." Molly held up a hand. "Don't worry about me. I can easily find my way back to the hotel. We'll talk later."

"Later?" he echoed.

Molly looked at him. He was being rather dense, but naturally he was upset. "Yes, later. After you've talked to your father and I've, er, had a shower and so forth."

"But—"

"No doubt, Fabrice, you will be taking Molly out to dinner," Fabrice's father cut in smoothly. "There is L'Orangerie, just around the corner. Or perhaps she would enjoy something more traditional, like Bofinger or La Coupole. I will reserve for you. Shall we say nine o'clock? Fabrice can pick you up half an hour before. *Hein*, Fabrice?"

"*Oui, oui.*" He pouted.

"Ha!" Molly gave a sardonic laugh. La Coupole was in her guidebook, under the "Expensive" heading. "I doubt whether Fabrice could afford that." She turned to Fabrice and said tenderly, "It doesn't matter to me where we go or what we do. I'm not hungry." Unfortunately, as she spoke the words, her tummy rumbled loudly. She was ravenous! She cleared her throat, hoping that no one had heard, then walked over to Fabrice's father and with cool politeness held out her hand. "Good-bye, Monsieur Lebrun. I'm sorry if we have, er, deranged you." (Was that the right word?) "I hope you will remember what I said and—and act upon it."

He shook her hand with equal formality. "I am not at all deranged. Quite the contrary. It has been enchanting to meet you." He held her hand for a fraction longer than was necessary, and seemed to smile at her with genuine warmth. Or was it a sneer? Who could tell with the French? Molly flickered back an uncertain smile, gave Fabrice a last glowing look, and left.

When she emerged into the courtyard below, she saw that night had fallen. It was dark, and spookily still, apart from the sound of her heels on the cobbles. Decorative box bushes she had not noticed on the way in loomed from the shadows like figures lying in wait. For a disconnected moment she felt the presence of ghosts from history, imagined the smoky flame of torches, servants running, horses sweating and stamping after some desperate dash. When she stepped through the outer gate and let it swing back behind her, it seemed to clang shut with the reverberations of centuries.

Where was she? There was a sign ahead, by the bridge. Molly walked toward it and dug a hand into her bag, feeling for her map. "Pont de la Tournelle": she had a suspicion she was going the wrong way. In a minute she would orient herself. But first she looked back to study the handsome house, now softly lit by street-lamps. How odd to think that even the illiterate would once have been familiar with the deities carved on its façade, which she, with all her education, could not recognize; and would have read at a glance the emblems of shields and leaves and strange beasts she could not decode. Lights glowed in the flat one story from the top. A shadow passed across the window, and she raised her hand to wave. But if it was Fabrice, he didn't see her.

# 17

Anguille fumés . . . pintade au cerfeuil . . . *lotte à la crème de safran . . . pommes mousselines . . . salade de fenouil aux girolles.* Molly held the stiff menu to her face, hiding her eyes from Fabrice as they skidded and slithered across pages of unfamiliar words. She'd never seen such a detailed list of dishes, so grandiosely presented, so bafflingly arranged: "*Menu Gastronomique*," "*Menu Traditionel*," "*Menu du Jour*." And no prices! Could there really be people so rich that they didn't need to inquire?

Neither the restaurant nor its glamorous clientele, in full cry after the pleasures of the table, seemed to be in any doubt of their own worth. The room was opulently large, like a very grand coach station, with greeny-blue walls decorated with murals, and slender columns that sprouted gold leaves at the top. Everything glittered in the bright lights: mirrors, wine-buckets, silver caskets leaking fragrant steam, cufflinks and buckles, necklaces and earrings, dresses of *lamé* and silk worn with sinuous assurance. The waiters were magnificent in black jackets and white ties, patrolling the aisles with the stiff deportment and smooth, inhuman speed of robots on castors. It was the smartest restaurant Molly had ever been to.

"Really, the food is nothing special," said Fabrice, "but the *ambiance* is quite agreeable."

"Oh, Fabrice, it's fantastic." Molly lowered her menu to smile at him, fearful that he had misinterpreted her silence as criticism.

Tonight he looked more beautiful than ever, lounging against the banquette opposite her in a pink silk shirt, cigarette drooping from his elegant fingers. The shirt, he'd told her, had been forcibly lent to him by his father, who was ridiculously old-fashioned in such matters and insisted he could not accompany Molly in his paint-stained T-shirt. "What a tyrant!" Molly had exclaimed, eyes flashing. "I wouldn't mind what you wore." Or didn't wear, she'd added privately, thinking of the bedtime treats that lay in store. Presumably she'd get to see his place at last. Even if it was a hovel, she'd be too happy to care. She hoped Fabrice didn't mind that she was still wearing the same red dress. There was nothing else remotely suitable in the conference wardrobe she'd brought to Paris, and at least she'd managed to pep up her outfit with a necklace and some not-too-businesslike black heels, though now that she saw the slinky numbers other women were wearing, the effect didn't seem quite so successful as she'd thought in her hotel room.

A waiter was gliding toward their table. Molly ducked her head again, hoping to be invisible. She had no idea what to order. She felt him stop at her shoulder, saw his twinkling black shoes execute a neat quarter-turn. Without even looking up, Fabrice dismissed him with a sweep of his cigarette. Molly shot him a relieved grin.

"One has to keep these people in order," he told her. "After all, we're paying, *non?*"

"Absolutely," she agreed, impressed by his cool mastery. French men were so good at this kind of thing; no wonder the

English had had to import the phrase *savoir-faire*. But the question of who exactly was paying preoccupied her. She couldn't bear for Fabrice to spend money he didn't have on something as silly as food, just because his father had bullied him into it. But with all the expenses of this weekend, her own credit card must be nearly out of juice, and she doubted that she could pay even for her own meal here, let alone both. The idea of having her card returned publicly by one of these haughty waiters made her toes curl.

Fabrice stubbed out his cigarette and leaned across the table to go through the menu with her. There was some kind of seafood platter they could share as a starter—would she like that? Molly agreed gratefully. She didn't particularly like seafood, but sharing would be cheaper, wouldn't it? Fabrice must be worried about the money too, for as a main course he decided on pigs' trotters. Her appalled face made him laugh.

As for herself, after making Fabrice explain a dozen complex dishes (including brains, eel and sauerkraut), she admitted that she'd be happy with steak and *frites*. Ah, but what kind of steak? *Contre-filet*, *faux-filet*, *pavé*, *tournedos*, *bavette?* And how exactly would she like it cooked? Would she prefer the *sauce béarnaise* or the *sauce au poivre?* Molly thought it mad but marvellous that anyone could care so much, and asked bluntly which was the cheapest.

"Don't worry about that. I managed to squeeze some cash out of my father."

"You didn't! How?"

But Fabrice just looked sly and snapped his fingers at a passing waiter.

At last the food was ordered, the wines selected and a bottle already nestling in a cooler, their cutlery whisked away and replaced with more appropriate tools, and they could talk. Exaggerating only slightly, Molly told him how she had walked out of her job and jumped on a train to Paris. Somehow this hadn't come up before, and she was startled and flattered by his reaction.

"But I adore this story," he said, taking her hand between both of his. "That is how life should be. Impulsive. Unplanned. One must follow one's spirit, not submit oneself to the petty exigencies of commerce."

Molly nodded, smiling to herself at the pomposity of the French language, which could make anything sound like high philosophy.

"You are a heroine," he told her.

"An unemployed heroine."

"That is of no importance. You are free. Tomorrow you can get on another train, for Rome or St. Petersburg."

"Tomorrow I need to go home and find another job." She sighed, wondering if he would beg her to stay in Paris, with him.

"A job." He frowned. "But why?"

At that moment an extraordinary object was borne to their table and laid upon it with a flourish, like some great trophy of battle. It was a three-tiered tray, the bottom one at least eighteen inches across, on which crayfish, scallops, dismembered crabs and oysters lolled on a bed of crushed ice, among various smaller crustaceans, fronds of parsley, and lemon halves carved into petals. The waiter returned with extra starched napkins, a sauceboat of melted butter, and bowls of warm colorless liquid in which lemon slices floated (fingerbowls, not soup: she knew that much). With swift, neat contortions of the wrist he laid out an operating theater's worth of steel tools, variously hooked and hinged, filled their glasses and withdrew.

Fabrice lifted a crayfish from the top tier and jerked off its tail. "A job is a prison," he declared. "It puts chains on the mind. A job is what people do who have no imagination, who cannot envisage the great possibilities of life. How many great men can you name who have worked in a job?"

Molly's mind blanked as she watched him run a thumbnail up the belly of the fish, peel open its coral casing and pop out the creamy flesh. The other crayfish seemed to watch her with black beady eyes, daring her to do the same. She chose a scallop. "I agree that jobs aren't always that interesting. Mine certainly wasn't. But we all need them."

"Why?"

"Well, to live. To eat."

"Oh, eat." He shrugged dismissively, dunking his crayfish in the butter.

"And they're not all boring. Some jobs are really worthwhile. They give people the sense that they're contributing."

"Contributing to what?" Fabrice demanded, reaching for a small snail. "The bank accounts of greedy businessmen? The egos of presidents? The destruction of the planet through pollution and the plundering of natural resources? These are delicious, by the way. Here, have one." He tossed a shell onto her plate. "That is why art is supreme. By 'art' naturally I mean also literature, music, performance, et cetera. Art contributes to nothing except ideas—ideas that enrich the soul and cannot be valued in money terms. It is beautifully selfish."

Molly gazed at him admiringly. How well he talked. It had not occurred to her before that selfishness could be a positive thing. She felt pedestrian and narrow-minded by comparison. With some difficulty she had managed to insert a hook into her shell, and now drew out a grey, squidgy body. It didn't look very appetizing, but that just showed how unadventurous she was. "Chains on the mind . . ." She raised the snail to her mouth, then paused as a thought struck her. "But surely even artists have to earn—"

"*Ah, non.* Artists do not earn, they *give.* Don't you see? It is so much more pure. One cannot be bought, one gives freely."

Not squidge, rubber. She held the half-chewed snail in her mouth, feeling her gorge rise. As soon as she could, she spat it discreetly into her napkin.

"One must never work for money, only for the glory of the work itself, because that is your vision. Otherwise the work is debased, and you find yourself the slave of someone like *ce type* Pig."

"Figg." Molly giggled.

"His name is of no interest. He is nothing, *nul,* an empty suit, his pockets stuffed with worthless diplomas."

It was thrilling to hear Malcolm so sweepingly denounced. (God! How was poor Alicia getting on with him?) Molly was glad she had not boasted to Fabrice about her first-class degree. She could see now that it, too, was worthless in the great scheme of things, even though she had worked very hard to get it. Was that bad?

Fabrice had helped himself to a sea urchin, and was elaborating his theory of the nobility of "real" work: "Take painting, for example . . ." Molly wrestled with a crab claw. She was getting the teensiest bit tired of hearing about art. Could it be true that *all* jobs were degrading? She squeezed lemon juice onto a chunk of white meat, copying the way Fabrice first stabbed the lemon with his fork. He did everything with such grace. Each time she looked at him—the dark ellipses of his eyelashes, his mobile mouth and white teeth, the triangle of butterscotch skin at his neck—she felt her body leap. They thought the same, really: it just sounded more pretentious in French. Obviously it was preferable to work for a noble goal, like art, than for a boring old paycheck. She herself had chafed at the drudgery at PLB, and even walked out after being called a stupid secretary. But perhaps Fabrice didn't realize that not everyone was as clever and talented as himself. What if you couldn't think of a noble goal, and had to just keep going until one occurred to you?

"No, Molly, the only valuation worth having is your own," Fabrice concluded, wiping butter from his chin. "Money itself is not important; it will follow naturally."

"I don't know. At least, I'm sure you're right. But it sounds too easy."

"On the contrary, it is much more difficult. To be a servant of art involves much harder, more painful work than that of the real servant who scrubs your floors."

His words evoked an image in Molly's mind: her mother's back, with its trailing plait, bent over seed trays as she moved down the polytunnel to examine the tiny green shoots that were her livelihood—watering, feeding, protecting, worrying, counting and re-counting the potential worth of each plant coaxed into saleable bloom. Molly felt a confusion she could not quite articulate.

"Well, anyway, I'm not an artist. I'm . . ." She hesitated. What was she exactly? Seated between opposing mirrors, she spied her own figure, an insignificant red blob, infinitely repeated in ever-decreasing size. The sensation of snail in her mouth still lingered. If she ate another sea creature she'd be sick. She laid her crushed napkin on the table and stood up. "Excuse me, Fabrice. I'm just going to the . . ." She waved vaguely.

She walked down the length of the restaurant, feeling the assault of blazing lights, clashing trays, overlapping conversations, and the clamor of her own whirling thoughts. In the privacy of the cubicle, she put her elbows on her knees, propped her face in her hands and closed her eyes. Fabrice, Fabrice . . . She wished they could stop talking and go home to bed. She was tired. She'd barely slept since arriving in Paris. No wonder she couldn't think.

As she was washing her hands she caught sight of her watch: nearly ten o'clock. Alicia must have been with Malcolm for more than two hours now—or dumped him already. Molly decided to text her to make sure she was okay. She got out her phone and switched it on. Oh! There was already a message waiting for her. She hoped she hadn't missed an emergency rescue call.

But the message wasn't from Alicia at all. "Molly: Important matter to discuss. Please contact urgently. A Friend." Molly frowned at the little screen. What did it mean? Who could it be from? She clicked to the end of the message, but the sender's phone number meant nothing to her. "A Friend": Molly stared at the words suspiciously. A real friend would give their name. And there was something stilted about the style of the prose; no normal person texted like that. Could it be somebody French? Or someone trying to disguise their identity for some reason? A disgusted expression spread across her features. She bet it was Malcolm, trying to trick her into replying so that he could torture her with some dreary question about the disk or the conference material. Malcolm: the nothing, *nul*, who had wanted to bring her to Paris so that he could get into her knickers, and was probably at this very moment pawing poor Alicia. Honestly, men!

There was a firm set to her mouth as Molly erased the message, and saw it consigned to the rubbish bin where it belonged. Then she quickly punched in a message for Alicia. "*ruok? sos* me any time." After a moment's thought she added: "At fab dinner with Fab! Prob his place tonite. xxx Molly." She watched the message insert itself into an envelope and fly off into cyberspace, then dropped her phone back into her bag. The battery was running low, but she'd better leave it on for an hour or two in case Alicia needed her.

She smoothed her hair in the mirror, feeling better. Her brain had begun to function again. (T. S. Eliot had worked in a job, as a publisher. George Orwell had washed dishes. So there!) And it *was* a wonderful dinner. She missed Fabrice already. She would change the subject, stop him banging on about art, get him to concentrate on her. She'd seen at least three couples kissing in this restaurant: not furtive little pecks across the table but long, intense, eyes-closed embraces, accompanied by such explicit fondlings of flesh that it seemed at any minute they would either go the whole way or burst into flames.

When she returned to the table the seafood platter had disappeared. At her place a round, pinky-brown steak lay dead center on a white plate. Molly stared at a trickle of blood running into the watercress garnish, and realized she was no longer hungry.

"Is it the way you like it?" Fabrice asked solicitously. "I think perhaps it is overcooked. I will order the waiter to bring another one."

"No, no, Fabrice, it's fine." She picked up her knife and fork, and sawed off a slice while he embarked on a detailed account of the time he'd had to send back his *magret de canard* three times before it was properly cooked. Three times! Such things were insupportable. Eventually she managed to steer the conversation back to herself. "You're so clever, Fabrice. What do you think I should do?"

"*Hein*?"

"About finding a job. I mean work. I mean—money, really." She gave an embarrassed laugh. "I know it's not very noble, but I've got rent to pay. I can't go home and sponge off my mother."

"Oh, one can always get money." He lit a cigarette.

"How?"

He gave her a knowing look. "The usual ways."

"What ways?"

"Molly, don't be naïve. You know what I mean. One can always sell something, borrow a friend's flat for a few months, cajole one's *papa* into paying for dinner." He nodded at her steak. "One can nick this and that when no one's looking. We all do such things."

"*I* don't." But even as she said the words she flushed, remembering the time she had found a twenty-pound note wedged between the cushions of the sofa at home and decided to keep it. She must have been about fourteen, bolshy and self-absorbed. There was a brand of jeans she wanted passionately that her mother selfishly refused to buy her. Everyone else was wearing them. She would die if she didn't get some too. If challenged, she would say she'd used her dog-walking and babysitting money (spent weeks ago). Already she could see herself swanking down to the bus stop where her friends congregated after school to mess around.

"You haven't seen a twenty-pound note anywhere, have you, darling?" her mother had asked a couple of evenings later. Molly, looking up from her book and acting the dreamy teenager for all she was worth, gave a bored grunt and shook her head. Accepting her answer, her mother turned back to her paperwork. Molly felt a lick of cold triumph. How easy it was! Anyway, it was only twenty pounds. A grown-up would never miss that.

But her mother did miss it. Molly found her searching for it in the living room, the kitchen, the greenhouse, riffling through the dirty washing to check her pockets. "What could I have done with it?" she wailed. Then, more frantically, "What am I going to do?" Normally her mother tried to shield Molly from money matters, but this time her worry was too great to conceal. It turned out that the note had been earmarked for some electricity bill that had to be paid in advance, by installment, or they would be cut off. It was the end of a lean month, one of the nursery's regular customers was late with its payments, and her mother's overdraft had reached its limit.

Molly had joined in the search, turbulent with guilt, conscious all the time of the note hidden between the pages of her lockable five-year diary. She watched her mother's face tighten with strain, listened to her castigate herself for her carelessness, even apologize to Molly for not buying her a treat after school. Molly tried to block out the memory of what she'd done, but her skin prickled with self-loathing, her chest burned as if she'd swallowed acid. She no longer wanted the jeans. She wanted her mother to smile again, and to be able to smile back freely. In the end she "found" the note, not quite daring to meet her mother's eye as she poured out a complicated story of how she had discovered it in the unlikeliest place. The crisis passed. For a few days Molly made an effort to stop grunting and be more helpful, then she forgot all about it. At school there was a new craze for a certain type of clumpy-heeled shoe.

"I did take something once," she admitted to Fabrice. "It felt awful."

"Were you caught?"

"No . . ."

To her surprise he was smiling at her—a gentle, caressing smile that seemed to make his whole expression glow with affection. "Ah, *la petite Sainte* Molly, with her innocent English face." He reached over and stroked her cheek. "You're a very clever girl, you know. My father liked you."

"He couldn't have. What do you mean? Why am I clever?"

But he closed his lips tight and gave her a mischievous, conspiratorial look, as if holding on to a delicious secret.

"What?" she demanded, half laughing herself as she waited for him to explain the joke.

He drew on his cigarette and blew the smoke out of the corner of his mouth. "Haven't you found it yet?"

"Found what?"

"The thing from the apartment?"

"What thing?"

"I put it in your bag while you were sleeping. There's a man I know who will give me money for it. It's perfect! My father cannot accuse me. He saw me himself, walking out of the apartment like this." Fabrice gestured at his clothes, as if to demonstrate that they concealed nothing.

"My bag?" Molly had already picked it up and was rummaging through it. She couldn't take in what he was saying.

"In the little pocket. Of course I won't get the full value, but the money will keep me going for a while."

Molly pulled open the zip of the inner pocket and peered into its dark, silky depths. Oh, God! "The candle-snuffer," she breathed.

"Brilliant, isn't it? He probably won't notice it's gone for weeks."

Molly zipped the pocket shut—quickly, before anyone could see. The restaurant seemed to be spinning round, a carousel of grinning figures with Fabrice's face at its still center, his eyes warm and complicit.

Molly put the bag back down on the floor then straightened to face him. She took a steadying breath. "No," she said.

"What do you mean, 'no'?" She saw the warmth dying in his eyes.

"I can't let you do this, Fabrice. I'm not blaming you, of course. It's just that I know it will be a mistake. We're going to take that . . . thing back to your father, right now. You'll thank me later, I promise."

Fabrice shoved away his plate angrily. "What are you talking about? Take it back? Don't you understand? We got away with it!"

"We have so far, I agree," said Molly. His anger made her tremble. "But later you'll regret it. You'll hate yourself. You won't be able to paint. I couldn't bear that."

"Of course I won't be able to paint without any money, without any materials! What crazy game are you playing? Do you want a cut, is that it?"

"Fabrice!"

Through a blur of tears she was aware of a looming black bulk. "It is finished?" asked a waiter. "You are taking dessert? Cheese?"

"The bill." Fabrice glowered.

Molly clasped and unclasped her hands under the table. "I know you're cross, Fabrice, and I'm sorry. But I'm right. You'll see. We'll think of a way of explaining: a mistake . . . a misunderstanding . . . I don't know. But I'll be there with you. I'll stand up for you." Tentatively she put out a hand to touch his arm.

He shook her off furiously. "What's the matter with you? I buy you a nice dinner. Now it's completely ruined."

"No, it's not. I loved it."

"It's only a little thing I took. Unimportant. It doesn't even properly belong to my father."

"No, to your mother," Molly reminded him.

When the bill came, Fabrice slapped down notes and stalked ahead of her out of the restaurant. Molly had almost to run after him, and smiled extra hard at all the waiters who turned from what they were doing to bow politely. "*Merci*," she cried gaily. Yes, everything was delicious. "*Bonsoir, bonsoir!*"

Outside, Fabrice stood by his motorbike, fuming. "My father won't be in. It's Saturday night."

"Let's go past and see. Please."

She put her arms round him as they rode through the streets, trying to radiate affection and reassurance, but it was like cuddling a refrigerator.

When they reached the house, Molly saw lances of bright light shining at the edges of the curtains in Monsieur Lebrun's apartment. They got off the bike in silence. Fabrice tapped in the code. The lock clicked open. "Go on, then." He jerked his head.

Molly realized he still had his helmet on. "Aren't you coming?"

"No."

"Fabrice, *je t'en prie*—I beg you! You can't let me go alone."

"It's your choice." He shoved his hands into his pockets and turned to stare sulkily at the river. "Go ahead, betray me. Blacken my reputation."

"No, it's the opposite. You don't want to be a thief, do you?"

He twitched a shoulder. "I thought you liked me."

"I do like you. You know I do."

"Then come back with me now." His eyes were on hers, soft and seductive, as he reached out and pulled her close. "Back to bed," he whispered.

Molly swayed against him, feeling his breath on her neck. It was only a candle-snuffer: only a silly old candle-snuffer nobody used. She could get back on his bike now and have a whole night with Fabrice, wake up with him to sunshine and love. She could take the stupid thing back tomorrow.

His lips moved against her ear. "Molly . . . my little *cocotte*. Come on. Come with me now."

She longed—ached—to give in. But her awareness of the

stolen object—in *her* bag—lodged like a burr under her breastbone. "Couldn't you wait for me here?"

"No. You must choose. Which is worth more to you, my feelings or your nice clean conscience?"

Her hesitation revealed to them both that she had already chosen. He dropped his hands and started to turn away.

"Wait! When will I see you again? Don't you want to know what happens? You can't just—I can't—" She lowered her head, feeling tears prickle her nose. "I *love* you, Fabrice."

There was a silence in which Molly could hear only her own desperate sniffs.

Then she felt his hand on her hair. "Silly girl." He sighed. "On Sundays I'm usually in the Café Balzac around one o'clock, two o'clock. Near the St. Sulpice church. You can come if you like." *Si tu veux.*

"*Je veux.*" She tried to smile.

His bike roared into life. Molly stood by the big gates, waiting to see if he would turn back. The red cyclops eye of his scooter waned, flickered as he leaned into a corner, then disappeared. He was gone.

# 18

Knockout. Poetry on legs. Tall, athletic, nice big arse, tight leopardskin minidress held together at one shoulder with a giant gold safety pin, a smile that could light up Wembley Stadium. Heads swiveled to clock Alicia's progress as they threaded their way through the tables toward the one he'd reserved, near the stage. Malcolm smirked. If all Australian girls were like this, he was emigrating. Not sure about the tattoo, though.

"What *is* that?" he asked, using the excuse to lean closer in the hot semi-darkness and stroke Alicia's upper arm. The design looked like a bulldog in an aggressive bow-legged pose. "Your guard doggy? I hope he doesn't bite. *Grrrrr.*" He snapped his teeth playfully in the air. Christ, he was on good form tonight.

Alicia gave a yelp of laughter. "No, that's my team. Australian Rules football, you know?"

Football, she said. She liked sport! "But it's not like proper football, is it?"

"Heaps better. There's a lot more action, and the guys wear these really cute little shorts. I expect you'd look good in a pair, Malcolm."

"Expect I would." Malcolm smirked. She was coming on to him, all right.

"So what about you, Malcolm? Have you got any secret tattoos hiding under that groovy suit of yours?"

Of course he hadn't. His mum would kill him. Anyway, a tattoo would not be appropriate for someone in his position. Malcolm leaned back in his chair and gave her his Jack Nicholson leer. "Tell you what, you can check me over later and find out."

"Hoo-hoo!" Alicia waggled her eyebrows excitedly.

Malcolm topped up her champagne. He couldn't believe his luck. She was worth the extortionate price he was paying for them to be here—and the naked girls were still to come! For a reckless moment he had even considered opting for the Crazy Horse "*Dîner Spectacle*," but the prices started at eighty quid: no female was worth that. Anyway, she'd had a chance to fill up on free peanuts at the hotel bar, where he'd taken her first for a couple of drinks. (Cunning plan: he'd be able to put the meal on his "entertainment" expenses.)

*It can't be her.* That's what he'd thought the minute Alicia strode into the hotel lobby, where he'd been loitering behind a palm frond as per his arrangement with the bloke on Reception. If she'd been a dog, he was going to do a runner. But she wasn't a dog—she was a . . . what was she? A leopardess, he decided. A gorgeous, sexy leopardess. A wild creature waiting to be tamed. Down, Figg!

Somehow he'd been expecting her black hair to be longer, and the description he'd been given of the girl who'd dropped off the disk hadn't said anything about the orange streak at the front. Even the guy at Reception didn't seem to recognize her until she asked for Malcolm. As he'd sprinted over to claim her before she did another disappearing trick, he still felt a lingering sense of disbelief.

"It was you that brought the disk this afternoon, wasn't it?" he asked her, once they were settled in the bar.

"It might have been." She smiled coyly.

"Why did you run away? Not scared of me, were you?" He gave her a roguish grin.

"What?" She was batting her eyelashes in puzzlement. Probably not too bright. Just the way he liked them.

"You disappeared just as I got to the desk," he reminded her. "Why did you give it to that doctor instead?"

"Oh, that . . ." She fiddled with her earrings. "I get shy sometimes. You may find that hard to believe after the way I spoke to you on the phone, but . . ." She raised her eyes, mesmerizingly round and blue in a circle of black eyelashes, to his. "You don't realize, Malcolm, how exciting it is for me, a simple Australian girl, to be asked out by such a high-ranking executive from London." She crossed her legs.

Malcolm felt his ears go hot, and tried to stroke his tie before he remembered he wasn't wearing one. *Of course.* He should remember how intimidating all this must seem to a simple girl from the colonies. He'd been meaning to ask how Alicia had got hold of the disk in the first place, and whether Molly was in Paris, and why, but somehow he got sidetracked into telling her about his many responsibilities at PLB. Alicia seemed to be fascinated—she'd even made some very helpful suggestions about a problem that had been troubling him, namely the annual departmental Awayday, for which he'd been asked to organize some "ice-breakers" to help knit the staff into a real team. It turned out that Alicia had worked as a holiday rep in Greece the previous summer, and knew some great games. For example, you divided everyone into teams and lined them up in rows, standing behind each other with their legs apart. The person at the back had to crawl through all the legs and sprint up to the rep (or Malcolm, in this case), who gave them a shot of alcohol. Then they had to run round a broomstick ten times, while holding the top of the handle glued to their foreheads and the broom bit pressed to the ground, before returning to their team and crawling through the legs again, at which point the person now at the back would do the same thing. The first team to finish won.

"But we never got that far." Alicia giggled. "Most people were so dizzy they couldn't even find their team, especially with all the sand that got kicked up. Everyone was staggering all over the beach. It was hilarious."

"Not a lot of sand in Basingstoke, of course," Malcolm said thoughtfully. The Awayday was to be held in a hotel off the M3. "But I believe it could be adapted to a ballroom situation."

"'Course it could."

That's what he liked: optimism, energy, the proactive, can-do approach. Here was a lioness—leopardess—who could drag home a ruddy buffalo carcass, crack a joke at the same time and still be dynamite in the den come nightfall. Look at her now, giving him that flirty smile. It was a good thing he'd managed to get those condoms.

But first, the show. He'd been a little surprised to find that the Crazy Horse Saloon wasn't a saloon at all, but a smart building in one of the most fashionable parts of Paris—not far, Alicia told him, from the tunnel where Princess Diana had died. On the outside it looked like an exclusive club, with a discreet entrance guarded by a uniformed doorman. Very tasteful: not a tit or bum to be seen. He wondered for a moment if they'd come to the wrong place. Could there be two clubs with the same name? Malcolm had a nightmare vision of sitting through an evening of highbrow rubbish while the girls were getting their kit off elsewhere. But no, his tickets were waiting for him at the desk. Malcolm purchased a glossy program—ten euros!—and ushered Alicia through the inner doors with a pat on the bottom.

The inside resembled a small theatre, but with tables packed tight around the stage and a curving bar at the back. Soft lighting, an abundance of crimson velvet and hothouse temperatures gave it a mellow, seductive atmosphere. It was like sitting in a warm red cave. A beam of light projected the words "CRAZY HORSE PARIS" onto the curtains, which rippled from time to time with intriguing backstage preparations. Malcolm imagined what lay behind those curtains and squeezed his thighs together. Life didn't get much better than this.

His hand trembled as he read the program, which told him he was about to see a revue called *Teasing*: "Twelve short scenes, some classical, some contemporary, are the perfect showcase for twenty statuesque dancers who will put on the most fabulous nude spectacle in the world."

* * *

Just then a tinny squeak began to play a tune Malcolm eventually recognized as "Waltzing Matilda." Alicia whipped her mobile out of her bag. He hurriedly retrieved his own phone and turned it off. He looked up to see Alicia grinning as she scanned a text message in the half-light. "Anyone important?" he asked.

"Not compared to you, Malcolm." She gave him a look. Blimey.

The lights were dimming. A hush fell over the room. Malcolm tingled with expectancy. A drumroll rose to a crescendo. The curtains swished back. Malcolm's mouth sagged open. To the sound of jolly military music, girls were marching onto the stage, wearing boots, bearskin hats, leather gloves up to their elbows—and nothing else, apart from dangly things like fly whisks over their you-know-whats. Look at those bodies! Long legs, bare breasts, acres of smooth skin gleaming in the lights. Trying not to gawk, Malcolm made a show of studying his program. This was billed as a "ballet" entitled "God Save Our Bareskin." Oh, ho, very good. He sneaked a glance at Alicia, wondering what she made of it all. She was loving it! The little tart. An image came into his mind of Alicia cavorting around his hotel room, wearing nothing but her tattoo. He wiped his forehead, and returned his attention to the stage.

The girls marched around in various formations. They saluted, stood to attention and at ease, wheeled left so that all their tits pointed one way, like pink noses sniffing the wind, then right, then did an about-turn so that their bottoms lined up like a row of luscious plums.

"Great choreography, isn't it?" Alicia said to him, under cover of the applause.

"It's not their choreography I'm looking at." Malcolm chuckled at his witty repartee.

"Oh, Malcolm, you crack me up." She threw back her head in a laugh, then leaned close to whisper: "I must say, this stuff really gives you ideas, doesn't it?"

Malcolm's heart lurched with excitement and mild terror. He smiled his sophisticated smile, and poured her another glass of champagne.

# 19

He does like me, Molly insisted, as the lift glided upward. His pride was hurt; that was all. Men had enormous egos. They couldn't help it: that was the way they were made. When their egos were threatened, they became angry, and anger made them cruel. Look at Sergeant Troy in *Far from the Madding Crowd*, who jilted the love of his life because she was late for their wedding, then suffered a broken heart until the day he died. Not that she wanted Fabrice's heart broken exactly, but he would probably be penitent tomorrow. She would forgive him, of course, in the end. She pictured herself in the Café Balzac, wistful and waiflike in black, being coaxed back to smiles. There would be enough time for them to make up properly before her train left. How did that poem go? Something, something, "and then you, lovely and willing in the afternoon . . ."

The lift bounced to a halt. Lights sprang on automatically in the empty corridor. It was very quiet. Molly stood outside the carved front door, gathering her courage. She felt very alone. What would she say? How could she explain, without betraying Fabrice? M. Lebrun was a bad-tempered tyrant. Her French was not up to the task. But it had to be done. She pressed the buzzer.

There were quick footsteps, the click of latches, and the door was pulled open. Monsieur Lebrun's impatient expression modulated to surprise, then curiosity. Dressed in dark trousers and a shirt with the sleeves rolled up, he looked less pin-perfect than he had this afternoon. There was a pencil in his hand. "Ah, Mademoiselle Molly. I'm sorry, I don't recall your other name."

"It doesn't matter. May I, um, come in a moment?"

"Of course." His eyes flickered momentarily to the corridor behind her, as if to check she was alone, then he stepped back to let her in and closed the door. "This way."

"I'm sorry it's so late. I saw the light on. I hope I'm not interrupting anything," Molly gabbled, as she followed him down the hall. Through an open doorway she caught a brief glimpse of a lighted room, very different from the rest of the flat, sparsely furnished in pale wood and chrome: a desk covered with papers, filing cabinets, a drawing board.

"I was working," he said, leading the way into the living room, "but not very profitably, it must be said. Now you have given me an excuse to have a cognac. You like cognac?"

"I don't know. But—"

"Then you must try."

"No. I mean, thank you, but I can't stay." Molly halted just inside the threshold. She felt sick. "Monsieur Lebrun—"

He turned sharply. "It's about Fabrice? Something is wrong?"

"No, no, Fabrice is fine. And thank you very much for giving him the money for our dinner. It was delicious. But—"

"The food was good? Really? I am glad. One cannot be sure, since the restaurant was taken over by a big group. Sometimes they are careless about the cheese. I was once offered a Reblochon that was an insult. One would think it had been purchased in the *supermarché!*" His handsome features contracted with disdain.

"We didn't have cheese," Molly said rather desperately,

clutching her bag. "Monsieur Lebrun," she went on, before he could quiz her further about the menu, "I have something to confess to you. Something very bad. This afternoon, when I was here, I—I stole something."

He looked at her in astonishment. Then his face cleared. "You mean the champagne. I told you, it is a gift. You must not think of it."

"Not the champagne. This." She put her hand into her bag and drew out the candle-snuffer. His face grew hard. She felt like a criminal. "You see, I'm very poor," she stumbled on. "I just lost my job. I came here and saw all your beautiful things and—well—I don't know what came over me. It was very wrong."

"But now you are bringing it back?" His face was like a mask.

"Yes. I was ashamed. The dinner and so forth. And you are Fabrice's father. So here it is." Somehow she managed to take a step and hand it to him. "I'm very, very sorry, Monsieur Lebrun."

He turned the snuffer this way and that in his hand for a moment, then pointed it at the sofa. "Sit down, Mademoiselle."

He spoke so sternly that she sank down obediently, watching with widening eyes as he walked to a corner of the room. She saw a telephone. Was he going to phone the police? "Monsieur . . ." she pleaded.

He laid down the snuffer and opened a cabinet. There was the chink of glasses. Solemnly he poured an inch of bronze liquid into two bulbous goblets, carried them over to Molly, and handed her one. "Please call me Armand. 'Monsieur' sounds so old. And of course I *am* old—old enough, certainly, to know that it was not you but my son who took this thing."

"No, honestly!" Her words fell thinly into a disbelieving silence.

He pulled up a chair and sat down, forearms on knees, confronting her. "It was Fabrice, wasn't it?"

Molly dropped her eyes. "He—you see, it belonged to his mother. He wanted to have something of hers."

"*Ah, non!*" Armand hit the arm of his chair so violently that Molly jumped. "Don't lie to me!"

Molly twisted the handle of her bag round and round, as if she was trying to shred the leather. "He was going to sell it," she whispered. "I knew he shouldn't. That's why I—that's why we agreed that I would bring it back."

"I suppose you're going to tell me he was too ashamed to bring it himself."

"Yes, he is! At least, he will be, I know."

"And is he waiting for you down there?" Armand jerked his head at the window, and the darkness outside.

Molly shook her head. "He was too angry." Without warning, she felt her face crumple out of shape, and had to grip her nose and squeeze her eyes tight to stop the tears bursting out.

"*Oh, là là,*" clucked Armand. "Drink your cognac. The world has not ended, I promise you."

"He didn't mean to take it," Molly wailed. "He didn't think. Perhaps if you gave him a little more money, were a little kinder to him . . ." Her words petered out. She raised the cognac waveringly to her mouth. The glass rattled against her teeth. Fumes scorched her nostrils as she tilted the liquid into her mouth. Ooh, how horrid! A firebolt shot down her throat, setting her chest aflame. Her lips stung.

Armand held his glass from underneath, fingers splayed around the bowl, and revolved it absently. "I am at the end of my patience with Fabrice," he said grimly. "The fact is that I give him an extremely generous allowance, probably more than I should. I have paid for many years of study, special tutorials, trips to Italy, to museums. He throws it all away. This afternoon you suggested that I had made it impossible for him to study. That is not true. Fabrice was dismissed by the *école* because he refused to take the examinations. He said the teachers were out of touch, blinkered—'Fascists'—and he refused to submit himself to their worthless opinion." He sighed. "I'm afraid he can be arrogant. And he is not always truthful—in many things. That is something you should know."

Molly stared at him. She wanted to protest. She wanted to disbelieve him, but the pain in his face told her he was speaking the truth.

"This is not the first time he has stolen from me," Armand continued. "I confess it with shame. The truth is, he is spoiled. His mother spoiled him when she was alive, as all mothers spoil their sons, and after she died Fabrice was so unhappy I wanted to make up for his great loss. It was hard to say no to him. Today you told me I neglected Fabrice—"

Molly's hands fluttered an apology. "That was very rude. I'm sorry. I thought—I felt—"

"You spoke your feelings honestly. That is admirable. You made me consider. It is true that I am very busy with my work. Perhaps I have given Fabrice too much money and not enough time. The exasperating thing is that he is truly talented: not a genius, *bien sûr* not a Corot or a Matisse, but there is a special quality to his work, an energy—" Armand broke off in frustration, tossing his hands in the air. "It's a terrible tragedy to waste a talent, don't you think?"

"I think he *wants* to do something good," Molly said slowly. "He took me to the Rodin museum today, and he wasn't just showing off, he was passionate about what can be done if you have a vision. He does show off a bit," she added, meeting Armand's eyes with a sideways smile, "but I don't mind."

Behind Armand's head she could see the mirror where she and Fabrice had looked at themselves, naked. She ached for that lost moment. It didn't matter that Fabrice could be a bit spoiled and self-centerd. He was so beautiful. Apart from his looks, what she liked about him best was his playfulness. She remembered the way he had grabbed her hand on the deck of the boat, the way he teased her about "culture," his lovely cartoon.

"Perhaps Fabrice doesn't know *how* to work," she said. "I realize that sounds strange, but sometimes people want something so much—they see what they want to be but they don't know how to achieve it." As she spoke the words, she realized that they could also apply to herself. "People can be so frightened of failing that they do nothing, or choose something so dull they have no chance of shining. And, of course, Fabrice sees you—very successful, very busy—and wonders if he will ever be the same." She frowned. "I did think it a bit odd that he brought me to your flat. I mean, why not his place? He was very nervous to begin with. He seemed angry with you, almost as if there was something he wanted to prove."

"Of course he can come here any time." Armand flapped his hands elegantly, not really answering her question. "That's why he has a key."

"Yes, but not—not to—" Molly started to blush. "Monsieur—Armand—I want to tell you that I don't usually—I'm not the sort of girl—"

"No, no!" he interrupted, aghast, palm raised. "That, of course, is none of my business. In France such things are understood. We are not like you English, who wish to print the story of every *petite amie* in the newspapers. *Enfin, l'amour, c'est l'amour.*" The way he waggled his head and puffed out little snorts of outrage reminded Molly of Alleluia, furiously shaking droplets from her coat after being plunged unexpectedly into water.

"It's just that Fabrice has been so kind to me, so much fun, so . . . everything." She smiled dreamily.

Armand had risen to fetch the cognac bottle. To Molly's surprise, her glass was empty. She held it out for him to refill. Even though she couldn't help wincing every time she drank the stuff, gradually it was spreading a warm contentment through her veins. Tentatively she smiled up at Armand. He wasn't so bad. It was funny how nervous she had been about coming here. Now she felt almost at ease with this old Frenchman, with his smooth manners and precise speech. "*Merci beaucoup*," she said.

"What a charming girl you are," Armand said. "And really, your French is not at all bad for an English person. Tell me, how did you meet Fabrice?"

She gave him an edited version of their meeting on the boat and the things they had done together. Under his interested questioning, she found herself explaining how she'd come to Paris in the first place. That led back to Phipps Lauzer Bergman, her problems with Malcolm and her current unemployed status.

"But of course you resigned! That is an absurd position for someone like you." His robust indignation reminded her of Fabrice. "One asks oneself why you would ever accept such a job. It is, to me, unbelievable." His lips pursed as if he had just tasted a supermarket cheese. "Tell me, what is your talent?"

While she sipped her cognac, Armand drew her out, asking her about university, her enthusiasms and ambitions, the books she enjoyed. Molly tried to explain to him the frustrations of living at home, and her desire to do something exciting and independent.

Armand apologized for not having heard of Minster Episcopi. He had visited Great Britain many times, naturally, over many years, though principally its cities—London, Edinburgh (*Ay-dan-boor*), Birmingham. He found it bizarre that a country with so many inventive, even brilliant architects should contain so many ugly buildings. It was an interesting paradox on which he must reflect further. Personally he would find it insupportable to live in the provinces in any country. What, he wondered, did her parents *do?*"

"My father's dead. He died when I was a baby. My mother's a gardener, I suppose. At least, she grows plants and sells them, and she runs the vegetable garden on a big estate near us, and a few years ago she trained as a landscape designer. She's finally getting commissions for that—in fact, she won some prize thing last year—but it's taken her ages. The trouble is, where we are, everyone wants box hedging and lollipops and pleached limes and herbaceous borders." Molly's French collapsed here into sign language, and elaborate phrasings rather like Dr. Johnson's dictionary definitions (the trees of which the branches are twisted together so that they resemble an elevated wall of leaves, the trunks serving as legs), though Armand seemed to understand. "Unfortunately, my mum's into concrete, and strange grasses, and huge fields of the same plant."

"But that is very fashionable now."

"Is it? My mum's not very fashionable, that's for sure." Molly yawned. She must go back to the hotel before she fell asleep. But she was so comfortably wedged into the corner of the sofa that she couldn't summon up the energy to stir.

"She sounds a formidable woman, your mother. I suppose she must still be quite young, to have so much energy."

"Oh, no. She's forty-two."

Molly's eyelids drooped lower and lower as she listened to Armand explaining that the interrelation of buildings and landscape was more important now than ever before, because of the invention of new materials. There was a revolutionary type of glass in development, strong enough to build office blocks with, that could generate and recycle its own heat. Naturally, she could imagine the savings in energy consumption and pollution levels. Unfortunately the glass had a tendency to shatter. "But I must stop talking," Armand broke off. "You are tired, Molly."

"A bit." She yawned again. "Sorry. I must go." But all she did was sit there, blinking sleepily.

Armand sprang gracefully to his feet. "I will give you a little coffee to wake you up."

"No, really."

"I insist. Wait there. Do not be afraid that the beans are not freshly roasted. I purchased them myself from a place of good reputation in the *sixième*. The *patronne* is very sympathetic." He was out of sight now, but his voice drifted back to her in snatches: ". . . really excellent taste . . . the aroma at once distinctive and marvellously smooth . . . East Africa, I believe . . ."

Molly let her head flop against the cushioned back of the sofa and giggled dopily at the ceiling. She loved Paris. She loved the French. She loved Fabrice. Her eyes closed as she pictured herself telling him that there would be no trouble about the candle-snuffer. He would be so happy. Everything was so much clearer, now that she understood him better. Tomorrow would be another golden day. Maybe it was tomorrow already . . .

Her head slipped sideways onto the arm of the sofa. Her breathing slowed; her fingers uncurled. She did not feel Armand slipping the shoes from her feet and easing her into a more comfortable position, or the touch of a blanket floated gently across her sleeping body.

# 20

"Ooh, I feel a bit smashed," giggled Alicia, as she swayed on Malcolm's arm in the hotel corridor.

"'For mash get Smash,'" Malcolm warbled fruitily, while he tried to extract the key card from his jacket pocket and press it into the electronic lock. The red light lingered for an irritating second, then turned green. He turned the handle and shoved open the door. "*Aunt-tray*, Madame!" He swept a welcoming hand, and stumbled slightly. He might be a bit smashed, too. Alicia tripped past him, giving him a saucy look. *Oh, yes*. She was as good as his. His plaything. His slave. He paused to hang the "Do Not Disturb" sign on the door.

"Gotta take a whizzer," she said, confusing him for a moment until he saw the way she was wriggling about.

"Over there." He threw her an indulgent smile. They had plenty of time. Alicia tottered into the bathroom and closed the door. Malcolm unbuttoned his jacket and hung it over the back of a chair, then poured himself a Scotch from the mini-bar, and sank into the two-seater sofa by the window. He kicked off his slip-on shoes. It was going to be a long night. And there was a strong possibility of more to come. His mind drifted back to their conversation in the taxi. Apparently Alicia was planning to come to England—if she could get a job. But she needed an employer to sponsor her so that she could extend her visa. Otherwise, she was off back to Australia. Hmm . . . A brilliant idea was forming in Malcolm's mind. His head whirled with possibilities.

There was a flushing sound, and a moment later Alicia appeared round the bathroom door. She smiled beguilingly at him. "What a great show that was," she said. "We've got nothing like that back in Oz. I'm so grateful to you for taking me."

"How grateful?" He smiled wolfishly, and patted the space beside him on the sofa. "Come and sit down."

"I can't. Not yet. I feel so revved up. So . . . inspired by those beautiful girls. Don't you?" She rummaged in the boxes of Phipps Lauzer Bergman merchandise, pulled out an umbrella and opened it up, then danced around in a passable imitation of the now-you-see-it-now-you-don't number at the Crazy Horse. " 'I'm singing in the rain, just singing in the rain . . .' Hey, where's your hat, Malcolm?"

Excited, he jumped up, found the Crazy Horse baseball cap he'd purchased after the show and put it on.

"No, other way round," said Alicia, wrenching it round so that the peak was at the back. "Yay, you look like Leyton Hewitt. He's Australian, you know."

Malcolm bounced on his toes and swished an imaginary serve.

"Ace!" yelled Alicia. "Fifteen—love."

Malcolm attempted another full-blooded serve, but this time he overbalanced, cannoning into Alicia. She staggered and dropped the umbrella, but stayed on her feet. Good. He liked them strong. He grabbed her bare shoulders and swayed, trying to get his eyes to focus. "What would happen if I undid this safety pin, I wonder?"

"Why not try it and see?"

Feeling breathless, Malcolm fumbled with the pin. As he withdrew it, her dress slipped from her shoulders to the floor.

She was wearing matching black bra and thong. "God, Alicia, you're—" The words died in his throat. She was undoing his shirt buttons. "Eeny . . . meeny . . . miney . . . *mo*!" In one fluid movement she had peeled off his shirt and was waving it like a matador's cape. Malcolm put his fists to his head, stuck out his index fingers like miniature horns and charged. Just as he reached her she swayed to one side and he blundered past, falling head first onto the bed. "*Olé!*" Alicia tossed the shirt aside, rolled him onto his back, then unbuttoned his fly and began to draw his trousers down his legs. Christ! She didn't hang about.

"What groovy underpants, Malcolm." She gazed admiringly at his jockeys. "Is that the Red Cross? Help! Help! I need emergency treatment." She scampered round the room, flapping her hands. Malcolm, beside himself with excitement, leapt off the bed and strutted after her in his pants and socks, waving an imaginary sword. "My name is Maximus Dickus. Son of Thickus Dickus. Loyal servant of the Emperor Caesar Saladus," he growled in his *Gladiator* voice. "And. I. Will. Have. My. Bonk!" He tripped over the umbrella.

"Hey, wow. Good imitation. Russell Crowe's Australian, you know."

Glowing at her compliment, Malcolm decided to repeat his trick. "My name is Maximu—"

"No, Malcolm. I think it's time for another game, don't you?"

"Woof!"

"All right, then." She gave him a stern look and pointed to the bed. "Lie down."

"Yes, Mistress." He hurled himself onto the bed, bouncing happily. "Come and get me."

"Not yet. I'm afraid you're a little too lively. I may just have to restrain you."

Malcolm goggled at the ceiling. This was unreal!

"Now, what have we here?" Alicia was rooting through her bag. Malcolm watched in frozen horror and delight as she drew out a pair of handcuffs and whirled them experimentally round one finger. Passively he allowed her to swing back his arms and lock them to the slatted wooden bedhead. He lay there spread-eagled, watching her with mingled nervousness and anticipation. No one had ever done this to him before. Now she was climbing onto the bed, crawling across to him, throwing one leg over until she was sitting on his abdomen. She began tracing little patterns on his front, starting just below his neck and moving lower . . . lower . . .

The telephone rang. Malcolm convulsed, as if he'd been electrocuted. "Oh, shit! Quick! Untie me!"

But, to his horror, she reached calmly across his body and picked up the phone. "Hello? . . . Yes, he's here. May I ask who's calling? . . . Oh, Mrs. Figg! How're you doing?"

Malcolm kicked furiously, but Alicia kept her balance easily. They were probably used to bucking broncos in Australia. Her voice didn't even wobble as she said, "Of course. I'll hand you over."

She leaned forward, pressing her chest to his, and held the phone to his ear.

"Hello, Mum," he said, in a wavering voice.

"Whatever are you doing, Malcolm?" she asked suspiciously. "Who's that girl?"

He could picture her exactly, smoking a fag at the kitchen table, with her feet tucked underneath in fluffy slippers and her *Jumbo Book of Crosswords* open.

"I hope you're not doing anything you'd be ashamed to tell your mother," she said, taking an audible puff of her cigarette.

"No, no. Ha, ha. That's—that's—that's my new secretary." At these words Alicia bucked up and down on top of him and shot her arms triumphantly into the air, whisking the phone away. Malcolm jerked his head pleadingly. With a penitent smile she cradled it back against his ear. "We've, er . . . got a lot of work on," he said, trying to sound businesslike. "I told you, Mum, I'm giving a very important speech tomorrow."

"Oh, Malky, it's a wonder you're alive, the way that company works you. Now, how are you coping with that Paris? No trouble with your plumbing?"

"I'm fine, Mum," he mumbled.

"You can never tell what they're going to put on your plate in a foreign country. Did you find the Marmite sandwiches I packed for you?"

"Yes, Mum."

"Well, mind you look after yourself. Get that secretary of yours to order you some nice hot cocoa. Good night, then. Kissy-kiss."

Malcolm grunted.

"I said, *kissy-kiss*."

"Yeah . . . er . . . kissy-kiss," he muttered, barely moving his lips.

"Aw, isn't she sweet?" said Alicia, replacing the phone. "Now, where were we?"

Malcolm turned away his head. Talk about a passion killer. He felt as limp as a windsock with no wind. Alicia lay down on top of him again and stroked his hair. "Don't worry. I'll make you a lovely secretary." She gave him a smoochy kiss under his ear, on his jaw, at the corner of his mouth. "Who's a sulky boy?" she crooned. Slowly he turned his head back. He felt her lips on his. Maybe this would be all right, after all.

The phone rang again. Malcolm jumped. "Don't you bloody answer that!" he shouted.

"Goodness, you're busy. It's lucky you have me," Alicia told him, raising herself up and reaching for the phone again. "Hello? . . . yes . . . I'm afraid he's a little tied up now." She gave Malcolm a naughty wink. "Can I help?"

Her expression grew concentrated as she listened. "Who? . . . Oh, I see . . . Yes, as a matter of fact I do."

Malcolm thrashed wildly. What if it was Jerry?

"I'll be right down," she said, and hung up.

"Who was that? Down where? You can't go now."

But she had already climbed off him and was starting to put on her dress. "Sorry, Malcolm, but I can't stay. We'll have to continue our game another time."

Malcolm stared at her in disbelief, then yanked at his bonds in fury. "You bitch! Let me go!"

"Now, now, Malcolm, you know I don't like bad language. Trust me, you'll soon be unlocked." She smiled at him winningly. "You and I are going to make a great team. I just know that we're going to work *sooo* well together." Now she'd found a pen and was scrawling something on a pad. "There we go: my phone number. I'll put it by the bed. Call me when you have a hand free."

Malcolm roared with rage and rattled his handcuffs.

"Oh, yes." She reached inside her bag and took out a small silver key. "Hmm, where shall I leave this?" Her eyes fell on his jockey shorts. "There," she said, slipping it inside as Malcolm writhed furiously. "That should be easy enough to find."

She fastened the safety pin over her shoulder, then turned to go. "Oh, I nearly forgot. Your cocoa!"

"I don't want any cocoa!" he shouted. "Let me go! You can't leave me like this."

"You're absolutely right." Alicia picked up the phone. "Hello, Room Service? Could you please send up some hot chocolate? Yes, right away. *Tout de suite*. Oh, and bring a pass key, would you? Monsieur Figg is indisposed and can't get out of bed."

She blew him a kiss and swept out of the room.

# 21

Hurry! He was waiting for her. She mustn't be late.

Molly was on the streets of an unfamiliar city, struggling through a dense, swirling crowd. Her progress was agonizingly slow and effortful. The gray road in front of her turned into a rocky gorge, then a river, which she had to swim. Stumbling up the far bank she tried to squeeze the water from her hair. There were gallons of it, pouring as if from a fountain. Panic gripped her. How could she turn up with wet hair?

Now the building was in front of her, with an imposing façade and stone steps leading up to the entrance. But they were so steep! How inconsiderate of the architect to design them like this. She had to haul herself up with nails and knees. Inside, it was a cavernous, uncompleted shell, littered with planks and rubble. High gantries crisscrossed above her head. The rickety staircase she was climbing had no banisters. Never mind. *Quick!* She must get there on time. At the end of a long, featureless corridor, she could see the door she wanted. An official waited to check her documents. But where had they gone? She searched in her bag, which had turned into a huge suitcase full of extraneous objects: her school science overall (what was that doing here?), Alleluia's squeaky toy in the shape of a rubber Christmas cracker (so *that*'s where it had gone). "I'm Molly," she insisted, through tears of desperation. "Molly Clearwater. He's expecting me."

Suddenly she was out on the streets again, chasing the back view of a figure walking briskly away from her, already half lost in the crowd. "Wait!" she called. "I'm coming." But her limbs were impossibly heavy, as if weighted with wet sand. She couldn't see properly. Her eyes were gummed half shut. She pulled at the lids, trying to stretch them open. A warning siren sounded urgently. That was the departure signal for his train. He was leaving! She was too late. Too late . . .

Molly woke with a gasp. Her face jerked free of some soft material pressed to her nose. What was that noise? Where was she? She sat up, heartbeat scudding. The shapes around her resolved themselves into Armand's furniture, standing calm and solid in the seeping morning light. This was Armand's sofa; she must have fallen asleep here last night. The noise was her phone, but even as she looked round for her bag, the beeping stopped. Molly rubbed her hands over her face and pushed back her hair, damp with sweat. Sinking against the cushions, she blew out a great sigh of relief, and waited for her pulse to slow. It was only a dream. The Dream. It came from time to time, maybe every few months, maybe once a year. Though the details varied, there was always the same dreadful mix of anxiety, frustration and despair, and always the same strange gray half-light that seemed to foretell the hopelessness of her quest.

She threw off her blanket and stood up, wanting to escape the mood of her dream. She crossed the room in bare feet, opened the windows, then the shutters, and leaned out. Her heart lifted at the ravishing scene laid out before her: trees and domes, curving bridges, boats on the river. It was another sparkling day, tinted gold and blue. The air was fresh, and joyful with the sound of church bells. Of course: it was Sunday.

There was a knock at the door. "Molly? Are you awake?" It was Armand.

"Yes. Come in," she called, and turned back into the room. She could already smell the coffee that he now carried in on a tray. There were two large, steaming cups, a bowl of sugar lumps, and a small basket of croissants and brioches. Armand looked dapper in a pale gray suit with a navy shirt. Molly tried to pull her dress straight. Sleeping in her clothes had given her an unpleasant, sticky feeling, as if her skin had gone moldy. Her mouth felt furry.

"You slept well?" he asked, setting down the tray.

"Very. I can't believe I fell asleep. Thank you for the blanket."

He shrugged, releasing a waft of cologne so strong Molly almost flinched. "What are your plans for today?" he asked. "May I drive you somewhere?"

Molly munched the crispy tail of her croissant. It was the most delicious one she'd ever tasted, sweet and buttery under its nut-brown glaze. "I don't know," she said vaguely, trying to gather her thoughts. "Oh! My phone. There was a message," she explained. "Do you mind if I look?"

She located her bag, pulled out her mobile and jabbed the button with her thumb. "Pik u up ur hotel 10.30. DON'T BE L8! Loads 2 tellya. xxx Alicia." Molly gave a squeak of panic. God, Rollerblading! She'd forgotten about that. What time was it? To her relief it was only nine fifteen, but she needed to return to the hotel, have a shower, get changed. "I've got to go in a minute," she told Armand, hastily stuffing more croissant into her mouth and swilling it down with milky coffee.

"I will drive you."

"No, please. It's not very far. I'm sure you have other things to do."

But he was insistent. His car was parked just outside. He liked driving in Paris—when, that is, the roads weren't shut off for cyclists and those *foutu* Rollerbladers. The mayor was an idiot. His latest crazy scheme was to turn the main riverside highway into a beach every summer—a *beach*, in the name of God, with thousands of tons of sand dumped on the pavements, full-grown palm trees in pots, sun-loungers, parasols, children making sandcastles, their parents drinking, even *dancing* in outdoor cafés, while the rest of Paris fumed in traffic jams. Imagine! Molly made tut-tutting noises. She thought it sounded wonderful.

Armand's car was small but luxurious, with deep leather seats and the sort of absurdly loud engine noise men seemed to like. He drove insanely fast, apparently oblivious to traffic lights, bollards and pedestrians, keeping one hand permanently poised on the horn. It was too hair-raising to watch the road; instead, Molly looked out of her side window, surprised to see how many people were out on the streets and how formally dressed they were. Sunday in England was a relaxed, unbuttoned day for car-washing, going to the pub, or constructing some infernal DIY kit in the back garden. Here, pairs of women in old-fashioned black dresses walked composedly arm in arm, presumably to church. Children were immaculate in white leather shoes, pressed shorts, beautiful dresses with smocking and full skirts. She saw both women and men, elegantly dressed, bowling down the street with gaiety in their step, dangling beribboned boxes. Having stopped to gaze at the displays in *pâtisserie* windows, she could guess what would be inside: a perfect fruit tart, the slices meticulously arranged in concentric circles and shiny with glaze, or perhaps a cake topped with a layer of chocolate as smooth and hard as ice, decorated with a spider's web of spun sugar. All the small shops seemed open. There was a pleasing bustle in the air. Only the tourists shambled about in trainers and sloppy clothes, encumbered with bulging bags.

With a squeal of tires Armand veered off a broad avenue, then turned up the street where her hotel was, racing between twin rows of parked cars as if they were walls of flame. When Molly pointed out her entrance, he came to a rocking halt, reversed onto the pavement opposite and yanked up the handbrake in front of a no-parking sign. She was still trying to find the door handle when he came round to usher her out of the car and across the street, deaf to her protestations. "*Oui, oui.* The roads are so dangerous here. Some people, you know, drive like maniacs."

One of the hotel cats sat on the reception desk, haughty and still. Behind it, Madame was shelling beans on her broad lap. Seeing Molly, she set them aside and rose to her feet. "*Bonjour*, Mademoiselle," she said, in the high-pitched chirrup that seemed common to all French women.

"*Bonjour*, Madame. The key, if you please." Molly rather liked the formality of these exchanges. She had turned to Armand with a smile, already formulating the words to thank him, to apologize for yesterday's hotheaded words, when she became aware that there was a problem.

"It's room fifty-eight, isn't it?" Madame asked.

"Yes, that's right."

"But the key is missing! Look for yourself." With a grunt of effort she twisted her squat body to point at an empty hook above her head. "Perhaps you took it with you yesterday evening?"

"No." Molly shook her head, suppressing a sigh of impatience. She was in a hurry and she felt grubby.

"*Mais alors*. Where could it have gone?" Madame raised her shoulders in a gesture of outraged amazement.

Armand stepped up to the desk, puffing out his chest. How could the key be missing? he demanded. His friend was a young woman, alone. There were issues of security.

Madame understood completely. Perhaps her husband knew something. Unfortunately he had just gone out to the market to buy a Bresse chicken.

A Bresse chicken? Armand's attention sharpened. Chickens from Bresse really were the best, weren't they? The flavor, the succulence—especially with a little spoonful of vermouth added halfway through the cooking. He kissed his fingertips.

Madame had never tried vermouth, though she had heard people speak of it. She preferred lemon.

Really? Lemon was, of course, traditional, especially in the South, but—

Molly shifted restlessly. "Er, the key . . ."

Of course, the key. Yes, yes, the key! It was possible that the maid had taken it for some reason, though that was irregular since she had her own set. Still, that must be the explanation. Probably she was in the room now, doing a *petit* tidy.

As Madame was reluctant to leave Reception unattended, it was agreed that Armand should accompany Molly upstairs to check that this was the case. They rode up together in the creaking lift. Lemon was all very well, he told her, but there was no question that vermouth was superior. He confessed to being very much surprised by what Madame had said.

Molly had noticed that the maids usually left the doors open when they were cleaning, so it was with a sinking heart that she saw her own door was shut. How was she going to get in? Worse, what if someone had lifted the key and pinched all her belongings? A burglar might be in there right now! She stood irresolutely in front of the door. "You knock," she said to Armand. He reached out and gave a peremptory rat-tat. Molly heard a thud, a scuffle of feet, a hand fumbling at the latch. Then the door was flung open by a woman with bare feet, stripy blonde-brown hair clipped awry on top of her head, and a long ethnic-print skirt that Molly recognized only too clearly. "*Mum!*" she shrieked.

The next minute she was smothered in hair and a familiar smell of organic lavender soap. "Oh, Molly darling, where have you been? I've been so worried. Thank goodness you're still alive."

"Of course I'm still alive! What are you doing here?" Molly struggled to escape from her mother's embrace.

"But how was I to know? You didn't ring. You didn't answer your phone. No one would tell me where you were. I was frantic." She cupped Molly's face in her hands and stroked her cheek. "My little Molly. My darling. My baby. Where on earth did you get that dress?"

"I am not a baby! For God's sake, all I did was come to Paris for a bloody weekend."

"But not with your work. That Figg person told me he'd fired you."

"So? I came anyway."

"Why didn't you tell me?"

"Why should I tell you?"

"I'm your mother! I love you. I've been lying awake all night, imagining the most ghastly—" She broke off suddenly, catching sight of something over Molly's shoulder. Her skin paled. Her features tightened into a grim mask. "Who," she demanded, "is that man?"

Belatedly Molly remembered Armand, who was hovering in the corridor with a polite half-smile on his face, apparently fascinated by the architrave detailing of her door. "I'm so sorry, Armand." She took his arm and drew him forward. "This is my mother. *Ma mère*." God, what language was she supposed to be speaking? "Mum, this is Armand. I spent the night at his place, okay?"

"Oh did you?" Ignoring Armand's outstretched hand, Molly's

mother threw back her head and stepped up to him like a rooster confronting a peacock. "And why didn't she sleep in her own bed last night, may I ask? Have you seduced my daughter?" A tuft of hair, poking out of the clip, trembled furiously. "You should be ashamed of yourself. A man of your age. Do you realize that my daughter is only twenty-one? *Twenty-one!*"

"Mum!" Molly yanked desperately at her mother's arm.

"How could you take advantage of a young girl, far from home, abroad for the first time in her life? No doubt it was easy to dazzle her with your sophisticated French ways. I admit my values seem old-fashioned to some, but I know what's right and what's wrong, and I am not afraid to speak my mind."

"For God's sake, shut up!" Molly yelled, crimson with embarrassment. "We have not been to bed together," she hissed into her mother's ear. "He's the father of someone I met. *Father*, got that? I fell asleep on his sofa. He's been extremely kind to me."

"Oh." Her mother looked disconcerted for a moment. Then she gave the daft laugh that other people thought was so charming but made Molly cringe in public, and held out her hand to Armand. "I'm so sorry. Very nice to meet you."

Armand was magnificent. He acted as if the previous minute had simply not existed. Gallantly grasping Molly's mother's hand and giving his most urbane smile, he said in dreadful English, "You are ze muzzer of Molly? *Impossible*." Now he turned to Molly in wonderment, his eyebrows practically at his hairline, and stage-whispered, "But she is so young! Now I see where Molly gets her character," he continued, piling it on thick. "She is a most charming girl, Madame Clearwater. I congratulate you."

"Oh, please, call me Fran." Her mother was practically simpering. This was pitiful. Molly longed to get rid of them both.

"Of course you are concerned about your daughter, Fran." Without Molly quite understanding how, Armand had steered them all into the bedroom and drawn her mother across to the window. "I, too, worry about my son, Fabrice, with whom Molly has spent a little time this weekend. He is twenty-three. A very talented boy, but, *euh*, *têtu*, you know?"

"Stubborn?"

"*Exactement*. But you speak French, Fran!"

"Not really."

"The young are so difficult to advise, these days."

"Oh, I agree . . ."

Blah, blah. Off they went on the usual parentspeak: the modern world, so many temptations . . . so much more dangerous . . . spoiled . . . materialism. When they were young . . .

Molly scowled at them, feeling aggrieved. Armand now had her mother pinned against the window, mesmerizing her with his repertoire of shrugs, pouts and weaving hands. They made a hilarious pair: Armand, man of the world, ridiculously smart, not a hair out of place; and her mother in that dreadful old T-shirt that had shrunk to nothing, looking absurdly healthy and wild-haired as if she'd just run in from the garden. Molly felt a sudden wrench of fondness. She did love her mother. It was lovely to see her. *But not now*.

She stomped over to grab her sponge bag and towel, avoiding an object dumped on the floor. Her mother had brought her backpack! How embarrassing. "Sorry, everyone," she announced, "but I'm going to have to change now, or I'll be late."

"Where are you going?" fluttered her mother. "Now that I'm here, can't we go out and have coffee or something?"

"No. I'm going Rollerblading—"

"Rollerblading! But, darling, that's so dangerous."

"Ah, yes, these appalling *patineurs*. They are ruining Paris. One takes one's life in one's hands, simply walking down the pavement."

"As I say, I'm going Rollerblading. Then I'm meeting Fabrice. After that I'll—well, I'll be busy."

"Doing what? Haven't you any time to spend with me?"

"My train goes at quarter to seven, Mum. I'll be rushing as it is."

"I'll see if I can change my ticket. Then we can travel home together and have a lovely chat."

For a moment Molly wondered if she had screamed aloud. Then she realized that a message had bleeped onto her phone. It was probably Alicia, already *en route* to pick her up. She must hurry! What was she going to wear? It wouldn't be possible for her to change after Rollerblading, and she had to look nice for Fabrice. And she had to pack! And check out of the hotel! Her mind spinning with anxiety, Molly clicked up the message. "Molly—Must see you. Important. Will be waiting in the Luxembourg Gardens today 3–4 p.m. by pond. Please come. A Friend."

Molly gave an exasperated sigh. Who was this weirdo? She didn't even know where the Luxembourg Gardens were. There wouldn't be time for anyone this afternoon except Fabrice. Too bad. Nevertheless, there was something heartfelt in the tone that touched her. It didn't sound like Malcolm.

"Who was that, Mollypops?" her mother asked nosily.

"No one," Molly snapped, clearing the screen. The clock on her phone read 10:19. "I must get a move on."

"*Alors*, Fran." Armand laid a coaxing hand on her mother's elbow. "Molly has much to think about. As for me, I have a very boring day ahead of me. It would give me much pleasure to show you Paris, to compensate for your terrible worry."

"Oh, well, that's very . . . But I don't . . ."

"We can rendezvous with Molly later. My car is outside. I will wait there while you prepare yourself."

"But I haven't anything . . ."

"Brilliant idea," Molly said firmly. "Go for it, Mum."

# 22

"So there he was, laid out on the bed like a possum on the barbie, when the phone goes again and the guy on the desk says there's a Mrs. Clearwater downstairs, asking about her daughter, and would Mr. Figg know anything about it? Bloody hell!" Alicia suddenly broke off. "Look at the size of those pumpkins, Moll."

They were walking together toward the Rollerblading place, along the same boulevard they had taken to Zabi's flat on Friday night, though today it had turned into a street market crammed with such sumptuous produce that Molly was stunned and enraptured. Back home, the "market" was a litter-strewn car-park tainted with burger smells and the whine of country-and-western music, where loud-mouthed hicks flogged off scabbed apples and dubious meat frozen into Family Packs, and you could buy loo rolls in bulk, polythene-wrapped bricks of gelatinous "Cheddar," and T-shirts that disintegrated at the first wash, printed with witty messages like "I Just Did It" or "Barbie Is a Slut." Its Paris equivalent was a sensuous wonderland of perfect greengages and figs, oysters and flowers, silvery fish still panting through crimson gills, chalky goat's cheese with cobweb crusts. Plane trees with mottled bark cast their shade on fresh walnuts, damp and wrinkled as newborn babies, grapes like translucent marbles, vine-tomatoes cascading from display stands, the pink gash of a watermelon split in half to show off its juicy flesh. The stalls were run by formidable matrons in snowy aprons, and fishmongers spruced up in sailor suits, conjuring with knives, who called everyone Madame or Monsieur. Instead of the pram-pushing moving mountains shouting, "If you do that one more time, Ryan, I'll kill you!" the shoppers here were keen as truffle-hounds, darting from stall to stall to sniff melons, taste cheese, savor an inky olive, or press a delicate thumb to the rumps of pears. Alicia was right about the pumpkins: some of them looked almost big enough for Cinderella to step right into and trot off to the ball.

"Never mind the pumpkins. Go on about last night," Molly urged.

"Well, naturally, I pricked up my ears at the name Clearwater, and nipped down to see what was going on. There was this poor woman practically in tears, convinced that Malcolm was holding you prisoner in his bedroom."

They caught each other's eye and spluttered into giggles. Molly was still reeling from Alicia's story of the handcuff trick.

"We shouldn't laugh," said Alicia. "Your mum was really upset."

"But she's such a fusspot! I'd barely been gone a day."

"Come on. She loves you. You're all she's got. And she looked so sweet and pretty standing in that huge lobby with her backpack and that funny old skirt."

Molly winced. "Her wardrobe hasn't changed since about 1980."

"I think she's cool. The hippie look's fashionable at the moment. Look at me." Alicia threw out her arms to show off her fringed jacket and tasselled cowboy boots, and accidentally bashed her hand into the arm of a man standing over a small brazier. "Oops. *Pardon!*"

"Look, he's roasting chestnuts," said Molly. "Let's buy some."

They watched him shuffle the chestnuts on the glowing heat until they attained the correct mixture of pale gold and charred black, then scoop them up with a perforated spatula and pour them into a cone of paper. "*Voilà,*" he said tenderly, offering the cone to Molly with a flourish. She handed over a coin and received the hot, sweet-smelling parcel.

"But why did you send her to my hotel?" Molly asked, through a mouthful of crumbly chestnut. "I could have been—you know—with Fabrice."

"She was worried about money, and she didn't know where to go. I blagged Monsieur into giving me your room key. Anyway, you told me you were going back to Fabrice's place to 'you know.' Honestly, Moll, why can't you say 'shag' like everyone else? How was it, anyway? Got any love-bites?" She flicked aside Molly's hair and peered at her neck.

"Get off." Molly smoothed her hair into place. "It was fine. In fact, it was wonderful." A smile curled her mouth as she remembered yesterday afternoon. She hesitated over telling Alicia the truth about what had happened afterward. It was too complicated to explain. Alicia wouldn't understand.

A delicious smell was wafting from some electrical contraption set out on the street, where glossy golden chickens roasted on multiple spits. They reminded Molly of something. "What about Malcolm? Wasn't he furious to be left tied up like that?"

"Yeah, he was pretty mad. He called me this morning and shouted a bit, but to tell you the truth I think he enjoyed it. Probably wants to get in touch with his feminine side." Alicia gave a whoop of laughter. "No, seriously, he's already talking about our next session—only he gets to tie me up. And guess what?" She stopped dramatically. "I'm coming to England!"

"No! That's fantastic." Molly threw her arms around Alicia, who hugged her back with enthusiasm. They swayed together, making excited little shrieks, while the French picked their way past, eyeing them with disapproval. "When?" she demanded. "How come? What about your visa problem?"

"Solved," Alicia said smugly. "Thanks to Malcolm I've now got a sponsor and a job."

"Brilliant! Have another chestnut. You deserve it."

But when Molly discovered exactly whose job Alicia had got, she couldn't help feeling secretly miffed. Alicia was great, of course, but she didn't have a degree, let alone a first-class one. Could she even spell?

"Do you think you'll be all right?" she asked, trying to be tactful. "I mean, have you got any, er, qualifications?"

"Bookkeeping, payroll, tractor maintenance, catering," Alicia reeled off. "Advanced word-processing, switchboard, first aid, life-saving, plus a few more I've forgotten. But that kind of job is just common sense, really, isn't it?"

"Mm," Molly said faintly. For the first time it occurred to her that she might not have been as brilliant an employee as she had thought.

"You're worried I don't know Shakespeare backward, aren't you?" Alicia teased.

"No, no. I'm not. I just wondered how you'd managed to learn all those things out in the bush."

"What bush?"

"Your little town, Tullmarino or whatever it's called."

At this point Alicia cracked up so much she had to cling to a lamppost and cross her legs to stop herself peeing with laughter. Tullamarine, she explained, was a suburb of Melbourne, site of the Melbourne airport; in other words, about as rural as Hounslow. And while she was at it, no, Australians did not really cook possums on the barbecue—although they wouldn't say no to a baby koala baked in tinfoil.

"Ha ha," Molly said grumpily, feeling foolish.

Alicia flung an arm affectionately across her shoulders. "You know what, Molly? You need to get out more. Stop reading so many books. Loosen up. Be brave. You're a gorgeous, crazy girl, with a brain the size of the Northern Territory, and the whole world is out there, waiting for you. At home in Tulla, I used to sun-bake out the back, watching those planes take off and land, land and take off, until I knew that if I didn't get on one I'd be stuck in Australia and the same old way of thinking about things for the rest of my life. And now look!" She stopped, and swept her arm in an arc as if to show off the view all round them.

Molly stopped too, and turned to face the way they had come. The market scene was like a wonderful painting, serene and yet full of life, composed of Matisse-like oranges and greens and dusky purples, and jolted into vibrancy by the figure of a statuesque black woman sailing toward them, dressed from head-wrap to heels in zinging yellow. In the other direction, a narrowing line of trees, interrupted here and there by the pearly gray of buildings and scarlet splashes of window-box geraniums, led the eye toward a column, on top of which a statue blazed gold against an azure sky.

"What is that?" asked Molly. "Who's the figure on top?" She'd seen a sign for place de la Bastille, and wondered if the monument had something to do with the French Revolution.

"I dunno. Probably some king or other. All I know is, they have a bloody good party there every July."

Soon they had left the market behind, crossed the square, and were walking along a street overlooking a marina formed from an inlet of the Seine. Small boats bobbed at anchor, their brightly painted hulls reflected in the green water. "That's where I'm kipping at the moment." Alicia pointed. "See that old wreck with the bike on top, and the Ozzie flag?"

"How romantic!"

"If you like damp, cold and rats, it is. It's just as well I'm coming to London before winter sets in."

"Er, yes. I've been meaning to ask you." Molly hesitated. "I'm sure you've got millions of friends in London, and my flat is very small, and not in a very exciting part of London—"

"Spit it out, girl."

"Well, if you wanted to sleep on my floor, or the sofa, I'd love it."

"Yay! Thought you'd never ask."

"When do you think you'll be coming?"

"Maybe in a month or so. It'll take Malcolm a little while to sort out the paperwork and send me a formal job offer. Anyway, I still have some traveling to do. I'm dying to go to Salzburg for the *Sound of Music* tour."

"What—you mean you're, er, keen on Mozart?"

"For God's sake, Moll, of course I don't mean bloody Mozart. *The Sound of Music*, capital letters. *Lederhosen*. Julie Andrews. Yodelling. Some cheeseball guide takes you on a bus tour to all the locations where the film was shot so you can take piccies. Everyone sings the songs, and you can dress up as a nun if you want. Or a Nazi—but that's pretty gross. Afterward, they give you a free packet of edelweiss seeds. I can't wait!"

Molly could now see a giant sign in the shape of a Rollerblade, hanging from a building ahead. Outside, a crowd of people milled around, trying on blades, screeching as they wobbled down the pavement clutching the wall, or showily spinning in the street, impudently oblivious of passing cars. Molly's stomach tightened. She had a horrible feeling she was about to make a fool of herself.

She followed Alicia inside a cavernous space that might once have been a garage but was now fitted out with a desk, racks of rollerblades, and long benches where people could try them on. Some kind of French rap music was playing on the stereo. Alicia said "hi" or "*salut*" to about a million people, and told Molly to pay the guy at the desk while she hunted out some blades and checked who was in her group today. Armed with a clipboard, she bristled with efficiency and natural authority.

Eventually, Molly was kitted out with blades, a helmet, and pads to protect her elbows and knees. As she sat on the bench, snapping the last clasp of her boots into place, she could see Alicia outside rounding up her flock, swaying up and down the street with effortless grace. It didn't look too difficult. Molly stood up boldly. A millisecond later, her legs shot out from under her and she sat down again, very hard, thumping onto the edge of the bench. It hurt like hell. "Lean forward a little. Bend your knees," advised one of the instructors. Very slowly Molly stood upright again and half shuffled, half teetered outside, feeling like a giant ape that had just celebrated its hundredth birthday. She cursed her mother for refusing to buy her Rollerblades—all the other kids had them—on the basis that it would be a ridiculous expense when Molly's feet were growing so fast.

Alicia was in charge of the so-called English-speaking group, which in practice meant anyone who wasn't French. Apart from Molly, it included two chunky American boys with floppy hair and at least a hundred teeth between them; a weird-looking Norwegian man with a forehead like a tombstone slab; and three over-excited Japanese girls, mewing like kittens, with cameras strapped to their waists in padded cases. There was also an

Italian girl and her boyfriend, both oozing sexiness in skintight leather, who stood moodily aloof from the rest, like movie stars unaccountably downgraded to economy class. Alicia gave them all a demonstration of some basic techniques and a brief safety lecture, then they set off down the pavement, a brood of ducklings stumbling and lurching after their mother. Molly was definitely the worst. Sport had never been her *forte* at school.

"Enjoying yourself?" asked Alicia, when they slithered to a halt at a pedestrian crossing and waited for the little light to turn green.

"It's great." Molly smiled through gritted teeth, hugging a lamppost.

"Don't worry. We'll be away from the cars in a sec, and you can let rip. Soon you'll be whizzing along like a pro."

Sure enough, they came to a metal barrier across the road, behind which cyclists and Rollerbladers sailed along an empty highway. Molly had to admit that the idea of shutting down whole areas of a city just so people could enjoy themselves was rather fantastic. According to Alicia, the French were besotted with Rollerblading. Every Friday night, as many as ten thousand people set off from somewhere on the Left Bank and roamed miles across Paris in one great, rolling tidal wave.

Molly herself was not rolling. She clumped, she lurched. She flailed and stumbled. Worst of all, she seemed to have attracted the interest of the Norwegian guy, who stayed glued to her side as she lagged further and further behind. "Hello, my name is Odmund," he said, in a weird, warbling accent that made his vowel-sounds skid sideways. "I like your body."

"Oh. Thank you very much." His eyes were the very pale blue of madmen and mystics. When he spoke, he had the unnerving habit of rolling them upward until the whites showed, and fluttering his lashes as if he was going to faint. He began to confide to Molly his theory that the lost island of Atlantis was located somewhere off the coast of Ireland.

His soft, creepy voice was suddenly drowned by a scream of rage. "Oy, you bitch! Come back!" The next thing Molly knew, a girl in a red sweater whizzed past her on Rollerblades, heading back toward the barrier. Behind her, in furious pursuit, raced a black-haired, slitty-eyed witch on wheels. "Alicia!" Molly called in astonishment.

"Janine! My Rollerblades!" Alicia yelled in explanation as she shot past. Her voice floated back to Molly in snatches. "Keep everyone here . . . don't lose . . . relying on you, Moll . . ."

The rest of the group, agog at the drama, had turned back. "Right," said Molly, as they approached. "Er . . ." No one was listening anyway. They were all watching the chase. Janine had passed the barrier now, and was heading for a brick archway under what looked like a raised railway line. But instead of continuing under it, she came to a jolting stop by one of the brick supports, and started clumping up a stone staircase. Alicia, who was about thirty feet behind her, did the same.

"It's not a railroad," said one of the Americans. "Look! I can see people and trees. Come on, let's go help Alicia."

"No. Please," Molly begged. "She wants us to stay here, to stay together. We mustn't just . . . no, seriously, you can't . . ." Her voice petered into hopelessness as the two boys headed determinedly toward the staircase, followed by the Japanese girls, who had taken out their cameras and were deliriously snapping photos of everything in sight. Meanwhile, Molly noticed that the Italians were sloping off in the opposite direction. "Hang on, where are you going?" she yelled desperately. The girl looked back and twitched her shoulder in a languid, who-wants-to-know shrug. To the café, she said. They needed an espresso.

Molly's head swung one way, then the other, then back again.

What should she do? The Italians could look after themselves, she decided, and plunged in the direction of the steps, closely accompanied by Odmund. By the time she got there, the Americans and Japanese had vanished. She didn't fancy climbing those steps on rollerblades. Besides, she'd just noticed a sign with a line drawn through a picture of a skating-boot. Rollerblading was forbidden: she didn't want to break the law. "We'll wait here," she told Odmund, glad that she'd be able to produce at least one member of the group when Alicia returned. She lowered herself carefully onto the bottom step. Odmund sat down uncomfortably close beside her, and fixed her with his mad eyes. The people of Atlantis, you see, had red hair (flutter, flutter). A mysteriously large proportion of Irish people had red hair, too, though they were supposed to be black-haired Celts. Had it never occurred to Molly to wonder whether, even now perhaps, the people of Atlantis rose from their sea-dwelling to mate with the natives?

Molly stood up. "Don't move," she commanded, raising her finger to Odmund as if ordering a dog to stay. Clinging to the hand-rail she dragged and panted her way to the top of the steps, and found herself on a broad tarmacked walkway, bordered with small trees and flowerbeds rampant with roses and shrubs. Obviously it had once been an elevated railway, now transformed for the people of Paris to enjoy a quiet stroll above the busy streets. She could see archways flowing with late clematis and flaming vines, the gleam of a shallow decorative pond, benches conveniently positioned to admire the view of rooftops and distant spires. Mothers pushed prams, toddlers toddled, lovers canoodled, women gossiped arm in arm, a solitary middle-aged man paused to smell a rose. It was all extremely charming. The only trouble was that the walkway led in both directions, and Molly had no idea which Alicia had taken.

She hobbled over to a bench and sat down, feeling defeated. Out of the eight people Alicia had asked her to look after, she now had charge of precisely none. What if one broke a leg and Alicia was fired for negligence? Molly sank her head into her hands and closed her eyes. *Have you met Molly Clearwater? The useless friend? The stupid secretary? The little baby whose mother chased after her to Paris, tee-hee? Leadership skills, zero. Rollerblading skills, zero. Oh, and by the way, she has a purple bruise on her bum.*

Molly sighed, and opened her eyes, blinking in the sunshine. At least she could practice her Rollerblading, and perhaps find some of the group at the same time. She stood up and decided to take the leftward route leading toward the pond. Lean forward, bend your knees, push one foot away from the other. She set off carefully. This wasn't too bad. Actually, she was doing rather well. It was easier if you went faster, and there seemed to be a bit of a slope here. Whee! Still: not too fast. Where were the brakes? Help! She'd forgotten how to stop, and was heading straight for the pond!

Everything now happened very fast. Molly tried to steer to one side of the pond, only to see a small child right in her path, examining something on the ground. Veering too sharply the other way, she lost her balance. Her arms windmilled wildly. At the same time a red blur shot out of nowhere. Molly could feel herself falling. She toppled sideways, legs sprawling, desperately grabbing at the air. Her fingers latched onto something solid, then a body crashed into her, spun away and disappeared. There was a shriek, then a loud splash. Scrambling to her hands and knees, Molly realized to her horror that she had tripped someone into the pond. "Oh, God, sorry. *Pardon, pardon,*" she said, to the thrashing, spluttering figure.

To complete her humiliation, Alicia arrived on the scene at this moment, looking like Boadicea on E and yelling something that sounded like "Rip her!" Since the Americans and Japanese had just straggled into sight, Molly wondered if she was urging them to tear her limb from limb. One of the Japanese girls darted forward, arms raised. Molly flinched, but the girl was only taking her picture. Then Molly noticed a funny thing. Alicia was smiling. In fact, she was grinning from ear to ear. "Ripper!" she repeated, her eyes shining with triumph and admiration. "Molly, you star! You've caught Janine."

# 23

Molly was so keen to see Fabrice that she tripped on her way up the stairs from the Métro, and fell ignominiously onto concrete steps littered with discarded tickets. She picked herself up and dusted off the knees of her jeans: more bruises. And what about her hair? She paused in the shelter of the exit to brush it vigorously, although her work was soon undone as she emerged onto the pavement of a broad, drafty street. "Boulevard St-Germain," read a sign: wasn't that supposed to be famous? A haunt of intellectuals? All she could see were cars and tourists. Having found her bearings, Molly turned up a side street, exaggerating the confident briskness of her walk to demonstrate (should anyone be watching) that she was herself virtually a native. She had a real French boyfriend—no, a lover: that sounded much more grown-up—gorgeous, sexy, charming (mostly), and an artist to boot. Ha!

Of course, he might still be a bit cross with her; she must expect that. Anyone would be embarrassed to be caught out as he had been, and perhaps she hadn't handled the situation very well. Molly felt a squirm of disquiet. Had she appeared priggish? Fabrice might feel—all right, he did feel—that she had gone behind his back and sneaked to his father. But she'd been right, hadn't she? He would understand that she'd done it for him, because she cared about him. Thinking about the way Fabrice's hair slithered down over his temples and the caress of his eyes, picturing his lean brown fingers reaching for her, made her ache to show him just how much she cared.

A square opened up in front of her, dominated by a white stone church of double-decker colonnades and arches, with Italian-looking belfries on top, gaily sprouting weeds. This must be Saint Sulpice. There was a grand fountain in the middle, where a couple of backpackers sat munching enormous sandwiches wrapped in paper. Water gushed from the open mouths of lions and cascaded over stone tiers into pale gold pools. Miniature rainbows danced in the spray. Once again Molly felt herself moved by the lavish beauty of this city. Every corner sprang a trap, ensnaring her eyes and heart.

But where was Café Balzac? "Near" Saint Sulpice, he had said. Molly set off to circumnavigate the square in case it was hidden behind the trees, and checked her watch in rising anxiety. It was nearly one thirty. She wished Fabrice had not been so vague. Catching her reflection in a shop window (Yves St. Laurent!), she realized that this was the first time in the whole weekend that she was dressed entirely in her own clothes: indigo jeans, a favorite long-sleeved T-shirt in pale pink splashed with funky roses, and cheapo Marks & Spencer boots in somewhat scuffed black suede. The contrast she made with the mannequins, staring back with the haughty conviction of their own skeletal elegance, was undeniable. But Fabrice liked her as she was, curves and all. She had "a sensational body." Molly repeated the treasured words, then groped in her bag and gave herself a boost of perfume, just to be on the safe side. As she cocked her head to avoid stinging her eyes, she noticed a white awning down a side-street, on which the word "Balzac" swayed in and out of focus on a gentle breeze. With a breath of relief, she hurried toward it.

The pavement outside was lined with bentwood chairs and tiny round tables, thronged with people. She could hear the lively ripple of conversation as she approached, and saw sunglasses flash in her direction as she slowed to scan the figures. None was Fabrice. Stepping into the entrance, Molly found her path blocked by a waiter stowing a corkscrew in the pocket of his long apron. He raised an eyebrow inquiringly. "I'm looking . . . I have a friend." She pointed vaguely to the interior of the café. He stepped aside with a professional nod.

Inside, the noise level rose. Molly was aware of a confusion of tables and people, the scrape of chairs on the wooden floor, a fug of smoke and wine fumes. It was hard to see properly in the comparative gloom. She took a few tentative steps in one direction, peering into dusky corners, then in another. A burst of laughter made her turn, and suddenly she saw a profile she recognized. Breaking into a smile, she stepped toward him with a smile, then paused, uncertain.

He was not alone. Molly saw with a pang of disappointment that he sat in a group of three others, all leaning close and cutting across each other's conversation in the manner of old friends. Fabrice lounged against the wall at the far end of the small rectangular table, which was scattered with beer bottles, glasses, ashtrays, and plates still bearing the remains of some snack. He was listening to a man with a ponytail, sitting opposite him, who was obviously in the middle of telling a story. Molly felt shy about breaking into their circle, but the sight of Fabrice so close, every detail of his body familiar yet intensely exciting, drew her forward. "Hello, Fabrice," she said, nervously fingering the edge of the table. One by one, heads were raised in her direction—a girl, two unknown men, finally Fabrice.

"Ah, Molly. *Ça va?*" He gave her a casual nod. "This is Molly," he told the others. "She's English. Here for the weekend."

They put out their hands for her to shake: the girl, with appraising eyes and curly black hair cut short (Sylvie), a guy with wire-rimmed glasses and a wispy goatee (Olivier), the ponytail man (Henri). "*Bonjour*," they said, with polite, fleeting smiles. Molly waited for Fabrice to suggest that his friends move round to make a space for her to sit next to him. But he didn't. There were no spare chairs anyway. She stood for an awkward moment, feeling foolish. Then Olivier jumped to his feet, and returned shortly with a chair, which he placed for Molly at the head of the table, with himself on her left and Sylvie on her right.

"Thank you very much." She gave him her best smile and sat down, trying to ignore a tightness in her throat. Fabrice, sitting on the far side of Sylvie, was once again talking to Henri. Perhaps he was still in a huff with her. But it was a good sign that he felt able to introduce her to his friends. If she acted normal and joined good-humoredly in the conversation, he would soon thaw. They could talk properly when his friends left.

Sylvie turned to her. "So, you are English?"

"Yes."

"From London?"

"Yes."

"You came just for the weekend?"

"Yes." Molly tried to inject a sparkle into these monosyllables.

"Have you known Fabrice long?"

"We met on Friday night. At a club."

The girl raised her eyebrows and turned to say, "Is that true, Fabrice? You went to a club?"

The others picked up on her words, and piled in with questions. They seemed to be teasing him. Perhaps he didn't normally go to clubs. Fabrice shrugged defensively, muttered something and gave a sheepish smile. Molly smiled, too, though she couldn't understand what exactly they were saying, and tried to catch his eye. *I'm sorry about last night*, she wanted to say. *Everything's all right. I love you.* But his eyes were lowered as he shook another cigarette out of a squashy packet.

Now they all started talking about clubs. They were great, *n'est-ce pas?* No, they were boring: you couldn't talk properly. It was better to go to a bar. But what about dancing? What about . . . ? Molly was losing the thread. They were talking too fast for her to follow. Slangy phrases ricocheted back and forth. "*Mais si, c'est de la balle*" . . . "*Quel con!*" Other words didn't even sound like proper French. She felt like someone who didn't understand the rules of tennis, watching the ball ping incomprehensibly from side to side. Her lips stiffened with the effort of keeping an interested expression in place.

Olivier glanced at her face and took pity on her. "They're speaking Verlan," he said. "You know what that is?" Molly shook her head. It was a kind of slang, he explained, in which the syllables of a word were reversed. *Métro* became *tromé*; a bottle wasn't a *bouteille* but a *teille-bou*; her own name would become Lee-mo. It had grown up in the tower blocks that encircled Paris, probably as a code to baffle outsiders, especially the police. Grass, for example, in the druggy sense—*l'herbe*—was known as "*beu-her*." But now Verlan was hip, and peppered the speech of most young people in Paris.

"Or is-Par," Molly quipped, trying to be witty, hoping that Fabrice would notice how well she was getting on with his friend. The Verlan thing seemed to mirror her own nightmarish sense that everything was back to front and upside down. Yesterday Fabrice had made love to her as if she was beautiful and desirable. Why was he neglecting her today? Perhaps he was embarrassed to be nice to her in front of his friends. But why? Though she tried to concentrate on Olivier, to whom she now began to explain Cockney rhyming slang, all her attention was tuned into Fabrice, as he joined in with the others, joking and arguing. She ached to hold his hand and nuzzle the warm skin of his neck, which she could practically feel—almost smell—from memory. She kept trying to catch his eye, but he barely looked in her direction.

"I had a very funny adventure today," she said abruptly, breaking rather desperately into the conversation. But her story of Janine and the Rollerblades seemed to fall flat. It was difficult to do an imitation of an Australian accent in French. She told them all how funny it was to see poor Janine up-ended in the pond, and brutally forced by Alicia to walk home in her socks, but no one laughed. Molly also realized, too late, that it was not very tactful to tell a story about pilfered Rollerblades in front of Fabrice. Her voice ground to a halt.

"Go on telling me about your English slang." Olivier leapt gallantly into the breach. At the same time Molly heard Sylvie saying, "Doesn't Gabrielle like to Rollerblade?" Soon the others were all talking about Gabrielle, whoever she was—where was she? when was she coming back?—while Molly struggled on to demonstrate that, in English anyway, apples and pears rhymed with stairs.

Suddenly she was aware of a waiter standing by her chair, head cocked as if waiting for a response to something. For the first time Fabrice looked at her directly from the far end of the table, and said, "Do you want another drink?"

"No, I'm fine." At least that's what she meant to say. But she felt such a confusion of feelings—surprise, delight, a desperate desire to make the right answer, hurt that he hadn't noticed she'd never had a drink in the first place—that what she actually came out with was, "I'm good." *Je suis bonne.*

There was a startled pause, then a snigger went round the table. Even the waiter was trying not to smirk. As Olivier moved in smartly to deal with him, Molly saw Henri Ponytail lean forward to give Fabrice a teasing poke in the arm. "Is that true?" he murmured slyly. "She's *bonne?*"

Molly felt herself blushing. There was some joke going on that she didn't get. Keeping her tone light and a smile on her face, she turned to Sylvie and asked, "What did I say? My French is so hopeless. Did I make a frightful mistake?"

Sylvie waved a hand as if it wasn't important.

"No, no, tell me," said Molly. "I like to know these things. Really."

Sylvie exchanged glances with Olivier across the table. Molly turned from one to the other. "Well?"

Olivier took a breath. "Sometimes—not in this instance, of course—but sometimes *bonne* is a short way of saying, *euh*, good to make love."

"Oh," said Molly, still not quite understanding. She turned back to Sylvie, who looked at her for a long moment with dark, unreadable eyes, then said in English, "It means fuckable."

Molly jumped as if she'd been hit. Her arm collided with the waiter's—he had reappeared to place something on the table. "*Pardon*," he said, as if he was at fault.

*Fuckable*. The ugly word reverberated in her head, crashing and squealing like a car out of control. Of course no one meant her. That stupid Henri was just making a stupid, chauvinist joke. Fabrice wouldn't—couldn't . . . But what was happening now? Sylvie had reached out to pick up a piece of folded paper from the table. She was rummaging in her bag. There was a general shifting and commotion. Molly realized that Olivier hadn't been ordering more drinks: he'd been asking for the bill.

"Are you going somewhere?" she asked Sylvie, feigning friendly interest. Thank God! They were leaving. At last she and Fabrice could talk in peace.

"To the cinema. There's a Polish film, very classic."

But now Molly saw that Fabrice had pulled out his wallet, too. He was throwing notes on the plate. He pushed back his chair. Molly's pulse was beating so fast she was almost choking. "Fabrice, you're not going, are you?" she called. Though she tried to sound casual, she could hear an undertone of shrill desperation. "I—I need to talk to you. About last night." She was aware of the other three watching them curiously.

Fabrice twitched his watch into view, then gave a petulant sigh. "Okay, you go on ahead," he said to the others. "I'll catch you up later." He subsided into his chair, tapping a hand on the table.

Molly stood up to shake everyone's hand in the formal French manner, determined to give the appearance of normality. "Very nice to meet you, Olivier . . . Yes, good-bye. Enjoy the film." Her fingers clung tightly to the back of her chair. She waited until the others shambled out of the doorway, then turned back and took the seat next to Fabrice. He had lit another cigarette.

"Hi," she said softly, daring to press a fingertip, just for a second, to one of his knuckles. "You're very quiet today. Are you still angry about last night?"

He wouldn't meet her eyes. "What do you want?"

Oh, God, he *was* still angry. "I—just wanted to talk to you."

"What about?"

"Well . . . you and me. Us."

He pulled on his cigarette. "Us?"

Molly pretended not to notice the coldness in his tone. Her own was upbeat, persuasive, almost jaunty, as she said, "I thought we might do something together before my train leaves. I don't need to be at the station until six fifteen. Or . . . I could stay on longer, if you wanted."

"What for?" he grunted moodily. She longed to kiss him

back to good humor, to stroke his hair and wrap her arms round his neck, but he was so touchy she feared he might reject her and make things worse.

"Look, I'm busy." He fiddled with his cigarette packet. "I've got things to do."

Molly swallowed, trying to keep her voice easy and light. "Couldn't we do them together?"

"No."

"Why not?"

He tapped the packet irritably on the table, glared over her shoulder, then glanced into her face and quickly down again. "Gabrielle's coming back tonight."

An invisible hand was squeezing her throat. "Gabrielle? Who—? Why—?"

But she knew the truth even before he said the words. "My girlfriend."

Molly was keeping such tight control of herself that she was scarcely breathing. "Oh, I see," she managed to say. She bowed her head.

Fabrice swept back his hair. "*Enfin*, Molly, what did you expect? I have a life here, naturally. No doubt you have someone back in England, *n'est-ce pas?*"

Molly forced herself to nod dumbly, staring at her lap.

"Let's not enact the big drama," he went on. "We're adults, after all. You're not going to tell me I forced you into anything?"

"No, of course not." Molly made herself look up into his face.

Whatever he saw in hers seemed to enrage him. He was scowling now, almost contemptuous. "You know, I am a little angry with you, Molly. I show you Paris, I take you to my studio, I give you dinner, and what do you do? You betray me to my father." He was becoming worked up now. His eyes burned with indignation.

"Oh, Fabrice, I'm sorry. I didn't—"

"Yes!" He slapped the table. "You try to tell *me* how to behave. Me, an artist! Who are you to give me lectures, *hein?* Just a stupid English girl here for the weekend, looking for a Frenchman to fuck."

Molly recoiled, her jaw slack with shock. *A stupid English girl*: that's what he thought. That's what he had always thought. She'd got everything wrong. Everything.

With a supreme effort she raised her arm and pretended to look at her watch. "Oh, Fabrice, I've just remembered. I'm supposed to be meeting someone. I'm awfully sorry." She pushed herself upright on stiff legs.

He stood up too, and slung on his jacket. Clutching her bag tightly, Molly stumbled through the blur of the café and onto the street. It felt as though she had rocks in her chest.

Outside, she turned to face him. Somehow she forced her features into a smile. "You'd better hurry and catch up with your friends."

"Yes." He shifted uncomfortably. "*Alors, ciao.*" He reached for her shoulders and kissed her swiftly on both cheeks, then walked away without a backward glance.

# 24

In the Jardin du Luxembourg the leaves were dying. Many had already fallen. They swirled in bright copper drifts and crunched under her feet as Molly turned through the open gates and stepped onto a wide sand-and-gravel path. She had not intended to come. She hardly knew how she had got here. It seemed that automatically, without volition, placing one foot in front of the other like a sleepwalker, she had arrived at the tall black railings, spiked with gold, that guarded this park, and followed them round until she was admitted inside.

The noise of traffic faded. She walked down a broad avenue in the hushed shadow of trees, so dense and closely planted they formed high walls of dark, mottled green. Her boots stepped in and out of puddles of sunlight. She was aware of trainers jogging past, the brisk strut of high heels, the erratic patter of children's shoes, bouncing under rubbery legs. But she kept her head bowed to hide the tears that squeezed from her eyes. Her arms were wrapped tightly round her ribs as if she was cold.

Stupid, stupid girl! How could she have ever imagined that Fabrice cared about her, even loved her? In his eyes she was just an easy lay, a casual fuck, *bonne*. To think that she'd worried if she was intelligent enough for him—as if he cared two hoots about her brain! To think that she'd stripped for him in the name of art, lapped up his flattery about her "sensational" body, willingly made love in a stranger's flat, then preached to him about morality! He must have been laughing himself sick all weekend. At this very moment he was probably regaling his friend Henri with the hilarious story of her gullibility. These English girls: what pushovers. One empty compliment, one smoldering glance, and they're anybody's. Luckily they all go home on Sunday night, ha ha.

Molly fumbled in her bag for something to blow her nose on, but all she could find was a leaflet from the Rodin museum. She blew her nose on it anyway, and dropped it into an elegant dark green urn that seemed to be a bin. Good-bye, Fabrice.

But how cruel he had been, to leave her without a shred of pride. She pictured herself as a figure on a high, sunny cliff, blithely walking along the edge, dizzy with happiness, eyes starry with her own fantasies, ignoring all warning signs—until he had simply reached out and casually pushed her over. "Just a stupid English girl looking for a Frenchman to fuck."

He must be right. As usual, she had romanticized everything, elevating their relationship to love. In his eyes there had never been any relationship in the first place: no meeting of minds, no spark of enjoyment, no "twins of sorrow." In fact, their "relationship" had turned out to be exactly the thing that had always seemed most repugnant to her: sex without feeling, a one-time bonk. Go on, say the word—a *shag.*

Molly felt sick, and lifted her head quickly to gulp in fresh air. To her surprise, a pony was ambling past, led by a rough-looking man with a bandanna round his neck. A small girl sat on it stiffly, just managing to contain her pride and excitement with a furious, quelling frown. Her parents walked by her side, alternately murmuring warnings and approval. Now Molly could hear a repetitive, echoing sound like corks popping, and turned her head to see white figures running and leaping behind a high, wire-netting fence: they were playing tennis. On the other side of the path a group of men stood round a *boules* court, grave as judges.

The park was coming alive around her. Half of Paris seemed to be out for its Sunday stroll: noisy families, elderly women still smartly dressed from church and Sunday lunch, young men with jackets slung over their shoulders, even a policeman, very spruce in navy blue, with a pale blue stripe around his chest and a Charles de Gaulle cap. She passed a leotarded woman practising *t'ai chi*, two men leaning over a chessboard, girls sitting with books on their laps and bare legs propped to the sun on a second chair. Most of all Molly noticed the couples, drifting with their arms wrapped round each other, kissing on benches, stopping in quiet spots beneath the trees to hold hands and stare into each other's eyes. Their happiness taunted her.

Up ahead, like the light at the end of the tunnel, was an open space where a jet of water sparkled in the sunshine. Molly remembered why she was here. "A friend." Could that be true? Was it a joke, a hoax? She stepped into the sunshine and paused by an urn at the top of a broad flight of steps. She was looking down on a large, ornamental pond, where children guided toy sailing boats back and forth with short sticks. Around its edge people sunbathed, read and gossiped on green metal chairs scattered between clipped orange trees and African palms. The whole area was encircled by raised stone balustrading, decorated with urns and statues. Molly could hear laughter, the splash of water, bees humming sleepily among the flowers. On the far side of the pond, a stone staircase, mirroring her own, led to a shaded avenue. To her right, another avenue provided a long vista to a distant domed building. Something about the scene, supremely artful yet almost comically alive, tickled a corner of her memory. This reminded her of something. What was it?

But now her eye had been caught by a palatial building to her left, where the French flag fluttered from a central turret. On a high pediment decorated with flying nymphs was a clock, with the hands standing at twenty minutes past three. *In the Luxembourg Gardens today . . . 3–4 p.m. . . . Important . . . A friend.* Molly touched a hand to her face, conscious that she must look blotchy and red-eyed. Did she really want to meet anyone in this state? She peered round the urn to scan the figures seated by the pond, or moving back and forth in front of the palace, but she was too far away to see clearly. There was no one she recognized. *Please come.* She began to descend the steps.

She was about halfway down when a figure detached itself from the anonymity of the crowd around the pond and made its way urgently toward her. When Molly saw who it was, she felt disappointment, a surge of exasperation. It wasn't anyone mysterious, only the doctor from the conference hotel, the stranger whose arm she'd grabbed to hide from Malcolm. What on earth did he want? The last time she'd seen him she'd been wearing that ridiculous wig! She already felt foolish enough for one day.

"Molly Clearwater? Is that you?" He peered at her intently. "You look a little different today."

"Hi." Molly scuffed a foot. "Look, I'm sorry if this sounds rude, but if it's about that bloody disk again, I don't want to know."

"No, no. All that's fine, I promise." He hesitated, looking into her face. Probably he could see that she'd been crying. She glared at the ground.

"I mean, I've left Phipps Lauzer Bergman. I couldn't care less about the conference and—and I'm having a horrible day."

"Poor you. I'm sorry." Her eyes flickered to him briefly. He was smiling a little, but not nastily. Actually, he looked quite kind. She remembered that he'd been kind before, at the hotel.

But sympathy was the last thing she wanted, or she'd start crying again. She folded her arms.

"So what's this all about?" she demanded. "All those text messages—what's the big urgency? Who are you?"

"My name's Jonathan—Jonathan Griffin." He put his hands into his pockets, then took them out again. It occurred to her that he was nervous in some way. "Do you mind if we take a little walk?" He gestured at the avenue that led away from the palace.

Molly glowered at him, ready to say no. Then she noticed his strained expression. He seemed to be trying to control some powerful emotion—although what it might be, she couldn't imagine.

She accepted his suggestion with a nod. Why not? She didn't have anything else to do.

They walked in silence. Molly wondered what on earth was going on. Perhaps he was a loony or a pervert? Could he possibly *fancy* her? She hadn't picked up any such vibe at the hotel, and now he didn't seem keen to do anything creepy like take her arm. If anything, he was concerned to keep his distance. And he was awfully old: forty, at least. Anyway, nothing much could happen to her among these crowds.

"What a perfect day," he said, taking an appreciative breath and looking around him.

Oh, right. They were going to discuss the weather. Molly turned her head away and rolled her eyes at one of the white statues of women—queens, to judge from their crowns—lining their route, who stared back from blank sockets.

But the sweetness of the air filled her nostrils. The sun warmed her face, and suffused everything with that golden intensity of light peculiar to autumn. Where it caught the turning leaves, the trees looked as if they'd been dusted with cinnamon.

It was impossible not to respond to the vistas so artfully designed to please. The slow, regular pace of their progress side by side was soothing. "Yes, it's lovely," she answered.

He began to talk to her about the park: how Simone de Beauvoir had played here as a child, with her hoop, how it contained an old-fashioned puppet theater and a miniature Statue of Liberty. "And beehives!" he added, flashing her a smile. "Shall we go and look?"

They turned off to smaller paths that wound through dappled shade, past statues of lions and stags, poets and mythological figures; past little enclosures of pruned fruit trees, where he pointed out how the individual fruits were wrapped in protective cloth. Here were the bees: "*Danger d'abeilles!*"—they exchanged a little smile at the sign. As they strolled he asked her gentle, undemanding questions. Had she been to Paris before? What did she think of it? Molly had the odd sense that he was biding his time. But for what?

"Look," she said finally, stopping at the edge of some kind of railed enclosure, "what's going on? What are we doing? What do you want?"

She saw his face fall, and felt a pang of regret at the sharpness of her tone. He was obviously a nice man. "It's just—I'm not in a very sociable mood and . . ." Damn! She was going to cry again. She took a few steps away from him and gripped the railings. She was aware of children's shrieks, the bright colors of climbing frames and swings, and realized that she was looking into a playground.

He came up beside her. "I'm sorry. Of course, this must all seem very odd. The thing is . . ." He paused for so long that she turned to look at him. He seemed agitated, struggling to find the words. "I don't mean to add to your worries," he said. "It's just that I've been wanting to meet you for a very long time."

"How could you? We only met yesterday. How do you even know my name? How did you get my mobile number?"

"Ah, that was Malcolm Figg."

Malcolm! She knew it. The vague friendliness she'd begun to feel for this man drained away. "I've had enough of this," she snapped. "I don't work for Phipps Lauzer Bergman any more. As my boss so kindly pointed out to me last Friday, I was only a 'stupid secretary' anyway."

"Molly!" he protested. "You've got the wrong end of the stick. I'm not interested in anything to do with Phipps Lauzer Bergman, or that godawful boring conference. I'm interested in *you*."

Molly's head whirled. "Me? Huh—what's interesting about me?"

"Everything, as far as I'm concerned."

She shook her head. "You've got me confused with someone else. I'm just an ordinary English girl over in Paris for the weekend. A silly girl who's made a mess of everything." Again the tears rose, and she hid her face in her hand. She thought that she would hit him if he dared to put his arm round her now.

"I'm sure it's not that bad."

"What do you know? What do you care? You know nothing about me." Molly rounded on him, moist eyes blazing. She knew that she was being unfair, that he was only trying to be kind, but she was so unhappy that she lashed out anyway.

He looked back at her with an expression of obvious distress. "Well, in a way that's true. But in another way I know quite a lot about you. I know your birthday, for example: the twenty-fourth of May. I know where you were born. I know that your middle name is Catherine."

"God, who are you? A detective or something?"

He shook his head and smiled.

"Well, how do you know my birthday, then? Are you some kind of creep who's found me on the Internet, maybe intercepted my e-mails?"

"Do you really think that?" He looked her calmly in the eye.

"All right, no. But how do you know so much about me—and why should you be interested in me?"

"Can't you guess?"

Molly shook her head. But an idea was stirring in her mind. A ridiculous idea. Impossible. She looked out across the playground and wrapped her arms round her waist.

He was silent for a moment. "Let me try to explain this another way." He took a deep breath. "Will you let me tell you a story?"

She nodded slowly, staring at the distant trees.

"Once upon a time, a long time ago, a very pretty girl and a rather thoughtless young man met and fell in love. They had a fantastic summer together. He thought she was great. But when the summer came to an end they went their separate ways. He had to go abroad, to work. And although he really, really liked the girl, he didn't think about her as much as he probably should have. And what he didn't know, because she didn't tell him, was that she was pregnant, and that eight months after he left she gave birth to a daughter. He didn't find that out until the child was nearly three years old, and by that time the mother had no use for him."

"What about the little girl?" Molly gripped the railings tight. "Didn't she have a use for him?"

"I don't know about that. You see, this man wasn't allowed to meet her. He didn't know where she lived."

"He could have found out . . ."

"You know what I'm telling you, don't you?"

"No! Maybe. I don't know."

"Molly. Look at me. Please. I've waited so long for this moment. I've thought about it, dreamed about it, feared it might never happen."

Molly resisted his plea, staring fiercely down at the ground, no longer seeing anything as her eyes misted over. Her heart thudded. A wild hope was growing in her mind. She felt dizzy, as if she could stand only by clutching these railings. "That young man. Was it . . . ? Is it . . . ?" Finally she raised her head. "You?"

He nodded. She saw that his eyes were shiny with tears, but they looked at her steadily. "And that little girl," he said, "was you. Molly, I'm your father."

# 25

Molly gave a wrenching cry and spun away from him. She couldn't see, she couldn't think. Her legs staggered. She put out a hand to steady herself, and felt the scaly bark of a tree under her fingers.

"I'm sorry. I know it's a shock." His voice was at her shoulder. Out of the corner of her eye she could see his hands hovering in mid-air.

"I'm fine." But she wasn't fine. She leaned against the tree, panting for breath.

"Come and sit down." His hand clasped her elbow, and she allowed herself to be led to a vacant bench under the trees. She rested her forearms on her knees and bent her head to the dusty ground, gulping in air.

"Are you all right?" He sat down beside her, not too close. She stared dumbly at his black leather lace-ups. She was aware that he had turned to face her, one knee riding up on the bench. Perhaps she choked, because she heard him say, "Let me get you some water. Don't move."

She heard the crunch of his shoes on the gravel. A moment later she raised her head and saw him loping toward a wooden building, the flaps of his jacket flying. At the entrance he looked back and raised a hand, perhaps to reassure her—or to reassure himself that she was still there—then disappeared inside. It seemed to be some kind of café or restaurant, housed in a quaint structure whose shingle roof and deep eaves reminded Molly of a woodcutter's cottage in a fairy tale. The people who sat at the windows, sipping from cups and raising genteel forkfuls of cake to their mouths, looked equally unreal.

In a minute he was out again, carrying a tumbler of water, trying to hurry, careful not to spill. Molly watched him approach—this stranger—her father. Could it be true? Out of all the men in the world, out of all the fathers she had fantasized into life, the choices had suddenly narrowed down to one middle-aged man in a tan jacket and blue shirt walking toward her.

"Here. Take your time." He bent to give her the water, then sat down beside her again, watching her face as she drank. She held the glass to her lips with both hands and took slow sips, trying to calm her spinning thoughts. At length she summoned enough control to lower the glass and turn to him. "Is it true?"

"Yes, it's true." His eyes were tender and anxious: blue eyes, she noticed, like hers. But that meant nothing.

"What makes you so sure I'm your . . ." She hesitated. It seemed too intimate to say the word aloud.

"My daughter? My daughter Molly?" Far from hesitating, his voice brimmed with joyous conviction. He laughed and pushed a hand roughly over his hair. Then he swivelled sideways on the bench to stare directly into her eyes. "Isn't it obvious?"

Molly looked away. This sudden intimacy with a stranger was too much for her. To cover her confusion, she fired more questions at him. "Why are you telling me now? Why here, in Paris? Why didn't you look for me earlier?" She wanted to say: *Where have you been all my life?*

"Because I didn't know how to find you. And for another reason I'll explain in a minute. You see, I'm here only because I happened to see your name on the conference bumf. Phipps Lauzer Bergman invited me months ago. I never intended to come. But I'm not very organized and I didn't get round to replying, so a few weeks ago they wrote again, asking me whether I was attending and including a list of everyone coming to the conference. I glanced through it, just to have a chuckle at the careerists and free-loaders among my colleagues, and was about to bin the lot when a name leaped out at me: Molly Clearwater. I couldn't believe it!"

"So you knew my name? You knew I existed?"

"I've known of your existence for nineteen years. But I didn't know where you lived, not even whether you were in England. Suddenly here was my chance to see you, to get to know you—if, of course, it was you. But Clearwater's an unusual name. I didn't really have any doubts. And now that I've met you I don't have any doubts at all."

Molly felt her own doubts melting in the sunshine of his confidence. An absurd hope was rising in her. She stared at him speechlessly, barely able to take in what he was saying.

"I could have simply phoned you up at work, or waylaid you outside your office," he continued, "but this is such a tremendous thing for me, meeting you at last. I was terrified of blundering in on your life in a way that might frighten you, and make you reject me. I thought that if we met in normal circumstances, on neutral territory, as it were, we'd have the chance to get to know each other a little before—well, before I sprang this surprise on you. I wanted to find out what sort of a person you were first, maybe even get a hint of your feelings about your unknown father."

"So you were, um, interested in me, sort of?"

"Of course I was interested! I nearly went mad waiting for this conference, and wondering what you would think of me. I had my hair cut specially. I bought this jacket. I know," he added quickly, brushing at the creases on his sleeve, "it doesn't look new. Something happens to clothes when I put them on. And I'm a lousy packer. But I can assure you that this is the first time I've ever worn it, in your honor."

There was such warmth in his eyes that Molly couldn't help responding with a faint smile. But she wasn't interested in his jacket. "Go on," she said.

"The minute I arrived at the hotel, I asked the front desk if you'd checked in. Not yet, they said. I asked again when I came down for dinner, and learned that your booking had been canceled, and you weren't coming at all. God, that was a low point. I nearly got on a plane and went home. Little did I guess that fate was going to lead you to me anyway, mysteriously disguised as a raven-haired Australian spouting French nursery rhymes!"

Molly put a hand to her hair, blushing as she remembered. That awful wig! In the many and various fantasies in which she'd staged a meeting with her father, the one constant had been her own poised and impressive appearance. "I must have looked ridiculous."

"You were fantastic! Resourceful, brave, delightful. You cheered me up when I was feeling depressed about coming to the conference for nothing. Of course I didn't know then who you were. But I worried that you were in trouble. As soon as I met the absurd Figg, I understood perfectly your desire to avoid him at all costs. By the way, his story is that he fired you."

"I resigned!" Molly said indignantly.

"Of course you did. Any intelligent person would. Though I shall always be grateful to him, since he was the one who inadvertently revealed that you were the girl I'd been looking for all along. And, thanks to him, I managed to get your number. My messages didn't frighten you, did they?"

"Not exactly. They were just, you know, weird. No one uses proper punctuation or spelling like that." She suppressed a smile, not sure yet if she could tease him.

"Don't they?" He seemed shocked. Then his face cleared. "Anyway, you came. That's the main thing."

"I nearly didn't."

They exchanged a look. The tension in his mouth and the softness in his eyes told her as clearly as words how much he had feared that she wouldn't come, and how overwhelmed he was that she had. There was no doubting that he cared.

But not that much, she thought bitterly, or he wouldn't have waited all this time to tell her so. Probably, in a little while, having satisfied his curiosity, he would remember that he had an appointment to keep, or a plane to catch. It had been so interesting to meet her. They must keep in touch. How dare he invade her life now, when it was too late? Molly looked away. She felt suddenly claustrophobic in the shade of these somber trees, whose perfectly spaced trunks hemmed her in like prison bars. The jingle-jangle of a carousel had started up nearby. In a patch of sunlight she could see prancing horses with scarlet nostrils and seafoam manes, swooping up and down. Small children clung to the gilt barley-sugar rods, and beamed seed-pearl smiles at their hovering parents. She stood up. "I'd better take this glass back," she said.

"No, no, let me." He jumped to his feet, and practically wrenched it from her hands. He looked at her worriedly, sensing her change of mood.

She could read in his eyes the fear that she might leave now, and felt an impulse to hurt him. "Did you say Griffith or Griffin? I can't quite remember."

"Griffin. Jonathan Peter." Though his voice and gaze were steady, she could tell she had upset him. He twisted the glass nervously. "Molly, I—I don't know what you've been told about me. I appreciate that you may not be interested in me. The last thing I want is to disrupt your life. If—if you don't want anything to do with me, I'll try to understand. But your existence has been very important to me for nearly twenty years, and now that we've met, *you* are very important to me." He broke off, frowning with the intensity of his thoughts. Emotions scudded across his face like shadows of clouds on a bright field, and she knew that he was choosing, discarding, editing his words, anxious not to get it wrong. He turned back to her. "You're grown-up now. I've missed your childhood. That's the brutal fact we both have to face. But I would like to explain why. I would like to tell you the story from my side—if you're willing to hear it."

"All right," Molly said, casually hitching her bag onto her shoulder, as her heart knocked at her ribs. Perhaps she had misjudged him? She walked beside him in silence to the café, scuffing leaves, thinking, This is my father. I am walking with my father in the park. *Je me promène dans le parc avec mon père.*

"Would you like something to eat? To drink?" he asked, as they reached the entrance, gesturing with the empty glass. "Hot chocolate? Tea? Cake? We could go inside, if you like."

Molly shook her head. "I'd rather walk in the sunshine."

He smiled agreement. "Me, too."

They took a broad path that led toward a large greenhouse in the distance. Molly felt the excitement wind tight inside her as she waited for him to speak.

"It was the summer of Princess Diana's wedding," he began, "Lady Di, as she was then. I was twenty-three, and had finally come to the end of my five years of medical training. A group of us used to fool around with comedy, and that year we took a show up to the Edinburgh Festival. We were pretty awful, I expect, but we had a great time. There were always parties to go to, and other people's shows to see, and such a buzz in the city that one felt on a permanent high. Plus, on my very first day, I met a beautiful girl with long blonde hair and the most gorgeous laugh, who was doing the sets for one of the other shows at our venue. We bonded over an enormous cut-out of Mrs. Thatcher that refused to stay upright. Frankie had a staple gun. I thought she was marvelous."

"Frankie?" Molly wrinkled her nose.

"That's what I called your mother. Frankie and Johnnie." He sighed. "Golden days. We were madly in love for about three weeks. When the festival was over, we sneaked off to Skye for a few days, lying to our parents that there was lots of clearing up to do. My mother was particularly furious because I was about to go off to work in America, and she'd organized various farewell dos, which she had to cancel." He grinned happily. Molly glimpsed how he must have appeared twenty-two years ago—eager, boyish, good-looking even.

"Anyway, finally we had to say good-bye. We talked about her coming to visit me in California. When I first got there I wrote to her practically every day, and rushed to my pigeon-hole every morning, looking for her letters. But my new life was so exciting. I wrote less often, and so did she. Then her letters stopped altogether." He glanced at Molly, and she could tell that this was difficult for him. "I won't pretend to you that I was heartbroken. My life had moved on. I was meeting new people, my work was interesting, I was even learning to surf—sort of. Then Frankie sent me this rather odd letter, only a few weeks before Christmas, saying that she was thinking of coming to California for the holiday, and what was I doing?" An embarrassed look came over his face. He fiddled with the hair above his ear. "This doesn't sound too good, but the truth is that a rather attractive girl called Kristal had invited me to spend Christmas at her family's ski lodge at Lake Tahoe. It didn't occur to me that there might be any urgent reason why Frankie wanted to see me. So I wrote back saying I was a bit tied up at Christmas, but if she was keen why didn't she come out at Easter?" He paused, and dug his hands into his pockets. "I never heard from her again."

By common consent they turned into the path that ran alongside the greenhouse. An orange tree sailed past them in midair. Molly saw that men on small forklift trucks were transporting them inside, pot and all, to keep them safe over the winter.

"I stayed in America for three years," he continued, "and then came back to take up a job at a hospital in Birmingham. After California, it was a grim life. I was working or on call practically all the time, and I didn't know anyone. I remembered that Frankie's home was in Shropshire, not too far away. Perhaps I still felt a bit guilty about the Christmas thing. Anyway, I trawled through my old address book for her number. Her mother answered the phone, and told me Frankie had recently moved away. She was quite cagey, wouldn't say exactly where, or what Frankie was doing, but she obviously sussed pretty quickly who I was and suggested I come to see her. Well, I say 'suggested,' but something in her voice made me think it was urgent."

"And you went? You mean you actually met Granny?" Molly turned to him eagerly. His story was beginning to take fire in her heart. This point of contact between her beloved grandmother and unknown father seemed supremely important.

"Oh, yes. In some ways I got to know Catherine extremely well. She was a lovely woman, and very kind to me. But . . . I'm sorry to ask, is she still alive?"

Molly shook her head. "She died when I was fifteen."

"Ah. That explains a lot. I'm sorry."

"I always thought she must know about you. Tell me. Please."

And so, digging his hands deeper into his pockets and tip-ping his head back in the way she now realized was characteristic, he told her about driving out of Birmingham, one harsh winter Sunday, and arriving an hour late for lunch, having lost his way in the folds of brown moorland hills, with the beginnings of a blizzard dusting them with white. In Catherine's cottage a fire burned comfortably, with some hairy dog— "Brando," Molly reminded him, "because he had pouchy cheeks like Marlon Brando in *The Godfather*"—okay, with Brando lolling beside the flames and the smell of roast lamb wafting from the kitchen. Mrs. Clearwater—Catherine—had settled him in an armchair with an enormous sherry, insisting that she was so thankful he was late because it had given her the chance to find out who the murderer was in her library book. Molly hugged her elbows as she listened to him evoke, with such affection and poignant humor, the woman she had loved. Over lunch, he went on, they had conversed normally about normal topics, then taken their coffee back to the fire to talk. "What I am going to say," she'd announced, "I tell you now in confidence. I want you to give me your word that you will not abuse that confidence." Impressed by her solemnity, he had promised.

"And that's when I found out that I had a daughter, Molly Catherine, aged two and a half." He stopped on the path for a moment, and turned to smile at her. "You."

"Wh-what did you think?"

"At first I didn't know what to think. I was shocked, confused, amazed. I was very lucky that your grandmother was such a wise and generous-hearted woman. She didn't condemn me, or tell me what to do, or insist I cough up money—nothing like that. She just told me to go away and sort out what I felt, although I think I knew straight away. I can remember driving back to the hospital on the dark, slushy roads, with my windscreen wipers going like crazy and white dots of snow swirling in the headlights, thinking, *I'm a father, I'm a father!* Catherine had given me a photograph. I remember pulling it out when I stopped at a service station, and just staring in astonishment."

"A photo? Of me, you mean?"

"Yes. Would you like to see it?" His hand was already travelling to his breast pocket.

"You've got it *here?*"

"I keep it with me always. Look, let's go and sit down on that bench, so you can look properly."

They sat side by side on the smooth wood, surrounded by flowerbeds gaudy with petunias. He flipped open his wallet and drew out a small, square photo with a thin white margin round the edge and corners worn to papery softness. As he handed it to her, their fingers touched. Molly was acutely conscious of the physical intimacy, of the masculine solidity of his shoulder so close to her own. It felt strange, but not unpleasant.

The photo showed a small girl in pink dungarees and a pink-and-yellow-striped T-shirt, hands stuck into her pockets, blonde head tipped confidently to the camera with a cheeky I-am-me-and-I-am-marvelous smile. Molly knew the photo from the album at home. But seeing it again in these strange circumstances, knowing it had been carried around for years and years by a man she'd not known until now, raised goosebumps down her back.

"The weekend after I'd been to see Catherine," he continued, "I went home and told the whole story to my mother, and asked her what I should do. She was pretty surprised, naturally, but she also asked if I was sure the baby was mine. Well, of course, I couldn't be sure, though I couldn't imagine anyone lying about such a thing, especially Frankie. But I showed my mother that photo. God! I can remember it so well—leaning against the fridge while she found her glasses, watching her hold the photo under the light for what seemed like hours. Finally, she looked up at me and said, 'I don't know what you can do about it, darling, but those are definitely the Griffin eyebrows.'"

Molly's eyes flew to his face. Recognition punched her in the stomach. Wonderingly, she touched a finger to one of her eyebrows, tracing the long, swooping line that tipped upward like a swift's wing, so distinctive that people often commented on them—the same line she could see repeated more emphatically on his face, the same line that was faintly but unmistakably duplicated on the face of the child in the photograph.

They stared at each other, rapt as lovers, awed by the potency of this tiny proof of genetic inheritance.

"Yours are rather more kempt than mine," he said at last, "but she was right, wasn't she? I'm afraid I've been staring at your eyebrows for the past hour or so."

Molly nodded slowly. This really was her father. She was his daughter. And at least two other people, her grandmother and his mother—another, brand-new grandmother—had known this for a fact. With every passing moment her dark secret was rising into the light. It was thrilling, frightening, disorienting. She bent her head again to the photograph, moved by the sight of the absurdly short legs and wide, innocent face of the child she had once been, wondering how he could have closed his heart to that tiny figure.

"So what *did* you do?" she asked at length.

"I rang your grandmother and asked if I could see you, or at least have some kind of contact with you—whatever Frankie thought was appropriate. Oh, and I sent her some kind of toy and asked if she could smuggle it through to you for Christmas."

"A toy?" Molly looked up.

"I know, I know." He winced, mistaking her sharpened interest for contempt. "It was a pathetic gesture. Selfish. Sentimental. I just needed to do something, to make it real for myself."

"But what was the toy? Do you remember?"

"Oh, yes. In fact, Catherine told me you seemed very keen on your 'special present from Father Christmas.' I realize now it was a rather odd animal to choose. Children generally prefer the obvious things—teddies, rabbits, tigers. But I wasn't thinking of you so much as myself, and I was determined to find something unusual that might impress itself on your memory."

"Like—" Molly could hardly bring herself to say the word—"Like a . . . badger?"

"Yes!" He looked delighted. "You can remember it, then?"

Molly nodded. Her chest felt so tight she couldn't speak. Bertie! He had given her Bertie, her companion for all these years, all those nights when she had lain in bed pouring her secrets into his ear, feeling his fur against her lips, wondering and wondering about her father. "He's a 'him,' not an 'it,'" she said. "He's called Bertie. I still have him, though I know I'm supposed to be much too old for . . ." She turned her face away. *I didn't want a badger, I wanted you!* But she couldn't say the cruel words aloud. "Here, you'd better have this back." She thrust the photograph into his hands.

He looked at it unhappily. "Oh, Molly, I'm so sorry."

"Why didn't anyone tell me?" she burst out.

He reached into his wallet again and drew out a letter. "I don't usually carry this about, but I brought it to the conference, hoping I'd meet you. It's from your grandmother. You'd better read it yourself."

Molly took the folded sheets and opened them up. It was a shock to see the pale gray paper her grandmother had always favored and her familiar neat writing in faded blue ink. She saw from the date that the letter had been written almost nineteen years ago.

*Dear Jonathan,*

*I've seen Fran and had a long talk with her. She was very angry to hear that I told you about Molly, but I can cope with that. I'm sure it's right that you should know the truth.*

*But I'm afraid that Fran is insistent that there should be no contact between you and Molly. As you know, Fran is a very proud, independent person. She took a brave decision in having Molly, and has coped marvelously with all the hard work a baby entails. Even you, I suspect, an overworked junior doctor, cannot quite imagine what it is like to raise a child alone, to be on call every day and be woken up every night, without remission.*

*As a result, Fran now feels that Molly is her child, and hers alone. She did not ask you for help, and doesn't want it now. Molly is happy and well balanced, and Fran cannot see the point of introducing a stranger into her life, especially one who is so busy and could only see Molly irregularly. She bears you no grudge, but she begs you to leave her and Molly to get on with their own lives.*

*I don't agree with Fran's decision. I feel the time may come when Molly needs to know who you are. But Molly is her child, and I must respect her wishes.*

*I'm sorry, Jonathan. I sense that you are not the sort of young man to shirk his responsibilities, but for the time being, at least, you must keep out of the picture completely. Rest assured that I will let you know if you are needed, and please feel free to contact me. I will be glad to tell you of Molly's progress, on the understanding that you do not try to seek her out. Content yourself with the knowledge that she is a happy little thing, with a loving mother who will do everything possible for her.*

*All the best,*
*Catherine Clearwater*

Molly was still trying to take in what she had read when he spoke again. "I always had the feeling that your grandmother intended to tell you one day who I was, or tell me where I could find you. I got very wound up around the time of your eighteenth birthday, and again on your twenty-first. But, of course, I heard nothing, and now I know why. Once you turned twenty-one, I reckoned that I was free to try to find you. Not all children want anything to do with their real parents—quite a number of adopted children definitely don't. I knew I had to be careful. I had just started to search, and suddenly I found you, in a place I would never have thought of looking."

Molly read through the letter again, her jaw tightening with resentment. "Happy and well balanced . . . no point in introducing a stranger into her life . . ." *No point?* How dared her mother decide for her? How did she know what it was like to see other children hoisted on their fathers' shoulders, to watch Abi's dad slip her a fiver with a wink and a whispered "Don't tell Mum," never to have the glare of her mother's attention deflected by a third person? It could have been so different. *She* could have been different. Now it was too late.

She refolded the letter, pressed it briefly to her cheek, remembering her grandmother with love, then handed it back to him. She stood up abruptly. "Let's walk."

Taken by surprise, he stowed the treasures away again and was still sliding the wallet into his inner breast pocket when he caught up with her. "Don't be too hard on your mother," he said. "She meant it for the best, and she's done a great job. Just look at you."

"Oh, yeah, just look at me." Molly thumped her boots down on the gravel.

"Has something upset you?" he asked gently. "Before meeting me, I mean. You said something earlier about a horrible day. Anything I can help with? I'd like to, if I can."

Molly felt her throat tighten with misery. "It's just . . . I'm not fit for anything. I don't understand anything. Other people seem to waltz through life, knowing exactly what to do and why they're doing it, and I keep making stupid, *stupid* mistakes. I mucked up my university, I mucked up my job. Even this weekend, I've made a total idiot of myself."

"Not with me, you haven't. I can't imagine another girl I'd be happier to discover was my daughter."

"What do you know?" Molly stopped and glared at him. "You haven't been around for twenty-one years. Well, let me tell you, I'm a freak. I'm a goody-goody. Everybody says so. Mum's brought me up to be that way, and every time I try to do something different, to do something on my own for a change . . ."

She jerked her head in frustration and stomped to the edge of the path, arms folded, scowling into the blurred greenery. Yet another statue glowed in the dappled sunlight, this time of a young girl offering herself, with roses, to a libertine painter. Molly's gaze focused on the details of her very low-cut dress and swelling breasts, her round face, the tiny feet emerging from a puffed-out eighteenth-century skirt. "There you go. That's me." She pointed contemptuously. "That's the daughter you've been so keen to meet."

"She's certainly very pretty," he ventured cautiously. "I'm not so sure about him. Does he deserve her, do you think?"

Molly stepped closer to the statue and rubbed at the lichen on the girl's foot. "I don't know," she muttered.

He moved to stand beside her. "Why don't you tell me what's happened?" he said softly. "Tell your old dad."

Molly opened her mouth to rebel at his use of the name he

had no right to, but instead she found herself telling him about Fabrice. "I didn't mean to betray him," she finished. "I thought I was helping. But he was so angry, so contemptuous. Somehow he made me feel like a prig and a slut at the same time. I don't know which is worse."

"Well, speaking for myself, I'd like to punch him on the nose. Of course you did the right thing! He's just ashamed of himself, and so he should be."

"Do you really think so?" Molly asked waveringly.

"Yes, I do." His conviction was wonderfully bracing. "And as for you, you don't strike me as either a prig or a slut." He stepped forward and gestured at the statue. "Look at that girl, with her sweet, trusting face. She might be making a mistake to fall for the artist, but it's a mistake, not a fault. People show their characters in the way they behave. It's his weakness, not hers, that he doesn't value her. How dare this Fabrice whisk you off on his motorbike and then not treat you properly? I hope you were wearing a helmet, by the way."

Molly had to smile. Amazingly, he was cheering her up. His kindness, his interest, his sheer bulky masculine presence made her feel protected and cherished. "So you don't think I'm totally useless?" she said. "You're not too disappointed in me?"

"*Disappointed?* Disappointed to find I have a beautiful, brave daughter, brimming with intelligence and integrity? I'm so proud I could roar. In fact, I'm going to roar. *Rrrrrah!*" He beat his chest for good measure. Molly blushed, laughed, looked away, half embarrassed and half pleased. A pair of impossibly chic women, with their scarves and handbags arranged just so, were walking past on the path. They turned their heads at this uncivilized noise, raised their eyebrows in ladylike astonishment and then . . . *smiled.* Suddenly Molly saw what they saw—a father teasing his daughter. It gave her a strange feeling.

"Mind you," he went on seriously, "it's not my opinion that counts. Nobody but you can dictate what sort of person you are: not your mother, not me, not your boss or your friends, certainly not some thoughtless young Frenchman on a scooter. Your mother may have instilled in you certain principles. I may have given you half my genes. But your identity is your own. Remember that, Molly."

His words poured into her head like a cool, clear stream. Her identity was her own. It was a liberating thought. At the same time another, more mischievous realization tugged at her. He was lecturing her, speaking disapprovingly of "young men," and warning her about road safety: just like a dad!

They stood in companionable silence, contemplating the statue and their own thoughts. A pigeon fluttered down, settled itself on the head of the painter and crapped copiously on his riotous locks. Molly caught her father's eye, and they both burst out laughing. "Portrait of the artist as a bit of a shit?" he suggested. "Come on, let's leave him to the birds."

It was not just the eyebrows they had in common, Molly reflected, as they walked on together. She liked his humor. She liked his quick intelligence. She liked strolling beside him, alive to the charm of the scene, and feeling that they belonged together. "I wish I'd known you before," she said impulsively. "Didn't you ever think of trying to find me, despite what Mum said?"

"Of course I did. I used to fantasize about meeting you one day by chance. I had dreams of heroically rescuing a little girl from drowning in the sea, then discovering she was my lost daughter. I imagined myself curing you of some disease. I dreamed that one day there'd be a knock at the door, and I'd open it to find you standing on the step. Crazy stuff!"

Not so crazy as believing herself to be the illegitimate daughter of the Count of Montepulciano, Molly thought. But it was a revelation that he, too, had made up fantasy encounters. She felt as if a long-locked secret door was swinging open. "I used to dream about meeting you, too," she said simply.

"Did you?" he asked, eyes shining. "Did you really?" He seemed to turn the thought over in his mind. "Oh, Molly, I won't say I thought about you consciously every day. But you were always there like a distant ache, or a wonderful secret—a great question mark hooked deep into my heart. Although I admit it didn't really begin to plague me until my wife and I started to have children."

"*Your wife!* You're married? You've got children?" The words tore out of Molly's throat. She tried to calm herself. It was natural, of course it was, that a man of his age would have a family.

"Rory's thirteen, Ben's eleven, and Charlie will be eight next week."

Molly could hardly take it in. Three human beings she had not until this minute known existed, all sharing the same genes as herself. Three little boys whom this man had hugged and played with, whose birthdays he had celebrated, whose bumps and bruises he had kissed—whom he had probably seen being born! Jealousy bit into her heart.

"My wife's called Georgie—Georgina. She's a doctor, too. Apart from my mother, she's the only other person I've told about you. Funnily enough, it was one of the things that bonded us together. It made me realize I must really love her to trust her with such an important secret. I proposed to her a week afterward. We've been married—uh, let's see . . . if Rory's thirteen . . ." He squinted into the sun, nose wrinkled, mouth awry, making the calculation, and again Molly felt a shock of recognition. ("Don't make that awful face, Mollypops. What if the wind changes?")

"Fifteen years," he concluded. "Blimey." He ruffled the hair over his ear and gave a small grin of wonderment.

"So your children don't know about me?"

"Not yet. But I'd love you to meet them."

Molly thought about it. "Georgina" sounded posh, a bit jolly hockeysticks. And three half-brothers . . . What if they didn't like her?

"Do you still live in Birmingham?" she asked cautiously.

"Christ, no. Didn't I say? We've lived in London for years. 'Clapham borders,' the estate agents call it, otherwise known as Tooting."

Molly gaped at him in disbelief. "But I'm living practically down the road—'Wandsworth borders,' otherwise known as—"

"Earlsfield!" they chorused.

"We could have passed each other in the street," she exclaimed.

"You've probably seen me on the common, practising my golf strokes."

"*Golf!*"

"Oh dear. Is that very bad?"

"Pretty bad." She was smiling now, confident that she could tease him. "Mum and I hate golf. It ruins the countryside. People wear peculiar trousers and wiggle their bums."

"Don't be golfist. Frankie always was a bit of a puritan. On Skye, I remember, she swam in this loch, where the water was so freezing I could barely paddle, and called me a wimp."

"Yep, that sounds like Mum." Molly kicked through a drift of leaves, feeling defensive, affectionate and angry about her mother all at the same time. Would it be disloyal, she wondered, to become involved with this man, whom her mother had kept away from her for twenty-one years?

When she was a child, there had been a school run between the village and the main road where the school bus stopped, a distance of perhaps a mile. The other mothers always went in the car; her own, of course, did things differently. "No need to drive," she scoffed. "We can take the shortcut through the woods. Fresh air and exercise, a run for Alleluia, and no pollution. It will be fun!" Molly was mortified. She wanted to be like everyone else, strapped into her seatbelt in the back of some clapped-out Honda with packets of crisps being handed round. Instead, her mother had brought bananas and misshapen shortbread, home-made with organic flour. She wore wellies and an embarrassing Australian sheep-farmer's hat, and often brought her battered bike so she could collect things in the basket and give the smaller children rides on the back. And yet it *was* fun, tramping back home on a mellow autumn afternoon like this, looking out for mushrooms, stopping to climb trees, collecting conkers. Sometimes they saw deer. In spring there were primroses and birds' nests to find. On the way they played spelling and times-tables games ("If we found five nests with three eggs each . . ."); it never felt like homework. On gray days she even got them to sing songs like "One Man Went To Mow" to keep their spirits up. "Your mum's weird," a boy had told Molly one day, "but I quite like her." Molly had sighed: her view exactly.

They had now looped round to the stone staircase overlooking the pond, where Molly had hesitated about meeting "A Friend" and almost turned back. Here again was the jet of water fizzing like champagne from a bottle, the giant stone urns casting hourglass shadows, the collision of extreme formality and almost pagan enjoyment that tickled the senses. Somewhere in the far trees a brass band was playing. Molly could just make out a collection of figures in uniform, their instruments winking in the sun. Once again she felt the flicker of an elusive memory.

"You know what this always reminds me of?" he said. "The pompous statues, the palm trees, the palace with its flag flying and everybody having such a good time—"

"The Babar books!" She'd finally got it. "Look, there are even those overlapping metal hoops around the edges of the grass. I can practically see Babar and Celeste coming out of that palace in their crowns and ermine robes."

"And Alexander and Pom in their sailor outfits, playing with the boats."

"Yes." Molly's smile wavered a little as she thought of all the children's books he would never read to her.

As they descended the steps, she caught sight of the clock on the palace pediment and was shocked to see that it was a quarter past five. "Oh, no! I've got to go."

"Already?"

"My train leaves in an hour and a half, and first I've got to collect my luggage and—and everything." It was too complicated to explain about her mother and Armand.

"Sit down with me a minute first. I want to say something to you." He led the way toward a couple of vacant chairs at the edge of the pond, although when they were seated he said nothing for a few moments, just gazed into her face with pleasure and amazement, as if she were one of the park's statues miraculously come to life. "I can't believe it, can you?"

Molly shook her head, returning his incredulous smile. She felt a little shy again, under his scrutiny.

His face grew serious. He leaned toward her, forearms on his knees. "Molly, I know it's too late for all sorts of things, but now I've found you I want to get to know you properly. I'd like you to be a part of my life—a part of my family—in as much as you want to be. You don't have to decide anything now. Of course you need to think, you need to talk to your mother—all that."

He reached into his jacket and brought out a card. "Here's where you can reach me, if you want to talk. Any time. Otherwise, what I suggest is that we meet for lunch next weekend, just you and me. I'll ring you in a couple of days to discuss where and when. Then maybe afterward, or maybe another time, depending on how you feel, I'll take you home and introduce you to the family. What do you say?"

"Okay." Molly took the card. It was just an ordinary business card, printed on one side with several numbers handwritten on the back, but she held it in her palm as if it were a treasure. This was the first piece of solid evidence about her father she'd ever possessed. More than that, it represented a commitment to the future—a future together. She blinked at his formally printed name. "Um, I know this is a funny thing to say, but what should I call you?"

He grinned. "Whatever you like. Jonathan will do for now. Can I walk you to wherever you're going, or would you rather be alone?"

"Alone, I think."

"Fair enough."

They stood up, took a few steps, stopped and faced each other.

"I don't know how we do this." He laughed. "Do we shake hands?" He stretched out his arm with a kind of embarrassed gallantry, and Molly slid her palm against his, feeling his fingers close around her knuckles. They stood like that in the soft sunlight, looking into each other's faces—shy, delighted—unsure what to say, neither wanting to let go.

Afterward, she couldn't have said who moved first, but suddenly they were hugging each other. He felt large and solid, and smelled of clean shirt. A part of Molly thought, *What am I doing with my arms around this stranger?* But a louder, jubilant voice insisted, *He's not a stranger. This is my father. I am flesh of his flesh.* He was not like any of the thousand fathers she had imagined, just an ordinary man: Jonathan Griffin. But a nice man. And he was *real*, not a fantasy, not a dream slipping away with the dawn. Her grip tightened on him for a moment. She could feel a rim of flab round his waist. Tut. Not enough golf. She smiled into the lapel of his jacket. Yes, this was her father, for better or worse. It was not impossible that she'd be doing more hugging in future. She'd better get used to it.

# 26

"Which way now?"

"*Tout droit.*"

"That means right, doesn't it?"

"*Attention*, Fran!"

"Or is it left?"

"*Non!*"

"No! For Christ's sake, Mum, *straight on*."

Armand's car swerved violently, slinging Molly across the back seat and narrowly missing a pair of petrified tourists stranded midway on a pedestrian crossing. Molly's mother straightened the steering wheel and sped onto a bridge in a blare of furious honking. "Hell's bells," she giggled.

"Very good." Removing his hand from his heart, Armand patted her shoulder. "You see, Fran? You drive like a true Parisian."

"It's your car, Armand—so fast, so responsive, and all these exciting buttons! What does this one do?"

Twin jets of water spurted into the air as the windscreen wipers leapt into action, spraying droplets back through the open sun-roof into Molly's face. "Oh, sorry, folks."

Molly dried her cheeks ostentatiously, and glowered at the back of her mother's head. "Mum, have you been drinking?"

"Only a bit of wine at lunchtime. Armand took me to a fabulous little *restaurant du quartier*. Way off the tourist beat. You'd never find it unless you knew it was there. I had snails!"

"Yeah, I can smell the garlic from here."

It wasn't true. All Molly could smell was perfume, an insinuating magnolia-like fragrance that wasn't exactly unpleasant, simply . . . unsuitable. Her mother used soap, not perfume. She ate lentils, not snails. What on earth did she think she was doing, driving Armand's car? Apparently it had been his idea. Her mother, he claimed, needed more "adventure" in her life.

In the hotel that morning, it had been agreed that Armand would drive Molly to the station, along with her mother and the luggage, the pick-up point being the entrance to some Arab Institute building that turned out to be a vast slab of steel and glass set on a windy corner by the river. Molly had been waiting for almost ten minutes before she heard the toot of a car horn and saw a glamorous blonde slow to a halt beside her. It was another ten seconds before she recognized her mother, wearing a slim-fitting jacket of dark green velvet with a silky white shirt underneath. "We've been shopping," her mother explained, her eyes skidding away from Molly's raised-eyebrow stare. "I went a bit mad." Again the loony laugh. Molly had climbed wordlessly into the back seat and slammed the door.

As well as shopping "in the Marais," wherever that might be, and lunching at the fabulous little restaurant, they had spent some time strolling through a botanical garden. "Such a treat for me." Molly's mother smiled happily at Armand.

"I've been to some gardens, too, as it happens," Molly announced portentously.

"What, darling? I can't hear you over the roar of this mighty engine."

"You are teasing me, Fran, I think. Now, here you must be

careful. Follow the blue Peugeot. *Non*, the Peugeot! *Voilà*. You see the new opera house? One says it resembles a hippopotamus in the bath, but some of the productions are magnificent. Perhaps . . . great pleasure . . . acoustics . . ."

"I used to . . . *Magic Flute*, of course . . . so busy . . ."

Burble, burble. Molly could see their heads turning toward each other, but as they did not have the courtesy to raise their voices, and since Molly felt it would be undignified to crouch forward like some eager doggy, their conversation reached her only in fragments. She folded her arms, sat back and jiggled a foot. *And how was your day, Molly? Oh, you met your father at last?* . . . *So sorry to hear how my rotten son treated you.*

But no. Now Armand seemed to be commiserating about the dearth of culture in what he called *Mince d'heure Épice-corps-pis*.

Yes, Minster Episcopi was a bit dull at times, agreed Molly's mother, but . . .

Molly gave her a wounded look in the rear-view mirror. What did she mean, dull? It was their *home*. And was that mascara she was wearing? Molly pinched her lips. She could wait. Soon she would have her mother to herself for three whole hours. Traveling back to London together had not been what she'd planned, but now the reproaches were bubbling up inside her like acid. I *wasn't* happy. I *did* need him. He thought about me *all the time*. He wanted to see me, and *you* stopped him! No wonder I know nothing about men. No wonder my love life's a mess.

Her mother's laugh rippled from the front seat. Strands of her long hair swirled in the rushing draft. The way she was behaving, anyone would think she was twenty-two, not forty-two. Why did she need that new jacket when she had a perfectly good Barbour? What on earth could she be saying to Armand—a sophisticated, cultured Frenchman—to make him respond with such attentive delight?

Molly cleared her throat, sighed heavily, stared mournfully into space. She rather thought she felt a bit car-sick—not that anyone would care. In the end she leaned forward until she was virtually kneeling on the hard metal bump behind the handbrake, plonked her elbows on the corners of the two leather seats, and thrust her head between the pair of them. Immediately they fell silent, almost as though she was interrupting something.

"How was the Rollerblading, darling?" her mother asked brightly.

"All right." Molly scorned this feeble attempt to make conversation.

"And . . . Fabrice, is it? Did you have a lovely time?"

How could she even ask? The insensitivity!

"I'll tell you on the train," she said, in a low voice, eyes downcast.

"Ah. Yes. Er, actually . . ." Molly's mother glanced at Armand.

"I have invited your mother to stay on in France for a few days," Armand took over smoothly. "It would be most interesting for her to visit some of the gardens here in Paris—Parc de la Villette, the rooftop of the Gare Montparnasse and so forth. Also, there is a project I am working on, a new centre of culture in Biarritz—on the Atlantic coast, you know? I am hoping Fran will accompany me on a visit to the site next week, and give me her opinion."

"Opinion on what?" Molly was flabbergasted.

"Landscaping, *bien sûr*. The relationship between structure and space, architecture and nature, *euh* . . ."

"Preserving the environment," her mother chipped in.

"*Exactement*."

"But—but—but what about your plants, Mum? And Alleluia? The chickens?"

"Oh, they'll be all right for a few days. I've done some phoning, called in a few favors. I just thought . . . now I'm here . . . and with this glorious weather. Though not, of course, if you need me, Mollypops."

Her selfishness took Molly's breath away. "If you need me?" Just when she had no job, no money, a broken heart, and was reeling from the most cataclysmic revelation of her entire life? She made a choking noise and was still casting around for a suitably stinging reply when Armand spoke up.

"*Mais quand même*, Fran, Molly has her own home, her own life. Why should you not enjoy a little holiday? There is an exceptional restaurant in Biarritz where one can eat baby wild boar cooked with mushrooms, bay leaf and just a *soupçon* of coriander."

"Mum doesn't eat meat," Molly objected.

"And the fish, of course, is superb. It is even possible that the sea may still be warm enough for swimming."

"Oh, I can swim in anything," Molly's mother said blithely.

"Yes, even a freezing cold Scottish loch." Molly gave the words bitter emphasis. "Isn't that right, Mum?"

"Is it? Ha ha. I—I can't remember."

Armand glanced from one to the other, and cleared his throat. "Speaking of work, Molly, I have an idea for you. An old friend of mine, an English woman of much charm and talent, is starting some kind of new festival of literature—where, I don't remember, but her office is in London. Soho, I believe. She requires an *assistante*—someone to send out the letters of invitation to the writers, organize the timetable, arrange their hotels and so forth. Naturally, I thought of you."

"*Me?*" Molly jerked in surprise. No one would give her a job like that. What if she had to ring up Martin Amis?

"Why not? You are intelligent, charming, honest. You interest yourself in literature. I am sure you work hard."

"Oh, she *does*. I remember when she was at Bloom 'n' Veg—"

Molly silenced her mother with a Medusa glare in the rear-view mirror.

Armand took a piece of paper from his breast pocket, and handed it to Molly. "Here are the details. She will be expecting your contact tomorrow."

"Tomorrow?"

"Monday, you know? When one recommences work?"

"Oh. Right." Molly took the paper wonderingly. *Intelligent, charming, honest* . . . Was she really? That's not what Malcolm had thought. But, then, her father had called Malcolm "absurd," and had seemed almost proud of her for resigning. Maybe she wasn't such a failure after all. Impulsively she stretched forward and kissed Armand's cheek. "Thank you very much, Armand. That's really kind of you."

"*De rien, ma petite*." He smoothed his already perfect hair.

Molly pushed herself off her knees, and sank back into her seat to stow the paper carefully in her wallet. As she did so, her eye was caught by the flickering light as trees rushed past. She was leaving Paris. The realization struck her with such a bitter-sweet pang that she shifted across to the window to gaze at what might be the last leafy avenue, the last green kiosk and red awning, the last café, with its clientele jammed elbow to elbow on the pavement outside, drinking, gesticulating, talking, talking, talking, while they soaked up the fiery rays of the evening sun.

And here was the place de la République again, where she had emerged on that first, scary night, and later— Quickly, Molly tried to block out the memory of pausing just there, by that traffic-light, next to that café, with her arms wrapped around Fabrice, but she could not prevent a wave of desire and nostalgia tearing through her.

"*Allez*, Fran! You have the priority."

"I do? Help!"

"*Vite, vite! . . . Bravo!*"

Honestly, they were behaving like teenagers. Now Armand was showing off the heated front seats. "Ooh, what luxury!" her mother exclaimed, tossing him a look that was, well, frankly flirtatious. Molly was scandalized.

A memory popped up from nowhere, unbidden but vivid and entire in every detail. She had been twelve years old, and it was Christmas time. One of the things Molly and her mother prided themselves on was that they made their cards and presents by hand. "Much more special than buying them from a shop," Mum always said. Instead of wasting their money on "plastic rubbish," they baked mince pies together, Molly weighing out the dried fruit, Mum wielding the sharp knife to cut it up, both vying later to make the best pastry decoration on top of each pie—Christmas trees, bells, ivy leaves, snowmen. Or they covered old shoeboxes with Christmas paper salvaged from last year, and filled them with layers of homemade truffles, wonkily shaped but delicious, and so rich that once Molly had been sick on the kitchen floor after licking all the bowls, saucepans, spoons and spatulas.

That evening they were sitting at the kitchen table by the Rayburn, with the King's College Choir pouring out carols from the stereo (or perhaps Mum's weird old records, like Blondie or Michael Jackson), and the tools of their trade laid out on sheets of newspaper: squat bottles of ink, phials of glitter, cotton wool for Santa's beard, fans of colored card—green, red, gold, silver—a dragon's hoard of felt-tips. "I was wondering about inviting Jem for Christmas this year," Molly's mother said casually—although Molly, alert to every nuance of her mother's voice, knew that the suggestion was far from casual. "What do you think?"

Jem was a local carpenter, rumored by the villagers to be an old Etonian although he lived a hippieish life in a yurt in one of Lord Spilsbury's fields, along with his dog Kip. The previous summer he had come to do odd jobs in the cottage—building bookshelves in an alcove, fixing a door that had warped in the damp and wouldn't close. Molly had quite liked him—his dark, unkempt roughness, the sureness of his hands as he snuggled wood into place, the half-teasing, half-flattering way he called out, "Good golly, Miss Molly!" when he saw her. One evening he'd worked so late that they'd invited him to supper. It had been a festive occasion, one of the best evenings of the year. Jem had cooked them pancakes for dessert, with much pan-shaking and extravagant flipping. He had made Kip do tricks. Afterward, he'd taught them both to play poker, using raisins for chips, and Molly had triumphed with a full house and gone to bed with twenty-six raisins under her belt. She had lain under the covers with Bertie, deliciously warm and tired, and fallen asleep listening to the low drone of their conversation and the rumble of laughter through the floorboards.

Jem had been around a lot after that. Molly came to recognize the sound of his pickup engine. Sometimes she came home from school and noticed something different in the house—a new shelf, a shed repaired. "Oh, yes, Jem's been round," her mother would say, her tone too offhand, her eyes too bright. Molly noticed she was suddenly out more—"just going to the pub," "just a little drinks party in the village," "just taking Alleluia out for a run." That summer she'd deserted Molly for two whole days to go to the Glastonbury Festival—in a big group of people, but it was Jem's truck they went in, all tumbled into the back with their tents and camping stoves, clowning around like primary-school kids. Molly disapproved. There was a new spring in Mum's step, a skittishness she found distasteful.

So that night, in answer to her mother's question, she had picked up a glue stick and carefully applied it to the back of a snowman shape. "Jem?" she said consideringly.

"Well, only if you think it would be fun, darling. I just feel a bit sorry for him, all alone in that cold tent."

Molly turned over her snowman and positioned him above a piece of red card, taking her time. Then she pressed the snowman into place and smoothed him flat with her fist. "I don't think it would be fair to Alleluia. She doesn't really like Kip. She always hides under the piano. Anyway, I like our Christmases the way they are, Mummy." She raised her eyes, wide and empty, to her mother's nervous gaze, both thrilled and frightened by the power that surged through her. "Don't you?"

"Of course I do, sweetheart." There was barely a hesitation before Molly felt her mother's warm hand on hers.

Molly smiled. "Molly and Mum." She began the familiar litany.

Obediently, her mother responded, "Mum and Molly."

And that was the end of Jem. Once or twice after Christmas, when Molly was out walking Alleluia, she saw his pickup coming down the lane and waited for him to shout, "Good golly, Miss Molly," but he didn't even slow down. Soon afterward he moved away—Cornwall, they said. Her mother never mentioned him again.

Now, watching her with Armand, Molly was aware of the same heightened energy, and felt the same instinct to extinguish it. She could still make her mother come with her, if she tried. A few tears on the station platform, a waiflike slump to her shoulders, and her mother would crumble to her will.

"*Alors*, now we approach the station, Fran. Pay attention to the taxis—they are brutes." Armand swivelled gracefully in his seat. "Molly, you will excuse us if we do not accompany you inside. I have promised to take your mother to a concert in the Sainte-Chapelle. We must hurry or we will be late."

Before Molly could gather her thoughts, the car had come to a halt outside the vast gray façade. Armand jumped out and opened Molly's door for her. "Come, I will take your case out of the boot." Her mother had climbed out too. She was wearing leather trousers!

"*Voilà*." Armand set Molly's case on the ground and slammed the boot shut, but not before she had seen the stash of expensive-looking carrier-bags inside. She barely had time to dart her mother a look of astonished reproof before Armand was kissing her good-bye—a firm smack on each cheek. "Come back to Paris soon, Molly. You will stay in my apartment, *hein?*"

Then he was back inside the car, tactfully leaving Molly alone with her mother. Except she didn't look like her mother, neither was she acting like her. Molly still couldn't believe they were just going to dump her here and swan off to some concert.

"Mum, are you sure about this?" she said, in a low, concerned voice. "Armand is nice, I agree, but he's *French*. He's probably got a—you know—mistress," she whispered.

"Dozens, I should think." Her mother trailed a hand through her long hair, a dreamy smile on her face. "All the sales assistants seem to recognize him. He even knows the best place for lingerie."

"Mum! You didn't—"

"Of course not." She started guiltily. Then her face softened and she stroked Molly's cheek. "Don't look so worried, sweetheart. This is just a little adventure. I know it's very wicked, but it's so . . . *lovely* having someone to look after me, instead of thinking of everything and doing everything myself. You don't mind, do you?"

"*Vous venez*, Fran?" Armand called impatiently. "We must hurry."

"Good-bye, lovey." Her mother wrapped her arms around Molly in a tight hug. Molly clung to her, eyes squeezed shut, wanting to burrow into familiar comfort and security. But she could feel her mother vibrating with tension and excitement that had nothing to do with her. The new perfume filled her nostrils. Eventually, she was the one who let go and stepped away, silently noting the eagerness with which her mother climbed back into the car. The engine purred into action.

"Good luck with the job!" Her mother grinned from the open window. "I'll see you soon."

The car rattled across the cobbles. A velvet-clad arm waved cheerily. Molly saw the two heads, backlit by the sunset, already talking. The left indicator blinked, shortly followed by the right. Eventually, the car shot straight ahead across the busy avenue and disappeared down a side street with an expensive roar.

Molly stood on the wide forecourt among the scuttling leaves. Then she picked up her case and trudged inside.

# 27

The queue shuffled forward a few inches. Someone's trolley banged the back of Molly's calves. "Sorry, love," called a husky Lancashire voice. Molly nodded in listless acknowledgement, turning her head just far enough to clock the woman's saggy green shell-suit, gray hairstyle reminiscent of rock formations following some prehistoric natural disaster, and tubby hubby wearing an "I Love Paris" hat. Mechanically, she rolled her own trolley forward and slumped against the handle.

So this was the end of her adventure. Good-bye to sunlight on the Seine, umbrellas on pavements, footfalls in cobbled courtyards, geraniums on balconies. Good-bye to dogs in coats, women in scarves, old men fishing on quays; to *pâtisseries* and *épiceries*; to monuments and fountains exploding into the air, and a tower woven from iron in the sky. Good-bye to gaiety, adventure, sparkle, romance. Good-bye to Paris.

Everything felt dreary. Everything looked brown. All was tedium and confusion, and the petty anxiety of tickets and timetables. The Eurostar departure area, located on a balcony under the roof, possessed none of the grandeur of the rest of the station. There was no charm, no style, just a seething mass of people and bags funneling into a narrow entrance, where a stewardess in her blue and yellow uniform checked tickets and waved passengers through to Passport Control. Echoing announcements numbed Molly's brain. Do not leave your luggage unattended. Smoking is not permitted. The train from Abbeville has arrived at platform eleven. The Eurostar for London departs in twenty minutes.

Soon she would be on her way back to dull, familiar England, back to Fat Sal and their scuzzy flat. Paris would fade to a dream, and so would the Molly Clearwater who had danced in a gold skirt with no knickers, and dared to show her breasts.

Already she was becoming invisible. No one was here to see her off; even her mother had abandoned her. "They flee from me that sometime did me seek," she quoted mournfully to herself. "I have seen them, gentle, tame and meek, that now are wild, and do not remember . . ."

She hadn't a single photo from her visit: no silly souvenir, not even a postcard—nothing but the ticket in her pocket and a rawness in her heart. It was probably raining in England.

A gap opened in front of her, and obediently she moved forward, one of the herd. The queue was becoming restive. There was only one official at Passport Control, processing passengers with a magnificent lack of urgency while the big station clock ticked off the minutes. French people queue-jumped with shameless *panache*, to British mutters of outrage. A touch on her arm made Molly shrink irritably away. *No need to push.* She felt it again, and snapped her head round. "Fabrice!"

"Molly! Thank God I am not too late!"

He had been running. His cheekbones were lightly sheened with sweat. Locks of hair spilled across his forehead. His helmet swung from one hand, with a package jammed inside. The ardor in his eyes made her head spin.

Molly gripped the handle of her trolley tight. "What are you doing here?"

"I wanted to see you—to talk to you."

"What about?"

He pushed back his hair in a passionate gesture. "You are angry with me. *C'est normal.* I behaved very badly. And I am ashamed. Truly."

Everything about him was fiery, urgent, physical. His leather jacket hung open. Molly could see the rise and fall of his chest under the thin shirt, the roll of his hipbones against taut jeans. She dragged her eyes away.

He pressed closer and laid a hand on her case. "This afternoon I have been in torment. In the cinema, all I could see was your face. I knew I must come here and find you."

Molly stared at his fingers, and it was as if she could feel them on her skin, claiming her, rekindling bonfires throughout her body.

"Excuse me, love, can you move up a bit?" said the voice from behind.

Molly jerked back to reality. The queue had advanced several feet without her noticing. *Concentrate.* She was going home. Paris was over. Fabrice was over. He had hurt her, humiliated her, made her feel stupid and worthless. She practically charged forward with her trolley, dislodging Fabrice's hand.

"Molly, please." His wounded tone reproached her. "I can't talk to you like this. Come. We will find a little corner, away from these people. I will push your *chariot.*" He seized the trolley, swung it out of the queue and set off toward the far wall.

"Fabrice, no! I'll miss my train."

But she followed as if he twitched an invisible leash. What was she doing? This was crazy. God, he was gorgeous! The station clock showed that there were twelve minutes to departure. Molly glanced back wildly. Mr. "I Love Paris" gave her a chummy thumbs-up and pointed to the floor ahead of him, as if to say that he'd keep her place. She flashed him a distracted smile.

Fabrice had tossed his belongings into the tray of the trolley and shoved it to one side. Now he grasped her elbows, swung her round, and crowded her against the wall with his body. "This is better, isn't it?"

"Is it?" Molly said breathlessly. A treacherous smile tugged at the corners of her mouth. "Listen," she rapped out, breaking free of his hold, "I'm in a hurry. What do you want?"

He bent his head and looked at her through smoky lashes. "I want to say I'm sorry."

Molly lowered her eyes to his shirt button.

"*Écoute* . . ." He hooked a finger into hers and swung her hand gently. "I know I said some foolish things, but I didn't mean them. I was angry—confused. My friends were teasing me. Please, Molly, tell me you forgive me."

*Just a stupid English girl here for the weekend, looking for a Frenchman to fuck*. Molly swallowed and shook her head.

"I know I hurt you. But when I hurt you, I hurt myself, too. Here." He smote his heart with his fist. "Until that moment I did not understand how special you are. Look at me, Molly. Tell me you forgive me."

Slowly she raised her head, registering the sensuous curve of his lower lip, the perfect cheekbones with their hemispheres of shadow, those velvety eyes. He was so penitent, so passionate, so irresistible. "All right," she whispered.

His smile was like a shower of fireworks. He raised her hand to his lips and kissed it rapturously. He was absurd—adorable.

"*Tu vois?* How easy it is to make me happy. And now—now I

cannot let you go." Reaching for her other hand, Fabrice wound both her arms around his back and pulled her tight to his lean body.

"Stay with me, Molly," he murmured. "Stay in Paris."

"I can't!"

"Why not?"

"The train . . ."

"*Bof.*"

"My ticket . . ."

"Silly girl." He bent to rub his nose against hers.

"And—and there's a job I'm interested in. In London. It's important, Fabrice."

"Of course. But a day or two won't matter, will it?" He rocked his hips teasingly from side to side. Her very bones seemed to melt.

Molly closed her eyes, trying to remember why exactly she must go home, why it was impossible for her to stay. All that happened was that her forehead sank against his chest. His shirt was warm and smelled of Fabrice. She could have torn it off with her teeth.

"Don't we have fun together?" His breath tickled her neck. "Don't you like me, just a little bit? Don't you remember, in bed, how you . . . ?"

*Yes, she remembered. How could she forget? How dared he remind her?*

"Stop it, Fabrice!" She tore herself free. "How can you come here, torment me, make a fool of me, pretend you care about me—"

"I don't pretend!"

"—when all the time you have—" it was humiliating to have to be the one to remind him "—when all the time you have Gabrielle."

"I swear to you, Molly—*je te jure*—it is over between me and

Gabrielle. I feel it in my heart. Now that I have met you I cannot think of her. She is just a girl, nothing special."

"But you said—"

He dismissed anything he might or might not have said with a toss of wild hair, and recaptured her hands. "You must not be jealous of Gabrielle. She does not touch me as you do. She does not have your beautiful blue eyes—your long blonde hair—your gorgeous breasts." (*Les seins superbes.*) He gazed down at them in open admiration. "You are a woman, Molly. Gabrielle is . . . *en-fin*, what one calls *la carte bleue*." He flicked his fingers down his own chest in an unmistakable gesture: flat as a credit card.

"Fabrice! That's so mean." But a giggle escaped her.

"So. You will stay?" His eyes were alight.

"What—just because you like my breasts?" Molly half laughed, half sighed with exasperation, twisting in his grasp, and caught sight of the couple who had been behind her, now disappearing through Passport Control. She had lost her place! The time was six thirty-seven. Her train left in eight minutes. "No, I can't," she said firmly, pulling her hands free. "You're not serious, Fabrice."

"But I am! *Écoute*, Molly. When I first saw you on the boat, of course I thought you were a very pretty girl. *Très sympa.* It was fun to take you on the scooter. But you are right. I was not *sérieux*. It was you who said, 'What shall we do tomorrow, Fabrice?' and you were so adorable that I was tempted. At the Rodin museum I had no idea . . . But then you touched my heart and, *enfin*, you made me want to paint you, to make love to you. And now you have tamed me, like the fox in *Le Petit Prince*. You cannot abandon me now."

Molly sighed. It was hard to resist the appeal in his eyes, the tumble of words from his kissable mouth. "You abandoned me," she reminded him. "You made me go to your father alone. Today you acted as if I was a stranger."

"But I was wrong! You are right. I am weak, but you are strong. That is why I want you to stay—not for your sake, Molly, but for mine."

*For his sake.* Dazzled by this thought, Molly barely noticed his fingers sliding back into her palm. He admired her! He needed her. He said she was right. It was practically her duty to stay; priggish to refuse. Who was she to deny him, however he might have behaved? Unconsciously her fingers twisted and curled in his.

"I will be different, Molly. Let me prove it to you. Just one more day . . . One more night. Then we'll see . . ."

"Oh, Fabrice, I don't know—I can't think!" Her voice rose in anguish. The final passengers had reached the stewardess, who hustled them through and glanced round for stragglers. Feebly, Molly flapped a hand to catch her attention. The stewardess widened her eyes and pointed urgently to her watch.

Fabrice leaned his forearm against the wall above her head, blocking out everything except his own slim, dark, seductive grace. He brushed a lock of hair from her forehead and smiled into her eyes. "Forget the train. Forget London. My scooter is outside. We can go now."

Molly gazed back, mesmerized, as his fingers trailed behind her ear, down her neck, across her throat. She pictured herself leaving the noise and confusion of the station, walking out with Fabrice into the fresh evening air. She would climb onto his scooter and wrap her arms around him tight, tight. Together they would speed back into Paris, with the sky fading to pale rose over the high roofs. There would be fountains and cafés, life and laughter. They would talk, and he would listen to her. Later they would lie in some dark room in a tangle of urgent limbs and the voluptuous slither of skin against skin, and finally she would fall asleep with her ear laid against his beating heart.

*Yes!* As he pressed closer, her body arched in surrender. What did it matter if he was weak? And a bit lazy. And a bit spoiled. No one was perfect. Mr. Darcy had humiliated Elizabeth. Mr. Rochester tried to marry Jane Eyre when he was already married!

She could have Paris. She could have Fabrice—for a little longer, anyway. It was worth it even for one day—one night—one hour. Wasn't it?

"Will all passengers for the six forty-five Eurostar go to the platform immediately? This train leaves in four minutes."

But Jane Eyre had waited until Mr. Rochester was free. Elizabeth had refused Mr. Darcy until she understood his true character. *People show their character in the way they behave.* Who had said that? Molly closed her eyes, trying to remember.

Now Fabrice was so close that their foreheads touched. She felt his breath on her lips. "*Viens*, Molly," he whispered. "Come with me?"

The seconds ticked by. Slowly, painfully, as if tearing skin, Molly raised her head away from Fabrice's and opened her eyes. "If you had asked me yesterday," she told him, "I would have said yes with all my heart."

"But what is different?" He clutched at her arm. "I am the same person."

"Yes. But . . . I'm not."

"I don't understand. You want to stay. I know you do."

She shook her head. "I'm going home."

"But why?"

"Because . . ." Molly hesitated. She saw her father standing in Luxembourg Gardens: *I'm so proud of you I could roar*. She thought of the photograph of herself as a little girl and the way he had handled it as if it were precious and important. "Because it's not enough for me—a day, a night, 'we'll see.'" She raised her chin and looked him in the eye. "I think I'm worth more than that."

She watched the emotions cross his face: incomprehension, disappointment, hurt, anger—perhaps a flicker of acknowledgement. Then the warmth faded from his eyes. He stepped clear of her and turned away.

"The Eurostar is leaving immediately," called the stewardess, glaring in Molly's direction.

"Fabrice, I'm sorry, but I must leave." Molly seized her case from the trolley. "*Je viens*—I'm coming!" she shouted to the stewardess. "*Au revoir*, Fabrice." She put a hand on his arm. Even now she ached for one last, obliterating kiss.

He twitched her away and stared at the ground.

"Say good-bye to me at least," she begged.

"Two minutes to departure!"

With a despairing sigh Molly turned and ran. The stewardess checked her ticket and frowned severely. "*Vite, vite!* You must run."

Molly was fumbling for her passport when she felt an arm hook round her neck, a scrape of stubble against her cheek, a frantic kiss on the corner of her mouth. "Here, this is for you." Fabrice thrust something into her hand. "Good-bye, Molly. *Je t'embrasse.*"

*Bang!* Her passport was slapped back on the counter. Molly jammed the package Fabrice had given her into her shoulder-bag, dumped everything on the X-ray machine and ran through the metal arch. As she picked up her belongings she caught a last glimpse of him, standing with one long thigh thrust forward, hands jammed into his pockets: a rebellious boy staring back with fierce, unsmiling intensity. She took a step backward, then another, finally turned into an archway, out of sight. She fed her ticket into a machine, pushed through the barrier and then was racing along a corridor, down some steps, and out onto the platform. Christ! It was completely deserted except for a man in uniform, wristwatch cocked, flag held aloft. Everyone else was on the train. Faces peered at her through the windows as she galloped clumsily past, case bumping against her leg, looking for her coach.

"The doors will close automatically in a few moments," announced a heavily accented voice from the loudspeakers.

A steward leaned from a doorway and grabbed her ticket. "Get on here," he said. "You'll never make it to your coach." She slung her case onto the high step and seized the handrail. Seconds after she had climbed aboard, the doors slid closed. A whistle blew. The train began to move. Molly stumbled her way down the aisle in search of her seat, panting with exertion.

"Well run, lass." She recognized Mr. "I Love Paris," comfortably ensconced by a window with a styrofoam cup of tea. His wife beamed a motherly smile. "So you decided to come home, after all?"

"Yes," said Molly, and burst into tears.

# 28

It was getting dark now. Molly sat with her chin in her hand, watching the plains of northern France skim soundlessly past the reinforced glass of the train window. The horizon rose and fell in gentle curves, feathered with poplar trees. Thumbprints of cloud smudged a shimmering opal sky. Idly, her mind elsewhere, Molly absorbed the unfamiliar details: steeples shaped like witches' hats, rather than the four-square towers she was used to; dainty, biscuit-colored cows instead of the black-and-white hulks that grazed the patchwork meadows at home; pylons stalking the railway line in towering cats' cradles of wire and steel. With every rushing mile, shadows deepened across the landscape. France was fading—retreating before her eyes. Paris had gone for good. She felt disoriented, in limbo, strangely sluggish after the emotional tempest of her departure.

For the first half-hour of the journey she had been too upset to take her seat under the curious eyes of strangers. Instead, she had first of all lurked in the luggage area between her coach and the next, head ducked to the window to torture herself with the sight of Paris slipping away. Each tall house with peeling paint and rusting balcony, each narrow street with scooters tilting through traffic, a glimpse of Sacré Coeur glowing pink in the sunset, brought a fresh gush of tears. She should have stayed with Fabrice, after all. No, no, it would never have worked. But he had looked so beautiful, and so sad. And she was so miserable. One thing was for sure: she would never fall in love again.

Then, just as the heart-wrenching charm of the view disappeared under an assault of tower blocks and semi-industrial clutter, a voice announced over the loudspeaker, in both English and outlandishly accented French, that the buffet car was now open. Molly realized that she was starving, having eaten nothing since her breakfast croissant with Armand. Wiping her cheeks with her sleeves, she made her way through the swaying coaches and found the owner of the voice, chirpy and smartly jacketed in white, presiding over a service hatch and a small area of waist-high tables bolted to the floor. It was odd to be speaking English again. She blew the last of her euros on hot chocolate and a ham baguette, and carried them over to an empty table by the window. The darkening fields flew past, overlaid by her own ghostly reflection.

What had Fabrice really felt about her? The tormenting question went round and round in her head. Had all that drama at the station been just another game—another whim, like taking her on his scooter in the first place? Molly munched her sandwich thoughtfully. She was proud of herself for having the courage to leave. But there was a cold feeling in the pit of her stomach that no amount of hot chocolate could warm. Fabrice—a fabrication? Had she made it all up—the romance, the attraction, the feeling that there had been something special between them?

So many wonderful things had happened to her in Paris. She had found her father. It was incredible what a difference it made simply to know who he was. The shadow of doubt under which she had lived for so long had finally lifted. There was no dark mystery, no shameful secret. On the contrary, she had a brand new family to meet—grandparents, half-brothers, perhaps a whole network of uncles and aunts and cousins. Damn! She should have asked if he—Jonathan—her father—had brothers and sisters. She *would* ask, when she saw him next weekend. She could even ring him up and ask him *now!* She wouldn't do it, of course, but the knowledge that she *could* was so dizzying that Molly clung to the edge of the table.

Her sandwich was finished, and she was tired of standing. She fitted a plastic lid onto the remains of her hot chocolate, retraced her steps and located her seat, one of four surrounding a gray Formica table. It was embarrassing to appear at this late stage. Molly whispered an apology to a Japanese lady, who had to stand up and move into the aisle so that Molly could slither into her window seat. Though she did so as unobtrusively as possible, she was aware of flickering glances from the other two passengers—a middle-aged woman clicking at her laptop in the seat opposite, and a youngish guy on the aisle, reading a book. But both were soon absorbed again, and the Japanese woman resumed her conversation with her friends across the aisle, leaving Molly to pursue her own meandering thoughts.

Alicia was coming to London: that was something else to look forward to. She pictured them going to bars and clubs together, having adventures, doing all the things Molly had thought she'd do when she went to London but had been too timid to attempt alone. But now she'd have a mate.

Oops! She'd just remembered Malcolm. She might have to see him, too, if Alicia persisted in her perverse attraction. That could be a bit embarrassing, though funnily enough the "stupid secretary" label no longer rankled. She knew now that it wasn't true. Anyway, by then she might have landed an exciting new job. Molly drained the last of her hot chocolate and sat up excitedly. A literary festival! She'd have to mug up on hot writers and popular taste. Her eye strayed to the guy diagonally opposite—mid-twenties, tousled brown hair, rangy build under a faded blue sweatshirt: what was he reading, for example? Something about the SAS, probably, or one of those novels about how vulnerable and fundamentally decent men were under the loutish exterior. Molly slid down in her seat until she was practically horizontal and cocked her head to squint at the title. Whoa, *War and Peace!* His eyelids suddenly flew up. Gray, amused eyes looked straight into hers. Molly turned away.

Where was she? Oh, yes, the new job as *assistante* to Armand's "old friend" (ho ho). Molly pictured herself in some lavish country hotel, sitting with Will Self over breakfast (or "oleaginous orgy," as he would no doubt call it), before running upstairs to check that Zadie Smith was quite happy with her pillows. It sounded perfect, but could she do it? What would she say at the interview? Who could advise her?

*She would ask her father.* The thought struck her as so brilliant and satisfying she gaped at her reflection in the window. "I asked my father," she practiced in her head. "Yes, my father said . . ." No, even better: "My dad . . ."

And what about her mother? How shocked she would be when Molly revealed her great discovery. But it would serve her right for being so cruelly secretive and overprotective all these years. Molly toyed with the idea of ringing Armand's flat later tonight and seeing if her mother was there. It would be fun to catch her out, explode a bombshell into her "little adventure." How guilty her mother would feel—how alarmed and exposed that her secret was out at last. There would be no more nonsense about Biarritz: she would jump on the next train home.

*Don't be too hard on your mother.* Her father's words reproved her. Molly shut her eyes for a moment, trying to imagine the girl he had described—Frankie: beautiful, carefree, twenty years old—who had found herself pregnant and given up everything to devote herself to her child. To Molly. It couldn't have been easy. It wouldn't be what one would choose. She might not have done everything right. But having made the decision, her mother had stuck by it with all the bravery and fierceness she possessed. Molly felt a rush of affection, and with it came a startling new perception. They were *both* caught in the old "Molly and Mum" trap. It wasn't just Molly who longed to escape: her mother did, too. That's what her bolt with Armand was all about. Molly had the power to recall her—but how much better to prize open the jaws of the trap and chuck it away for good. If she could let her mother go free, with love, to footle around with Frenchmen or do any other daft thing she fancied, wouldn't that prove that she herself was truly grown up and in no further need of smothering? Besides, whenever her mother went away, even for a night, she always brought Molly a present: the one from France ought to be spectacular.

Crikey! How could she have forgotten? Molly bent down and felt in her bag for the package Fabrice had given her. She drew out a long narrow cylinder wrapped in a plastic bag and secured with rubber bands. She snapped these off, pulled off the plastic and unrolled the paper inside. It was a drawing of herself—nude! More than nude—voluptuous, languorous-eyed . . . beautiful. Molly stared in wonder. Was this really her, this sensual creature with her rounded stomach and full breasts, lying with her hands clasped behind her head? The drawing was erotic, but there was character in it, too. Fabrice had captured her shy defiance and the kindling fire in her eyes, with delicacy and affection. He had signed and dated the drawing: this professional touch made her smile. But what moved her most was the inscription across one of the top corners: "*Pour Molly—la plus belle et la plus gentille de toutes les filles.*" For Molly, most beautiful and kindest of girls.

She sighed. The man in the sweatshirt glanced up. His expression was friendly, interested, even admiring—or did the drawing show through the paper? Blushing, Molly rolled it tight, fitted the rubber bands back on and put it away. But her heart was singing. Whatever his failings, Fabrice had not been cynical: the proof was here. More than that, he had given her a new way of looking at herself: not plump, but desirable; not shy, but confident; not protected and repressed; certainly not priggish. Boldly, Molly looked over at Mr. Sweatshirt, as if to test her new self. He smiled.

It occurred to her that she might have smudged mascara under her eyes—or a mustache of hot chocolate. Apologizing to the Japanese lady once again, she squirmed her way out of her seat and walked through to the loo to check. Oh dear. She took out her makeup bag.

Fabrice was probably at this very moment sitting in a noisy café, fondling some thin, perfect French girl while he dismissed rumors of a mysterious *Anglaise* who had been seen with him over the weekend. ("*Mais écoute*, Gabrielle . . .") There was a catch in her throat, halfway between a sob and a giggle. He *was* gorgeous—unpredictable, unreliable, absurd, melodramatic—but gorgeous. She would never forget him.

When she had brushed the shine back into her hair, touched up her eyes and rubbed some color into her cheeks and lips, she lingered at the mirror. No disguises anymore—no gold skirt, no black wig, no red dress. She knew who she was. Now she would be herself.

As she unlocked the door, the speaker system crackled into life and a voice announced that the train would shortly be entering the tunnel. Molly turned to look out of the window, but there was nothing to see except darkness. For a moment she felt a wrench of loss, thinking of all she had experienced and discovered in Paris, and everything it had meant to her: beauty, joy, enchantment, liberation, a sense of possibility that fizzed the blood.

Then her head seemed to fill with dazzling light, as if she was once again standing on Armand's balcony on the Île St-Louis, with the sun sparkling on the river below. How foolish she was! These things could not be taken away. They were in her heart. Wherever she went, whatever she did, she would take Paris with her.

She pushed at the handle of the door to her coach. It slid back with a hiss. The guy in the sweatshirt looked up. He had put down his book. Gazing serenely over his head, Molly stepped forward into her new future.

# Acknowledgments

My first thanks must go to Amanda Craig for suggesting the idea for this book: a characteristically generous gesture from someone who is herself a writer, and a loyal and valued friend.

Thanks, too, to Caroline, Eveline and Sylvie for a memorable evening in Montmartre; to Robert Parker for giving me a glimpse into "real" Paris; and especially Doug and Claudie for their opulent Franco-American hospitality.

A big cheer for the wonderful Ozzie girls who've sparked up the Sisman household (and enriched our vocabularies) over the last decade or so: Annabelle, Kelly, Jane, Georgie, Jo and Leah. None of them bears any resemblance to the fictional Alicia in this story, except in their boundless good humor and appetite for fun.

Liz Rigbey gave me brilliant advice when I needed it most. George Misiewicz explained the arcane rituals of medical conferences. Jonathan Lloyd, my agent, is like the Rock of Gibraltar, only lots more fun. Louise Moore continues to be a paragon among publishers.

My greatest debt is, as always, to my husband Adam, without whose encouragement, criticism, inspiration and unflagging practical support I'd still be chewing my pencil over Chapter One.